First published 2022

First printed edition published 2024 by Drollery Ltd.

Copyright © Alice Coldbreath, 2022

ISBN 978-1-916736-10-8

More books available by Alice Coldbreath:

The Vawdrey Brothers Series:

Book 1: Her Baseborn Bridegroom

Book 2: His Forsaken Bride

Book 3: An Ill-Made Match

The Brides of Karadok Series:

Book 1: Wed By Proxy

Book 2: The Unlovely Bride

Book 3: The Consolation Prize

Book 4: Her Bridegroom, Bought and Paid For

Book 5: An Inconvenient Vow

Book 6: The Favourite

The Victorian Prizefighter Series:

Book 1: A Bride for the Prizefighter

Book 2: A Substitute Wife for the Prizefighter

Book 3: A Contracted Spouse for the Prizefighter

I would like to dedicate this book to Hannah Belle, a very frequent visitor to Karadok. Thank you so much for your encouragement which has meant so much to me. ~ Alice

"The white shield with the black tree is the strongest competitor today… Sir Jeffree de Crecy." —Roland Vawdrey, *An Ill-Made Match.*

"De Crecy is handsome to be sure, but to my mind, his looks are somewhat marred by his manner… He always looks like his own moustache stinks…" —Lenora Orde, *The Unlovely Bride.*

"Me, I would say that always he seems like he has a stick up his bottom." —Queen Armenal, *Her Bridegroom, Bought and Paid For.*

May

Ganford Chase

"Hurry, Sabina!" her mother urged. "We must not keep the groom waiting overlong."

"I am here, Mother," Sabina replied mildly, bringing up the rear. Her parents flanked her sister on either side as they strode up the long, winding approach to Ganford Chase, the historic home of the Dukes of Bethencourt. Sabina cursed the impulse that had made her parents abandon their cart so far down the lane, for it meant they had been forced to walk for a good twenty minutes before they reached even this point, and there was still a good ten minutes before they reached the main entrance.

And really, it was such a foolish gesture, for who here would care if their wagon was shabby? It was not as though the duke's family and friends were unaware of their social standing. Everyone in the village knew the bride's family had fallen on hard times in recent years. But there, Mother had insisted they climb down and send Milford back to the farm with the wagon. *For you know his lordship is sure to send us back in one of his many conveyances*, Thora Burrell had twittered. *For he is so exceedingly kind and generous.*

Mother and Isemay had exchanged warm glances at this point, pressing each other's hands. *He is the best of men, is he not, Mother? Oh yes, daughter! The absolute best.* Sabina's expression had soured, for she remembered her mother expressing similar convictions at her own wedding three years ago. Mother had been convinced that Miles Hendry possessed every virtue desirable in a future husband. And only look how that had turned out!

Her mother twisted back now to look at Sabina anxiously. "You are not trailing your hem in the dirt, Sabina!" she fussed. "Really, your garb…" She frowned anxiously. "If only this fabric would have stretched far enough for us to make you a new gown for the occasion too," she fretted, glancing down at her own new outfit.

Sabina rolled her eyes. "No one will be looking at me, Mother," she pointed out needlessly. "Not when Isemay makes such a beautiful bride."

Instantly the petulant look dropped from her mother's face. "She does, does she not? I vow that never since time began has Ganfordshire seen such a lovely bride. Is that not so, Wilfred?"

Their father nodded enthusiastically, though he did not speak. Sabina suspected the long trudge up the drive had puffed him out. "Indeed, indeed," he wheezed when his wife shot him an impatient look.

"Sabina made a lovely bride too," Isemay pointed out, a frown on her beautiful face as she twisted back to look at her sister. Sabina shot her a reassuring smile. *Dear Isemay.* As though Sabina's appearance had been even remotely comparable to the vision of loveliness that her younger sister made.

"Oh, to be sure!" their father agreed hastily.

"Sabina looked very well," her mother conceded, her face immediately assuming the expression of tragic suffering that any mention of Sabina's ill-fated marriage seemed to induce in her. For some reason, Thora Burrell appeared to think the failure of her eldest daughter's wedding was a sad reflection on herself.

"It was Miles who did not make a worthy bridegroom!" Isemay continued stubbornly.

Their mother sucked in a shocked breath. "Isemay!"

"Well, well, let us not rake up such unhappy subjects now," Wilfred Burrell cut in hastily. "On this happy occasion!"

Sabina heartily agreed with the sentiment, and luckily, as they rounded the bend, Ganford Chase came into view in all its magnificence to distract them. Their party halted abruptly as they stood a moment catching their breaths and staring up at the imposing ancestral home of the Dukes of Bethencourt.

Thora Burrell turned misty-eyed. "To think that my little Isemay will be mistress of *such* a house!"

Their father breathed heavily and clutched his side. "Indeed," he puffed. "Indeed. A great day."

Sabina gazed at the gray stone monstrosity and hoped devoutly that her sister never put the duke's competent steward's nose out of joint. There was no chance that any of the tasks Isemay did about Tipton Manor would have prepared her for the running of such a huge household.

Briefly, Sabina thought of Morecotte, which had been her married home for a year and a half before she had returned to her father's house. What sort of disarray would the place lie in now? she thought bitterly. Miles had been a slipshod master even before he had descended into a life of drink and debauchery. And now his distant relative Alfred was in residence. He was just as bad as Miles only without the looks and charm.

3

Her bosom swelled at the injustice that a third sort of cousin five times removed could have usurped her rightful inheritance as Miles's widow. If only Morecotte could be returned to her, she could have some semblance of an independent life. It was not that she wasn't fond of her parents, but without Isemay there, she would suffer the full brunt of her mother's attention. And Mother could be so very *trying*.

"Let us make haste!" her mother urged, flapping her arms. "We must not keep his lordship waiting!"

Sabina thought sourly of the duke's wedding guests. Bethencourt by himself was tolerable, though he was a fussy old bachelor and could be rather querulous. Sometimes she worried that Isemay would regret binding herself to such a man. He was so much older than her vivacious sister, and then, there was his family… Sabina shuddered. Bethencourt's relations had started arriving at Ganford Chase a week ago, and the Burrells had been invited to dine there twice since. Sabina had not found the experience pleasant.

A more disagreeable and frostier crowd of miseries she had never met, looking down their noses at them with their flinty gazes. His nephew and heir, that horrible Sir Jeffree, was the absolute worst of the bunch in Sabina's opinion. She thought now of Sir Jeffree de Crecy's fair good looks and those very blue eyes. The monumental arrogance of the man slapped you in the face every time you so much as looked at him.

Thankfully, he considered the likes of a provincial widow entirely beneath his notice, so Sabina had managed to escape his critical regard most of the time she had been in his presence. Still, she had observed him and the duke's closest friend, that cold fish Sir Charles Ellis, exchanging meaningful looks when her parents had found themselves out of their depth amid all the talk of art and culture at supper.

4

Her bosom swelled indignantly as she remembered their matching sneers. Her father might be a provincial nobody, but he was a kind man who had never done anyone any harm. Sabina's greatest mistake in life had been naïvely thinking that all men were like him. Her marriage had been a harsh lesson in life, teaching her that was not the case.

By the time they reached the grand entrance, there were several attendants stood awaiting their arrival. The lead one, an individual in a yellow tunic with a superior air, was almost twitching with impatience.

"This way, this way," he urged in a thin voice, gesturing before them. "The guests are gathered as we speak in the Great Hall."

Sabina eyed the man severely. "Well, it is not as though they can continue without her now, is it? They can surely wait another instant while my sister catches her breath."

"Sabina!" Thora Burrell hissed, pinching her arm. "You will make a spectacle of us!"

Ignoring her mother, Sabina stepped forward and offered her arm to Isemay, who was fiddling with her shoe. Her sister seized hold of her gratefully and reached down to remove a stone from her slipper. "A moment to recover would be appreciated," the bride admitted with a wince. "The soles on my slippers are so thin that I felt every stone on the approach."

"A breather would be a boon," their father concurred, mopping his brow. "For it has grown rather warm."

Their mother tutted but, realizing she was overruled, flapped her voluminous sleeves in front of her face in an effort to dispel her heightened color and the faint beads of perspiration from her brow.

Sabina took the opportunity to look her sister full in the face to search for any signs of cold feet. He was rich to be sure, and Isemay would be a duchess, but Bevis de Crecy was three times Isemay's age. Noticing her scrutiny, her sister gave her a radiant smile. "I am ready," she said, straightening up. Sabina dropped back so their father could take her place and lead Isemay into the Great Hall.

*

"I *suppose* she is beautiful," the Lady Maud said doubtfully, gazing across the Great Hall at her former brother-in-law's bride. Her lip curled scornfully. "By current standards at least."

When her words elicited no response from her depressed-looking second husband or her brooding son, she continued. "In my day, of course, other considerations were given to such an appellation. Refinement, grace, elegance of mind," she listed. "These were thought *just* as important attributes when it came to feminine beauty."

Jeffree de Crecy shifted impatiently from one foot to another. His mother was being ridiculous. Even the girl's sternest critic could not deny she was a beauty. He gazed with cold disapproval at Isemay Burrell and felt an overwhelming black tide overtake him. He had been holding it at bay all morning, but now it engulfed him like a great wave.

After all, what was the point in trying to put a brave face on it? Jeffree was in a foul mood. Ganford Chase was usually his haven, the place he felt the most at home in all the world. But those days were numbered, past even. After today it would have a new mistress and it would be *her* son, not Jeffree, who would one day inherit the dukedom and the ancestral home.

Since he was a boy, his uncle and every other member of his family had encouraged him to look at Ganford Chase as being his eventually. *You are my heir*, Uncle Bevis had told him over and over. *One day you will be Duke of Bethencourt, my boy.* And now look at the old dotard.

Jeffree's gaze shifted from the radiant youth of Isemay Burrell to the countenance of his uncle. Bevis de Crecy, fifth Duke of Bethencourt, was a well-preserved fifty-nine years of age. But even well-preserved looked ancient stood next to a maiden of nineteen.

Jeffree huffed out a breath and swallowed down his resentment that he would have to bear witness to this travesty of a wedding.

"Apparently Burrell is nothing more than a country squire," his mother pronounced contemptuously. "One would scarcely require telling, looking at his barbarous appearance now."

Jeffree cast an impatient look at the father of the bride. He looked a short, stout little man with an almost fearful expression in his eyes as he cast about the huge Great Hall. "He looks what he is," he agreed shortly. "Overwhelmed."

"It is outrageous that his daughter thought to thrust herself forward into a role such as Duchess of Bethencourt." His mother sounded grieved. "Only *look* at the mother! You can see where she gets her presumption! Resting her hand like that on Bevis's arm!"

Jeffree declined to pay any more attention to the bridal party. Instead, he turned pointedly to gaze in the opposite direction. "I believe I shall go and have a word with my godfather," he murmured.

"Poor Sir Charles," his mother responded at once. "He will feel this insult to our family name *most* keenly."

Jeffree clamped down his temptation to remind her that she had not been a de Crecy since her remarriage fifteen years ago.

7

Instead, he nodded at Sir Dudley, who nodded glumly back, and made his way to where Sir Charles Ellis stood on the opposite end of the hall.

"My boy," Sir Charles uttered, flickering his flinty eyes over Jeffree. He was a tall, spare man of gaunt appearance with iron-gray hair. He lowered his voice. "A sad day for this house."

Jeffree gave a sharp nod and fell in beside him. "He will not be dissuaded," he said, his lips a grim line of disapproval.

"Such madness often takes men in the autumn of their life, or so I understand," Sir Charles responded with a faint curl of his lip.

Jeffree glanced about; Sir Charles Ellis had been a good friend of the family for years, and the close association of their families was long-standing. He would have thought on such an occasion that his godfather's son and heir, Sir Leland Ellis, would have been in attendance. "Leland is not here," he observed.

After his own father's death, Jeffree had been raised in his godfather's house. He and Leland had learned their lessons together. However, to say they were like brothers would not have been a true statement of fact. They had never been close.

Sir Charles's face grew even sterner, if such a thing was possible. "Leland disappeared last night, and no one has seen hide nor hair of him since," he uttered with frigid distaste. "No doubt his destination was the nearest tavern."

Jeffree made no comment. It seemed that in his son, Sir Charles's abstemious lifestyle was reversed. Where the father lived a life of strict discipline, retiring to bed early with an improving text, the son caroused and led a life of flagrant dissipation. It was a bitter bone of contention between the two of them.

8

Jeffree cleared his throat. "Well, it is not as though he will miss much," he said dryly.

Sir Charles had just opened his mouth when the banging of a door and raised voices distracted him from making a reply. Jeffree also turned his head to see who this late arrival was. Whoever it was had only just arrived in the nick of time, for the priest had moved to the front of the hall and had been about to start proceedings.

Whoever it was had damnably bad manners, Jeffree thought, casting disapproving eyes toward the door which was barging open. To his surprise, the latecomer was none other than Leland Ellis, who swaggered in with a bored expression on his face. What *was* surprising was the procession of sober-robed individuals who followed in his wake.

"What is this?" Sir Charles muttered sharply. "What is the boy about?"

Jeffree's eyes narrowed. To his mind, Leland's companions looked like officials of some kind; he cast a quick glance toward the priest, whose mouth had dropped open. Clearly, they had *not* been expected at the wedding.

Leland made his unhurried way into the center of the room, his mocking eyes trained on the bride, who was flanked by her kinsfolk: her bewildered-looking parents and her dowdy older sister. Once there Leland halted, and the loud mutterings of the assembled crowd died down to a whisper.

"What is the meaning of this rude interruption to my wedding day?" cried the Duke of Bethencourt from his dais. He was an unimposing figure of middling height, with sandy-colored hair and a neatly trimmed beard. "It's an outrage i'faith! Ellis? You overstep the mark, bringing this rabble into my hall uninvited!"

Rabble seemed an odd word to describe the company, Jeffree thought. To his mind, they looked more like clerics. Then he noticed the disreputable-looking character bringing up the rear. Who in hells was this? The fellow's doublet had clearly seen better days, the cuffs looked beer-stained, and he looked so green about the gills Jeffree thought he was likely to throw up before them all.

Had Leland brought some drinking companion along to his host's wedding? Jeffree was baffled. This reprobate looked no more like one of Leland's usual cronies than the rest of them. Though he ran with a vicious crowd, Leland's friends were always monied and usually titled. This fellow looked as much a yokel as the Burrells.

"My pardon, Your Grace," Leland replied in that well-bred drawl of his, and though he seemed to make no effort to raise his voice, somehow it carried effortlessly to the four corners of the room. "But certain facts have come to light at this late hour which cannot go unpunished. My companions here are the local questor, summoner, and magistrate of this parish." He paused a moment, letting the significance of his words sink in.

Leland had brought along an ecclesiastical court, thought Jeffree, feeling stunned. Brought them to Uncle Bevis's wedding. *But why?*

"The proceeding is a little irregular, it is true," Leland continued. "But it will serve." He swung around to take in the crowd, before returning to face the dais where the Duke of Bethencourt stood open-mouthed in his wedding day finery. "I am afraid I must put a halt to your wedding, Your Grace."

"What?" the duke bleated, reeling back and falling into his seat. His steward rushed forward to assist him, but no one present could drag their eyes off Leland's insolent face.

"There have been dark dealings afoot, which must be dragged into the light," Leland pronounced with something approaching relish. The crowd murmured, and Jeffree saw Sir Charles stiffen beside him. "The wrong-doers must be brought to book," Leland continued. His enigmatic gaze traveled over his rapt audience to rest a moment on Jeffree's own face. What the hells was this?

"Reparations must be made," Leland pronounced lovingly, still looking at Jeffree. Not for the first time that morning Jeffree felt the presentiment of imminent disaster. Why the fuck was this bastard looking in his direction? "There will be a reckoning," Leland promised. "And it starts now."

2

Sabina passed her arm around her sister's slim shoulders as Isemay shrank toward her.

"What is happening?" Isemay moaned softly. "I don't understand."

"Neither do I," Sabina started to reply before choking on her words as she caught sight of the spindle-shanked figure who had slouched in behind the court officials. Surely that was the current thorn in her side, her late husband's cousin, Alfred Hendry! She stared at him in astonishment. What was *he* doing here?

She knew of no link betwixt the de Crecy family and her late husband's. Indeed, Miles had always spoken of the Hendry family as hailing from just outside the southern capital. Sabina turned her head to see if her father had noted Alfred's presence, but Wilfred Burrell was gazing with fascinated dismay at the cool devil speaking who was holding everyone in the palm of his hands.

Sabina had briefly met Sir Leland Ellis in the past few days and her impression had been no more favorable than the rest of the bunch. He was tall and thin, with pale skin and curling black hair. He was certainly far too young for the annoying smirk and attitude of languid boredom that he adopted as habit, for he could be no more than four and twenty. His manner was very near as infuriating as Sir Jeffree's withering disdain.

She had seen the two of them about the neighborhood a few times over the years, for both Sir Leland and Sir Jeffree stayed with the duke often. However, both had considered themselves far too good to mix with the general populace of Ganfordshire, so Sabina had only ever seen them at a distance until the last week.

Her eye was naturally drawn toward Sir Jeffree as the tallest and grandest figure in the room. So strong was the look of supercilious hauteur on his face that it almost took her breath away. How did one ever get to be so contemptuous of one's fellow man? she wondered. Around these parts, everyone whispered that the duke's heir was as prideful as a devil.

As for Sir Leland, for someone currently smashing the duke's wedding to smithereens, he looked as though he was taking a dark sort of enjoyment from the task, Sabina thought with a shiver. Why was he doing this? He did not even have an iron in the fire, she reasoned, for he was not actually related to the Duke of Bethencourt at all. It was not as though he would be ousted from the line of succession as the nephew might be if the marriage produced issue. Sabina was wrenched from her thoughts when Isemay's grasp on her arm grew painful.

"Information has lately come my way," Leland Ellis continued in his smooth, compelling voice. "Implicating Mistress Isemay Burrell of lewd, immoral conduct. In short, of wickedly playing his lordship, the Duke of Bethencourt false."

Gasps and hisses filled the hall as she, Isemay, and their mother all cried out simultaneously, "No!" and "Nay! 'Tis not so!"

It seemed to Sabina that barely anyone present even deigned to acknowledge their reaction. It was as though everyone in the hall was straining to draw apart from the beleaguered bridal party.

Sir Leland did not even pause in his narrative. "This man," he said, raising his voice and gesturing toward Alfred Hendry, "bears witness to the infamy! One Alfred Hendry of this parish!

13

He has performed his civic duty this morning and informed the magistrates of what he knows."

"You shall not say so!" burst out Sabina's father, finding his voice. He took a step forward and pointed a shaking finger at Alfred Hendry. "That man holds a grudge against our family and seeks to discredit us!"

Sabina looked from her father's indignant face to those of the magistrate, questor, and summoner. As she took in their self-important expressions, she realized with a sinking heart that she had no faith in such men as these with their long faces and sober robes.

It was men like these ones who had been stalling for months now over her own inheritance claim, making very little progress in their judgment. Finally, her father had told her they were likely holding out for a bribe, and the only reason there had thus far been no ruling was that neither they nor Alfred Hendry could afford to sway them in their favor.

It was true, this was not the same court, for ecclesiastical courts held sway over moral transgressions, not property claims. Still, thought Sabina, narrowing her eyes, they were the same *type*. Turning from them with disgust, she sought out that craven cur Alfred Hendry. As always, he avoided her gaze with his shifty, watery eyes. Miserable creature that he was! How dare he besmirch her sister's name with this vicious slander, the lying knave!

Sabina's soul burned as she turned her head to seek out the duke with her accusatory stare. What was he doing while Isemay's name was dragged through the mud? Bevis de Crecy, the fifth duke, was staring open-mouthed at the spectacle unfolding in front of him. He sat slumped into his seat, holding a pomander to his nose as though to ward off anything

14

unsavory. Bitterly, Sabina realized they could expect no rescue from that quarter.

She let her eyes travel over the onlookers who stood drinking in Sir Leland's words. Already she could see their shock transforming into more hostile emotion as they glanced at poor Isemay's blanched face. Isemay's lovely mouth quivered. *Do not cry*, Sabina willed her silently as she pressed her sister's slender shoulders. *Do not let them see any sign of weakness for they will take it as confirmation of guilt.*

Sabina knew what it was to face ostracization and judgment. She had withstood the scandal of returning to her father's roof after the failure of her marriage. It had been hard, even for one as stalwart as she. Only respectable widowhood had brought her back from the brink of social ruin. Isemay would never survive the disgrace of this, she thought with certainty. She must *do* something.

Hardening her resolve to foil this foul plot against her sister, Sabina turned back to listen to Sir Leland with careful attention. His lying words teased and tantalized but gave no proof apart from the say-so of the dissolute Alfred. She did not need to see Isemay's bewildered terror to know it for naught but a tangle of lies. Her sister was blameless. This was a conspiracy against her sister's good fortune in catching a duke's eye. No doubt it had been trumped up by his superior family and friends, she seethed. *The pack of jackals.*

She had to find a loose thread to take hold of and unravel the plot in front of everyone now before it grew out of control. Squaring her shoulders, Sabina accepted the fact that in the face of such insurmountable odds, only something drastic could reverse the tide at this point. It did not matter. She would do whatever it took, unflinchingly.

15

Finally, it seemed Sir Leland had tired of toying with his prey and was set to deliver the killing blow. "Who, you may well wonder, is the coconspirator in this foul act of wickedness?" he drawled, swinging about to take in his avid audience. "Whose soul could be so blackened as to behave in such a depraved way toward so exalted a personage as his lordship? For make no mistake, this was the most treacherous act of disloyalty by both parties.

"My witness," he said, once more indicating toward the wretched Alfred, "Alfred Hendry, hath his own reasons for keeping an eye on the inhabitants of Tipton Hall, who would deprive him of his rightful inheritance."

Sabina spluttered at yet another falsehood and heard her father's startled protest at the home of his ancestors being brought up so scurrilously.

"Imagine his surprise, when he witnessed night after night the figure of a man creeping under cover of darkness to the Burrell home, climbing the shrubbery to gain admittance to this woman's bedchamber." Again, he gestured toward the pale Isemay.

Leland's voice rose against the faint murmurings of the scandalized crowd. "Finally, giving in to his curiosity, Alfred Hendry followed the guilty party back from whence he came. You may imagine his astonishment when he found him bound for this very residence." Sir Leland spread his arms wide, indicating the walls around them. "The hallowed halls of Ganford Chase!" The mutterings grew as people looked from side to side at their immediate neighbors, wondering who the culprit could possibly be.

"Speak!" Sir Leland demanded theatrically, turning back to a startled-looking Alfred. "Speak up and shame the guilty party, I say!"

Alfred coughed and scratched the back of his neck. Sabina felt a sudden, savage satisfaction when she saw the look of irritation that flashed across Sir Leland's face. He had chosen poorly in his false witness at least. Alfred Hendry had never given satisfaction to anyone in his life, it was unlikely he would start now. Alfred mumbled something, and Sabina strained her ears to hear him.

"What was that you say?" Sir Leland asked sharply, clearly angry that his dramatic effect was being ruined. "None present can hear you!"

Alfred's expression turned sullen. "It were that Sir Jeffree de Crecy," she heard him mutter. Sabina's eyes widened. So, this was an attempt to discredit the duke's heir as well? Her gaze sought out Sir Jeffree, who must not have heard the accusation, for his face still wore its habitual expression of disdainful hauteur. Unless, thought Sabina with sudden fury, he was in on the plot too!

Suddenly, with horrible clarity, the situation made sense. The rotten swine had been unable to bear the thought of the title and property slipping through his privileged fingers, so he had cooked up this wicked and slanderous charge with the help of his friend! Sabina felt breathless with affront. He would rather seem a nasty sneaking lecher than be disinherited!

"Speak up, man!" Sir Leland barked. "Point out the culprit to us! Let us see who is lover to the fair Isemay."

Alfred straightened his slouching figure and raised a shaking hand, flapping it ineffectually in Sir Jeffree de Crecy's direction. "'Tis Sir Jeffree de Crecy!" he bleated and then took

17

a quick step behind Sir Leland so that he stood a barrier between himself and the imposing Sir Jeffree, who looked suddenly frozen to the spot, his eyes starting from his head.

An unpleasant smile curved Sir Leland's lips. "And this is where I come into the tale," he said slowly. "For last night this man and I did fall into conversation at an inn known locally as The Blue Boar. Alfred Hendry did seek to unburden himself to me of his uneasy secret, and armed with this knowledge, I confronted Sir Jeffree last night when he was in his cups and his lips loosened. Then did he confess he had taken Mistress Isemay to his bed."

"No!" Isemay cried out in distress, half tearing herself from her sister's arms. Sabina allowed herself one last glance at Sir Jeffree, whom the accusation appeared to have transformed into a frozen statue, and decided enough was enough. Catching hold of her sister, Sabina thrust her firmly toward their mother and took a step forward.

"Gentlemen!" she said rousingly. "I'm afraid you have the facts all wrong in this matter." She kept her tone calm, though she lifted her voice so all could hear. "Though you have uncovered an intrigue, it is true, you err in identifying one of the principal players of this sad tale." She paused a moment, ensuring everyone had followed her thus far, before continuing in a ringing voice. "For 'tis I who have been playing the whore to Sir Jeffree and *not* my innocent sister at all."

For a moment, the hall was so silent you could have heard a pin drop. Then the onlookers dissolved into an expostulating, outraged rabble.

"Quiet!" roared a voice, which Sabina was surprised to see emanated from the dark-robed summoner. He did not look as though he should possess such a booming voice. He struck his staff against the flagstones and turned toward his fellows. The white-bearded magistrate cleared his throat.

"Madam, your name?" he asked, directing a coldly disapproving look in her direction.

"It is Sabina Hendry, formerly Burrell."

The magistrate's snowy eyebrows rose, and he shot a quick glance at sulky Alfred. "And your relationship to the witness is?"

"The witness is some manner of distant cousin to my late husband, Miles Hendry."

"And you now reside at this place, this…" He turned to look at his colleague who murmured a prompt under his breath. "Tipton Hall?"

"I do," Sabina confirmed, aiming her voice to the rafters. "My late husband's property is currently a matter of dispute between myself and your *witness*, so I am unable to take possession of my rightful home."

"Why you scarcely lived there when he was alive, you hussy!" fired up Alfred fretfully.

"Quiet!" the summoner roared again, and Alfred cringed.

"So, you, then, are sister to the accused," the magistrate mused. "It seems strange, madam," he continued, "that Hendry does not seek to heap the blame upon your shoulders if the two of you are in contention as you claim."

Sabina shrugged a shoulder. "As to that, sir, you have just heard, have you not, how he calls me hussy and casts aspersions on the state of my late marriage. I can assure you his tongue has been busy wagging with such tales for the past twelvemonth. He has done his best besmirch my reputation already."

19

She let her cool eye travel impartially over the listening audience. She was not sure how many were acquainted with her own family troubles. Most of them, apart from the servants, were not local, for they were nobles who had traveled far and wide to attend the wedding.

"My sister's reputation is stainless. Doubtless, this knave saw a chance to inflict more damage upon our family name this way. Or mayhap he simply mistook the bedchamber window in his nighttime vigils creeping about in our shrubbery. Perhaps he just meant to add some additional spice to his tale, by adding in a cuckold when relaying it to the drinkers at The Blue Boar."

There were gasps and a muffled laugh at her cutting remarks, and the magistrate whipped around at once to seek out the miscreant. Everyone stared back solemnly. Sabina had the oddest suspicion that it was Sir Leland Ellis who had laughed. He was watching her now with amusement and an appreciative gleam in his eye. Her bosom heaved. How dare he find this a source of amusement! she seethed. Her sister's life! Her family's reputation!

The questor and magistrate clearly shared her suspicions for they were also now glaring at Sir Leland. They had not appreciated the reminder of the role the tavern had played in the proceedings. She risked a glance at the proud Sir Jeffree, who still stood rigid with shock, no doubt at her intervention at the eleventh hour of this wicked plot. Likely he was struck dumb that she would dare to mount a defense against such exalted company and fight back. Well, he was wrong!

Sabina took a steadying breath. She needed to remain calm in the eye of the storm. Lifting her chin, she turned back to the magistrate, who had given a polite cough.

"Your tale, Mistress Hendry, is an interesting one," he said. "Yet I see a flaw. Why should Sir Jeffree mislead Sir Leland by telling him it was the younger sister he was trysting with?" he asked. "Answer me that!"

"As if he would look twice at you!" Alfred put in spitefully.

Sabina felt her color ebb and flow at this jibe, for well she knew Isemay was the beauty of the family and not she. Still, her voice was steady when she replied gravely, "As to that, sir, I am afraid I cannot say. My sister is generally considered far more beauteous than I. Perhaps Sir Jeffree did not wish to own his lover was so plain of face."

A murmur went up at that, and Sabina knew she had struck the right note. Most men here could well understand such a face-saving lie, and Sir Jeffree was known most of all for his monstrous pride.

"Sir Jeffree?" the official probed. There was a heavy silence. Sabina took a deep breath and brought herself to glance once more at Sir Jeffree, who was now, she noticed, brick red. She thought it was with anger, and certainly, the glance he turned on her was full of bitter recrimination and loathing.

"I hardly know what to say, save this," he said through gritted teeth. "That Mistress Isemay Burrell is innocent of all these false accusations."

"Jeffree, my boy!" It was the Duke of Bethencourt who cried this as Isemay openly wept with relief. Sabina wanted to go and comfort her, but she forced herself to remain rooted to the spot. There may be more questions, more lies to tell before her sister's honor was restored. She would not take her seat until she knew Isemay was in the clear. Stiffening her spine, she stared straight ahead, ignoring the hue and cry all around her.

21

3

Jeffree was fuming. He could not believe what his life had descended to in the past hour. Now everyone thought he had been sporting in bed with the elder sister while boasting of bedding the younger! He looked *ridiculous* and the blow to his pride could not be borne. His name bandied about and sullied in the most degrading manner possible. And what's more, in front of his entire family! He could *slaughter* Leland! He still might.

He glowered at the bastard now as he stood listening in sardonic amusement to something the court officials were saying to him. He did not look remotely shamefaced about the role he had played. In three steps, Jeffree could seize a good hold of his neck and shake him like a dog with a rat. He had always been the bigger and stronger of the two of them.

"Hold, Jeffree," his godfather cautioned, shrewdly guessing his thoughts. He kept a hand clapped to Jeffree's shoulder in an iron grip, but they both knew that would not hold him if he truly went for Leland. "You still need to keep a cool head about you, my boy," Sir Charles continued. "We are not clear of the woods yet."

Jeffree whipped his head around to pin the older man with a savage glare. "I am aware of that!" he answered furiously. "The repercussions from this day will likely never die down!"

"Look," the older man cautioned, nodding toward the three black-robed court members. "They will expect to exact some punishment for the wrongdoing they believe they have uncovered this day. You can bribe them, it is true, but you must wait for an opportune time. For the moment, at least, you must appear to accept their ruling."

Jeffree bristled. "I am not the one deserving of punishment!" he pointed out angrily. "That would be Leland and that false bloody witness of his!"

Sir Charles clicked his tongue sympathetically. "You know Leland of old. My son was ever a wild, rash youth."

"Youth?" Jeffree was incredulous. Leland was twenty-four years of age. "He's only four years younger than me!"

"I can understand why he thought to intervene," Sir Charles spoke thoughtfully. "But alas, this scheme was as ill-advised as the majority of Leland's stratagems."

Infuriated, Sir Jeffree shrugged his mentor's bony hand from his shoulder. "Ill-advised?" he repeated in thunderstruck tones. "Good gods, man, he has dragged my name through the mud, and if I don't end up in a pillory or under sentence for a flogging, it will be no thanks to him!"

Sir Charles opened his mouth, but Jeffree was in no mood to hear his cautious counsel. Losing all patience, Jeffree strode over to where the bridal party was stood arguing with one another while the court officials stood looking on in disapproval.

"If you will only come away with us now, Isemay," the mother was imploring her youngest daughter. "And leave this business to be settled. His lordship will surely want to fix when your vows are now to be made."

The bride shuddered and wrenched her arm free of her clinging mother. "Indeed, I will not, Mother!" she answered with spirit. A good deal more spirit than Jeffree thought was proper. He would have thought, under the circumstances, she would have been better employed swooning somewhere in a corner as became a modest maiden. At the very least, she ought to have

23

been weeping at her betrothed's side, begging his forgiveness for the wretched spectacle the wedding had descended into.

Where was his uncle anyway? A quick scan of the hall showed the duke still being fussed over by his steward. Even from here, Jeffree could hear the duke's peevish tone of voice as he complained of his ill-treatment. *His ill-treatment?* No one had accused him of being a lecherous adulterer! At least…he supposed that was not precisely the charge. The graceless wench had claimed herself a widow. Where was she anyway?

Jeffree surveyed the gaggle in front of him. The Burrells seemed to be staging quite a scene. Even the officials could not seem to impose any order on them. The bride had two spots of high color in both her cheeks and her eyes sparkled with indignation. "You think I will languish on the sidelines while my sister, who has championed me this day, is meted out with harsh punishment?" she asked shrilly.

"Isemay!" her father replied, glancing around nervously. "Calm yourself, child! What will this fine company think?"

"I no longer care what they think!" Isemay responded hotly, then burst into impassioned tears.

"Child, child!" her mother quavered, looking just as embarrassed as her spouse. "Shhhh!"

Someone cleared their throat, and that was when Jeffree noticed her. The woman who had compounded the lie and boldly claimed him for her lover. His chest swelled with indignation. Sabina Hendry looked so far from the picture of a fallen woman that it was almost laughable.

She stood there in her prim, outdated wimple, her hands on her hips, looking steely-eyed and unrepentant in the midst of the throng. There was something unnervingly bold about her, he decided. You would think she would scarcely dare to look him in the eye after her outrageous lie, but there she was, facing him bold as brass.

"You need have no concerns on my account, Isemay," she said calmly enough. "Do go with Mother now; there's a good girl. Father will stand by me and see I am not dealt with unjustly."

Isemay sniffed. "Well, so long as no one suggests you are branded or your ears cut off," she said tearfully. "Like they did with that bawd from Leckington last winter."

Jeffree stiffened. Though of tender years, clearly this sister was just as unschooled in her tongue as the older. Both were wayward and cared not a whit for the superior company they now found themselves in. He was shocked to his core to hear the hallowed halls of Ganford Chase polluted with such talk!

"Isemay!" her mother shrieked. "The very idea! The things these children do hear," she twittered, towing her daughter away. Isemay cast a worried backward glance over her shoulder as she was led toward her betrothed, and Jeffree shook his head. His uncle had chosen ill, attempting to link the lot of the de Crecys to these ill-bred Burrells.

Jeffree let his narrowed gaze return to his true quarry. As a rich man, he could afford to bribe his way clear of any consequences, but that was not the case when it came to Mistress Sabina Hendry. Was she really as calm as she appeared? He found it hard to believe. The punishments for sexual misconduct were harsher for women, and with no gold to grease their palms, these ecclesiastical courts could be brutal.

As though she felt his accusing glare, she looked up at him a moment, their gazes clashing. The eyes that met his own were coldly impersonal and not so much as a blush stained her cheek. Then, just as quickly, she seemed to dismiss him altogether, her

25

gaze returning to that of the bearded magistrate, who was conferring with his fellows.

Jeffree glanced toward her father, Master Burrell, hovering close by with an anxious expression on his round face. "I pray you gentlemen will spare my child," he quavered. "This past year has not been kind to her what with losing her husband and her home—" he began but was cut off by the loud-mouthed summoner.

"Silence!" he barked, and Master Burrell lapsed once more into unhappy silence, practically wringing his hands.

"This matter is a grave one," the questor started solemnly. "A very grave and serious matter indeed, which has led to grievous outcomes. As such, my colleagues and I can only see fit to mete out the most severe of punishments at our disposal—"

"Just one moment," Jeffree interrupted loudly, drowning out the fellow's speech. "I desire some speech alone with Mistress Hendry."

There was an awkward silence as everyone stared boggle-eyed at him.

"Some might say there has already been a surfeit of desire and alone time betwixt the two of us, Sir Jeffree," Sabina Hendry replied, confounding him for a moment with her audacity.

He glared at her. She gazed back, a cool challenge in her gray eyes. He had never seen anyone look less like a temptress in that frumpy headdress, but she had nerve, he would give her that. An abundance of bloody nerve. "Nevertheless, madam," he ground out once he could catch his breath. "I would have an audience with you."

"Alone, I fear, *cannot* be permitted at this point, Sir Jeffree," the magistrate interrupted. He wilted a little under Jeffree's

26

angry answering gaze but looked resolute on this point. Ridiculous, in Jeffree's opinion, as clearly they believed that horse had already bolted.

"Apart, then!" he flung at them angrily, gesturing to a far corner of the room. "You can surely observe us from a distance."

"I am afraid that it is impossible, Sir Jeffree," one of his fellow officials intoned gravely. "If you have aught to say to this woman, it must be here and now, in front of witnesses. It has already been proved that your motives in seeking her out are far from pure."

Jeffree ground his teeth and turned toward Sabina Hendry. "Well, then, madam. It seems we must converse in front of all present." She made no response and that needled him. "Come now, you are surely not afraid of me, not after all we have meant to each other," he said nastily and was pleased to see a slight flush mount her cheek, even as he heard the indrawn breaths his words had caused. It was worth it though, to put a dent in her blasted composure.

Sabina Hendry cleared her throat. "As you say, Sir Jeffree. It would be disingenuous for me to play coy with you now. What is't you would say to me?"

He sent a vaguely hunted glance from left to right. Was he really going to have to do this? "In light of all that has passed," he said gruffly, "it seems that only one path lies before us. One that would lead to the restoration of our reputations in any case."

His words seemed to mystify her, a crinkle appearing between those gray eyes. "I don't think I quite—?" she started, but he threw up a hand to silence her, even as his soul rebelled against the words he was struggling to utter.

"You will have to marry me," he said abruptly, forcing the words past his lips. "At this juncture, neither of us has much choice in the matter."

Her reaction would have been comical if so much had not been at stake. Jeffree was not exactly known for his sense of humor at the best of times, and at this precise moment, he couldn't imagine ever laughing again.

Sabina Hendry's mouth dropped open. She stared at him as her father went off in a paroxysm of splutters and coughs. Once her father's labored breathing had subsided into gentle wheezing, she took a deep breath. "I am afraid that is quite impossible for I have vowed ne'er to be wed again, Sir Jeffree."

"*You have vowed?*" he asked sharply, feeling winded by her words. "*You* have vowed?" His voice rose in anger. "I care nothing for your vows, madam," he said. "I have lived my whole life under a sacred vow I made in my eighteenth year!" He struck his chest with his palm. "I have never deviated from that solemn vow by word or deed not once, since that day. Never has my devotion been brought into question or disrepute—not once until I met you! You have made an open *mockery* of the life I have lived and brought my reputation into outright ridicule!"

She was listening now, her eyes wide and alarmed. "Sir Jeffree—" she started resolutely. "I hardly know of what vow you speak—"

He cut her off impatiently. "My celibacy, of course, what else!" He paid no attention to the embarrassed coughs and uneasy shufflings of feet all around him, for he cared not a whit for what any of these people thought. "You have compromised me, madam, and I demand you take responsibility for the damage you have wrought on my reputation and my virtue," he

28

thundered. "And I demand you do it now, in front of these witnesses here present. I will accept no other compensation. Indeed, there is none other that would suffice."

The color had now drained from Sabina Hendry's face. She looked aghast. "Sir Jeffree, you cannot possibly mean for us to be joined as man and wife! Only consider—"

"That is exactly what I mean!" He swung about to look at the court officials. "Am I not justified?"

The questor cleared his throat. "Madam, by your own admission you have lain with this man and afforded him the rights and privileges which should belong only to your husband. Why should you cavil now, when you are offered the role of wife, in place of wanton? It is more than the likes of you deserve!"

Sabina's mouth opened and closed, as well it might, Jeffree thought contemptuously. She could make no answer to that, not after her previous bald-faced lie. "It is madness!" she cried, looking about wildly. "I won't do it! You cannot make me!"

"Stubborn, willful woman!" the magistrate exploded. "I can scarcely believe mine ears! This man, whose virtue you stole by way of your wicked wiles, is willing to give you the protection of his name, and you turn your nose up at the opportunity!"

"I barely know him!"

"You *know* him in ways, madam, that would make a decent woman burn with shame!"

"Young woman," the summoner put forth. "If you are so foolish as to reject this proposal then I feel it is only fair to warn you that you face public punishment of the most stringent kind. By method of a skimmington ride, culminating in the ducking stool."

Sabina Hendry's breath came very fast. "You would do that to me? The daughter of a Burrell of Tipton Hall? I am no village lass!"

"You have shown yourself no better than the lowest village lass, who resides in the gutter," the summoner responded with venom.

Sabina flinched as the words sank into her flesh like barbs. "I cannot marry this man," she said in a low, trembling voice. "It is not reasonable to ask it of me!"

"Sabina," her father said hoarsely. She turned to him at once. "Child, you speak of being a Burrell of Tipton Hall, and yet, if you do not take this step, if you do not accept this man's offer then…" His words trailed off before he could bring himself to utter his dire warning, and he turned his face, now wet with tears, away from her. "Do not ask your mother and me to live through the shame of seeing you publicly lambasted for a harlot."

Well, thought Jeffree, the implication was clear enough. She would be cast out from the ancestral home and the bosom of her family. Her father's words seemed to have made more of an impression on her than his own, he noticed sourly.

Ceasing her protestations, Sabina cast a deeply despairing look in his direction. "However repulsive we both find the notion?" she asked brokenly.

Jeffree snorted. Gods above, but she was an ungrateful bitch! He could not remember disliking a person more in his life. He was coldly furious as he gave his short nod of agreement, his mouth tight with anger and his eyes hard and glittering. He felt as though he could strangle her.

"Very well, then," she said hollowly, with the expression of one greeting the pronouncement of the hangman. "I suppose I have little choice in the matter and will have to marry you."

4

Afterward, Sabina remembered the events of the next quarter of an hour as a miserable blur. After being hustled into an antechamber, they got through the formalities with scant ceremony. For all his insistence it must go ahead, her new groom seemed to have as much trouble as her in forcing the vows through his tight lips. Sabina found it best not to look him full in the face, but rather to focus on a spot just to the left of him.

The three officials stood as witnesses, along with her shamefaced father. The priest engaged for the duke's nuptials had instead to turn his offices to theirs. Despite the Great Hall being full of his relatives, Sabina noticed that Sir Jeffree had not asked a single one of them to stand beside him now and see him joined in matrimony.

She wondered suddenly how many of those disapproving nobles even knew what was happening in this small chamber, mere yards away from where they stood gossiping over the morning's events? Well, the duke had certainly thrown a banquet to remember, she thought bitterly. Would the priest now go next door and join Isemay with Bethencourt?

Would she have to reenter the Great Hall at Sir Jeffree's side? Sabina was distinctly uneasy at the prospect. She only had so much bluster and she had used up today's allowance to the full. Seizing the bull by the horns, she turned to her new husband. "What now?" she asked forthrightly and saw him give a violent start. Of course he would think a wife should only speak when spoken to!

He opened his mouth and then shut it again, as though drawing a sad blank. She realized Jeffree de Crecy had no more notion of how they should continue than she had!

"I am not staying in this house," she started pugnaciously.

That roused him alright. "You will stay wherever I see fit, madam!" he retorted, blue eyes blazing.

Jarringly, Sabina realized that now they were indeed man and wife, this was no more than the truth. She bit the side of her mouth as her father regarded them with unease.

"I shall have to go in search of your sister and mother," Wilfred Burrell muttered, looking harried. "The gods only know what has become of them and how they are coping!"

"Yes," Sabina agreed dismally. Mother always did tend to think herself the most affected by any given situation. She sent another glance Sir Jeffree's way and saw the magistrates were now taking their leave of him. He looked rigid with affront as they issued whatever final words they saw fit on such an occasion. Likely an entreaty to sin no more. Giving them a stiff nod, Sir Jeffree watched them leave the chamber, his large body radiating hostility from every pore.

Then his eyes flickered to meet Sabina's, and her breath caught to see them flare with such loathing. What had she done, she wondered with a spurt of alarm, linking her lot in life to this man? Fighting down the rising panic, she turned back to her father. "Go, then." She forced a smile to her lips. "You had better see they have come to no ill."

Her father cast a quick look at Sir Jeffree, blanched, and beat a hasty retreat, leaving them alone together. An uneasy silence ruled for all of one minute. Then he spoke. "We had better go out there and face them," he said with a marked lack of enthusiasm. Significantly, he left the *together* unvoiced, and Sabina considered this a moment.

"You are probably right," she conceded. "However, I should tell you now, Sir Jeffree, that I will not be paraded and humiliated to appease your friends and relations."

"What?" he barked. By this point, Sabina was starting to think his handsome face wore a permanent expression of outrage. It must be exhausting, she thought, always being so offended.

"If you will give me your arm," she continued with as much calm as she could muster, "and treat me with civility, then I will accompany you back into the Great Hall right willingly."

"You will accompany me back into the hall, madam, because I say you will," he returned harshly, but after a heartbeat or two, he stalked over to her. Looking at his face, she braced herself, thinking he might shake her until her teeth rattled. When he reached her, however, he halted abruptly and offered his arm. True, he was stony-faced when he did so, but under present circumstances, she found this understandable.

Taking a deep breath, Sabina laid her hand on his forearm. She felt him stiffen beneath her touch and tried to keep her clasp on his decorated sleeve as light as humanly possible. His tunic was an elaborately embroidered affair, covered with gold thread. She could only imagine the contrast they would present to the company at large.

Her own dress had been in her possession for two years at least and had been worn on many occasions, as the fraying braid on her cuffs attested. Any spare monies her father had were spent on Isemay's attire. After all, she reflected wryly, today was not supposed to be *her* wedding day.

Pressing her lips together, Sabina steeled herself for the ordeal ahead of her. None present would ever know how much it cost her pride to walk back into that hall, whose rafters had heard her defamed as a shameless woman, a self-proclaimed strumpet no less.

She reentered it now as Sir Jeffree's despised bride. Everyone would draw their own conclusions about that, seeing them leave the room with the members of the ecclesiastical court and then reenter, respectably wed. No doubt they would conclude he had married her under sufferance, under threat of punishment no less.

Should she disabuse them of this fact? Protest she had wanted no part of him, that he was the one who had insisted on this ridiculous union? She dismissed the notion almost at once. They would ne'er believe such a thing, she thought dully. Instead, they would all think her a nasty little schemer, a woman of loose morals, triumphant at the outcome of catching such a husband.

Even as they crossed the threshold into the large flagstoned hall, she heard the whispering start, saw the cold, hostile stares. *Oh gods, what had Isemay been thinking, wanting to be joined in marriage to this despicable lot?* There was not one friendly face among them!

Sabina swallowed and found herself clutching at Sir Jeffree's arm. To his credit, he did not make so much as a murmur of protest as he led her across the Great Hall, headed for a woman in her late forties, dressed in a dark blue brocade. If she had not such a sour expression, Sabina would have thought her a handsome woman despite the many lines at her forehead and about her mouth. She guessed they were from years of frowning and pulling down her mouth into a disagreeable sneer.

35

At their approach, she turned flashing eyes on Sabina. "Why do you bring this woman into my presence, Jeffree?" she asked in freezing accents. Instead of moderating her tone, she raised it, making her words clear to those standing about them.

Only by the greatest effort of will did Sabina not react. Perhaps those two mortifying years of marriage to Miles had stood her in good stead after all? For they had prepared her to meet this fresh torment now with an appearance of unruffled outward calm.

"I bring her to you as a dutiful son, presenting his spouse," Jeffree replied, his voice lifted to match her own.

So then, this was his mother. Sabina recognized those very blue eyes, though it looked like that was the only physical trait he had inherited from her. His mother was dark and slight, not fair and tall. Was the man stood next to her with the stooping shoulders his father, then? she wondered. If so, it was hard to believe when Jeffree's own were so very broad. Whatever else he might be, her new husband was a fine figure of a man.

His mother choked on whatever words had hovered on her lips, as all around them gasped and hissed. "You cannot be in earnest, my son!" She faltered.

"I assure you that I am," Sir Jeffree replied woodenly. "This is my mother, Lady Maud Vyse, and her husband," he added as an afterthought. "Sir Dudley Vyse. Present your curtsey." He said the last without turning his head, and for a moment, Sabina was not sure who he was addressing. Then her wits kicked in and she sank down into her most graceful curtsey.

Jeffree's mother gave her only the most cursory nod of her head by way of response. Sir Dudley bobbed his thinning head, shooting an alarmed look first at his wife and then Jeffree, speech apparently beyond him.

36

To Sabina's dismay, her husband did not move immediately on to the next group of relatives. Instead, Jeffree remained where he was as though they might pass some more words by way of conversation. The silence grew oppressive. All about them, it seemed as though people craned their ears to hear their exchange.

"How remarkably well this has turned out for you," her new mother-in-law said finally, addressing her in a voice as cold as ice. "You are to be congratulated, it seems, as well as rewarded for your *conduct*. Punishment, it seems, must wait for the hereafter."

Some might say this marriage was punishment enough, Sabina thought, but left the words unspoken. She did not know the lengths this latest husband might go to by way of retaliation. For all she knew, he might box her ears or haul her out and beat her with the nearest stick.

Instead, she forced a small, answering smile of equal coolness to her own lips. "How right you are, Lady Maud. As the gods know, we will surely reap that which we sow."

Jeffree's mother's eyes widened, and two spots of hard color appeared in her gaunt cheeks. She seemed almost to stagger for a moment at her new daughter-in-law's effrontery. Her husband reached out a steadying hand to catch her elbow. Shrugging him off angrily, she straightened herself. "Move away now, Jeffree. There is only so much a mother can tolerate," she said bitterly.

He inclined his head and moved on to the next group without another word. Sabina kept her tight smile in place for the next half hour as they made their way slowly about the room, Jeffree formally introducing her to a myriad of de Crecys and their connections. Few ventured more than superior stares in

37

exchange and minuscule nods. Sabina did not trouble herself to remember their names.

They had performed almost a full circuit of the hall when they finally approached the dais. The Duke of Bethencourt was seated, speaking plaintively to his dour-looking friend, Sir Charles Ellis. Of his vile son, who had made the wicked accusations, Sabina could see no trace, nor of her mother or sister. Frowning slightly at their absence, Sabina allowed herself to be escorted into their presence.

"Uncle," Sir Jeffree said. "Allow me to introduce my wife." She turned a deaf ear to the faint trace of scorn she heard in his words at addressing her thus.

The duke eyed her doubtfully. "Er, yes, I have met—er—Mistress Hendry on several occasions." He clammed up as she performed a curtsey low enough for a duke. "All most irregular," he fretted. "I could wish you had chosen a less underhanded method in your wooing, Jeffree!"

Sabina's eyes widened, and she could not forbear a sidelong glance at this. Sir Jeffree's chagrined reaction would have been almost laughable if the situation were not so dire. She waited for him to strenuously deny that he had ever wooed the likes of her, but other than a hot slash of color appearing along his cheekbones, he did not react.

"Poor Mistress Isemay has been treated shamefully," the duke tutted. "All a misunderstanding, so Ellis tells me." He indicated his friend who stood by looking like he was carved out of granite. "Leland got the wrong end of the stick. Or at least, that wretched fellow from the tavern misled him or got his facts muddled up, I hardly know which."

An awkward silence reigned for a moment. Had the father been trying to excuse his son's behavior? Sabina wondered scornfully. If so, she would never be convinced that Sir Leland had acted in good faith. A craven cur like Alfred would never have dared to cook up such a story left to his own devices. No, he had been put up to it by Leland Ellis, Jeffree de Crecy, and very likely this upstanding gentleman, Sir Charles Ellis.

"Alfred Hendry," Sir Charles Ellis said suddenly, as though seizing on something previously overlooked. "A relation of yours by marriage, I understand," he said to Sabina, fixing her with an accusing stare, before directing an enigmatic look at her husband. She felt Jeffree stiffen beside her.

And just what did Sir Charles mean by looking like that? she wondered indignantly. Did he mean to suggest to the duke that *she* had set the little worm up with his tale of spying neath her window? *Ridiculous!*

"Only the most tenuous of familial links existed between my late husband and Alfred Hendry," she said steadily, and once again saw the same reaction as Lady Maud had given her. Sir Charles drew back, looking as though she had offered him mortal insult. Did none of them think she had a tongue in her head to make a reply?

Did they truly expect her to stand meekly by while they made their barbed comments and not retaliate? More than likely, they expected her to be tongue-tied in their magnificent presence, she thought with gathering resentment. Well, they could think again! She was not so easily intimidated.

Sabina gazed back at Sir Charles, more than ready to defend herself. She was no sniveling child, but a full-grown woman of five and twenty who knew her own mind. If he had meant to get his son off the hook by selecting her for his scapegoat, then he could think again! "I am surprised to find your son no longer center stage, Sir Charles," she opined coolly. "He seemed so at

39

home in that spot, I wondered if performing to a crowd might be in his blood."

Sir Charles's gaunt cheeks filled with hectic color, and Sabina felt a rising satisfaction that her bolt had struck home. Sir Charles was a proud and autocratic type, 'twas plain to see. He gave her a stiff nod. "My son was *mortified* to have falsely accused the duke's intended on the information he received in good faith."

Sabina let her lip curl. Men like Leland Ellis were never mortified. Having seen his wicked plot fail, he had either fled from repercussions or had grown bored and sauntered off in search of further sport. Personally, she suspected the latter.

"Well, well," huffed the duke fractiously. "The damage is done. This Hendry fellow is clearly a mischief-maker of the highest order, or else a most muddle-headed individual," he tutted. "Shouting accusations from the rooftops when he would be better counseled to have stayed at home!"

"He is lucky he was not horse-whipped," Sir Charles agreed haughtily.

"*He* is lucky?" Sabina cut in. "If he is, then he is not the only one."

Sir Charles looked almost apoplectic at this rejoinder, and Sabina felt Jeffree's arm turn beneath her own and his fingers grip her there warningly. Sabina almost gasped aloud at this unexpected contact. Instead, she pressed her lips together firmly and lapsed into silence. No one spoke for a full minute, and Sabina took the opportunity to gather her scattered wits.

"Might I enquire, Your Grace, the current whereabouts of my family?" she asked at last.

The duke gazed about in bewilderment. "Naseby!" he cried, and his ever-attentive steward hurried forward. "Where is the Mistress Isemay and her parents?"

"They have been taken into an adjoining room, Your Grace. For the ladies to—er—*recover*," he said with a small bow. "I would be happy to lead Lady de Crecy there, if that would be agreeable." He directed a polite glance Sabina's way, and both she and Jeffree had started violently at this form of address.

Lady de Crecy? Sabina gave a shudder that she wasn't sure was not echoed in Jeffree's tall frame. Gods, was that to be her name from now on? Heavens forbid!

*

In a daze, Sabina allowed herself to be led by Naseby into a small adjoining chamber where she found her mother lying on a wooden settle bench with her head on a cushion, moaning. Isemay's slender form was pacing up and down the floorboards. She swung about on hearing the door open. "Sabina!" Her sister flew across the room to embrace her.

"So!" her mother said, striving to sit up. "You're here are you! Well, I hope you are proud of yourself, that's all I can say! I have never been so ashamed in my life! Announcing in front of everyone that you've been acting like a—like the veriest *trollop*! In front of all the duke's fancy company too!" her mother wailed.

Sabina released her sister and approached the bench. "Mother, please!"

"I don't care what your sister says," Thora Burrell sniffed, swinging her legs onto the floor. "It was utterly *humiliating*, and I will ne'er be able to show my face abroad again!"

"Mother—"

41

"My own father would have beaten me soundly for daring to act in such an abandoned fashion, but not your father—oh no! Won't lift so much as a finger to put our reputation to rights!"

"What do you mean?" Sabina asked carefully. Surely her mother did not believe the ridiculous tale of her acting as Sir Jeffree's paramour? *Nay, it could not be so.* "If you mean Father won't banish me, then he did threaten that, if it makes you feel any better."

Her mother sniffed. "You deserve to be soundly whipped and put from our door!"

Sabina felt her shoulders sag. "Mother, please," she said wearily. "Father has done everything he could, indeed it was at his insistence that I went ahead with—"

"Quite *ruining* your sister's wedding day, you wicked creature!" her mother continued, heedless of her interruption. "Well, it's all come to naught now, thanks to your conduct! Isemay is too mortified to go ahead with the ceremony. She will ne'er be wed now! Oh, you have disgraced us all!"

Sabina's heart thudded. *Had it all been for naught, then?* For a moment she felt quite bereft. Then she remembered she had succeeded in clearing Isemay's name. "Nay, Mother, Isemay has emerged from this ordeal with her reputation untarnished," she pointed out desperately.

"Untarnished?" her mother raged, clutching her fists. "With her own sister branded a—"

"That's enough, Mother!" Isemay said fiercely, crossing the room to stand beside Sabina. "Father and I have explained it to you a hundred times!" She took a firm hold of her mother's arm and shook it. "You are being foolish and refusing to listen to reason. Sabina saved me, and I shall forever be grateful to her."

42

Turning, Isemay reached for Sabina's hand and gripped it fiercely before continuing, "If I hear you maligning my sister again, I vow I will *never* forgive you, Mother. Not ever!"

At these vehemently spoken words, their mother collapsed into a heap of heartrending sobs. Isemay pulled a wry face. "She's overwrought; do not listen to her. She is beside herself that I did not marry Bethencourt."

"It is true, then; you do not mean to be married this day?" Sabina asked, feeling dumbfounded.

Isemay pressed her lips together. "I do not," she said firmly.

"Is the duke—?"

"I sent Father to speak to him and explain that he means to take me home forthwith." Isemay cast a darkling look over her shoulder. "I can hardly be expected to remain amid such company where I have been so vilely slandered and abused."

Their mother let out another low moan. Sabina's head reeled. Isemay returning home with their parents, and she left behind a new bride? "Isemay—" she started urgently.

"Will you be ready?" her sister continued. "Father will not be many more minutes. The duke has very delicate sensibilities. He will understand why we will not tarry."

Sabina stared at her in abject misery. "Did Father not tell you?" she asked despairingly.

The color drained out of Isemay's face. "What?" she gasped. "Oh, tell me quickly! They do not mean to punish you?" Blindly she reached for Sabina, who caught her hands in a firm grip.

43

"No, no," Sabina said swiftly. "Nothing like that. I am to be spared." She licked her lips which were suddenly dry. "'Tis only that… We were forced to take rather…drastic measures."

"Drastic measures?" Isemay repeated faintly. "What can you mean, sister?"

"I… That is…Sir Jeffree de Crecy hath been forced to marry me," Sabina managed to croak at last.

"*What?*" their mother squawked at once, bouncing up from her seat. "Married?"

"Shhhh! Keep your voice down, Mother," Sabina begged. "They will hear us in the Great Hall."

"I do not care if they hear me as far as Kilmarton town!" their mother retorted with spirit, advancing on Sabina and grasping hold of her other hand. "Is this true, Sabina? Are you indeed the wife of this man, the duke's nephew?" Her puffy eyes fixed anxiously on her eldest daughter's face and Sabina relented.

"Yes, Mother," she admitted bleakly. "We just exchanged vows in full view of the priest, and the court representatives acted as witnesses."

Her mother's plump fingers squeezed her own so tight that Sabina winced. "Then he's bound right and tight. Oh, saints be praised!" Thora Burrell moaned. "I never doubted your father for an instant. Doubtless he threatened to punish the villain! Seducing my poor daughter and under our own roof too, the knave!"

Sabina closed her eyes briefly. Isemay sank into the chair her mother had abandoned with a horror-stricken expression on her lovely face. "Oh, Sabina, no!" she uttered faintly.

"Now is not the time for such die-away airs, Isemay!" their mother scolded her youngest daughter roundly. "Sabina has done the right thing. Men—they're all the same!" Thora Burrell's bosom heaved. "But he won't get away with it! Not this time!" She nodded fiercely. "He can pay the fiddler for playing his tune!" Abstractedly, she patted Sabina's arm. "Well done, daughter," she murmured sagely. "Very well done. I am glad to see you behaving sensibly for once."

"Mother!" Isemay reproached her. "How can you say so? Does not everyone in the county agree that Sir Jeffree is the most arrogant and vainglorious man in all Karadok?"

"Oh, hush now! Fie! 'Tis foolishness to dwell on such things now that circumstances have changed! He is rich, handsome, and well-connected." Thora Burrell recited the only virtues she knew of her son-in-law and straightened the bodice of her gown. "Those are not things to turn your nose up at. Where can your father be?" she tutted. "I shall need to visit with your aunt Mabel before nightfall."

"Visit with our aunt?" Isemay's face fell as she and Sabina exchanged looks. "Mother, we hardly want gossip of this day to spread!" Aunt Mabel had a livelier tongue even than their mother.

"Nonsense!" their mother preened. "Sabina is married, of course, I must tell my sister!"

Isemay opened her mouth again, but Sabina caught her eye and shook her head. After all, the visiting nobles might not spread word in the vicinity for none of them were local, but certainly, there had been servants drifting in and out of the hall. They would soon carry the news to their relatives in the village and to the patrons of The Blue Boar. Perhaps, after all, it might not be

45

the worst thing for Aunt Mabel to spread a less salacious version of events.

A look of horror dawned on Isemay's face. "They will let you return home with us, will they not? They surely do not mean for you to remain here?"

"Stupid child!" Their mother rounded on Isemay. "Where else is a wife's place, but at her husband's side! You surely do not expect Sabina to abandon a *second* husband?" she said pointedly. Sabina's face flamed red.

It was at this point that there was a faint knock on the door, and two men appeared outlined in it. One the small, slightly rotund figure of her father and the other the tall, imposing figure of her new husband. Sabina's heart sank all the way down to her somewhat worn slippers.

"Thora, Isemay," her father said, rocking back on his heels. "His Grace has kindly condescended to send us home in one of his conveyances. We must take our leave of Sabina now." Sir Jeffree stood stony silent beside him, saying not a word.

Thora Burrell glanced fleetingly at her new son-in-law, then seemed to decide against whatever she had been considering saying. Instead, she hurried to Sabina and clasped her in her arms. "Do not lose heart now," she murmured beneath her breath. "Not when you have him where you want him!"

Sabina could not withstand the grimace that passed over her face. Clearly, against all odds, her mother now saw her in the light of some intrepid husband-catcher. "Do not worry, Mother," she managed to reply as they drew apart.

Then she found herself fiercely hugged by Isemay. "We will think of some way out of this mess!" her sister whispered. "Just...do not consummate the vows!"

Sabina cast a quick glance over her shoulder at Sir Jeffree. Somehow she did not think bedding her was uppermost on his mind. He looked more likely to fling her in a ditch! "Do not worry," she repeated numbly. "All will be well."

Her father nodded at her from the doorway, clearly too discomfited by everything that had passed to embrace her now. Sabina lowered her eyes as her family passed out of the room. She swallowed hard before looking up again. Jeffree de Crecy was stood in the doorway, looking about as tractable as a figure carved from marble.

"What now?" she asked, feeling suddenly exhausted. It had been a long day.

Wordlessly, he gestured for her to pass through the door before him. Squaring her shoulders, Sabina followed his command and they walked down the passageway, to where he indicated she should climb a flight of stairs.

Sabina did so and he followed her up. At the top of the stairs, he led her along a corridor until they reached a door which he flung open and marched inside. Sabina hesitated on the threshold. The door had opened into a large bedchamber with a big, canopied bed covered and draped in luxurious blue brocade. Her eye traveled over a handsome square table and two chairs, a carved bench, and a large trunk before reaching the massive unlit fireplace with the de Crecy arms displayed above it.

"Where are you going to sleep?" she asked pointedly.

"That is *my* bed."

"Then where am I to sleep?" Sabina asked, gritting her teeth.

He nodded his head toward a door on the far wall. Her head held high, Sabina marched across the room and opened the door, stepping into another large room that seemed stuffed to the brim with cabinets and trunks and suits of armor. One entire wall was covered in a variety of battle weapons, decorated shields, and standards, all bearing that image of the black tree on the white field. Sabina pulled a face. It seemed the de Crecy family would be in no danger of forgetting their family crest.

Hearing a footfall behind her, Sabina turned about to see Sir Jeffree had followed her. Walking to a large armoire, he unlocked the doors and drew out a small truckle bed. Then he opened another door and extracted a pile of blankets which he slung on top of it. "Here," he said briefly.

This, she realized, was to be her bed. "Who usually sleeps in here? Your servant?" Sabina asked, curious despite herself.

"No one," he replied. "Osborn sleeps in the servants' quarters when we stay at Ganford Chase."

"So, this room is for all your possessions, then?" she asked, startled at such a large room being used for that purpose alone. She had not realized Sir Jeffree had his own rooms at the duke's residence. Though perhaps she ought to have, considering he must have been the heir for over twenty years.

"You flatter yourself," he replied with a curl of his lip and stalked back out. Sabina stared after him, puzzled a moment until his meaning trickled through. Of course he would think she should be honored to belong to him, she thought, slowly shaking her head. Pompous ass!

Sabina spent a couple of minutes making up the cot, though in truth, it could be no later than six o'clock. The bed felt as though it would be comfortable enough to sleep in, though it was rather narrow. It was only as she twitched the last blanket into place that she heard a knock and Sir Jeffree answering his bedroom door. Though she lifted her head, she could make out

48

no words of the murmured conversation. The door shut again, and she heard his footsteps advancing.

"They will serve us our supper up here," he said coldly from the doorway. "You will join me at the table next door." It was not a request, but an order, and he turned sharply on his heel after issuing it and disappeared. Reluctantly, Sabina straightened up. It was not as though she had a better occupation for her time, and besides, now she thought about it, she had not eaten for several hours.

This and this alone was what prompted her to walk back into his bedchamber and drop down into one of the seats at his table. Sir Jeffree was stood staring down at the unlit hearth, one hand resting on the mantel. He did not turn when she entered. He did not acknowledge her in any way. Sabina cast her eyes around the vast room, with its impressive views over the duke's extensive grounds.

Moments later the door was knocked again, and Sir Jeffree lifted his head to shout, "Come in!" Three servants appeared carrying a variety of dressed dishes. As they were set down, Sabina guessed they were a sample from the fancy wedding banquet that had been planned for this evening. Would the rest of the duke's guests be dining in the Great Hall even now? Despite the fact there was no bride or groom to sit in the positions of honor?

Jeffree came and sat opposite her for their meal and indicated the servant should serve them wine. Sabina's stomach rumbled as she gazed upon the fare. He did not dismiss the servants once the dishes were set out but instead expected to be waited on. If it seemed strange to Sabina to be waited on by three servants when dining privately in your own bedchamber, she held her tongue and tried to ignore the servant stood silently at her elbow.

When she drank down her goblet of wine rather fast, it was instantly refilled without her having to ask. The first course was a loin of veal covered with some kind of rich sauce, gilted plums, and pomegranate seeds. Jeffree scraped the plums and seeds from his meat and ate it with an expression of acute dislike, but Sabina tucked in hungrily. Unsurprisingly, the duke's cook was first-rate; she did not know when she had ever eaten such luxurious foods.

The second course was a dish of creamed fish served with glazed root vegetables in a carmeline sauce.

"Must everything served from my uncle's kitchen be drenched in sauce?" Jeffree asked irritably. "It makes the dish well-nigh unpalatable." He threw down his knife and demanded more water be added to his wine.

In Sabina's opinion, it was almost wicked to add water to such a delicate and fragrant wine, but she supposed Jeffree was privileged to the point he thought it nothing special. The next course was a fine mature cheese served with round, thin, fried crackers dusted with saffron and a jelly crafted into the shape of a fowl and decorated with real feathers.

Jeffree's mouth grew pinched and tight when he saw the elaborate jelly and he waved this away and partook only of the cheese and crackers. "Is there no bread?" he demanded, and when the servant made as though to go and fetch some, he bade him irritably to stay where he was.

Sabina tried a mouthful of the jelly and found it filled with berries and flavored with nutmeg. To her surprise, it was delicious with the cheese. "This jelly is wonderful," she said aloud. "You should try it. You would not expect it, but it really complements the cheese."

Sir Jeffree sent her a withering look and did not bother making any reply. Sabina turned to the servant hovering nearby. "Please present my compliments to the cook." The servant bowed and refilled her goblet. How many had she had now? She had better make this her last one or she would be growing far too outspoken. She did not know why she was bothered to speak to him at all, save that it seemed a little awkward to sit through an entire meal in stony silence with servants present.

The final course was stewed pears in rosewater drizzled in honey. Jeffree eschewed this sweet course altogether, demanding more watered wine, and quit the table, striding to the window where he stood with his back to her as Sabina finished her bowl of pears.

"That was truly delicious," she said, setting down her spoon once she had finished. "Thank you." The servants responded with bobbed heads and wan smiles as they finished tidying away the dishes.

"I shall expect my bath in the next half hour," Jeffree said over his shoulder as they bowed their way out of the room and shut the door behind them. Sabina could only guess at the additional strain the household staff must be under with so many guests staying with them at present. The de Crecys could not be an easy clan to accommodate.

"You can retire next door now," Jeffree said aloud, still not deigning to look in her direction. *Rude beast.* Sabina pushed back her chair and rose without a word, making her way into his storeroom. She supposed she would be brought some water to wash at some point. Then again, perhaps not. Carefully removing her wimple, she set the pieces of crisp white linen down on top of a flat-topped trunk and then unpinned the coiled braids from about her ears.

51

She had just set her hair pins down beside her headdress when she heard the door knock next door and murmured voices. *It must be His Highness's bath*, she thought sourly. She was just unlacing her cuffs when she heard the rap on her own door.

"Are you decent?"

Sabina rolled her eyes. "Yes," she answered.

The door opened, and he stood in the doorway holding a bowl and steaming jug. Sabina looked at him; he looked at Sabina. It dawned on her that he was not going to stir another step, so with a sigh, she walked toward him to take the washing water from him. To her surprise, he took an almost alarmed step back.

"What is it?" she asked with surprise.

"You are undressing," he said stiffly, hot color suffusing his face.

Sabina's jaw almost dropped at such prudishness. "I have only removed my headdress," she pointed out, and he bridled like some sort of maiden aunt, thrusting the ewer toward her so violently that a good deal of it sloshed out into the basin.

Sabina grabbed it and retreated into the room as he slammed the door shut. She shook her head. He really was the oddest man she had ever met in her life! Carrying the basin to the nearest armoire, she set it down and found a ball of soap flakes and a cloth inside. Undressing briskly down to her shift, she slung her gown over the nearest chest, had a good wash, and clambered into the truckle bed.

She was relieved about the separate sleeping arrangements, though not for one minute had she imagined he would fall on her with lust as soon as they were alone. He had made it clear he viewed her with cold contempt, and anyway, if he had been speaking true when he demanded her hand in marriage, then he simply was not inclined that way.

Incredible as it might seem, with such a body and handsome face, Sir Jeffree must have no taste for fornication. Sabina could only be thankful for that fact, even though she bore no faith whatsoever in Isemay's words from earlier. There could be no way out of this union that did not involve her absolute ruin— consummation or no consummation.

She had barely managed to scrape through her estrangement from her first husband. Only his death had freed her from the stain of a reputation as an undutiful wife. Flinging a hand behind her head and rearranging herself on the small cot, Sabina considered the path before her in the failing light of the summer's evening.

It had clearly not occurred to Sir Jeffree to provide her with a candle and the room was now growing dark. Her tired eyes drooped. Likely she could soon leave this wretched place. Sir Jeffree could stash her in his own home, wherever that might be. Some godsforsaken spot in a far-flung corner of Karadok. Doubtless, he neglected it shamefully while toadying up to his uncle.

With a bit of luck, she could be settled there independently while Sir Jeffree was off…doing whatever it was that Sir Jeffree did. That way, this disastrous marriage need not be quite so inconvenient after all! Maybe she could make it her home. Of course, she would never feel about it as she did Morecotte.

The thought of Morecotte filled her with the familiar feeling of loss, the home she had loved far more than Miles. Beautiful Morecotte. She had thought she would grow old there, surrounded by its orchards full of blossoming and fruitful trees.

She would always regret Morecotte. Sabina's eyes closed, and she fell into an uneasy and fitful sleep.

5

Jeffree snatched open the door and paced back inside. "Well?" he demanded of his manservant, pulling the drying cloth from his hair and throwing it into the chair before the fire. "What did you find out?"

Osborn shut the door quietly behind him and dragged his hat off his head before clearing his throat noisily.

"Be quiet, can't you, man!" Jeffree snapped, motioning for the servant to join him at the fireplace. "She will hear you."

When Osborn's eyes tracked over to the empty bed, Jeffree let out an irritated huff. "She's in my dressing room next door," he said scathingly and then felt annoyed he'd had to explain himself to his own servant.

"Oh." Osborn sniffed and wiped his cuff across his bulbous nose. "It's on account of how parched I am, Master Jeffree," Osborn explained soulfully. "My throat is awful dry."

"Parched?" Jeffree repeated. "You have spent the whole evening in the local inn!"

"It was a mortal long way back," Osborn sighed.

"Fool!" Jeffree scowled, but he gestured toward the remaining pitcher of wine anyway from which Osborn hastened to pour himself a goblet, filled to the brim. He walked slowly back over to the fireplace to join his master, careful not to spill as much as a drop.

Jeffree rolled his eyes and asked himself for the thousandth time why he put up with the scoundrel. Once Osborn had drained half the cup and smacked his lips, he wiped his mouth with the back of his hand and relaxed into his habitual slouch.

"Well?" Jeffree barked. "What do they say in the village about Mistress Sabina Hendry?"

"Plenty!" Osborn replied with a chuckle which made Jeffree's blood freeze. "She's only been widowed a twelvemonth, but before that she'd set tongues wagging in the county with her froward, headstrong ways! They do say as Hendry had his hands full with her and rued the day he took her to wife! Only lived with her a year he did, before he threw her out for a nagging scold and set her packing, back to her father's house with a flea in her ear."

Jeffree, who had frozen with his arm half raised to the mantel again, relaxed. "A scold?" he repeated coolly. It was certainly true she had a wayward tongue. *A nagging scold.* Well, he supposed, it could be worse. There were certainly graver vices for young, handsome widows to indulge in.

He had not actually realized she was handsome until he had seen her with her long honey-colored braids hanging down to her waist just an hour ago. Why had he thought her hair would be dark beneath that wimple? Likely, he had thought she would resemble her sister in that respect. That and the fact her eyebrows were so dark and that small black mole just above and to the left of her mouth.

Realizing Osborn was watching him shrewdly, he pulled himself together. A shrewish wife was not such a daunting thing to him after all. She would be ill-advised to practice such tricks on him. "So, she's thought a shrew locally, is she?" he asked.

"Aye, Master Jeffree," tutted Osborn, shaking his head. "There's many a local lass has felt the brunt of her temper. Wouldn't suffer a pretty face to serve her at table, she wouldn't. A veritable termagant, she was by all accounts. Up she would fly and drive the poor maids from her door, if she thought her

56

husband's eye tarried too long on them. A nasty tongue and a suspicious nature, so they say."

Jeffree blinked. So, Mistress Hendry was the jealous type, was she? His lip curled with disgust. He could not stand women who loved creating vulgar, petty scenes. A commonplace mind, he supposed must be the fault. "Anything else?"

"That cousin of Hendry's has taken possession of the widow's property—they's been in dispute over which of them is the true owner, ever since the husband cocked up his toes and died. A pretty little property next to Langley Woods. They do say as possession is eleven points in the law when it comes to property, so mayhap he has already won the battle. Or as good as."

Jeffree shrugged contemptuously. "Some paltry land dispute is hardly my concern. You say she returned to her father's roof directly after her husband cast her off?"

"Aye," Osborn agreed, "that's right enough. Old Burrell had to have her back at his table, poor old sod. He's well-thought-of locally, is Burrell. A fair landlord and a good master though he's no head for business and suffered many losses these past five years what with one thing and another. They do say his income has more than halved. It must have been a blow to have his daughter returned in disgrace, another burden on his purse."

Jeffree grunted. The Burrells had the look of people struggling to keep up appearances. The finery of the youngest daughter's bride clothes had contrasted heavily with her older sister's shabbiness. Likely they viewed the beauty as the means to restore her family's fortunes. "Is that all?" he asked as Osborn drained his goblet to the dregs.

"It is, Master Jeffree," said Osborn, glancing hopefully toward what was left of the wine.

Jeffree waved him toward it. "Help yourself," he said dryly. "How goes the feasting below?"

Osborn poured his cup with his tongue sticking out of the corner of his mouth in concentration. "Dismally, Master Jeffree. How but dismally, when a wedding feast lacks both bride and groom?"

"What?" Jeffree's tone was sharp. "The wedding did not go ahead as planned?"

"Only you was married in the house this day," Osborn replied. "The Burrells carried off Mistress Isemay in great umbrage at the dishonor done to her. By all accounts, the duke don't blame 'em one bit."

"What of Master Leland?" Jeffree frowned. "Has he remained under my uncle's roof?"

"Oh-ho! Not he, the rascal. He showed a clean pair of heels and cleared out when everyone was distracted. Powerful put out, Sir Charles was about it, though everyone agrees young Master Leland could not have stayed put, not after the trick he played."

Jeffree grunted. He supposed that was true enough. If Leland had not the money to put up at an inn, for his father kept him frequently short of funds, he had a friend in the next county whose place he could make for at a pinch. Mallenby would no doubt think this latest mischief of Leland's a grand jest. None of Leland's friends had any morals to speak of.

Dismissing Osborn, Jeffree bolted the door after him. He shrugged off the robe he had wrapped himself in after his bath, climbed into bed clad only in a pair of braies, and tried to forget that tonight was his wedding night to the biggest shrew in Ganfordshire.

*

"Wake up, damn you!"

Someone was shaking her arm. Someone insistent and gruff. Sabina gasped and sat up abruptly, nearly bumping heads with the half-naked man crouched beside her cot. It took her a moment to recall who this man was and why he had access to her bedchamber at some ungodly hour in the morning.

"Come on!" Jeffree scowled at her, flinging back her blankets.

His hissed breath made her glance down to find her shift had ridden up her legs as she slept and was now tangled at her thighs. Sleepily yanking the hemline down, she allowed herself to be half dragged out of the room and into Sir Jeffree's bedchamber next door.

"Get in the bed," he said in an urgent undertone, his hand at her elbow, propelling her in the direction of the bed.

This brought Sabina up short. "What? Why?"

"I can hear the household stirring." He scowled. "Servants will be lighting the fire and bringing us washing water. You had best be in the marital bed by then, or there will be even more talk."

His tone, as usual, was irritated, and Sabina was too tired and muddled to demand an explanation, though she opened her mouth to attempt it.

"Just get under the covers," he snapped impatiently, thrusting her toward the huge bed. Sabina shrugged and climbed onto the mattress. She crawled up to the top of the bed and then slipped under the sumptuous blankets, burrowing down into the soft comfort with a sigh.

The truckle bed had been rather hard in truth, and she had woken in the early hours feeling cold. The spot she had gravitated toward felt so warm; she realized she must be lying directly where Sir Jeffree had been sleeping. She was so comfortable, she did not even care. Rolling onto her side, Sabina closed her eyes and allowed herself to drift back to sleep.

When she woke again, it must have been at least an hour later, for it was a lot lighter in the room and two servants were crouched over the large fireplace, feeding the blaze. Sir Jeffree must have overestimated his ranking among the duke's houseguests, for clearly, he was way down the priority list for them to have left him waiting so long.

Either that or they were trying to give him some extra time in his eager bride's arms, she reflected, pulling a face. Two more servants entered with steaming ewers of washing water which they set carefully on the table. Sabina felt herself prickle all over at the curious stares that were turned her way.

Rolling onto her back, she turned her head and found Sir Jeffree lying not even an arm's length from her. To her surprise, he was sprawled out on the bed with abandon, most un-de Crecy-like. Not only was his chest uncovered and his arms flung wide, but he had one well-formed leg lying on top of the covers. Despite his arrogant coldness, his body must run hot, she thought, for there was not a goose pimple in sight even with the amount of bare flesh on display. Likely sleeping in such a huge bed had given him bad habits.

She considered him critically a moment. There was no getting around the fact, he was a fine figure of a man. Not just tall and well-built, but heavily muscled too, which surprised her. Her first husband enjoyed hunting and archery, but he had certainly not had a physique like this one.

Her eyes ran over Sir Jeffree's golden hair and short curling beard. Even disliking him acutely as she did, she was forced to

60

admit he was probably the most handsome man she had ever seen at such close quarters. In truth, she could see no fault in his looks, though some might say it was a pity that his eyelashes and eyebrows were as fair as his beard. His face did not lack distinction for this, all the same. Even without those piercing blue eyes opened, he had a heart-stopping face. Shame he was so absolutely loathsome in his character.

Seeing him stir, Sabina turned hastily away to study the vaulted ceiling which was crisscrossed with beams. She wondered if the fireplace, however vast, could warm such a huge bedchamber in the winter. Turning back, Sabina found Sir Jeffree's very blue eyes trained on her. He said not a word. The absurd notion flashed into her head that Sir Jeffree must never have woken with a woman in his bed before. She cleared her throat and sat up.

When he averted his face so quickly, she glanced down, thinking she must have slipped out of her shift. But no, she was still decently covered. He was just hugely prudish.

"Have you not finished that yet?" he shouted suddenly, making Sabina jump. She had practically forgotten all about the dallying servants. "Get out!"

Footsteps scuffed across the floor as they hurried out, shutting the door behind them.

"Are you always so unfailingly rude to everyone?" she asked, though deep down she already knew the answer. Of course he was.

Clearly, Sir Jeffree thought the question beneath contempt, for he ignored it, rolling out of bed, and stalking into the next room where she supposed one or more of the many cabinets were stuffed with his clothes. He slammed the door behind him, and

Sabina sat there, in the middle of his huge bed, wondering what she was supposed to do now.

She was just debating climbing out of the bed and starting her own ablutions when he marched back into the room carrying a pile of fresh clothes. He seemed annoyed by the sight of her still in the bed, but she was quite convinced he would have been just as put out to find her stood in the center of the room. She turned a blind eye to this and slid out of bed. Seizing one of the pitchers of warm water to her chest, she made her way gingerly into the next room.

Sabina took her time over her wash, rebraiding her hair and pinning it into place, then donning her best dress and wimple once again. She almost felt armored when she had the severe white headdress in place. She knew it made her look older and a good deal more formidable. Sat with her braids down in that massive expanse of blue brocade she probably looked a nervous little fool.

Now she beheld herself in one of the mirrored cabinet doors and thought she looked practically middle-aged. She primmed up her mouth and looked severe. If she was to face a legion of de Crecys again, it was just as well she felt fortified. She was going into battle after all, and she certainly wasn't going to meekly lie down and take their snubbing, rude behavior, however much they might expect it as their due.

When she could delay no longer, she rapped on Sir Jeffree's door and walked in to find him once more gazing out of the window, resplendent in a tunic of scarlet decorated on the sleeves with seed pearls. Sabina blinked at him, wondering what the occasion was. Then again, maybe he always dressed like that. Yesterday's outfit had been a more sober color, a subdued plum with gold threadwork, though now she thought about it, it had been just as sumptuous in its own way.

He turned and frowned at her, but in an abstracted fashion. "How far is your father's abode from here?" he asked.

"Don't you remember?" she asked waspishly. "From our midnight trysts. Not very thorough of you to neglect that detail when you were cooking up your nasty little story."

"*My* nasty little story?" he snapped. "You were the one who labeled yourself my whore!" He turned redder at these words than she did, she noticed as she marched over to the carved wooden settle and plumped herself down. "I would have refuted Sir Leland's claim," he said stiffly. "Had you but given me half a chance."

"You said nothing!" she flung at him. "While your good friend Leland Ellis maligned my sister in the foulest way!"

"God's teeth, madam!" he shouted back at her. "I was in shock that Leland could even *think* to utter such a depraved thing! Not everyone's tongue is so ready as yours!"

"I do not believe you," she answered woodenly. "So much did you hate the thought of being disinherited that you would have swallowed that wicked lie and let my family fall into ruination."

He stepped forward hastily at that, his fists clenched. "You shall not say so!" he seethed.

"I heard what you've all been saying about us even before the wedding!" she responded angrily. "What jumped-up bumpkins we Burrells are. How *dare* we presume to aim as high as the noble family of de Crecy! Looking down your long noses. But you soon stopped being so aloof when Ellis started with his sordid little tale. Then you were all rubbing your hands together with glee and lapping up it up, thrilled to your cores!"

Sir Jeffree's face froze, and Sabina could see he was both shocked and struggling to find a response. Good gods, had no

63

one challenged him to his face before? From his flummoxed expression, it appeared not. He turned his face aside, and when he spoke, his voice was low and gruff. "I own we were less than gracious. Saying such things was…beneath our dignity."

Silence reigned for a moment, and when he spoke again, his voice had returned to its former formality. "My only defense is my bitter disappointment in the match. Even you must see how it affects my expectations. I was…venting my spleen. Whatever I thought and said of the match…it was not my place to judge His Grace's decision." Every word seemed to be dragged from his unwilling lips.

Noticing Sir Jeffree had fallen short of begging her pardon, Sabina snorted and folded her arms. "You insulted my family," she responded coldly. "Why in hells should I care now about making reparation to your sainted reputation?" She noticed with satisfaction how shocked he looked at her use of the word *hells*. *Good!*

"Because," Sir Jeffree countered, practically gnashing his teeth by this point, "can't you see? I was angry and resentful, speaking poison about your family was the only means I had to relieve my feelings! If I had known there was some nefarious plot afoot, wouldn't I have been reconciled to the wedding and speaking fair? Wouldn't I have been biding my time and making it widely known that I bore no malice?"

Sabina shrugged a shoulder. "How should I know? I should think that 'speaking fair' would have alerted everyone you were up to something. From what I can make out, you have never 'spoken fair' to anyone in your life!"

Sir Jeffree looked incensed. "Madam," he said stiffly. "You scarcely know me. And I have not acted so very poorly toward you despite the fact you would have wriggled out of your obligation to me if you could have."

"What obligation?" Sabina asked.

"After blackening my name, need I remind you, you had the *temerity* to turn down my proposal of marriage in front of witnesses?"

Sabina snorted. "What of it? I cannot see that I have done anything so wicked as to deserve such a punishment as marriage to *you*!"

"You ruined my reputation!" he flung at her.

"No," she replied steadily. "*You* did that when you agreed to go along with Leland Ellis's scheme!"

"I? Agree?" He seemed to have difficulty catching his breath for a minute. "I agreed to no such thing!" he all but roared.

Sabina clapped her hands to her ears. "*He* was the one who named you in his work of fiction, not I!"

That gave him pause for a moment; she saw him raking back over the words spoken. Suddenly his gaze narrowed. "You named me also," he said, bringing up his chin. "And compounded the lie!"

"I merely deflected the blow from my blameless sister!"

"By flinging yourself in its path," he said bitterly.

"That may be so," she conceded. "But I could only work with the materials before me to try and mitigate the consequences as best I could. You have doomed us to this marriage and you alone!"

He huffed out a breath, placing hands on his hips. "And just what do you think would have happened to you, madam, if I had not married you?" His tone was scornful.

"Well, that can only be conjecture at this point," she said, tossing her head.

"I seem to remember the magistrate spoke of consequences. Dire consequences if my memory serves me well."

She stuck her nose in the air. "As my father is a man of some note in the district, they would not have had the free rein such men revel in when it comes to the punishment of women."

"Oh? Spared you a scold's punishment before, has he?" he asked in a cool, hateful tone.

"Pardon?"

"I hear that is your reputation locally," he continued with a sneer. "A shrewish nag whose first husband put her from his door."

Sabina shot out of her seat, breathing hard. "You know *nothing* about it!" Suddenly, she was the one struggling to draw breath. So, even the godlike de Crecys knew all about her bitter failure of a marriage. Maybe they had all thoroughly discussed it last night at supper when she was sleeping in a storeroom. Or mayhap they had known about it before then when they were picking over Isemay's family background and finding them all wanting. The failure of a sister who could not keep a husband.

She wheeled about and lurched blindly for the bedchamber door, wrenching it open and practically falling into the corridor outside. She did not think Sir Jeffree called after her, at least, she would not have heard anyway above the buzzing in her ears. She just fled—*hurry, hurry*—along the corridor. Was that a flight of steps? It was not the wide staircase she had climbed

66

the night before, but the last thing she wanted was to end up in a main part of the house where all the guests would be gathered. This was likely a servants' stair; it was so narrow and would serve very well for her purpose. She plunged down it, emerging into a narrow corridor which she picked along stealthily, hearing a babble of conversation which seemed to come from the adjoining room which she guessed was either the buttery or a kitchen pantry.

"He never!" said a country accent warmly. "And her his paramour the whole time?"

"Bold as brass she were, Sidney said. *'Tis I be his whore, not my fair sister, only he won't own it on account of my plain face.* And that proud Sir Jeffree, he didn't know where to put himself! That's what Sidney said. His face turned red as fire, they do say."

"As well it might!" the first voice rejoined wonderingly. "Well, good on 'er, I says. Least she never let 'er sister get the blame for 'er wrongdoings."

"Get the blame!" her companion derided. "She wanted to get his pledge in front of the magistrate, that's what she wanted."

"And who can blame her?" the first said stoutly. "The poor lady. Right prettily she spoke about her supper last night, Badrick said. And that Sir Jeffree, he wouldn't even try that jelly what Mr. Copling slaved over to prepare for the fine folks. Let the bridal couple have it, that's what the kitchen decided, and he were downright ungrateful for the gesture!"

"Mr. Copling had a tear in his eye when he heard what she said about his jelly. Perfectly sets off the cheese she said, and he heaved a great sigh. *Mistress Edland,* quoth he, *there ain't a man alive in this mausoleum what appreciates my genius, but this scorned bride, she sees my vision.* His Grace only eats like

67

a bird and that Sir Leland's more for the drink than his victuals. As for that Sir Jeffree, well…"

But Sabina was not destined to hear any more about Jeffree's exacting tastes. With burning ears, she flung open the first door that opened out into the grounds and stumbled along the path skirting the kitchen garden. She was going home. Not to Morecotte sadly, which was infested with Alfred Hendry's loathed presence, but to her father's house. She had fled to Tipton Hall when her first marriage broke down and it seemed she was doing it now a second time.

A slightly hysterical laugh bubbled up as she scanned the horizon for landmarks. This situation was hardly comparable, for this second marriage was the joke of a cruel god. Spotting the sprawling mass of Langley Woods to the right of her and the first of the standing stones at Rossley Bligh, Sabina got her bearings. *As the crow flies, it must be a twelve-mile walk*, she fancied. It could be no later than ten o'clock. Squaring her shoulders, she hitched up her skirts to avoid the wet grass and started walking.

6

Jeffree was in a vile mood. Actually, he felt like he had been in one for days. Now he couldn't find the bloody woman anywhere! She had disappeared. He hadn't worried when she first stumbled out of the room looking like he had slapped her. After all, where was she going to go? She didn't know Ganford Chase or anyone in it. Then, after he had sent servants scrambling from the cellars to the attics, had bawled at his uncle's steward and finally accepted she was not beneath its roof, he set out muttering for the stables and saddled his horse. The grooms assured him no horses were missing and gave him the directions for Tipton Hall and he duly set off. At the start of the journey, he felt belligerent and hard done by. He would never have gone along with Leland's infamous smear campaign against Isemay Burrell, but he supposed, in truth, her sister was not to know that. The wretched woman had then sacrificed him to save her sister's skin. Herself, too, he acknowledged, but that was her own affair. He failed to see why he should have been implicated in her version of events.

Still, he supposed there were small opportunities for young, dispossessed widows. She saw an opportunity to better herself and leaped at the chance to snare herself a rich husband. There was no question she had quick wits. You only had to consider how swiftly she had interceded to divert all blame for her sister. A quick temper too, more's the pity.

She had flown off that bench earlier and looked like she would happily have flown at him. He felt a reluctant stirring of interest in how that would have played out. He had no experience with harpies or the subduing of them. What would he have done if she had flung herself at him? For some reason, even though she had been fully dressed at the time, he imagined her with her braids flying and nothing on but her shift.

When she had blazed at him so indignantly, he had felt jolted to his core. It was as if something sat up inside him at recognizing some quality in her. In the battlefield, something similar alerted him to a worthy foe. He had never encountered such a thing with a woman before. He had been half inclined to sit back down and engage with her, but something held him back.

Mayhap it had been the murderous gleam in her eyes. He had noticed how tightly her fingers were wrapped around her napkin, as though wringing the life out of it. It wouldn't take much to get her flying out of the chair in a fury. That really shouldn't excite him, he reflected with a quick shake of his head. His tastes must be getting warped. It was getting ridiculous if even a show of temper had him aroused.

His mind was likely disordered after the happenings of the previous day. It wasn't until he was nearing the property that he started wondering what he would tell her family if it turned out she was nowhere in the vicinity. It was precisely at that point when he spotted the lone figure trudging over the field to the left of the sprawling half-timbered manor house the Burrells called home.

There was something familiar about that flapping white headdress and blue dress. He did a double-take. Was it her? It *was* her. He felt an overwhelming tide of some strong emotion that he couldn't identify for the moment. To his surprise, it felt like something close to relief.

In his mind's eye, he had pictured her flagging down some cart or wagon on the road, not walking cross country. She might know a shortcut, he conceded, but she still must have walked some miles. Her hem was wet and mud-spattered. She had a high color in those cheeks and sparkling eyes.

Dismounting, he led his horse to the fence and tethered him there, before vaulting over to join her in the field, approaching her cautiously. He saw her step falter as she noticed him looming on the horizon. Then she drew herself up, doggedly keeping her course straight for Tipton Hall.

"You should have told me if you wanted to collect your things," he said aloud. "I would have brought you over." No reply to that, just a more upward tilt of her chin. "And I would have appreciated word of where you were going," he added doggedly. "I have turned Ganford Chase upside down this morning in search of you."

That did make her start. She turned on him a look of burning reproach, though when she spoke her words were calm, flippant even. "I am sure your family congratulated you on losing such a shrewish wife so quickly. That is quite a feat. It took my first husband fully a twelvemonth to do so."

Jeffree bristled. "I did not lose you. You ran off."

"I thought I would spare you my scolding ways," she answered after a heartbeat. "Besides, the result is the same. Estrangement. As far as I am concerned, we cannot reach that state fast enough."

He let out an irritated huff. "We can scarcely be estranged after so short a period of time. You would make us look ridiculous." To his annoyance, he sounded sulky and sullen. He had no earthly idea why.

Her eye kindled. "*I* would make us look ridiculous? I was not the one shouting and scowling the day after we were married for all to see and draw their own conclusions! I also did not listen to unfounded gossip and repeat the most hurtful thing I could possibly say, flinging it in your face before you had so much as broken your fast!"

For an instant, Jeffree considered telling her his own character was quite unblemished, but after the previous day, he could no longer claim that with perfect truth. Then, too, he could point out she had gone on to create a much bigger scene than he had. Instead, he forced himself to weigh up the best course of action. "I apologize," he said stiffly.

Sabina blinked. "For what?" she asked after a moment's silence, narrowing her eyes.

"For…shouting before you had broken your fast," Jeffree answered with a trace of uncertainty. He could point out that he had not been shouting at her, but she might not consider that a valid point. His mother also detested raised voices and insisted on silence at random times of the day.

"For repeating rumors about your character despite the fact I do not know their veracity," he added grudgingly. *Though what I do know of your personality, I do not like,* he added silently. Those honey-colored braids did not count, nor how she filled out her shift.

Sabina expelled her breath as though he had taken the wind out of her sails. "Thank you," she said, surprising him again. "I still want to return home though. There can be no point in my remaining at Ganford Chase when my sister did not even marry the duke."

"You remaining at Ganford Chase has absolutely nothing to do with your sister or my uncle," he heard himself point out. "You are there, madam, because I am. And I happen to be your husband."

72

Sabina's eyebrows shot back up again, and they stared at one another, as though sizing each other up anew. "Sir Jeffree," she began in what she clearly thought to be a reasonable tone. "I think we need to have a frank discussion as to how—"

At this point, they were interrupted by a shriek from the direction of the house. "Sabina!"

Jeffree swung around with a murmur of annoyance to find Isemay Burrell heading determinedly toward them, her dark hair loose and her arms full of freshly cut herbs.

"Sister!"

Isemay broke into a run and Jeffree turned back to Sabina. "Do not give your family any false expectations, wife," he warned.

His words seemed to startle her. "What sort of false expectations?"

"Of you returning home anytime soon," he replied tersely.

Isemay Burrell pulled up by the fence and rested her elbows along the top of it. "Is all well, sister?" she called anxiously.

"Perfectly," Sabina responded, perhaps a little too quickly, for her sister's perturbed look sharpened. She glanced quickly from her sister's face to his and then back again.

"You are coming into the house, of course," Isemay said with a challenging note in her voice.

"Of course," Sabina assured her. "We—er—wanted to collect some of my things," she said in what would have been a creditable lie if her sister had not been so observant. As it was, he noticed Isemay's eyes take in first Sabina's muddied hem and then his horse tethered nearby. Her sister had not been fooled and clearly believed he had been trying to head Sabina off.

73

When Sabina walked to the fence, Jeffree seized her waist and lifted her so she could swing her leg over the top. She gave a tiny yelp at the contact, and he nearly begged her pardon. But damn it all, he had every right to touch what was his, he thought, biting back the apology. She scrambled over the top and dropped down beside her sister looking rather flustered.

"Thank you," she murmured, avoiding his eye. He followed her over and grabbed his horse's reins as the sisters linked arms and started toward the side of the house. It was only as they walked right the way around that he realized they were leading him to the stables.

To his surprise, despite it being a decent size, no stable hand emerged to take over and they clearly expected him to see to his horse. After leading Radax into a stall large enough to house his destrier, he followed them back to the house where they led him in through a kitchen door.

A plump woman was sat up to the table chopping onions. Sabina greeted her as Isemay plunked down her herbs next to her. The servant cast the sisters only the most cursory of glances as they passed through, but he was subjected to a keen stare which he felt burning into the back of his head as he followed them into the passageway.

The interior of Tipton Hall was surprisingly dark and gloomy, seeming mostly to comprise of passageways and little poky rooms. Isemay placed a finger to her lips as they passed one chamber from which he thought he could hear loud snores emanating.

"Mother is resting!" she murmured and tipped her head significantly that they should carry on to another room. Jeffree's eyebrows shot up, but he kept his tread light all the same. The room Isemay led them to was filled with dark wood

74

furniture and murky wall hangings. Barely any light seemed to penetrate the window, and he almost tripped over a footstool before righting himself.

"Where is Father?" Sabina asked once Isemay had shut the door after them.

"He has ridden out with Hodgson this morning to look over the crops. He should be back soon."

When both sisters looked to him, he cleared his throat. "Hodgson is your father's steward?" he asked, unsure of his cue.

"Hodgson fulfils many roles," Sabina answered. "Steward is just one of them."

"Father has had to let so many of his staff go these past couple of years," Isemay piped up. "Everyone has had to take on more duties."

Thinking of their mother's snores, Jeffree made no comment, though he noted he had seen only one servant about the place so far.

"Please be seated and I will fetch us some refreshment," Isemay said with a formality that seemed to surprise even her sister. "And then we can discuss what is to be done about everything." She then whisked out of the room, and Jeffree turned to Sabina, who was lowering herself onto a love seat. Deliberately, he walked and sat beside her on the two-seater bench. Sabina turned to him, but before she could speak, he forestalled her.

"I think we need to be on the same page before your sister returns," he said bluntly. "She seems determined to put her oar in."

75

"Do you find that surprising, all things considered?" she asked coolly. "Yesterday was supposed to be her wedding day, not mine."

Jeffree regarded her frowningly. "I do not understand why their marriage did not take place," he admitted finally. "Our own union should not have been a bar to it."

Sabina folded her hands and set them in her lap. "As to that, I was not there when any decision was reached," she said with a shrug. "Have you spoken to your uncle this morn? Does he still desire it?"

"I have no idea." Speaking to his uncle had not been high on his priority list. "I do not see why he should have changed his mind."

Sabina regarded him with a stunned look. "The day now has been tainted with…certain associations. Your uncle is a good deal more delicate in his feelings than you, it seems."

Jeffree found himself bristling at the implied criticism. "What would be the point in postponing their wedding, only to have to go through the whole rigmarole a few months down the line?" he asked, he thought reasonably enough.

Sabina made no reply, instead turning her head sharply as though she heard some footfall. Sure enough, her sister came sailing through the door, carrying a jug and three cups. She was so out of breath, Jeffree guessed she had run the whole way, as though she feared he might tuck her sister under his arm and carry her off like a marauder!

"Here we are," Isemay said blithely, sloshing the ale into the three cups. "Now," she said, sitting down opposite them. "What is to be done?"

"Done?" Jeffree echoed tetchily. From what his uncle had let slip about his prospective bride, he had imagined her to be some demure, retiring maiden. Not this interfering young woman who seemed determined to thrust herself into their business.

"About Sabina."

"Sabina is my wife," Jeffree responded. "There remains nothing to be 'done' about that. The matter is done and dusted."

Isemay straightened in her seat. "I do not see why Sabina's life should be blighted," she began with what Jeffree could only believe was a staggering disrespect, when a muffled shriek came from the direction of the doorway.

"Isemay!" Thora Burrell squawked, rushing into the room. "You stupid child! What are you saying!" She flapped her hands at her youngest daughter, rather as though she were swatting away flies. "You must excuse her, Sir Jeffree," she said, turning back to him. "Isemay's—er—disappointment over what happened yesterday, or rather what *failed* to happen, has sadly disordered her wits."

"My wits are perfectly fine, thank you, Mother!" Isemay sniped from behind her mother's bulk, only to be ignored.

"We are, of course, sensible to the honor you have done us by marrying into our family and repairing my daughter's honor," Thora Burrell twittered, her eyes solely trained on him. Jeffree inclined his head. Perhaps the woman was not as bad as he initially feared.

"What is this?" his mother-in-law asked sharply, her eye falling on the pitcher of ale. "Isemay! You did not serve Sir Jeffree that weak ale! Why, that is not fit for visitors! You should have brought out the honeyed!"

77

"I thought you said he was family now, not a guest," Isemay pointed out with a toss of her head.

"Do not be so provoking, child! Go and ask Hildeth for the honeyed ale at once and the best goblets!"

Isemay's face grew tight, but she rose from her seat and left the room, looking back over her shoulder at her sister and wriggling her eyebrows expressively. Really, Jeffree could not understand what his uncle had been thinking wanting to wed the girl. If Sabina was a shrew, then assuredly, Isemay was unbecomingly headstrong.

"And how is your dear uncle, His Grace the Duke of Bethencourt, this morn?" asked their mother, happily unaware of his thoughts.

"He's—er—keeping to his rooms this morning," Jeffree managed to dredge from his memory. "Apparently, he took a chill sitting in the Great Hall all day yesterday in a draught."

Thora Burrell's face fell. "Oh, the poor, dear man!" she cried, sinking into a chair.

"Did he really say that?" Sabina enquired with a curious look on her face.

"So Nasby told me," Jeffree said with a shrug, naming his uncle's steward. "Why?"

"No reason," she replied evasively, but he wasn't sure he believed her. There was a definite hint of disapproval on her face.

"My uncle has always been susceptible to chills," he heard himself say defensively.

"And Ganford Chase is such a very large residence," Thora Burrell lamented. "There are sure to be so many draughts."

78

"Yes," Jeffree agreed, turning to look at Sabina's profile. Was she daring to suggest his uncle was a malingerer? The woman's effrontery was quite breathtaking. Her chin was far too pronounced in his opinion. It hinted to a headstrong will.

"Father has gone out this morning, I hear," Sabina said.

A spasm crossed over her mother's face. "I wanted him to stay and comfort me, but no, nothing would do but that he had to go out with Hodgson," she said petulantly.

"Pray, why were you in need of comfort, Mother?" Sabina asked coolly.

Thora Burrell opened her mouth, then closed it again, her eyes darting from her daughter to Jeffree. She cleared her throat. "Such a very *odd* day yesterday, to be sure," she muttered. "And Isemay's wedding came to naught..." She trailed off, fidgeting in her seat.

"Well, well," Jeffree heard himself say briskly. "You still saw one daughter married after all."

Thora Burrell's expression lightened. "That is very true, Sir Jeffree," she said, nodding with satisfaction and settling back in her seat. "There is that comfort."

Sabina made some sort of muffled exclamation, but when Jeffree turned toward her, she was staring straight ahead once again.

"Where is that girl with the honeyed ale?" his mother-in-law fretted. "We should have a toast to the newly wedded couple. I think I will just see where she is..." Rising from her chair, Thora Burrell made her way out of the room with many nods and encouraging smiles toward them.

"I am not coming back to Ganford Chase," Sabina said as soon as her mother closed the door behind her.

"What?" Jeffree was startled.

"I am not wanted there, and I have no desire to inflict myself on everyone. I would be much better at home."

"You are being absurd," he scoffed. "And this is no longer your home."

"Where, then, is?" she asked, turning toward him. "You must see that it is quite impossible for me to remain at Ganford Chase, in light of all that has happened."

He made no immediate reply to that. In truth, he could not deny there was a certain awkwardness to the setup. His mother and the rest of them were likely to be no more reconciled to the match this morning than they had been yesterday.

"I do not know your situation, Sir Jeffree," she persisted. "Is it possible you have a home of your own somewhere?"

He could reply to that at least. "I do not. Most of the year-round I travel for the tournaments. It has never seemed necessary for me to purchase my own estate." Then, too, he had been raised as Bethencourt's heir.

Sabina blinked. "So then, Ganford Chase is your main residence?" She sounded dismayed. He did not have the chance to reply with anything more than a nod when she placed an impetuous hand on his arm. He stiffened. "Wait!" she said breathlessly. "I have an idea!"

She shot out of the seat and began agitatedly pacing about the room. Jeffree watched her with resignation. What wild start was this? Finally, she swung about to face him. "Doubtless you heard something of the inheritance dispute between myself and Alfred Hendry which was touched on yesterday."

Jeffree shrugged. Of course, Osborn had mentioned it to him the previous evening, but he was in no hurry to admit possession of the facts. "He is the cousin of your late husband," he responded cautiously.

"A distant cousin," she stressed. "Miles barely acknowledged the connection and Alfred only stayed at Morecotte with us once prior to my...that is, to our estrangement. On that occasion, Miles kicked him out after he outstayed his welcome and offered a grave insult to one of our servants."

Jeffree recalled Alfred Hendry's sullen face and found he did not find it difficult to believe.

"He has no legitimate claim to Morecotte," Sabina insisted. "Miles settled the place on me when we married. He intended for the property to pass directly to me and any children which we might have had. The fact we did not have any should not factor."

"On his death, by your own admission, you were estranged."

"We were," Sabina agreed. "But nothing had been done officially. My father has retained the betrothal papers where my dower was agreed. In the event of his death, Morecotte was to become mine outright." She looked at him significantly. Jeffree gazed back at her blankly. He could not see how this had any bearing on anything. She took a deep breath. "Sir Jeffree," she started determinedly. "If you could only see your way clear to espousing my cause, then I think I can see the perfect solution to our predicament."

"Solution?" Jeffree echoed, frowning. "What predicament?"

"If you would only throw your weight behind my claim, then the authorities will surely recognize my rightful ownership of Morecotte."

"Why should the disposal of your late husband's property concern me?"

Sabina pressed her lips together a moment and surveyed him grimly. "It is *my* property, Sir Jeffree," she pointed out. "That is what I have been telling you." When he continued to look unimpressed, she plunked her hands on her hips. "What if you tried considering it as an asset that I should have brought into this marriage?" she tried, using a different tack.

Jeffree snorted. What was it Osborn had said about the property? Some piddling estate. It was hardly up to his own standards, he who had been heir to Ganford Chase for twenty-eight years!

"Only consider," Sabina urged, "how convenient it would be for me to have a home near that of my own family and not too far from Ganford Chase for appearance's sake!"

Jeffree huffed. "Appearance's sake?" he echoed. "So, you envisage yourself living life there, unencumbered by a husband, do you?" Even though the idea had decided merit, for some reason, it riled him that she should be trying to find ways to get rid of him already.

"Oh, that is a good idea!" exclaimed Isemay from the doorway. Directly she had said it, she placed a finger to her lips and looked back over her shoulder. Sabina grimaced and slipped back into her seat beside him as his mother-in-law returned to the room bearing a platter of spiced gingerbreads.

"Did I just hear the door?" Thora Burrell said, setting down the gingerbreads next to the honeyed ale that Isemay had brought.

"That will be your father." She bustled back out again, calling "Wilfred!" loudly down the corridor. Sabina leaned forward and started filling the cups.

"What will you do about ridding yourselves of your uninvited houseguest?" Isemay hissed, her eyes gleaming with anticipation. "And by that, I mean Alfred Hendry," she explained to Jeffree quite needlessly. He wondered if his sister-in-law thought him lacking in intelligence.

Sabina cast him a sidelong look. "We have not had much opportunity for a council of war," she admitted. "But I am sure we will hit on some stratagem."

Jeffree opened his mouth to point out he had yet to pledge himself to the cause, but as Thora Burrell chose this moment to reenter the room, dragging her husband in her wake, he shut it again smartly.

Wilfred Burrell patted his daughter on the shoulder, cleared his throat, shuffled his feet, and managed to greet Jeffree without quite meeting his eye.

"Mayhap you'll grace us with your presence at supper this evening at Tipton Hall," his new father-in-law suggested, clearing his throat.

For some godsforsaken reason, Jeffree found himself murmuring some agreement. Maybe he *was* lacking in wits. When Sabina rose from her seat moments later, he shot out a hand to detain her. "Where are you off to?"

She looked down at her arm in surprise and he released her. "I thought I would go up to my room."

"To pack your things?"

A look of annoyance crossed her face. "If we are staying to supper, should we not stay the night here with my family?"

Jeffree suffered an unpleasant jolt, realizing three pairs of eyes were now trained on him with varying expressions of anxious anticipation for his reply. "We could, I suppose," he answered begrudgingly, and instantly his mother-in-law's face was wreathed in smiles.

"Isemay, Sabina, we must go at once and make the bedchamber ready, for you know the bedspread in your room is not fit to be seen by decent company. We must take the canopy from the guest bedroom at once."

"Why can Sir Jeffree not just be set up in the guest bedchamber?" Isemay asked ingenuously. Her words were met with a heavy silence.

"Stupid child!" her mother upbraided her, recovering first. "The very idea that newlyweds should be put in separate chambers! Come now, girls, let us make ready!"

To his intense discomfort, Jeffree was left to make awkward conversation with Wilfred Burrell.

7

Their mother talked nonstop as they shook out and changed the bedding in Sabina's bedchamber. So much so that neither of the sisters could get a word in edgeways.

"I do hope Sir Jeffree finds the room comfortable," Thora Burrell fretted. "'Tis a vast pity that the view is not a prettier one from this window."

"I always rather liked the view," Sabina commented mildly. "You can see Langley Woods in the distance on a clear day."

For her part, she was more worried about the fact she had no truckle bed or dressing room to stash an unwanted spouse in. She could not be so blatant as to refuse to share a chamber with him, so she would have to simply try to remake the bed so their sheets divided them.

"Do you think Sir Jeffree will be satisfied with a plain pork pie for supper?" her mother carried on uneasily. "I am sure they are used to far grander pies at Ganford Chase. Roasted venison and the like with the pastry all set out in their family crest."

"He did not seem terribly appreciative of the fine supper he was served last night," Sabina admitted distractedly.

Nothing would then do, but she had to recount what they had been served, course by course. Sabina did not admit that they had eaten in the confines of her husband's bedchamber, for she did not want to give the impression she had been cowering there, too afraid to face the de Crecy family.

She thought from the look on Isemay's face that her sister guessed she had not been a guest of honor at the duke's table. Their mother, though, despite regretting the fact she had missed the banquet, seemed to derive some satisfaction from the idea of her daughter presiding over a grand wedding feast. Sabina saw no reason to disillusion her.

Stepping down off the chair she had been balanced on to hang the curtains from the ceiling canopy, Sabina looked about the bedchamber. She could not help but reflect how shabby and bare Sir Jeffree would consider the space in contrast with his own magnificent rooms at Ganford Chase. As though guessing her thoughts, her mother directed Isemay to fetch the small table and chairs from the guest bedchamber.

"For you know, he may find a use for them when he is taking off his boots," their mother said vaguely.

Sabina gave her a forced smile. "Yes, mayhap," she agreed. Her mother beamed back at her, completely oblivious of any underlying tension. Sabina tarried awhile, tidying her things away as her mother watched with approval, clearly under the impression she was seeking to please her new spouse with a neat room.

Sabina sighed; she supposed she did want to get on Jeffree's good side momentarily. If he had one. If he would only agree to support her in the effort to reclaim Morecotte, then she felt she could overlook even his worst character flaws. Being trotted out once in a while to play the role of dutiful spouse would be tolerable if she had her own bolthole to retreat to when it was over. Morecotte was not large, but there were rooms enough for them to have separate sleeping arrangements.

When Isemay tried to have any further private words with her, their mother prevented it by sending her youngest daughter to pick flowers for the room. "I won't say your sister has not every right to be disappointed," Thora Burrell admitted once Isemay had departed, a look of frustration on her lovely face. "But she

86

could have married Bethencourt yesterday if she had not been so scrupulous in her manners."

Sabina looked up curiously at her mother's chagrined tone. "You surely do not think exchanging vows in such an atmosphere would have been ideal?"

"Why should they not?" her mother demanded indignantly. "You did, did you not? And on this occasion, at least, I think you have acted with a good deal more sense than your sister."

Sabina gazed back at her, not knowing what to say. "I—it is not really the same thing, Mother. Our circumstances are quite different," she managed after a moment's awkwardness.

"I do not see how it is not entirely the same thing," Thora Burrell sniffed. "His Grace the duke could scarce have refused to honor his vow, all things considered, same as Sir Jeffree could not. But there! Isemay would not hear of it, and now the opportunity is squandered." She shook her head mournfully. "I doubt they will ever be wed now!" she concluded bitterly.

Sabina was startled. She closed the cabinet door and turned around to face her mother. "Why do you say so? Did Bethencourt say something to indicate he had changed his mind?"

Her mother's eyes avoided hers. "The Duke of Bethencourt said everything that was expected of him," her mother said. "But you mark my words, it will all come to naught. Under such circumstances as your sister's, it is better for the groom to know as little as possible about the bride's character."

Sabina blinked. "What circumstances might those be?"

Her mother smoothed her skirts. "Marriage to a fussy old bachelor," she answered frankly.

87

"Mother!"

"I speak nothing but the truth, Sabina," the older woman replied sagely. "Isemay has a perfect form and face. She plays the lute and sings like a regular songbird. His Grace has admired her from afar and set her on a pedestal." They moved toward the door together, and Thora Burrell indicated for her daughter to go before her. As they started toward the stairs, she linked arms with Sabina. "Under such a courtship, overfamiliarity is fatal. It shatters the illusion of perfection."

Sabina winced. "I think Isemay's character is far more laudable than her face and form."

Thora Burrel snorted. "You are alone in that opinion!"

"Mother!"

"Isemay is growing sadly willful!" her mother complained as they started down the staircase. "She listens to me less and less as she gets older. Now she is no longer dazzled by Bethencourt's title and wealth, it will all fall by the wayside. You will see."

Sabina remembered her own burning indignation at the duke's seeming inability to defend his bride-to-be, the way he had wallowed in self-pity in the aftermath. She bit her lip. "If there is no affection between them, or even true respect, then perhaps it would be for the better if they were *not* joined in matrimony."

Her mother gave her a pointed look. "As you love and respect your own husband, I suppose?" she asked skeptically.

Sabina turned a dull shade of red. "We had our hands forced, Mother. Our circumstances were different, whatever you may think." In all honesty, she was so stunned by her mother's shrewd words about Bethencourt that she was not as vehement as she might have been. For all her effusive praise of the duke, it seemed Thora Burrell had been all too aware of his flaws.

"Oh well!" her mother concluded, throwing up her hands as they reached the bottom step. "The duke has slipped through our fingers. But never fear, daughter, for you have secured the next best thing in his heir. I daresay Bethencourt will never marry now, and I will live to see one of my daughters a duchess still."

Sabina had just opened her mouth to rebuke her mother's words when she noticed with horror that the door leading to the sitting room was wide open. Looking up, her gaze focused on the upright figure stood rigid and gazing out at her with hard, angry eyes. Closing her own briefly, Sabina uttered a silent curse and almost missed her footing. She would have slipped, were her mother's arm not entwined with her own.

"Have a care, Sabina!" her mother scolded. "You will have the both of us over!"

Perhaps it was no surprise that the rest of the afternoon was constrained. Wilfred Burrell offered to show Jeffree about the house and grounds and was accepted, albeit rather stiffly. Not caring to be further cornered by either her sister or her mother, Sabina tagged along like a dutiful wife, an action her father clearly approved of, for he patted her on the shoulder twice.

"I think you will do well with him," her father whispered when they returned to the house. "He may be reserved, but when he does speak, he talks sense."

As she had seen Sir Jeffree address only one question and a handful of rather critical remarks to her father, Sabina thought he was being wildly optimistic. Still, it could have been worse, she reflected. In any case, both her parents had been thoroughly charmed by her first husband, who had turned out to be an untrustworthy scoundrel.

To her surprise, Sir Jeffree ate expansively at the supper table that night, and though he offered no extravagant praise, neither did he complain or refuse any dish set before him. His consumption alone of the plain fare put him in good stead with her delighted mother, who beckoned to her after the meal.

"And to think," Thora Burrell said, looking gratified, "that by all accounts he is so hard to please, yet there he sat and tucked into Hildeth's pie as if it were roasted swan!"

Sabina nodded, her own suspicions forming about Sir Jeffree's picky palate. She cleared her throat. "Perhaps Isemay would grace us with some music now we have finished eating?" she suggested.

Isemay, when asked, did not seem keen to show off her talents. When she did fetch her lute, she performed three extremely tragic ballads, ending with one which told of a scorned woman who revenged herself on her lover by drowning him.

As the last plaintive notes died away, Jeffree cleared his throat and declared his intention of retiring for the evening. Sabina dutifully rose, and her mother handed her a candle to take up to bed. He responded to her parents' wishes for a good night with a terse nod and allowed himself to be led up the staircase and along the passageway to her bedchamber.

Once there, Sabina lit another candle and then returned belowstairs to heat some water by the kitchen fire for his wash. She found Hildeth yawning by the hearth with a pan of water already bubbling.

"The mistress says ye're to take the first lot of water."

Sabina thanked her and filled a large ewer which she carried upstairs, pausing before her own bedchamber door, and knocking softly before opening it. To her consternation, Sir Jeffree had already stripped down to his braies. "Oh!" she exclaimed stupidly and stood there a moment like a startled deer. "You do realize this is my bedchamber?" she asked, before shaking herself and turning and shutting the door after her.

"What do you expect me to do? Sleep fully clothed?"

She could not see his expression clearly in the shadowy room, but his voice was sardonic.

"Well, no…" she answered lamely, setting the ewer down on a side table. That *was* what she had imagined though, the two of them remaining fully clothed all night. It was not practical, of course, but the thought of lying next to him and vulnerable in sleep was unthinkable. "I will keep mine on," she said aloud.

He snorted. "You have *nothing* to fear from me, madam."

Sabina flushed, for his tone was scathing. It was one thing to know she was nothing special, quite another for someone to tell you they find you repugnant. Even Miles had not done that. "Oh, very well, then, have it your own way," she answered and, without ceremony, divested herself of her headdress, casting it onto a chair.

She busied herself, removing her shoes and belt for the next few minutes, and heard Jeffree move to the table to take his wash. When she had unpinned and uncoiled her braids, she ventured a quick glance in his direction and found him turned with his back toward her, drying his neck. Swiftly she loosened the ties at her neck and wrists and wriggled out of her gown, so she stood in only her stockings and shift.

Jeffree turned about and glanced toward the bed. Then he threw down the cloth and made for it without any more ado. Sabina moved to the table, picked up the basin, and carried it to the window to empty out his water. Then she returned and emptied the remaining water in the ewer for her own wash. When it was time to dry off, she had to pick up the discarded cloth from the floor. She did so, muttering under her breath.

When she turned toward the bed, Jeffree had already extinguished his own candle and rolled onto his side, showing her his back. Sabina walked to the bed, trying not to drag her feet. Gritting her teeth, she climbed in beside him and blew out her own candle. Earlier she hadn't the time to separate the sheets out and her bed was not a large one. Still, if they lay back-to-back until morning, then surely they could get through the indignity.

"You don't have a fire lit?" His voice coming out of the dark startled her. For some reason, she had thought there would be no talking while they were so closely sequestered.

"Not in May, no," she replied, using the time of year as the excuse rather than the lack of money and resources. When he made no reply, she added, "Are you cold?" He did not reply at once, so she lay tense, waiting for his response.

Finally, she could stand it no longer and turned, looking over her shoulder at him. It was a fruitless exercise as the window to her room was so small it barely admitted any light. "Jeffree?" She heard him hiss out a breath. Realizing she had addressed him informally for the first time, Sabina felt her face grow hot.

"No," he answered after a heavy pause. "I'm not cold."

Sabina dropped her head back onto her pillow and squeezed her eyes shut. She had a bad feeling sleep would not come at all for her this night.

"Is that the window I am supposed to have climbed through?" he asked dryly. "I should not think my shoulders could even fit."

"It is surprising what people will believe, when they want to," Sabina answered lightly, and realized this was true even of herself. Only look at how blindly she had gone into her first marriage. Her parents had assured her Miles was everything she could hope for in a spouse. He had turned out to be the absolute opposite.

How she wished she could forget that disastrous period of her life, but it felt like a festering wound. And now she'd had another husband inflicted on her. She huffed out a sigh. Nothing ever turned out the way you thought it would in life.

"Were you in league with Alfred Hendry?" he asked suddenly, his voice harsh.

Sabina shot upright and twisted about in the bed to face him. "No, I was not!" she retorted angrily. "I loathe and despise that man and he feels the same way about me; you could ask anyone! If you imagine for one minute that he would help me to snare a rich and well-connected husband, then you, Sir Jeffree, are a lackwit!"

He was silent, and it was only when she felt his breath on her face that she realized just how close she was to him in the dark. Uttering an exclamation, Sabina recoiled, rearing back in alarm. Unfortunately, the fact her legs were caught up in the bedclothes foiled her retreat, and instead, she pitched forward, landing sprawled on top of him.

"Oof!" Jeffree grunted, and Sabina felt his arms catch hold of her. She froze, then flinched and braced herself to be thrust away. Instead, he held her fast, one hand at her waist and the other gripping her thigh in an almost bruising clasp. *Oh, my*

93

gods! She was glad it was dark, or she would die of mortification on the spot! "I beg your pardon!" she heard herself gasp. "Let me just…"

"Hold still!" he answered tersely.

Sabina froze again in the act of trying to reach down to untangle her legs. "If I could just—!"

"I said hold still, damn you!"

Sabina blinked at the note of panic in his voice. Why was he so alarmed? It was not as though she would inflict an injury on his much larger body, she thought, unless she inadvertently kneed him in the ballocks. But as a matter of fact, neither of her knees were in contact with any part of Sir Jeffree right now, because they were splayed on either side of his muscular thigh. That was when she felt it, against her hip. *Oh.* For a moment she had thought it was his hand grazing her there. But she knew where his hands were; they were gripping her so tightly. That left only one possibility.

Dragging in a shocked breath, Sabina gazed down blankly into the darkness and felt his hot breath on her face. So, she thought dazedly, it was disinclination rather than inability that had kept Sir Jeffree chaste. His hands slid up her sides until they were under her arms, and very carefully, he lifted her off his body and deposited her on the bed beside him.

Sabina collapsed onto her back and lay there, feeling winded. "Sorry," she croaked, her mouth suddenly dry. "That was clumsy of me."

He made no reply, but she could hear his harsh, uneven breathing clearly enough. The awkwardness of their situation had become a hundred times worse! Squeezing her eyes shut, Sabina strove to catch her own breath. Her mind was reeling.

Of course, it meant nothing, she reassured herself. Men were sadly indiscriminate when it came to such things. Marriage to Miles had taught her that much. Then again, Sir Jeffree was apparently celibate. Maybe that was why he had been so…easily inflamed. She turned her head as though to seek out his face. A pointless exercise, as it was so dark in the room.

Well, she had apologized, and he had not responded. Sabina thought it permissible for her to lapse into silence now. She lay there awhile like a stunned fish, disbelieving that her life had come to this. That this man, lying in the dark beside her, was in truth and fact her husband. After a time, she rearranged the bedclothes to make sure every last bit of her was covered, and exhausted, fell fast asleep.

When next she woke, she found herself surrounded by a muscular male. For a moment, she hovered in that space between waking and dreaming. She frowned. This was not right. Even in the early days of her marriage, she and Miles had not lain like this. Both had preferred their own side of the bed and their own space.

Not only could she feel the press of a body, much larger than any she had known, up against her back, but there was a brawny arm slung about her waist, holding her firmly in place, with— was that a thigh? Wedged against her hip? Reluctantly, she opened her eyes, blinking at the shaft of morning light coming through her casement window.

Sabina glanced down at the arm wound snugly about her waist and swallowed. There was no escaping the fact that she was being tightly embraced by a sleeping Sir Jeffree de Crecy. She cast a slow glance over her side and spotted his knee and bent leg. She was not even sure if *embraced* was the right word, considering how indecently he was covering her backside!

He will be mortified when he awakes, she thought and felt a little guilty about the fleeting satisfaction she derived from that. It was purely because of his own disgusting superiority. By day he might find her entirely beneath his notice, but by night, apparently, he wanted nothing more than to find her beneath him!

She had the grace to blush at her own indelicacy of thought, but after all, he was insufferable, and she was only human. There would be precious few opportunities for her to gain the upper hand over Sir Jeffree, but apparently, while his thinking mind slept, his body liked her well enough to seek her out, despite her flaws.

She would not be flattered, for men were base creatures, and doubtless his own self-inflicted privations were at least partly to blame. She still found it hard to believe that he practiced abstinence, but he was a strange man all around. Otherwise, why would he be so often seen abroad in the company of that human icicle, Sir Charles Ellis?

It was not often she had seen him about the county, of course. Sabina's path had not often crossed that of the illustrious inhabitants of Ganford Chase until her sister had caught the eye of the duke, that is. But when she had caught fleeting glimpses of Sir Jeffree, or he had been excitedly pointed out to her, he had been with the flinty-eyed Sir Charles. Remembering the look of scalding revulsion the older man had directed at her the previous day, she winced.

If she were a man of Jeffree's fortune and privilege, she would certainly find more congenial company than *that* to while away the time with. It was a mystery to her, like the rest of him, she thought with a shrug. The arm about her waist tightened, and Sabina went very still. After a moment, he relaxed again, and Sabina breathed out with relief.

Should she try to extricate herself? She squinted at the window again, debating the hour, when a sudden knock at the door startled her. She and Sir Jeffree flinched as one. Sabina lifted her head as the door creaked open and Hildeth poked her head around it.

"Hildeth?" she quavered uncertainly, feeling Sir Jeffree freeze behind her.

"Your mother bade me bring hot water to your room, on account of your guest," the servant responded promptly. "Only I didn't want to walk in and catch you unawares." She cast a jaundiced eye over their entwined bodies. "I knows what newlyweds is like."

Sabina felt herself turn red as Jeffree snatched back his arm and rolled onto his back, putting some distance between them. Hildeth snorted and bustled in with the ewer. "I wasn't born yesterday!" she added for good measure, setting the jug down with a thud.

"Thank you."

The servant disappeared through the door and Sabina coughed. "Will you wash first, or shall I?" A heavy silence greeted her words, and it seemed Jeffree was at a loss how to answer. "I apologize that I have no dressing room for one of us to retreat to for modesty's sake."

He cleared his throat. "I will turn my back. You go first." He rolled onto his side, facing away from her, and Sabina almost leaped from the bed in her hurry to escape any awkwardness. She rushed her wash and dressed in such haste that she did not even rebraid her plaits. Instead, she simply wrapped them around her ears for a second day and pinned them into place before donning her wimple.

97

It was slovenly, and far from her usual practice, but Sabina felt horribly aware of Jeffree's presence in her bedchamber. He surely begrudged every minute, she told herself as she tightened the laces in her bodice. "I will see you belowstairs," she said, still red-faced as she whisked herself out of the room and slammed the door shut behind her.

She waited a moment with her back to the door, her eyes shut fast, collecting herself before venturing below. She took the stairs at a slow, plodding step, to give herself time to collect herself. By some ill timing, her family drifted out of various rooms to watch her descend.

"Of all the gowns to choose, Sabina," her mother commented critically. "You would choose that one!"

Sabina glanced down in surprise. In truth, she had just grasped the first she could reach from her cupboard.

"All Sabina's gowns are shabby," Isemay pointed out in defense of her sister. "I have remarked on it before, and you said it did not signify what she wore now she was a widow."

Their mother bridled. "Well, and so it did not! But she is not a widow anymore. She is the wife of a knight of renown from one of the foremost families in the land. It is not fitting that she should trail around looking so shabby."

"It is to be hoped that her new husband can bear the expense of clothing her adequately," their father put in hopefully. "As the expense of Isemay's bride clothes have well-nigh left my coffers empty for this month."

"Bear the expense?" his wife echoed. "To be sure he can! Why I have heard tell—"

"I have plenty of serviceable gowns in my possession, thank you," Sabina put in, wishing to cut short such talk. She stepped off the bottom step, and Isemay seized hold of her arm as they made their way toward the dining chamber.

"I would give you one of my gowns if I could," her sister whispered.

Sabina squeezed her arm. It was a kind thought, but her sister was slight of build and slender as a reed, where Sabina was a good deal more substantially built. "I doubt I could fit one leg in your gowns," she remarked wryly as they were seated about the table.

"I do hope Sir Jeffree does not disapprove of breaking one's fast so early in the day," their mother fretted. "I know it is frowned on to eat before midday in the best circles. Only common laborers and infants require sustenance at such an hour."

Their father snorted and helped himself to some toasted bread and roasted fish.

"I do not know Sir Jeffree's views on such matters," Sabina confessed, realizing her mother's eyes were fixed on her enquiringly.

"But surely you know at what hour you broke your fast yesterday, child!" her mother retorted crossly. She only ever addressed her grown daughters as such when she was agitated.

"We did not eat yesterday morn," Sabina admitted, neglecting to mention that she had absented herself not long after rising. "But if he disapproves of such a practice then he need not join us, need he?"

Her mother drew in a sharp breath, looking scandalized, but as her father gave a satisfied nod, their mother let the matter drop. "I trust Sir Jeffree took a good night's sleep," she commented as she buttered some bread.

99

Sabina lowered her cup. "I believe so, Mother," she answered shortly.

A smug look passed over Thora Burrell's face. "Hildeth said the two of you looked vastly cozy when she brought you your washing water first thing."

Sabina plunked her cup down on the table, her cheeks burning. "Did she indeed?" She could feel Isemay's wide-eyed look of concern burning into her as she reached for some toasted bread. If only Mother would cease talking, she felt sure she could get through the morning and regain her lost composure.

"If you carry on being agreeable then I am sure Sir Jeffree will be only too glad to buy you some gowns that would put Isemay's wardrobe quite in the shade," her mother rambled on. "Did you see some of the silks and satins at Ganford Chase the day before yesterday? I daresay some of them cost a pretty penny. That one lady, in the blue, now pray what relation was she to Sir Jeffree? She looked very distinguished," Thora Burrell rattled on. "I daresay, she looked as noble as a duchess herself."

"I am not sure who you mean," Sabina answered after a moment's pause. "I do not remember how anyone was dressed. I had other matters on my mind at the time."

"I should think so!" Isemay agreed spiritedly. "Why, poor Sabina almost ended up on a ducking stool! Who cares what robes some haughty, disagreeable woman was wearing?"

"That is no way to speak of your sister's in-laws!" their mother replied indignantly. "Why, my own mother-in-law would address me as nothing but 'wretched girl' for the first twelve months we were married, but I never said a word against her, did I, Wilfred?" she said, turning to her spouse.

Wilfred Burrell lowered his spoonful of roasted fish. "Not quite how I remember it, my dear," he answered dryly.

"Well, mayhap I said one or two words to you, but as my husband, you were the proper person to address my woes!"

"Yes, dear."

Isemay gave a hasty cough, and looking up, Sabina saw Jeffree stood on the threshold with the disagreeable look on his face she was starting to think was habitual.

"Oh! Good morning, Sir Jeffree," her mother twittered. "Will you not join us?"

He came stiffly into the room, and Sabina's father rose to draw out a seat for him.

Stealing a look at his face, Sabina wondered with a sinking heart just how much of their discussion he had overheard.

He sat down, studiously avoiding looking in her direction as her father pushed the dishes toward him and her mother poured him a cup of weak, foamy ale.

"A manservant of yours came to the house after we had all retired last night," her father said, addressing Sir Jeffree. "Hodgson admitted him."

Sir Jeffree blinked. "Osborn?" he asked with a frown.

"Aye, that was his name," Wilfred Burrell agreed.

"What did he want?"

"Your uncle, the duke, was anxious to discover your whereabouts."

Jeffree's eyebrows rose. "I would have thought it obvious." Sabina looked up with surprise at that. *Would he?* "Did he remain or return to Ganford Chase?" he asked, still sounding annoyed.

"Returned forthwith bearing tidings you were safe and well," her father answered.

Jeffree grunted and tucked into his plateful. It seemed, after all, that he was not too well-bred to break his fast in the morn, for he made a good meal of it, finishing off the loaf with plenty of butter.

"We had better return this morn," he said, addressing Sabina at the close of the meal.

"So soon?" Isemay asked, looking up with dismay. Privately, Sabina agreed with the sentiment. She turned to look at him, the same question in her eyes.

"A good deal of my relations will depart today," he explained grudgingly.

"And is my presence required for that?" she asked, remembering how thoroughly hostile clan de Crecy had been toward her.

"Thora! Isemay!" her father said, drawing back his chair. "Let us leave these two to discuss their leave without our presence impeding them."

Dragging their feet, her sister and mother complied, though they did not look happy about it. She thought Sir Jeffree offered her father the most infinitesimal of nods as they departed.

Sir Jeffree turned to her as soon as the door closed behind them. "Your presence is of course required," he said coldly. "It is your duty to present yourself at my side as my wife."

"Indeed?"

He narrowed his gaze. "If you can behave yourself in a seemly manner, maybe I could be induced to purchase you some new gowns that are fit to be seen in." His gaze scanned her faded red gown with derision. He must have heard at least part of their conversation.

Sabina squared her shoulders. "I want no gowns for an incentive, Sir Jeffree. I have already told you my desire." His face turned blank, and he stared at her with an odd expression. "Morecotte," she reminded him, feeling slightly annoyed it could have slipped his mind so quickly.

"Morecotte?" he repeated, clearly none the wiser.

"My home! The one that Alfred Hendry hath dispossessed me of! I told you of it yesterday."

"Oh, that." He made an irritated gesture with his hand. "That is nothing to me."

"As is politely sending off your relatives nothing to me!" Sabina countered smartly. When he looked instantly irate, she continued quickly, "You want a wife to conduct herself as you see fit and I want my home. Can we not reach some agreement, Sir Jeffree, where both of us get what we want?"

"Your duty, madam, should dictate that you try to please me in all things."

Sabina folded her lips, lest her wayward tongue provoke him further. When she had herself in order, she tried again. "Sir Jeffree—"

"Very well!" he cut in, taking the wind out of her sails. "I will look into that other matter."

"You will?" Sabina caught her breath and scanned his face. He gave a short nod. "As a priority?"

That brought forth a thunderous frown. "I have given you no reason to doubt my word, madam."

Sabina gazed at him a moment. "That is true enough," she conceded. "We have struck a bargain, then." His refusal to meet her eye made her uneasy. "Can we not shake hands on it?" she persisted recklessly.

He met her gaze at that, a fire kindling in his eye. "It seems you still think yourself a widow, madam, that must draw up contracts and deals. The fact is you are a married woman who should take your husband's word as law."

Only by the greatest effort of will did Sabina manage to choke back her instinctive reply. Jeffree narrowed his eyes at her. "You do not trust my word," he said. "Very well. How far is Morecotte from here?"

Sabina blinked at him uncomprehendingly. "It is but a twenty-minute ride from here."

"Well, then," he said, standing abruptly from the table. "We will set out in half an hour. Make sure your bags are packed and ready."

Sabina's head reeled. "For Morecotte?" she repeated, suddenly breathless. "Or Ganford Chase?"

"Both," he answered succinctly as he made for the door.

"Wait!" Sabina called after him. "But surely you mean to approach the magistrate first, or attempt some formal route?"

"To what end?"

"To make matters perfectly legal."

"You mean as Hendry did?" he asked sarcastically.

104

"Well…"

"Possession is eleven points in the law," he said briefly.

Sabina's eyebrows snapped together. "You mean for us to take possession of Morecotte now?" she asked shrilly. "But we—we have no men with us to—to—"

"You have me," he said simply. "I am the only man you have need of."

Her mouth was still hanging open as he passed out of the door. Sabina tore upstairs and packed in a hurry, and truth be told, she did not have much by way of personal possessions. Isemay helped her carry her things down the staircase, though she was far too distracted to answer most of her sister's chatter.

"But what will you do once you get there, sister?" Isemay asked as they walked out to where Sir Jeffree was waiting with his huge destrier.

"I hardly know," Sabina admitted, before raising her voice. "I have no horse of my own," she warned her husband as she passed him the first of the bags to strap to the horse's back.

He barely paused. "Then I must have you up before me," he answered with a shrug. "I daresay Radax can bear the additional weight."

"Not the most chivalrous way of putting it," Isemay murmured as she passed her bag to Sabina. Fortunately, their mother hurried out, preventing Sabina from having to reply.

"Do make sure you give our regards to His Grace, the Duke of Bethencourt," Thora Burrell gushed. "I hope he did not miss you at his table too much last night."

105

Sabina ventured a glance at Sir Jeffree's face and looked quickly away. "Thank you, Mother," she said hurriedly before he could snub her parent.

Sir Jeffree led his horse to the mounting block, and by an undignified combination of leaping and scrambling, Sabina managed to get onto the massive charger's broad back. Jeffree joined her moments later, making it look effortless, and Sabina steeled herself not to cringe away from his solid bulk surrounding her. For a moment, it brought vivid memories of waking that morn with his body wrapped around hers. She managed a brief wave at her mother and Isemay, and they were off.

8

Neither of them spoke until Tipton Hall was out of sight, and then Jeffree cleared his throat. "You will have to instruct me," he said. "For I have no idea in which direction this Morecotte lies."

Sabina was startled. She swiveled about in the saddle to look at him. "Are you truly in earnest about making for it now? And taking matters into your own hands?" she demanded.

"I see no reason for delay."

Sabina was so astonished by this assertion that for a moment she had no words. "Sir Jeffree," she expostulated. "This is reckless. This is ill-thought-out. I had not thought you so impetuous of nature."

"You are only just getting to know me," he pointed out dryly.

Which was true enough, Sabina acknowledged, but somewhere along the line, she had gained the impression he was stuffy and would be careful always to observe the laws and legalities of the land. Erroneously, it now turned out, for scanning his face, she could see no sign of wariness. He was completely calm about whatever opposition he would face at Morecotte.

She bit her lip. "I do not know what manner of staff Alfred Hendry is maintaining," she said urgently. "He keeps low company, and I would not be surprised if he retains some villainous servants to do his bidding. No decent ones would have remained on in such a man's service." He made no response to this. "What will we do if—?"

"How about you let me worry about how we deal with Hendry?" he suggested.

"But you don't look remotely worried, Sir Jeffree; that is what is bothering me!"

He gave a short laugh, at which she turned her head to stare at him. "I know how to deal with men of his ilk," he said grimly.

Sabina felt her face grow warm and turned to face forward. *You have me*, he had said. *I am the only man you have need of.* The astonishing words were still ringing in her ears. It would be foolish to set any store in them, she told herself. This was sure to end in disaster!

She was still convinced of the fact when they started down the dirt track that led toward her old home. It had not been maintained, and tall weeds were now choking up the lane. Not that it bothered Sir Jeffree's large destrier, who simply trampled them beneath his huge hooves, but it did make Sabina wonder about tradesmen's carts. Was Morecotte no longer on anyone's rounds? The place was too small to support a staff of more than five or so servants. Certainly not enough to produce all the provisions a functioning household would require.

When the house came into view, she felt the customary swell of affection and longing for the place. Curious how it did not seem in any way tainted with her bitter memories of Miles. It did make a beautiful picture surrounded as it was by blossoming trees and flowering hedgerows, even if they had been allowed to encroach upon the house.

Jeffree made no sound of appreciation at the pretty picture Morecotte made, and Sabina tensed as he dismounted and tied his horse to a convenient tree. "You stay here," he ordered.

Sabina, still sat upon his steed, bristled. "But—"

"I won't be long," he added sternly and strode toward the house, flinging open the door and starting down the passageway.

Sabina sat in an agony of indecision. What was she supposed to do? Even if she did manage to slide down off this massive horse, what would be her next move? Mentally, she pictured the rooms and layout of her old home. It would not take him long to stride about the place. Morecotte was not a large property; it had no more than six bedchambers if you did not include the attic rooms where the servants slept.

What would he do? she wondered. Go striding in there and demand to speak to Alfred? She wondered how many of the old servants remained. From the untended state of the gardens, she guessed not many. Suddenly she sat up. Surely she had heard some sound, like a muffled shout and then a crash? She turned to stare at the door expectantly, and moments later, Sir Jeffree burst from it, dragging someone by the scruff of his neck before depositing him into the water trough with a huge splash. After an astonished moment, she realized it was Alfred Hendry.

Sabina gaped as two burly manservants emerged from the house, rolling up their sleeves. Sabina opened her mouth to yell a warning but found Sir Jeffree had already turned and was striding now toward them. Sabina shut her eyes, heard a few dull thuds, doubtless body blows, and muffled grunts of pain. There was a splash, followed by another splash.

Another figure emerged from the house, an older, scrawnier servant with a stooped back. He surveyed the horse trough impassively and then squinted at Jeffree. Sabina recognized none of them. She cleared her throat. "Where is Master Carter who was head servant here?" she asked.

The old man shrugged. "Never 'eard of 'im," he admitted.

Jeffree disappeared back into the house in search of further quarry. "Is there anyone else within?" she asked.

The old man spat on the ground, though whether from insolence or habit, she was not entirely sure. When she realized he was not willing to answer her, she turned back to where the drenched manservants were clambering out of the trough. Alfred was coughing and sputtering up a storm, but he made no move to extricate himself. Likely he was still sotted from the previous night's excesses if she judged him on past form.

"Help me, you dolts!" he screamed impatiently, kicking his legs. The two manservants looked at one another with raised brows and then fell back, feigning deafness.

Jeffree reappeared once more over the threshold, and the old man straightened up at once. "Good master," he said in a wheedling voice, clasping his hands together in supplication. "Surely you will not throw an old man out of the only home he's ever known." Sabina's eyebrows rose at this palpable lie. She had not set foot in Morecotte for two years, but this man was not one of Miles's original staff.

Jeffree ignored him, turning to Sabina. "This is the entire household, save one woman in the kitchen," he announced as a stout middle-aged woman stepped out of the front door, still wielding her broom. She looked from the horse trough to the dripping servants with interest. "What would you have me do?"

"Dismiss them all," she answered at once. "I'll have none of them! Anyone who would willingly serve such a villain as Alfred Hendry must be a wretch themselves."

The servants had just broken out in a babble of protest when Alfred seemed to notice her for the first time. He gave an indignant yelp. "You! I might have known!"

"You might indeed!" she responded coolly. "As the rightful owner of this house, it is only right and proper that I should reclaim my home."

"Harlot!" Alfred railed at her, his face turning purple. "Shameless, unnatural woman. Who would—?" He got no further, for Jeffree cuffed him roughly about the head. Alfred let out a howl and cringed back in the trough, clasping his ears.

"Watch your mouth when you speak of my wife!" Jeffree barked. "I will suffer none to scold her save me." Sabina blinked at this but kept her head held high. "You heard her!" he roared, glancing around at the loitering servants. "Get you gone!"

One of the burly men slouched toward the water trough and heaved Hendry out in a grudging manner. After a moment, the old man hobbled over to join them, muttering under his breath. The three of them squelched resentfully down the weed-choked path, muttering complaints but not daring to raise their voices high enough for anyone to hear.

The woman hurried in her direction at once. "Milady," she appealed. "I beg you will give me the chance to keep my position. Indeed, I have no love for Master Hendry. He has ever been a poor master and done little to inspire loyalty."

Sabina surveyed her dispassionately. "Did you serve under the old master?" she asked with a hint of dread.

The woman's gaze did not falter. "That I did for a sixmonth, but as you can see, I am not the type as would have caught his fancy."

Sabina forced herself not to flinch. The woman was right. She was plain-faced and on the wrong side of thirty. Miles's taste did not run in such directions. "Is your family a local one?" she persisted.

"Aye, milady. My brother runs the pottery at Little Ganford. Until he married, I kept house there right comfortably for him. I daresay, a good deal more competently than that wife of his do now."

"And your family name?"

"'Tis Chawton, milady." She hesitated. "Though my married name is Lancer. Penny Lancer." She cast a quick look over at the remaining manservant who was stood emptying out his boots of water before setting out for the village.

"If I might make so bold, you might consider keeping on Lancer, milady. If you was to keep one of them on for the heavy work, I mean." Penny colored slightly and glanced away. "He be my husband, if truth be told."

Sabina glanced toward the man who looked rough-hewn and sullen. "He is your husband?" she asked softly. Penny nodded. "Do you stand witness to his good character?"

"He ain't all bad," Penny answered awkwardly. "Leastways, he's the best of a bad bunch."

Sabina sighed. She had heard of the Chawtons at least. They were a local family of good name. "Very well, Penny, you shall have your chance and so shall your husband."

A look of immense relief swept over the woman's face. She bobbed a curtsey. "Thank you kindly, milady. You won't regret it. Without those knaves cluttering up the rooms, I'll be able to bring some order to the place."

It was true, there was likely a good deal of work to be done. "You there!" Sabina called impulsively. "Lancer. Is that your name?"

The fellow looked up. "It is, milady," he answered gruffly.

"Your wife has put in a word for you. You may stay on if you wish for a trial period in our service."

Lancer shot a startled look at Penny before he gave a nod of acquiescence. "Right willingly, milady."

Jeffree moved forward at this point from where he was stood wearing a sardonic frown. "So much for your having none of them," he uttered scathingly. "You do realize you have now retained half of Hendry's staff!"

"If the outside appearance of my house is anything to go by, then the inside will need a good deal of work," Sabina observed. "There is no point in cutting off my nose to spite my face." Jeffree snorted. She held her arms out imperiously. "Can you please lift me down from this outlandishly tall horse?"

Jeffree's eyes flickered, and for one moment she thought he would churlishly refuse her. Then he strode forward and held up his hands. Sabina inched forward, took a deep breath, and plunged over the edge. He caught her firmly about the waist and swung her down to the floor, where he released her at once. There was no reason for her to feel so unaccountably flustered. Sabina straightened her wimple and smoothed her rumpled skirts.

"You must own the largest horse in Karadok," she commented. Again, enough time lapsed for her to think he would snub her before his response came.

"Radax's size is not unusual for a charger."

113

"Oh." She dropped her hands. "Well, shall we go inside?" she ventured.

He gave a brief nod, looking, she noticed, far from enthusiastic. Sabina squared her shoulders and strode into her old home. Mayhap it was all her imagination, but she felt sure the house was welcoming her back within its walls. True, her heart quailed moments later when she saw how unkempt and shabby everything was looking within, but she did not lose the sensation of coming home at last.

They proceeded from the entranceway straight into the Great Hall where the rushes strewn on the floor were covered in grime and grease and dried mud. Heaven only knew when clean rushes had last been put down. Seeing the way Jeffree's nose wrinkled, she knew she was not the only one to notice their evil smell.

Not only that, but many of the features of the room she was familiar with seemed to be missing. Only the great soot-blackened fireplace remained, and a large scarred dining table scattered with crumbs and leftovers. Where were the large wooden dressers with their display of silver candlesticks and gleaming tankards?

Where were the oiled weapons which Miles had displayed proudly from every wall? The truth dawned on her slowly as Jeffree inspected the filthy wall hangings with an expression of distaste. Alfred Hendry had sold everything that was not nailed down. Jeffree poked his finger through a hole in the tapestry and Sabina's eyes widened as she noticed the strange patina of holes which riddled the wall hangings.

Frowning, she turned about to face the tapestry behind her. At one time it had been a beautiful piece, depicting a sea battle on a storm-tossed ocean. Now, like the others, it was dirty and

114

damaged. She examined the slashes and tears. They appeared to be deliberately inflicted rather than moth-eaten or some other natural phenomena.

"What on earth happened here?" she asked, turning back to the servants, who had followed in their wake.

Penny glanced down at her feet, shamefaced. "I can hardly say, milady, as I was scarce allowed free roam of the house. Master Alfred did not permit me to leave the kitchen most days."

She turned to look back over her shoulder. "Lancer," she said, addressing her husband, who was bringing up the rear. "Milady asks what happened to the tapestries."

"'E shot 'em," Lancer growled in response. "For sport."

"Shot them?" Sabina repeated incredulously.

"With a bow and arrow."

"Alfred Hendry did?" Sabina asked, startled. She found it hard to imagine Alfred with a bow in his hand. He just was not the sporting kind.

"Nay, not Master Alfred, but Master Miles." Sabina pressed her lips together. Miles had wrought this damage on his home. *Miles?* Clearly, Lancer took her pointed silence as a statement of disbelief, for he added reluctantly, "He were drunk, of course, when he done it, milady. He were drunk as a lord most nights I knew 'im." The manservant shrugged.

Sabina sighed and turned about to survey the ruins of the Great Hall. Miles had always overindulged, but he had not been drunk every night in the twelve months they had been married. He must have really gone to rack and ruin in the last year of his life.

115

Catching sight of movement beneath the table, Sabina halted in her progress and stared at the two shaggy dogs lying under the scuffed dining table which was still littered with what she could only suppose was the previous night's meal. As they were lazily gnawing on bones, the dogs seemed in no hurry to make her acquaintance and ignored the newcomers.

"I do not recognize these hounds," she commented. "Do they belong to Alfred Hendry? I am surprised he did not take them with him."

"They wasn't 'is to take," Lancer responded quickly. "They'm mine, milady."

"I see. What happened to my late husband's dogs?"

"Master Alfred sold 'em," Lancer said bitterly. "Good dogs they was too. They'm sorely missed about the place."

Sabina nodded. Miles had been vastly proud of his hounds. "Alfred had no right to sell them," she said, lifting her chin. "Those animals belonged to me. What of Miles's horses?"

Lancer hesitated. "Sold also, milady," he said with obvious regret.

"The chestnut that was my husband's favorite? With the white star at her brow?"

"Blitha were sold first of all, milady," Lancer admitted. "She were too spirited for a worm like Master Alfred to ride."

Penny coughed loudly, letting her husband know he was overstepping a mark by criticizing his old master to his new one. Lancer's face turned instantly blank, but really, Sabina was hardly likely to object to such talk. Alfred Hendry *was* a craven worm as far as she was concerned.

116

It was then she noticed that, though he stood with his back to them, one arm braced against the mantel, Sir Jeffree's back was rigid with affront. Very likely he stood more on ceremony than she when it came to such matters and was not so free with servants.

"Let us see the rest," she said and led the way through to the kitchen, larder, and pantry which she was delighted to see looked a lot cleaner and better maintained than the Great Hall.

"This is my domain," Penny said eagerly. "And you can see, milady, that I am not slovenly by nature. I weren't given no free hand to interfere with the master's quarters, you see, but back here, all is as it should be."

"I can see that," Sabina agreed soothingly. "You have kept things in good order." She noticed, though, that the pantry was ill stocked, and while there were many herbs collected from the gardens and hung about to dry, there were few sacks of grain or flour and not a wheel of cheese or pat of butter in sight.

In the larder, there were some birds and dead hares strung up, but it was far from the abundance of meat that Miles delighted in piling up after his hunting trips.

"Are there no barrels of salted meats or fish?" Sabina asked, looking about.

"No, milady," Penny admitted regretfully. "We've used up all that was stored these past months. Master Alfred always waved such matters away. Oftentimes he took his meals at The Blue Boar," she said, naming the inn in town.

"I see." Sabina's eyebrows rose. No wonder Alfred had inspired no loyalty among his servants, not with their stores dwindling away and he wholly uncaring. When they descended to the cellar, which had functioned as a buttery in Sabina's day, they found only three dusty casks of ale remaining and no wine at all. Remembering the virtually impassable lane, Sabina guessed these must have been delivered some time ago.

"The cellar used to be stocked floor to ceiling full of wine back in Master Miles's day," Lancer commented, shaking his head. "But it's been long since drunk dry."

Sabina made no comment, simply marched back to the steps, and led their party up the staircase to the living quarters. The state of things there made her blanch, and she could not look in Jeffree's direction. Alfred Hendry had been living in absolute squalor.

"Throw open the windows," she commanded, covering her nose with her sleeve. "The air in here is foul and unwholesome!" Lancer and Penny ran to the casements and opened the few windows that allowed it. "This mattress and bedsheets will have to be burned!" she choked, turning away from the filthy pit that Hendry had slept in.

"The room will have to be stripped bare and a bonfire lit," Jeffree put in cuttingly.

She did not have the heart to argue with him. Besides, the only furniture that remained was an overturned footstool. The remains of a small table were lying in the fireplace. Sabina pursed her lips with disapproval and strode about the other bedrooms which were not quite as bad as the main bedchamber, though their furniture had likewise been looted. They stood practically bare, stripped even of bedframes, though one did have a mattress and showed signs of recent occupation. She supposed even a social pariah like Alfred must have some cronies.

One of the windows seemed to be broken and was covered in a blanket. There was a nest of mice in the smallest of the bedchambers which sent Sabina hurrying backward so fast, she stepped right into Jeffree, who caught her upper arms and set her from him carefully.

"I think we have seen enough for this day, have we not?" he asked through gritted teeth. "Much needs to be done before possession can be taken of this place."

"Well, I agree it would serve no purpose to disturb the servants by prying into their attic quarters at this point," she answered.

"We should set forth; 'tis almost midday," he said, his gaze flickering to the window. "Doubtless, my mother and Sir Dudley will be setting off shortly."

Sabina gazed back at him blankly. "You surely do not expect me to abandon Morecotte now," she answered with spirit. "Lest Alfred Hendry should return and try to take possession again. 'Twould be better if you left me here to supervise and guard against him."

Jeffree's gaze narrowed. "Indeed, I will not," he answered roundly. "We can send my man, Osborn, over from Ganford Chase and a couple of my uncle's servants to help out if needs be. Your place now is by my side, taking leave of my family."

Sabina bridled, opened her mouth to argue, then relented. After all, he had obliged her by restoring Morecotte to her. "Oh, very well," she murmured. "Though I cannot see that any of them will appreciate my presence. Indeed," she added, "they are far more likely to resent it!"

119

9

Sabina stayed close to his side and spoke little as they moved about the Great Hall, bidding farewell to his relatives. If anyone addressed her directly, she replied with civility, otherwise, she held her tongue. As it was, only his cousin Frederick and an aunt who was very deaf attempted any exchange of words with her. Jeffree suspected the aunt's deafness meant she had not fully grasped the events that had led to their marriage three days before.

Jeffree did not pay much heed to his aunt Justina's offer for them to come and visit with her next spring, but he scowled at Frederick, who he thought overstepped the mark by peering into Sabina's face with undue curiosity. He noticed how his cousin kept glancing over to him with puzzlement before returning his gaze to his wife.

It was that alone which had prompted Jeffree to take a firm hold of Sabina's arm and draw her in close. She had looked startled by the move but made no comment to finding herself suddenly clamped to his side.

"Where are your parents?" Sabina asked, looking about once Frederick had faded away.

"Vyse is not my father," Jeffree found himself retorting. "He is my mother's second husband."

"Oh." She shrugged, looking wholly unconcerned about her slip.

"They have two boys," he added, "who take a good deal of organizing. Doubtless, that is why they are late down."

"Your half brothers?" Sabina asked with a flicker of interest. "They were not present at the…at what happened three days ago?"

Jeffree grimaced. "Thankfully not. They were abovestairs at the time. They are but ten and twelve years of age."

"I see. And what are they like?"

"Like?" Jeffree was taken aback. A strange question, for they were naught but boys.

"Well, they are not de Crecys," she pointed out. "So, I might actually *like* them."

Jeffree snorted. "I have no interest in children. In my opinion, they are wholly unformed at that age and hardly worth the time or effort of getting to know."

"What a peculiar attitude," she responded at once. "I daresay you know what you were like that at that age and thought yourself worth the knowing."

Jeffree frowned down at her. "I was squired to Sir Hereward of Wolmer Hall at thirteen. That was when I made the transition from boy to man."

He felt her eyes on his face, but when he turned his head, she glanced away. "Was Sir Hereward a member of your uncle's party? Only I don't think I remember anyone pointing him out."

"He was not," Jeffree replied shortly. "Our association with that family was through my grandfather, not my uncle. The connection has grown distant. I have not seen him in two years at least."

She made no reply to that, and looking up, Jeffree was almost relieved to see his stepfather ushering his two half brothers into the hall with a harried expression on his face. The boys gave their father the slip almost at once and came hurtling in their direction with poor Sir Dudley hurrying in hot pursuit.

"Is this her?" Jasper asked, coming to a skidding halt directly in front of Sabina. Or was it Crispin? Jeffree sometimes forgot which of his brothers was which.

"Stand up straight and present your bows," Jeffree responded sternly. Both boys stopped, shuffled their feet, and gave untidy bows.

"This is my wife, Sabina de Crecy," Jeffree intoned gravely. "These are my brothers, Crispin and Jasper Vyse."

"I am Crispin," the shorter of the two proffered. "I'm ten."

"And I'm Jasper," the other added, not to be outdone. "I was twelve on the feast of St. Vester."

"How nice to meet you," Sabina responded at once with what Jeffree could not help but notice was a warmness heretofore lacking in her manner. "I am vastly happy to make your acquaintance."

"You are our sister-in-law now, Lady Sabina," Jasper pointed out, quite needlessly.

"We have not had one of those before," Crispin chimed in.

Jeffree was just about to ask them not to make asinine remarks when Sabina responded thoughtfully with: "Nor I, a brother." She regarded them with every evidence of interest and approval. "It will be a most interesting experience for us all."

This response seemed the right thing to say, for both boys beamed at once.

"Your pardon, Jeffree," Sir Dudley panted, catching up with them. "They are slippery as eels!"

He nodded and Sir Dudley attempted a grab at Jasper's shoulder, only to grasp at thin air for the boy twisted nimbly out of the way.

"Will you come and stay with us at Longacre?" Jasper panted, dodging his way in between Sabina and Jeffree as he continued to elude his father. "We have our own ponies and there's trout in the river that passes through Long Marsh."

"We can show you the best spots to try and tickle them," Crispin offered generously.

"That all sounds wonderful," Sabina answered easily, as though no ill will existed between his mother and herself. "But I have only recently retaken my own home which was wickedly stolen from me by an out and out villain. Your brother restored it to me only this morning and I have much to do to bring it back into repair."

Jeffree saw the startled look that stole over his stepfather's face at this news.

"Did Jeffree challenge him to a duel?" Crispin asked with a spark of interest kindling in his eyes. Jasper stopped bobbing and weaving his way around them to listen avidly.

"No, he did not," Sabina responded, and Jeffree saw both boys' faces fall. They glanced toward him disparagingly as though to say: *Nay, he would not, the dull dog!*

"He employed far more rough and ready methods, I assure you," Sabina continued. "Why he pulled Alfred Hendry from his bed and shook him like the rat he is. Then he dragged him down the stairs, so he bounced on every step, then threw him in the water trough and bade him never darken my doorstep again!"

123

Crispin gasped and both boys turned their heads to stare at him, a quite different expression dawning on their faces. Almost Jeffree asked how she could possibly know about his shaking and bumping Hendry on every step, as she had been outside the property.

"Did you break his pate, brother?" Jasper asked eagerly.

"Nay." Jeffree shook his head and cleared his throat. "He was a miserable cur, hardly worthy of the effort."

"What if he should return?" Crispin asked breathlessly. "Would you run him through with your blade?"

Jeffree frowned. "He wears no sword at his hip. Such an action would not be worthy of a knight."

"You would throw him in the horse trough again?" Jasper suggested with relish.

Jeffree considered this a moment. "Most likely," he agreed.

"But what if he should bring a band of hired swords?" Crispin suggested. "Would you fight in earnest, then, brother?"

"Assuredly I would."

Sabina looked alarmed. "Do you think that is likely?" she blurted, looking horrified.

Jeffree opened his mouth to say in his opinion it was most *unlikely*, but his brothers forestalled him with their excited clamor.

"He's sure to," Crispin said excitedly. "If he is a craven cur. You should boil some oil, sister, in order to fling it down on his mercenaries."

"And have some bows and arrows ready to shoot at them," Jasper added. "Crispin and I have bows and arrows at Longacre. We could ride out to your aid."

Crispin hastily echoed the sentiment, lamenting the fact he had lost half his arrows in the long meadow. "But likely I can make some more if old Mullins will give me a lend of his knife."

Jeffree opened his mouth to lambast this foolishness but was prevented once more from getting a word in edgeways.

"That would be most kind of you boys," Sabina answered gravely. "It certainly sets my mind at rest to know we have such able allies to our cause."

Instead of snuffing out this nonsense with a few sharp words, Jeffree found himself distracted by the twinkle in her eye which gave the lie to her serious tone. To his surprise, he saw Sir Dudley concealing an answering smile.

"Well, well," his stepfather said briskly, catching sight of his own expression. "That is enough now, boys. Your mother awaits us abovestairs. She is—er—wholly unable to face everyone today as her head is aching fit to split."

"What a pity," Sabina responded lightly. "You must convey our hopes for Lady Vyse's speedy recovery."

Sir Dudley reddened but nodded gratefully and made his bow. "I think we will be setting forth on our journey before midday, so this is our farewell, Lady Sabina. Perhaps when you are in our neck of the woods, you will visit us at Longacre. I know you sometimes compete in the vicinity, Jeffree, at Lord Blandivar's event. That must be coming up soon, I think?"

Jeffree looked evasive. "My plans are not yet certain," he prevaricated. "I will bear your invitation in mind." He bowed and his stepfather responded in kind before taking a step back.

125

"You will send word to us if the invasion should go ahead?" Jasper asked anxiously, finally allowing his father to grab his arm.

"Most definitely."

"I will make more arrows as soon as I reach home," Crispin vowed, twisting around as they were led away. "So we are ready for battle."

"We will be eternally grateful," Sabina called back. Jeffree regarded her with bafflement. "What delightful boys. I had a feeling I should like them."

"They are a pair of impudent knaves."

"They are enchanting young scamps," Sabina corrected him. "Fine boys. Thus far I like them best of all your family members."

"You seem to have forgotten your prospective brother-in-law," he pointed out dryly. "I am sure you do not prefer the likes of Jasper and Crispin to the duke himself."

Sabina snorted. "And I say that I do! His Grace is pleasant enough." She shrugged. "But after two minutes in his company, I am ready to seek out other."

Jeffree drew in a shocked breath, glancing about him. "You stand in his home, woman."

Sabina rolled her eyes. "I am aware of that, Sir Jeffree. Do you think a person's worth is wholly determined by their rank? I am sure there have been many who bear titles who are entirely contemptible and, even worse, extremely forgettable."

He blinked. "Even worse?" he echoed uncomprehendingly.

"Certainly." She nodded. "For there can be nothing worse than a complete bore."

Jeffree cast a quick glance around. "It is unseemly of you to say such things in present company," he said tightly. "You speak out of turn."

"Nonsense! I speak not of particulars, merely from my observations of the world."

He scoffed at this. "I daresay you have never been out of Ganfordshire, woman!"

Her eyes flashed. "I have seen enough! There was a baronet lived not five miles from my old home that drank himself into an early grave and beat his wife and daughter near every night. Does he deserve my respect because he was born with every advantage?"

"I have always made it my practice to avoid such vices that would lead to ruination," Jeffree answered stiffly. "All men are capable of sinking into degradation. Even those born into privilege."

"So, because you have always avoided women and drink that means you are beyond reproach, does it?" Sabina asked.

"That is not what I said," Jeffree answered frustratedly. "You twist my meaning."

"You were the one who made this about you," she pointed out. "I was merely praising your brothers."

Jeffree's brows drew together. "They are a pair of young jackanapes," he pronounced heavily, though he did not know why it annoyed him so much to hear her speak highly of them.

"What were you like at their age? Were you just as delightful before you were bundled off to Sir Hector's tender care?"

127

"Hereward," he corrected her automatically. "And there was precious little tender about his care, I assure you!"

She paused at the heat of his response. "Was he cruel to you?" she asked in an oddly stricken voice.

"No," Jeffree responded at once, though he did not know why he should reassure her. "He was a bluff, old country type. He liked wine, roasted meats, and hunting songs. Most nights I had to drag him to bed by his heels, while he sang raucously at the top of his lungs or he would have choked to death facedown in a vat of wine."

Sabina gave a smothered laugh. "At least he enjoyed life," she mused. "So then, it was not he that beat the joy out of you. Then it must have been someone else. Who was it, I wonder? Not your stepfather, for he seems a most mild-mannered man."

Jeffree regarded her with exasperation. "I was nothing like Jasper and Crispin. At their age, I was wholly given over to my studies."

"A sober-minded boy?" Sabina commented, gazing at him as though she were trying to picture him at thirteen.

He cleared his throat. "Sir Hereward thought I was a young prig," he admitted.

Sabina laughed again, and Jeffree realized that everyone still present in the hall was turned their way and staring at them with unabashed amazement.

"Jeffree, my boy!"

He turned his head to see his uncle had come into the hall at some point and was now seated before the fire in a burgundy robe. Stifling his disinclination, Jeffree led Sabina in that direction. "Your Grace," he greeted his uncle.

"Sit ye down, sit ye down," the Duke of Bethencourt urged them, gesturing to some seats that had been placed down beside him. "All of these farewells are most fatiguing. I vow, my voice has grown quite hoarse from all the endless repetition."

Jeffree released his hold of Sabina and saw her seated before he took the neighboring chair. "You are otherwise well this morning, Uncle?" he asked briskly, hoping that way to ward off any catalogue of complaints. No such luck.

The fifth duke tutted and adjusted the length of silk about his throat. "I fear I may have taken a chill," he quavered. "Naseby promised me a posset forthwith, but the wretched fellow has slipped away and abandoned me to my sufferings."

Sabina drew in a breath and Jeffree tensed. "If Naseby is your steward, Your Grace," she piped up, "then I believe he is stood in the entryway, directing people's baggage to their conveyances." There was a hint of reproach in her voice, which made Jeffree squirm, but his uncle seemed wholly oblivious to it.

"Oh, is he?" Bevis de Crecy murmured. "Well, then, I suppose I must not begrudge him if he is helping my guests on their way." He tugged fretfully at his moustache. "You spent the evening at Tipton Hall last night, I think?"

Jeffree found himself bristling. His uncle knew full well where they had spent the night, after sending servants to enquire. "We did," he growled.

"I hope it was not under some misapprehension that you were not welcome at Ganford Chase," his uncle continued, surprising him.

"Certainly not," Sabina responded. "But we wished to reassure my own parents as to our…" She hesitated a moment. "Marital accord," she settled on, refusing to meet Jeffree's eye.

"Yes…er, yes, I suppose that is understandable," his uncle replied begrudgingly. "May I ask, Mistress Sabina, how you found your dear sister yester'een?" Jeffree stiffened slightly. Could no one address his wife correctly? "I should not be surprised if she were to go into a sad decline," the duke continued mournfully. "Many a beauteous maid has done so, under far less provocation."

"I do not believe so," Sabina answered stoutly. "Her constitution is not so enfeebled." Jeffree darted a warning glance at her, which she completely ignored, lifting her chin. "She was affected, of course, by such rude treatment, but Isemay's reaction was more of indignation than lamentation."

The Duke of Bethencourt blinked, looking anything but gratified by this news. "I would have thought that any delicately reared maiden would have been stricken to her very core by such allegations!" he said, shuddering slightly. "But there, I daresay I am sadly old-fashioned and out of step with current ways."

Jeffree cleared his throat, seeing Sabina open her mouth on a retort. Catching his meaning, she lapsed into silence again, though he saw the flash in her eyes, indicating she had plenty more to say on the subject.

"Has my godfather taken his leave of you this morn?" Jeffree asked his uncle after a short, awkward silence.

"I've not seen hide nor hair of Charles," the duke responded peevishly. "He and Leland were going to stay on for a few weeks originally. Now, of course…" He spread his hands wide.

"That would be exceedingly awkward under the circumstances."

Jeffree's eyebrows rose, but he found himself entirely unable to make a polite rejoinder when it came to Leland. He supposed his godfather must still be some whereabouts the premises. With his punctilious manners, Sir Charles would never have departed without taking his leave of the duke.

"Your mother came and bade me farewell last night." The duke sighed and shook his head. "Dear lady," he tutted. "She felt the dishonor done to the de Crecy name most keenly."

"Strange," Jeffree retorted, "as she has not borne it in so many years."

His uncle looked taken aback. "Well…no," he conceded. "But you, my boy, her eldest son, bear it proudly."

"Sir Dudley made a better impression on me this morning," Sabina put in suddenly. "His personality has more opportunity to shine when his lady wife is not present."

The duke clearly took exception to this point of view. "Sir Dudley is a decent sort of man, by all accounts," he responded without enthusiasm. "But he cannot possibly be compared to my brother, Gaius, the Lady Maud's first husband. He outshone him in every respect."

"He sounds a perfect paragon," Sabina responded blandly, and though he might have taken this statement at face value at one time, Jeffree was no longer fooled. "But then I would expect no less from the sire of one such as Sir Jeffree," she concluded sweetly.

"Quite so," Bethencourt responded, seeing nothing suspect in her statement. "We de Crecys have always been a superior breed."

131

Jeffree felt his face grow hot and turned hastily toward Sabina to quell whatever retort was rising to those impertinent lips. She ignored his chastising glare. "Have you heard, Your Grace, how Sir Jeffree hath championed me this morn?" she asked in an abrupt change of subject.

"What's that you say?" his uncle asked, throwing a startled glance his way. "What have you been about now, Jeffree?" He looked alarmed, as though one of his previously docile hounds had snarled at someone.

"It was naught," Jeffree insisted. "She exaggerates."

"Nonsense! You were my perfect hero," Sabina responded fervently. "I only wish you could have championed my cause a twelvemonth ago and I would not have had all that fuss and pother with Alfred Hendry."

"As you would scarcely have been in the position to marry me, then, madam," he retorted scathingly, "my intervention would have been most improper."

"Why? Oh, you mean as I was so recently widowed?" For once, she had the grace to look somewhat abashed. "I suppose that is true enough, though some people do not let the grass grow under their feet." She bit her lip and dropped her gaze to her lap, lapsing into abrupt silence.

For some reason, Jeffree found himself just as displeased by her withdrawal from the conversation as he had been by her thrusting herself into it. He regarded her moodily until some pointed remark by his uncle roused him from his thoughts. "What was that you say, Uncle?"

"I said—oh, never mind, Jeffree! I know you are a newlywed, but it really is too bad!"

"What is?"

"If all you can do is sit and stare at your new bride, then you are hardly fit company for the rest of us!"

So startled by his uncle's irritated words was he, that all Jeffree could manage was an outraged splutter. Luckily, the arrival at his side of Sir Charles freed him of the necessity of replying.

"There you are, Charles!" Bethencourt hailed him. "We were just wondering where you had vanished to."

Sir Charles nodded all around. "I rode out abroad this morning to make some enquiries." Jeffree's ears pricked up. *About what?* he wondered. Scanning his godfather's face, he guessed they must have pertained to the whereabouts of his missing son. "Thought you would have enough bodies about the pace this morning, Bevis, without me adding to the crowd," Sir Charles said wryly as he let his eyes travel over the people bustling in and out of the Great Hall.

"I certainly have," the duke responded. "I am exhausted by all the comings and goings about the place. The draughts blasting in and out will be the death of me!"

Sir Charles inclined his head. "You have had a lot to contend with of late," he agreed gravely.

Sabina made a stifled noise, and Jeffree turned his head to look at her sharply. Her expression was perfectly composed, but he was not fooled. She had sniffed. He drew back his chair. "Perhaps we ought to withdraw—"

"Jeffree, my boy," Sir Charles interrupted. "Could I have a word? Privately," he stressed, his gaze once more flickering over the three of them sat before the fire.

Jeffree cleared his throat and stood up. "Of course."

133

Together they walked to the opposite end of the hall before the older man spoke. "I cannot find any trace of where Leland can have got to," Sir Charles said bluntly. "I've not heard so much as a word from him."

Jeffree glanced at his godfather and noted how haggard he was looking. Always a rather colorless man, today he looked almost gray. "Likely he has ridden into the next shire," he pointed out. "His friend Mallenby's estate lies across the border in Halfordshire."

A hopeful look filled Sir Charles's eyes, and Jeffree marveled that he could be so concerned about his son, who had long since reached his majority. Then, too, Leland had always been something of a liability. "You really think that he might have made in that direction?" Sir Charles said, perking up visibly.

"More than likely," Jeffree replied offhand. He was damned if he was going to worry his head over Leland. "He and Mallenby were thick as thieves six months ago when that business went down with Warrington."

Sir Charles winced. Warrington had been another of Leland's wild friends. Six months ago, he had eloped with another man's wife and then wound up perishing ignobly on the sword of her outraged spouse. "Leland had nothing to do with that," his godfather pointed out, two spots of color appearing on his gaunt cheeks.

"Aye, I know," said Jeffree dryly. "Mallenby testified that he and Leland were gambling till dawn and knew naught of Warrington's plans after he left them at midnight." Still, knowing what a loose-tongued braggart Warrington was, Jeffree found it hard to believe he had not told his friends what he intended. Knowing both individuals involved, Jeffree did not believe they would have even attempted to dissuade him from such a disastrous course of action.

Sir Charles avoided his eye and bit the inside of his cheek. "Halfordshire," he muttered. "'Tis some thirty miles from here, should you say?"

Jeffree nodded, narrowing his gaze. "You will not set off on some goose chase, surely? If you are uneasy in your mind, why not write to Leland, care of Mallenby?"

Sir Charles tipped his head, appearing to consider the suggestion. "I should not feel easy in my mind abandoning you here in your own predicament, my boy," his godfather hedged. "I need hardly say how shocked and appalled I am by all that has transpired. That you have been forced to take such a step grieves me. That my own son should have been instrumental in your misfortune is deeply regrettable to me."

"What are you talking about?" Jeffree interrupted him.

"Your enforced marriage," his godfather answered forthrightly. "What else?"

Jeffree waved a hand. "What is done is done."

Sir Charles blinked. "You are too fatalistic, Jeffree. It may be that you could be freed from this yoke, even at this late point. We must put our heads together and determine your best course of action."

Jeffree regarded him blankly. "Your pardon, Sir Charles, but we have not done such a thing since I passed boyhood. Besides," he added briskly, "I know how I am fixed for the next few weeks. I begin my training for the Summer Tournament on the morrow. Part of that preparation will be attending Areley Kings in a weeks' time."

"And—er—what, then, of Mistress Hendry?" his godfather asked with a frown.

Jeffree drew himself up. "That is not her name," he retorted loudly.

His godfather looked startled. "Jeffree, my boy, none could blame you for the action you took, not under such extenuating circumstances. It was naught but a matter of expedience. Now that the moment of crisis has passed, cooler heads can prevail. With your connections at court, an annulment would certainly not be out of the question."

When Jeffree did not speak at once, a look of dawning horror spread across Sir Charles's face. "You have not consummated—! No, I will not believe it! You cannot have been so rash!" He shook his head disbelievingly. "Nay Jeffree, I cannot believe you have fallen for such a trap and tied yourself to such a woman."

"That is enough!" Jeffree glanced away, his face reddening.

Sir Charles looked shocked. "I credited you with better sense," he said bitterly, "and more worldly wisdom. First Bevis, now you! Oh, these Burrell women are formidable indeed!" Jeffree pressed his lips together. "You judge Leland harshly, yet where you find it convenient you let others off the hook!" Sir Charles railed angrily.

"How else am I to judge Leland's behavior?" Jeffree demanded, firing up at once. "His behavior was execrable!"

"He was trying to help you!"

"Help me?" Jeffree repeated incredulously. "*Help me?*"

"By preserving your inheritance!" Sir Charles said with dignity. "Ganford Chase, the title of Duke of Bethencourt, both are rightfully yours!"

"He grossly slandered my name! Not to mention his attempt to destroy the reputation of a blameless young woman!"

Sir Charles's face froze. "As to that, none of us know that young woman's true character," he said stiffly. "Her family threw her in the way of Bethencourt in the hopes of snaring a rich and titled husband."

"That is not a crime," Jeffree pointed out. "None of us know any ill of Mistress Isemay, *including* Leland."

"That man, Alfred Hendry—"

"Is a craven liar, who I dragged from his own filth a mere hour ago. There is a property dispute betwixt himself and the Burrells, and Leland decided to take advantage of that ill feeling and use the fellow to achieve his own ends."

"You are determined to think the worst of Leland!"

"And you not to!" Jeffree retorted.

A troubled silence descended. "It seems we shall not agree on this matter," Sir Charles said haltingly.

"Apparently not."

"Mistress—I mean, *the Lady Sabina* has been busy these past couple of days, poisoning you against those you were raised with."

"Is that what you really think?" Jeffree asked sardonically.

"I am shocked your loyalties could be so easily swayed. This woman, she is hardly in the same league as the Lady Meliora."

Jeffree looked up sharply. "Lady Meliora is no more. She joined the cloister and took a different name and a different life," he reminded Sir Charles. "Devoting herself to her god."

"Even so... One does not simply renounce a devotion to such a caliber of woman in a mere matter of days! I had thought better of you, my boy." Sir Charles's tone was bitter.

Jeffree regarded him stonily. "Well, I, too, thought better of you, Charles," he answered at last. "I had not realized your views were so...*biased* where your son and heir was concerned. I suppose it is not to be wondered at, but you always took such pains to present yourself as a rational man of impartial judgment."

A hectic flush mounted Sir Charles's hollowed cheeks, but he made no reply to this, and after a curt nod, Jeffree turned on his heel and marched back across the hall. He found his uncle sipping on a foul-looking concoction of milk and egg which he had urged Sabina to partake a cup of. From her expression, Jeffree could tell she was not enjoying it. For some reason, this brightened his mood considerably.

"Jeffree, my boy, come and take a cup of this excellent posset. It has just a sprinkling of nutmeg which makes it most efficacious."

Jeffree demurred, but Sabina held up her own cup toward him. "Here, finish mine. It is very rich, Your Grace," she said, turning to his uncle. "I fear I cannot stomach the entire helping."

The duke tutted but accepted her excuses. Jeffree took the cup, mostly because she so clearly expected him to. He was not in the habit of drinking people's dregs. Still, he gazed at it a moment with disfavor before draining the cup with a grimace.

"I am sure, as His Grace said, it will do you a power of good," Sabina said cheerfully. He narrowed his eyes at her, but the duke was already vehemently agreeing with the sentiment. "Well," she continued after a moment of silence. "Have we said your farewells to everyone?" Her gaze strayed over his shoulder to where Sir Charles was flinging out of the door, shutting it behind him with a slam.

Jeffree found himself wondering if any of their exchange had been overheard. Both he and Sir Charles had been rather heated in the moment. He answered her question absently. "I believe so, though I did not see my Launceston cousins."

"The lot from Hever Foy?" asked the duke, his ears pricking up. "They barely waited for break of day before packing up. None of us saw them leave save the servants." He sighed. "Most injudicious to travel when the grass is still damp."

"Well, in that case…" Jeffree shrugged. "I have done my duty." He eyed her resignedly. Doubtless, she would now start clamoring to return to her blessed Morecotte.

She took a deep breath. "Can we—should we have some speech now between the two of us?" Sabina asked in a low voice, her gaze darting warningly toward his uncle, who was sniffing dubiously at an orange studded with cloves.

Jeffree felt strangely reluctant to accede to the request. He stood up, though, showing himself willing in body, if not in spirit. "Very well, then."

139

10

To Sabina's surprise, instead of repairing to Jeffree's own chambers, he led her into the small parlor off the Great Hall which they had been married in. She gazed about a moment, overwhelmed by the unpleasant associations before bringing her attention back to his tense features.

"Well?" he asked, folding his arms.

Sabina cleared her throat. "I heard you telling Sir Charles you had plans," she admitted. "Will you share them with me?"

"You heard that?" he said quickly, his brows drawing together in a frown.

"Only a few phrases were audible," she admitted and noticed he seemed to relax at her words. Should she be concerned? She regarded him dubiously.

"I start my training on the morrow," he answered at last. "For the next tournament."

"Oh? When is that?"

"Areley Kings. In a week's time."

Sabina nodded as though she knew what this entailed. She had never even heard of Areley Kings. Was it the name of the place or the actual tournament? "You—er—*joust*?" she ventured, deciding against displaying her ignorance.

"I do."

"Is it far from here?"

"You have to pass through the mountains. 'Tis a five-day ride at least."

"Oh, so when will you leave?" Her mind was full of Morecotte and establishing herself there without challenge. If Alfred Hendry brought officers of the court along, it would be awkward indeed with a husband *in absentia*. It was a moment before she noticed the narrow way he was regarding her, his face all tight and displeased looking. What had she said?

"*We* leave tomorrow," he informed her cuttingly.

Sabina gaped back at him. "We?" she repeated. "You expect me to accompany you?"

He drew himself up. "That is what I said."

"But *why?* And what of Morecotte?" she objected strenuously.

"I will speak to my uncle and have some staff sent over to assist with its overhaul. It is scarcely fit for habitation as it stands."

"I could make do!"

"Your place, madam, is by your husband's side."

Sabina opened her mouth. "Sir Jeffree, I—"

"And that is all I have to say on the matter," he cut across her, turning his back as he made for the door, flinging it open and exiting abruptly.

"Whereas I still have *several* more things to say!" Sabina called after his retreating form. He made no response, and she hurried out after him. "Sir Jeffree!" He ignored her, disappearing down a corridor, leaving Sabina behind, staring after him with exasperation. *Well!* She plunked her hands on her hips.

"Lady Sabina," a voice said nearby, causing her to wheel about. To her astonishment, it was Lady Maud Vyse emerging from the direction of the Great Hall.

141

"I had not realized you were up and about," Sabina exclaimed. "Sir Dudley said—"

"Yes," her mother-in-law responded briskly. "I had thought to sit quietly this afternoon to conserve my energies for the journey, but duty has ever been my primary consideration."

Really, thought Sabina, she could make no response to that. She supposed the other woman must have some reason for seeking her out. "Should we…?" She gestured back toward the chamber she had emerged from, and Lady Maud consented with a tilt of her dark head. Sabina shut the door after them and waited for the older woman to speak.

However, the Lady Maud seemed to have no ready speech to launch into. Instead, she stood a moment, smoothing her skirts, apparently considering how best to proceed. Eventually, she treated Sabina to a long, hard stare. "You must possess some curious charm that eludes me, Lady Sabina," she mused at last. "My sons all seem to find some strange fascination in your presence. I have heard that is true of some women, though I had scarcely believed it until this moment."

Sabina gave a startled laugh; the notion was so ludicrous. "Well," she said, determined not to take offense. After all, what was the point, when the woman was leaving for parts unknown on the morrow? "I will admit I was similarly taken with both Crispin and Jasper," she replied lightly, leaving Jeffree wholly out of it. "They seem delightful boys."

Lady Maud brightened in spite of herself. "You are fond of children?" she asked. "Dudley told me you were charming with them."

Sabina was a little taken aback to hear such strong praise from Sir Dudley. "I like children well enough," she admitted cautiously. "Though I have not had much to do with the raising

142

of them. I have only one sister and no nephews or nieces to speak of."

Lady Maud hesitated. "I did not have much to do with Jeffree's upbringing," she said surprisingly. "As Bevis's heir, the family did not agree he should continue with me after my remarriage. Sometimes, I think, I rather regret that fact. He did not have the carefree boyhood that my younger two sons enjoy."

"If he was not raised by you...?" Sabina started tentatively.

"He was raised in the household of his godfather, Sir Charles Ellis," her mother-in-law replied. "A most estimable man, but not...warm." Lady Maud drifted over to the window and gazed sightlessly out of it. "No, not warm," she repeated absently. "Dudley says he would not have him raise his own two boys, not for the wide world." She was silent a moment, before continuing. "Jeffree has turned out so very *reserved* and Leland so very *wild*. In Dudley's opinion, both extremes stem from Sir Charles's authoritarianism."

Sabina found herself largely in sympathy with Sir Dudley's opinion but thought it wise to hold her tongue. "How interesting," she replied instead. Strangely, she *was* interested. Also, she was surprised to find the Lady Maud so clearly held her second husband in such high esteem. For some reason, she had not gained that impression previously from seeing them together.

"Jeffree has shown precious little interest in his younger brothers over the years," Lady Maud continued, turning from the window back toward Sabina. "That has always pained me. If I could believe they might grow closer in time..." She shot a contemplative look toward Sabina.

"You think that *I* might be instrumental in bringing the brothers together?" Sabina asked with some skepticism.

"It would go a long way toward reconciling me to your marriage," the older woman replied frankly.

Sabina lowered her gaze. She supposed that ought to hold sway with her. If she were in a *normal* marriage, she would court her mother-in-law's approval. But this strange state of affairs that existed betwixt her and Sir Jeffree was proving hard to navigate. "Just how do you imagine I would bring such a thing about?" she asked.

"I had always thought that my second or third son would enter the church," the Lady Maud admitted with a sigh. "But alas, neither of them show the disposition, whatever my husband thinks. Very likely, Dudley and I must soon start looking about us for a knight who will take Jasper for a squire." She gave Sabina a significant look.

Oh. "And you have not broached this subject already with Jeffree?" Sabina asked slowly.

Lady Maud's expression soured. "The chance would be a fine thing. Jeffree has not visited us at Longacre in an age. He does not," she added in aggrieved tones, "even tell us when he is in the vicinity."

A memory stirred in Sabina's mind of something Sir Dudley had said. "There is a tournament that Jeffree competes in that takes place near where you live?" she asked.

"There is, not that we attend such things."

"What is the name of it?" Sabina asked.

A pucker appeared between Lady Maud's finely arched brows. "It is held in the grounds of Lord Blandivar's estate, for he is its patron," she said slowly, as though trying to recall the details to mind.

"We are leaving for something called Areley Kings on the morrow," Sabina admitted without enthusiasm.

"Areley Kings!" Lady Maud repeated in astonishment. "But that is the one! Yes, it is practically on our doorstep!" She looked instantly thoughtful. "This is all *most* fortuitous. I must speak to Dudley at once. Why, it would make perfect sense for us all to journey together on the morrow! That way, we shall not need to employ any additional guards to escort us. Two men are sure to be adequate for our party, and we have our manservant, Hadley, and Githa too, of course, to drive the cart."

Sabina felt a twinge of misgiving. Clearly, Sir Jeffree had not intended traveling with his family or even admitting to being in their neighborhood for the next two weeks! Seeing the Lady Maud stepping briskly toward the door, Sabina was half inclined to call after her. But then what could she say?

Her hand on the latch, Lady Maud turned back. "Leave it with me," she said authoritatively. "Men will drag their feet so when it comes to arrangements." She flashed the merest ghost of a smile in Sabina's direction and was gone.

Well, thought Sabina, certainly Lady Maud had force of character. She dawdled a moment before following in her wake. She had no wish to be present when Jeffree learned that they were to make up a family traveling party. Instead, she sought out Naseby and asked if she could be led to pen and ink and a quiet, comfortable corner to write letters. Bethencourt's steward led her obligingly into a small chamber where she was furnished with such objects, and she proceeded to spend a pleasant hour writing a missive to her family.

First, she let them know she would be away from Ganfordshire for at least three weeks as she was to accompany her new husband to an upcoming tournament. She then gave them the good news that Morecotte was once more in her possession. She bade her father, if he had the time or inclination, to ride over and check on the Lancers, who would be in charge of the place while she was away.

She made sure to keep her tone light and to let none of her misgivings show. Isemay, she knew, would be sure to read between the lines where she could. She was just signing her name when a brief knock on the door heralded the arrival of Sir Jeffree. It swung open and he stood on the threshold. "Here you are," he said sourly and entered the room, a martial light in his eye. "What's all this about you reorganizing my travel plans?"

Sabina twisted around in her chair. "Your mother sought you out, then?" she asked. "She's a very determined woman. I could scarcely get a word in."

"It seems you got in several as you were the one who revealed I was competing at Areley Kings."

Sabina bit her lip. "Yes," she admitted. "I suppose that was indiscreet of me. I did not realize it was on their doorstep though."

He folded his arms. "Didn't you?"

"In truth, I know next to nothing of your family, Sir Jeffree. Next time you must warn me if I am not to betray you on some vital matter." He snorted. "Will it be so very inconvenient? To travel with them on the morrow? I thought duty to your family was your byword."

"When did I say that?"

She waved a hand vaguely. "If you did not, then it sounds very like something you would say."

His brows snapped together. "I am a de Crecy, not a Vyse."

Sabina eyed him severely, rising from her chair. "If you would deny the bond between mother and child and brother to brother, then your notion of family is a very strange one indeed. Or mayhap it is only to your titled relatives that you feel honor bound."

Seeing the way his eye kindled, Sabina hastily changed the subject. "If the prospect is so very disagreeable to you, then why do you not refuse?" Jeffree had just opened his mouth to respond when another knock was heard on the door.

It was Naseby, who had come to collect her letter for delivery to Tipton Hall. She folded it hastily and handed it over. "Thank you, Naseby."

"I will have Colton take it over directly," the efficient steward responded, disappearing back out of the room.

"What was that?" Jeffree asked grudgingly.

"A letter to my parents informing them of our going away."

He grunted. "Perhaps you had better put together a few lines of instruction to that woman of yours over at Morecotte."

Sabina turned quickly toward him. "Did you send over any of your uncle's servants yet?"

"A party is leaving shortly. Some men and a couple of maids to get the place straight. If you write your note now they can take it with them."

Sabina sat herself back down and reached once more for the pen. She wrote a few hasty lines, predicting her return in some three weeks or so. She hoped devoutly this was not a rash promise. Surely after a couple of weeks of her constant company, Sir Jeffree would be only too glad to be rid of her? Casting a quick look at his frowning face, she thought it would not be long before he would be glad to banish her to Morecotte and forget he even had a wife.

The deputation of servants was dispatched, and they ate supper in the Great Hall with the duke that evening, though the table was sparsely populated for most of the de Crecy clan had now departed. From the pointed comments the duke dropped and his injured air, it seemed Sir Charles had now also taken himself off. Sabina could only be glad to be freed from the icy disapproval of his presence.

To her surprise, the Vyses did not join them at table, instead preferring to take their meals in their rooms. Watching how fussily Bethencourt turned away his dishes and complained about "a faint scratching noise" that was giving him palpitations, Sabina could only guess how two boisterous young lads at table might disquiet him. She thought overall that Sir Dudley and Lady Maud were wise to absent themselves.

Jeffree, too, turned away a good deal of the dishes with a thunderous frown. "This fowl is practically inedible," he muttered, pushing away a dish of goose which had been stewed in ginger, saffron, and pepper, and gilded in gold leaf. "What is the point in gold-plating it? I want to eat it, not display it on a shelf!" He threw down his knife in disgust.

"A choleric disposition such as mine should never eat goose," Bethencourt complained querulously from the head of the table. "My physician has begged me many times to avoid it like the plague. It unbalances my humors. Naseby, have a care to inform Cook." His steward promptly abandoned his fruitless search for a mouse under the table and straightened up to relay the duke's message. Sabina felt a stab of sympathy for the duke's superior kitchens. Did they never receive any praise?

"These capons stuffed with grapes are extremely tasty," she said loudly. "Will you not try one, husband?" It was only when Jeffree looked so startled that she realized she had likely not addressed him as such before.

He reached across and stabbed one of the capons with a knife and plunked it on his plate. Naseby gave her a distracted smile as he scurried away. "The stuffing is too sweet," Jeffree grouched after eating a mere mouthful. Sabina rolled her eyes. She had never met so many people who were so hard to please.

They retired early and Sabina found her bags had been carried up and placed in Jeffree's rooms. She transferred them into his storeroom, collected one of the jugs of hot water, and wished him a speedy good night before he could say anything to further irritate her.

Once alone, having hastily washed, undressed, and lain down in the truckle bed, she breathed a sigh of relief. She would savor this quiet moment to herself before they set out on the morrow. She was not sorry to see the last of Ganford Chase, for all it was so grand.

The Duke of Bethencourt was a finicking old woman, Sabina decided. If Isemay should consent once more to become his wife, then she would need the patience of a saint to put up with his constant stream of complaints. The fact they were so gently expressed made it ten times worse in Sabina's eyes, for it meant he did not feel strongly about any of them.

At least with Jeffree, he genuinely did not seem to favor fancy foods. He had tucked into her parents' plain fare without quibbling. She suspected for all his privileged upbringing, his palate was not really refined at all. That was probably a good thing if he was ever to eat from her own table at Morecotte, which she supposed he must do on some few occasions at least before they distanced themselves.

Sabina rolled onto her side and hitched her blankets up to her shoulder. How she wished they could simply reach that stage in their negotiations already where they could be frank with one another about what they hoped to salvage from this disastrous marriage.

At the moment though…they were far from that point. She sighed. There was still plenty of tiptoeing around each other to do before then. It was vexing, but there it was. Her eyelids drooped. He had returned Morecotte to her; she would have to focus on that and grit her teeth over the rest of it.

Sabina woke herself early the next morn, hearing next door's occupant moving about and muffled voices. When the soft knock on the door came, she opened it quickly and took the jug of hot water from Jeffree with thanks. As always, he hastily averted his eyes from her shift-clad form and backed out of the room as though fearing he might catch something.

Sabina readied herself and redonned the faded red dress, which was certainly fit for a day's traveling if not much else. She had not unpacked her things the night before, save for a comb and a clean shift, so she had precious little else to do by way of preparations. She was just lowering her circlet over her veil, fixing it firmly in place, when another knock sounded on her door.

This time Jeffree was accompanied by a stout-looking servant. "Osborn needs to pack my things," he said briefly and held the door open for her. Sabina glanced at the servant and found him looking fixedly straight through her. Someone else who did not want her around, she thought, suppressing a sigh.

"Very well." She passed through the door and found that some small repast had been set out on the table before the fire.

"We can break our fast here this morn," Jeffree said, clearing his throat and waving a hand toward it.

Sabina sat down and helped herself to some toasted bread. After a moment, Jeffree sat opposite her. "We set out in an hour," he said. Sabina nodded. "Lancer's here."

"*Lancer*?" Sabina looked up quickly, hearing the name of the servant from Morecotte. "What is he doing here?"

"He brought over your horse."

"Horse?" Sabina stared at him.

"And your hounds."

"My hounds?" she echoed incredulously. His blue gaze flicked to meet hers a moment and he nodded before attacking the butter with his knife. "I have no notion what you are talking about!"

"I tasked Lancer with reclaiming them from whomever it was Alfred Hendry sold them to," Jeffree replied casually.

Sabina's eyes widened with astonishment. "You did?"

"Of course. Yesterday, you seemed firmly of the opinion they were your property."

"Well, yes. They are!" she spluttered.

"There you are, then."

"But why has Lancer brought them here?" Sabina persisted as Jeffree tucked into a plate of roasted fish.

151

"Naturally, he brought them to his mistress. You have need of a horse. My uncle does not keep extensive stables. He barely rides and keeps mostly carriage horses."

"And the hounds?"

"Will need to be reacquainted with you, presumably."

Sabina thought fleetingly of Miles's prize hounds and felt her heart quail. She'd had little to do with them back in the day, but from what she could remember they had needed frequent feeding and exercise and firm instruction.

"I did not expect you to…" Words failed her. Her mind raced to more practical matters. "We will take the dogs with us?" she asked dubiously. Jeffree nodded. At least the exercise should wear the brutes out, she thought. "Shall I go down and speak to Lancer now?" she asked, half rising from her chair.

"No, finish your meal and we will go down and inspect them together."

Sabina found her appetite had fled. The horse could be one of several, but the one she had particularly enquired about had been Blitha. Surely Jeffree had not repurchased the beautiful chestnut for her with the star at its brow? Blitha had been Miles's pride and joy, but he certainly had not permitted Sabina or anyone else to ride her.

When they made their way downstairs, half an hour later, Sabina found Lancer seated to the one side of the huge hearth in the Great Hall, looking very ill at ease. He sprang to his feet when they entered the room, looking vastly relieved to see them.

"Milady!" he said. "They'm out in the courtyard, awaiting you."

Sabina was duly led out to find a groom holding Blitha and two stable lads trying to restrain the hounds. They broke free at their approach and circled about them enthusiastically, though she was not sure they sniffed any more at her than they did at Jeffree.

"Hello, Feste; hello, Brisis," she greeted them, managing to pet their sleek heads as they weaved about, snaking their muscular bodies between their legs.

"Which is which?" Jeffree asked, extending a hand for Brisis to sniff.

"The gray is Brisis and the white is Feste."

"Fine dogs."

"That they are, sir, the finest hounds in Ganfordshire," Lancer opined. "A pretty penny Fred Martin had me spend of your'n to get 'em back. I had to use both purses," he added regretfully.

Jeffree grunted. "He would have been a fool to take any less," he said, squatting down and letting Feste sniff his face.

Sabina noticed a new look of respect dawn in Lancer's eyes. "Will they come back to Morecotte with me now, sir?" he asked hopefully.

"No," Jeffree answered shortly. "They will accompany their mistress to Areley Kings."

Sabina opened her mouth, then closed it again. After all, mayhap he meant to leave her unattended when he competed and that was why he thought she had need of the dogs. She eyed their muscular haunches doubtfully. Keeping them in line was the part that worried her. Still, they were at least two years older than the last time she had seen them. Perhaps they were not quite so unruly as she recalled? One could only hope!

153

She walked over to Blitha and reached a hand up to stroke her neck. "Still a beauty," she murmured. Blitha whickered and lowered her nose to be petted.

Jeffree turned to the groom. "His Grace presumably has some riding saddles and tack? My lady's horse needs equipping, and I have not had time yet to procure such things."

"Aye, Sir Jeffree," the groom replied, casting an admiring look over Blitha. "Though, likely none that would do her justice. She's a fine horse."

Brisis was pawing at Sabina's skirts, so she knelt down to stroke the dog's sleek blue-gray head. "Do you remember me, Brisis?" she crooned. The dog's tail wagged. "I think you do," Sabina mused, tipping her head to one side. A crafty tongue brushed her ear and Sabina squeaked, turning her head to find Feste muscling in for some fuss.

"I'll leave them with you, then, milady," said Lancer regretfully as Sabina laughed and scratched the white hound's head.

"Thank you. And please convey my regards to your wife. I sent a note over to her yesterday…"

"Aye, she got it," Lancer responded. "She's following your instructions to the letter, don't you worry, milady."

Sabina nodded and straightened up. Jeffree had wandered in the direction of the stables with the groom leading Blitha. She glanced down at the dogs, who seemed happy enough to gambol about her feet, rather than follow Lancer, who took his leave of them with a last regretful glance over his shoulder. After all, Sabina thought with a frown, he did have his own dogs back at Morecotte!

"Come on." She whistled the dogs and walked after Sir Jeffree. The dogs followed along happily, swinging their tails so hard their whole bodies wagged.

Jeffree was just emerging from the stable. "Your horse is being saddled," he said briefly and reached down to pat Brisis.

"What must we do next?"

"Naught. Osborn will bring down your bags along with mine."

"What of your parents?" she asked hesitantly. "I mean, your mother and Sir Dudley?"

As though she had conjured them with her words alone, she heard excited voices and the rumbling of wheels as a covered cart was brought about, driven by a burly manservant.

"This is their conveyance now," Jeffree answered as his two half brothers came spilling into the yard.

"Lady Sabina!" shouted Crispin, noticing her first. His brother Jasper looked up to echo the sentiment before both boys were distracted by the dogs and came running over.

"Are these your dogs, brother?" Jasper asked eagerly as boys and dogs became enthusiastically acquainted.

"Your sister-in-law's," Jeffree answered distractedly.

"Your dogs, Lady Sabina?" Crispin gasped admiringly.

"Why, they're as fine a pair of hounds as I ever did see!" Jasper exclaimed, crouching down and giving a laugh of delight as Feste licked his face.

"Father keeps no dogs at Longacre," Crispin said sadly. "Though old Mullins has one in his cottage that he lets me and Jasper take out sometimes."

155

"Is this the same old Mullins who lends you his penknife?" Sabina asked, earning a pleased look from her young brothers-in-law and a startled one from Jeffree.

"That's right," Jasper answered. "He's as old as the hills and been at Longacre since Father was a boy."

"What is his dog like?"

"Lark is old too," Crispin said cheerfully. "But still good for some sport."

"He has a dark brown coat that curls," Jasper volunteered. "And doesn't like anyone to touch his feet."

As these confidences were exchanged, two coal-black horses were led into the courtyard.

"Those are our parents' horses," boasted Jasper. "Beauties, aren't they?"

"*We* still have to ride in the cart with Githa," Crispin added glumly.

"Even though I can ride as well as any boy twice my age." Jasper sounded aggrieved.

"I too!" his brother chimed in.

"I daresay that is very tiresome for you," Sabina murmured, noticing her in-laws had come out into the yard. "But it is a long journey, is it not? I expect your mother likes to know you are safe."

"That's enough!" Jeffree cut in when both boys took a spirited exception to this view. They lapsed at once into silence, squinting up at him with doubtful expressions. Sabina thought they viewed their older brother as a strict authority figure and

156

supposed that was not unexpected considering the age gap between them.

Lady Maud and Sir Dudley exchanged subdued greetings with them, and Sabina saw at once that the Lady Maud was not a morning person. She looked pained whenever her children spoke too loudly and winced a lot as the boys skipped around while their things were loaded onto their cart.

"Careful, boys!" their father admonished as he consulted with a wiry-looking manservant he addressed as Hadley.

Githa, the Vyses' female servant, turned out to be a stout young woman in her early twenties. When Crispin tried to dodge past her, she reached out and caught him with very little apparent effort, bundling him into the cart. Jasper, deciding discretion was the better part of valor, obligingly swung himself up behind his brother. "That's it, Master Jasper," Githa encouraged him placidly. "There's a good lad."

Then Osborn arrived and Sabina was distracted, for he brought her own sack of clothing down as well as several neat-looking bundles which Jeffree started at once attaching to his own massive horse.

"Where is your steed, Lady Sabina?" Crispin asked, leaning over the edge of the cart.

Sabina turned her head and saw the groom leading the gleaming Blitha out, now saddled and harnessed. "This is Blitha," she told the round-eyed boys. She could tell her horse and her hounds had risen her stock considerably with her brothers-in-law. Then again, her shabby dresses were likely of little consequence to a ten- and twelve-year-old.

Jasper whistled, and he and his brother exchanged glances.

"Do you own a hawk, sister?" Crispin asked hopefully. Sabina shook her head, and he sighed philosophically. "You cannot have everything," he said sadly.

"My first husband owned a hawk," Sabina admitted as she picked up her bag of clothing and wondered if she could fasten it behind her saddle. "He was a keen huntsman."

"You had a husband before?" Jasper asked with interest. "What happened to him?"

"He was gored to death by a wild boar he was harassing," she answered absently, examining the decorative saddle for loops. Hearing the boy's gasps, Sabina looked up quickly to see if she had alarmed them, but they looked more enthralled than aghast.

"Did it have big tusks?" Crispin asked in awestruck tones.

"Did you see it happen?" demanded Jasper, his eyes agleam.

"Boys!" Sir Dudley's shocked accents startled the three of them out of their conversation. "Those questions are far from seemly. Apologize at once!"

Sabina made haste to explain she was far from offended. "I was not there at the time," she said quickly. "And Miles and I were living separate lives by that point." If anything, she thought Sir Dudley looked even more shocked by her response. As for the boys, they looked as though they had even more questions trembling on their unguarded lips.

She threw them a cautioning frown. *Ask me later*, she conveyed with a waggle of her eyebrows and could tell they had understood her by the way they lowered their brimming gazes and pressed their lips together. *Pair of young imps.*

"If you have quite finished entertaining the boys," Jeffree said scathingly, appearing in front of her so suddenly, he made her jump. "Then we can perhaps finish our packing." He plucked the bag from her hands and carried it over to his waiting horse. Sabina watched in silence as he secured it with the rest of his packs and then swung back to help her mount Blitha.

Placing a hand on Jeffree's muscular shoulder, Sabina felt strangely flustered as he swung her up and onto the saddle. She remembered Alfred Hendry's two large manservants flying through the air and landing in the water trough. Sir Jeffree was a powerful man. Even his fancy tunic could not hide that fact. Today's outfit was a stunning shade of lapis lazuli trimmed with gold thread. Did he never dress down, even when on the road?

It was not long before they set off, and Sabina was pleased to find Blitha an almost effortless ride after the horses she had grown up with. She was attentive, responsive to commands, and had a smooth, even gait. She seemed just as gleaming and handsome as when she had been Miles's most prized possession. Whoever it was had owned her the past year had clearly looked after her well.

Despite the fact she had no interest in reaching their destination, Sabina found herself enjoying the ride. It did not grow uncomfortably warm until midday, and by then, they had reached the lower slopes of the Bitterleys, the range of hills that separated Ganfordshire from the neighboring county of Leighminster. As the slopes were tree-lined they were given plenty of shade after this point and the blazing sun did not affect them. The dogs ran happily alongside the horses, their tongues hanging out of their mouths as they bounded along, keeping easily apace.

Luckily, they were not looking to scale the highest point, the impressive Midsummer Mountain from which three cathedrals could be seen on a good day. Instead, they were heading for a pass that cut through two of the lesser hills, Old Foy and the Jaggedstone. They climbed their slopes gradually until, by midafternoon, their route started to get a little more challenging.

At Sir Dudley's request, they halted around three o'clock and some provisions were shared around, and the horses and dogs were given water. Jeffree concerned himself with his own charger and Sabina's mount as Sir Dudley's manservant, Hadley, and Osborn saw to the rest. Sabina sat on a grassy bank beside Lady Maud, Jasper, and Crispin and accepted a share of the barley cakes and cheese that their servant Githa handed out.

"I don't think much of this mountain range," Crispin said disparagingly, his mouth full of cheese. "If that is what the locals call it." He cast a quick look at Sabina. "The ones near Kellingford are *much* grander."

"Old Foy is not a mountain," Sabina agreed calmly. "It is one of the smaller hills belonging to the Bitterleys, but if you were to climb Midsummer Mount, then you could say you had climbed the tallest mountain in all Karadok."

"Is that so?" Jasper responded, sitting up with interest, shielding his eyes with his hand. "Which one is Midsummer Mount?"

Sabina turned and pointed to a blue-gray looming peak in the distance. "That one."

"I don't believe it is the tallest in the land," Crispin muttered, looking to his father for confirmation. Sir Dudley frowned at him but did not back up Sabina's claim.

"I assure you that I am familiar with the facts of my home county," Sabina was stung into responding. When Jeffree approached to grab another waterskin, she appealed to him. "Husband, will you not support me in this?"

Jeffree looked startled, then hid his reaction with a frown. "With what?" he asked, taking a sip of the water.

"My claim that Midsummer Mount is the highest peak in all Karadok."

"Every boy knows that," he retorted in a withering tone.

"Apparently not," Lady Maud responded as both her sons started protesting the rival claims of the Sehoran mountains.

"Nonsense," Jeffree corrected them, turning to his mother. "What manner of tutor have you employed that they should be so ignorant in basic geography?"

Crispin looked mutinous, and Sabina began to wish she had not raised the matter with Jeffree at all. He had an unfortunately combative nature which seemed to turn everything into an argument. At this point, Sir Dudley had joined the fray, mildly but doggedly defending the man they had employed for their sons' lessons. "Master Hibbold studied under the Bishop of Hudde himself and came most highly recommended."

"He sounds unfit for anything but the cloister," Jeffree concluded damningly. His stepfather looked pained.

Lady Maud sighed. "Alas, neither of the boys shows much aptitude for their books." She shot a significant look at Sabina, clearly seeing an opening for her to take.

Sabina cleared her throat. "Do you think perhaps that the boys might be destined for a different type of career than that of the clerical life?" she asked lightly.

"Certainly, they will not *both* go into the church," Sir Dudley said uneasily, shooting a glance at his wife. "Jasper must inherit Longacre; it is for Crispin I have always intended…"

161

An awkward silence descended on the group. Sabina saw a tense, worried look come over the younger boy's face. "I cannot imagine Crispin in holy robes," she mused loudly. Jasper gave a shout of laughter, and Crispin's impish face relaxed into a grin.

"I cannot think of anyone less suited," Jeffree said sourly. "He would be thrown out of the seminary within a sennight!"

Even Lady Maud smiled at this, though Sir Dudley protested that Crispin would grow steadier with age. The mood having lightened, they made their way back to the horses and set forth once more.

To her surprise, after an hour, Sabina found Jeffree dropping back to ride beside her. She scanned his profile, expecting him to direct some comment or issue, some command at her, but to her surprise, he rode on in silence. Was this for appearance's sake, then?

She turned her head quickly to look at her in-laws, but Lady Maud and Sir Dudley were occupied with their own conversation and the boys were absorbed in dropping bits of cheese over the side of their cart for the dogs to scavenge. Hadley had ridden ahead, and Osborn was bringing up the rear, so it was not as though anyone else would pay attention to their closeness or lack of it.

"You ride well," he said finally, breaking the silence between them, but still not turning his head to look at her.

Sabina was startled. "Thank you," she said. "So do you."

Jeffree snorted and finally cast her an appraising look. "You display to advantage in the saddle." He stated it as a plain statement of fact, no admiration in his tone, but to her annoyance, Sabina found herself starting to turn red.

162

"I am country-bred after all." He made no response to that, and she cast him another baffled look. "I suppose you were born in Caer-Lyoness," she hazarded. "Or Aphrany," she said, naming both the summer and winter capitals.

"Then you suppose wrong. I was born at Ganford Chase."

Sabina was surprised. "So then, you consider yourself a native of Ganfordshire?"

At her startled tone, he shrugged. "Where else?"

She did not know how to answer that; she knew only that she would not have considered in a million years that the proud Sir Jeffree hailed from her own home county. "Somewhere a good deal grander," she answered at last.

"Ganford Chase is very grand," he pointed out.

"Why so it is," she agreed lightly. "Most likely it is the grandest residence hereabouts. Still…" She hesitated.

"What?"

"You were seen but rarely about the countryside. One time you were pointed out to me at Ganford cathedral," she recalled. "And I was introduced to you once at the Bishop's Palace." His eyes widened at this, for he likely had no recollection of that occasion. As he had barely afforded her a glance let alone a reply, she was not surprised. "I daresay you have barely set foot in the village, though it lies only some five miles from Ganford Chase."

"The village?" At his incredulous tone, Sabina realized she had been right.

"I suppose a duke's heir has no need of a village," she reflected aloud.

163

Jeffree frowned. "I was not raised at Ganford Chase, but in the home of my godfather, Sir Charles Ellis, in Sutton St. Bolston." Sabina merely nodded. She already knew this, thanks to her mother-in-law. "On my visits to my uncle I have ridden all about this countryside, I assure you. When we return," he added, "you can show me this village. If you think it so noteworthy."

Now it was Sabina's turn to be startled. "Little Ganford? I am sure it is entirely beneath your notice. There is naught there but a smithy, a mill, and a duck pond!"

"Yet from your words, it seemed I could not claim to be Ganford-born if I had not a passing acquaintance with this duck pond."

Sabina laughed. She could not help it. Jeffree watched her with a curious look on his face which sobered her somehow. "I don't know why your indignation always strikes me as funny," she confided suddenly. Possibly it was because he was so proper.

"Always?" he echoed with displeasure.

She considered this, tipping her head to one side. "No," she admitted after a moment. "Not when I admitted to being your lover. I was not amused then and *you* looked as though you had turned to stone." Half fascinated, she watched the color creep along Jeffree's cheekbones. He turned in his saddle, as though to check if anyone was listening to them.

"You are...reckless, madam," he muttered. "Do you never consider the consequences of your wayward tongue?"

"Reckless?" Sabina blinked. "Do I seem that way to you?"

"Extremely reckless. Dangerously so."

164

"But you really know nothing of me, Sir Jeffree," she pointed out. "Heretofore, my life has been lived on a very quiet and peaceable scale."

He snorted. "That is not what I have heard."

Sabina forced herself to take a deep, calming breath, rather than react to the probing of a still-sore wound. "You mean," she said steadily, "because I left my marital home to return to my father's house. Society, being male-led, would be bound to blame me, I suppose."

"You believe yourself to be blameless in the matter?" He sounded skeptical.

"I believe the fault lay firmly in my late husband's lap."

"What did he do?"

The question was so direct that it almost took Sabina's breath away. She answered before delicacy of feeling could prevent her. "He would not stop fornicating with any willing wench who strayed upon his path," she answered forthrightly. "I could never enter a room but that some maidservant had to spring out of his arms. He expected me to turn a blind eye to his philandering, but I could not do so."

To her embarrassment, these last few words sounded half-choked. Sabina turned her head away from him a moment and forced herself to take steady, even breaths. "In the end, I asked only that he respected his marriage vows under our roof," she continued in a low tone. "But even that was too much to ask." The words were bitter on her tongue.

The crowning injustice was how ashamed *she* felt by Miles's conduct. Of course, everyone wondered what his wife lacked that she could not inspire faithfulness in his bosom. Even her mother seemed to think that if Sabina had only hit on some way of pleasing her husband, then he would not have strayed so flagrantly.

"He sounds like an uncouth, mannerless dolt," Jeffree said at last with a curl of his lip. "You should consider yourself well rid of him."

His words were so dismissive of the great tragedy of her first marriage that Sabina again felt a wildly inappropriate impulse to laugh. Instead, she bit her lip. "He was well-liked by his friends and acquaintances. In general, his neighbors had nary a harsh word to say of him. Even my parents..." She trailed off.

"They approved of him?" Jeffree's tone was sharp.

"They thought him a well-favored man of pleasant speech and goodly aspect. They believed he would make me a good husband."

Jeffree's eyebrows rose. "And when he did not?"

"They were...sorely disappointed. In both of us," she added quietly, thinking of how dismayed her parents had been. How they had encouraged her again and again to overlook Miles's womanizing and to end the estrangement.

"Doubtless, they were also disappointed with themselves," Jeffree said, surprising her greatly. "They should have guarded against such a thing. They were as taken in by him as you. Daughters should be protected against such men."

Sabina turned her head to stare at him. "I...yes, I suppose that is true."

"Unless you married him in the face of their opposition?" he suggested with an edge to his words.

Sabina shook her head. "Far from it. Our wooing was very straightforward. My father introduced us and negotiated the match not long after Miles moved into the area. Perhaps if he had been Ganford born and bred, we would have had warning of his true nature. Then again..." She shrugged. "Perhaps not." At Jeffree's quizzical look, she added, "It is considered customary, is it not, for young men to 'sow their oats' before marriage?"

His face was once again stiff with disapproval. "Not by me."

Sabina studied him in silence. "That is an unusual attitude for a man in your position to take, Sir Jeffree," she mused.

"What position is that?"

"A position of wealth and privilege, with the world at your feet."

He shrugged. "I have always held myself to a high moral standard. My guardian expected it."

"May I ask—?" She broke off awkwardly. But after all, she had confided in him the facts of her own past. Why could she not ask him about his own?

"Ask what?"

"Why...why it was that you made that vow? On the occasion of your eighteenth birthday, I mean." Was it purely her own imagination, or did he turn a little redder? "Did you...wish to take holy orders?" she asked tentatively. "But your position as the duke's heir prevented it?"

Jeffree cleared his throat. "I had no inclination for a holy life," he admitted grudgingly. "There was another reason."

"A disappointment?" Sabina ventured. "You were...disappointed in love?" However unlikely it seemed that staid, aloof Sir Jeffree could have nursed some thwarted passion in his bosom, she could think of no other reason why someone

167

should make so life-altering a vow, on his eighteenth birthday no less.

Jeffree's lips pressed firmly together, and her conviction grew. "You were!" she blurted in astonishment. "Did the lady die?"

"No, no, nothing as melodramatic as that!" Jeffree snapped. After a moment, he added with reluctance, "She was the one who took holy orders."

Sabina blinked. "Rather than marry you?" she asked, rather tactlessly.

He huffed. "She felt a calling," he said stiffly, "to another life."

Sabina felt her mouth fall open and closed it quickly again. *Good grief! The woman really had chosen a convent over marrying Jeffree de Crecy!* "I—I see," she stammered, struggling to hide her reaction.

"The lady was a noble and honorable woman who felt duty bound to take the veil," he said stiffly. "She was not the type of woman to shirk her duty, or the power of her convictions, however inconvenient they might be to her family and friends."

Inconvenient? Sabina stared at him. "You were acquaintances of long-standing?" she asked finally, unable to stem her curiosity.

Jeffree gave a short nod. "Since we were thirteen or thereabouts. Her family's lands bordered my guardian's."

"Sir Charles Ellis, you mean?"

"Yes."

"And he arranged the match?"

"On my fifteenth birthday."

"And three years later, she broke it to enter a convent?"

He gave another nod.

"That must have been a blow." He said nothing to this, but the pinched expression on his face made speech unnecessary. "How very inconvenient of her god," she added. "Which one was it by the way?"

Sir Jeffree's eyebrows snapped together. He regarded her a moment with deep suspicion, as though she were making a May game of him. "Goddess of the hearth," he said at last. "She bore a local name for her in Sutton, Meliora," he added tonelessly. "As though her parents devoted her from birth. Doubtless, that is how she saw it."

"Oh."

"Why?"

"I just thought it would be more fitting if it had been one of those fierce, virginal ones that scorned marriage," she answered truthfully.

Jeffree made a spluttering sound. "Do you always speak aloud your every thought, however wildly inappropriate?"

Sabina shook her head. "I apologize if I was inappropriate. You must forgive me; I am not used to moving in such exalted circles." Again, he turned his head to regard her narrowly. "After all," she added cheerfully, "if you are so determined to drag me around Karadok with you, you should be prepared. I am not some grand lady used to behaving with the utmost decorum."

"So, that is it, is it? You mean to disquiet me with your provincial frankness?" He gave a short laugh. "You will not so easily embarrass me, for all you think I am so staid."

169

He sounded so supremely confident in this that she turned her head to look at him. A moment of doubt crept in. It was true that Sir Jeffree was perhaps not quite as stuffy and proper as she had first thought. The water trough popped back into her mind, reminding her that he did not shy away from rough and ready methods once in a while.

Still, she *had* brought vivid color to his cheeks that day already several times with very little conscious effort, whether from embarrassment or annoyance. If she truly meant to show him up, she did not think she could fail to do so. Not with his notions of how a wife should conduct herself.

No doubt this Lady Meliora was some perfect paragon of womanhood, and once she had made herself unavailable, the youthful Jeffree had decided, in his disappointment, that no one would ever meet his high and mighty standards. It must have been a crushing blow to find himself now married to the likes of her, Sabina reflected without rancor. She had few illusions about her own merits.

Stealing a sideways glance at him now, she thought there could be worse stratagems than giving herself free rein to thoroughly irritate Jeffree de Crecy on this trip to Areley Kings. It seemed to come naturally to her after all. That way she would avoid being compelled to attend any more of these plaguey tournaments in future.

Sabina's spirits rose. Perhaps this trip was a providential opportunity after all.

11

They reached the start of Kilmarton Pass at about six that evening. The boys were bored and irritable and the dogs were panting hard. Jeffree dismounted briefly to lift the dogs into the back of the cart. His brothers instantly brightened, having Feste and Brisis to fuss over.

Sir Dudley dismounted and joined him as Hadley started handing around the waterskins. "Do you think we will reach the inn at the other side by nightfall?" he addressed Jeffree, looking up anxiously at the pink and red sky.

"We're sure to," Jeffree answered briefly. After all, it did not turn dark at this time of year until about ten o'clock.

His stepfather looked harried. "Your mother is worn out."

"She could always sit in the back of the cart."

"And be jolted around and driven half-mad by the boys' incessant chatter?" When Jeffree did not bother to answer this, Sir Dudley sighed and cast a look in Sabina's direction. "Your wife must be tired also," he commented. "Is she—er—used to arduous travel?"

Jeffree's eyebrows rose. He hardly thought this counted as "arduous travel." "I've not thought to ask. I think it doubtful she has even left Ganfordshire before."

Sir Dudley tutted and cast him a look of reproach. *A considerate husband would have asked*, his disapproving silence seemed to convey. Strange to say, Jeffree was now curious about that fact and let his gaze sweep across to where Sabina was sat atop her horse sipping water.

The setting sun cast a pink glow about her head and shoulders and invested her with an air of—something he had not associated with her before. He could not find the right word for it. It was not beauty. No, assuredly it was not beauty. How anyone could look beautiful with that unbecoming and all-encompassing headdress jammed on top of her head he could not imagine. But her profile was displayed to some advantage despite it, and the way she held her head and shoulders and the proud line of her back looked well this evening as the sun went down.

As he approached his horse once more, he pondered what it was exactly about her headdress that was so unflattering. It might be something to do with the flat, undecorated band she wore across her forehead, obscuring her hairline and so much as a peek of the abundant hair that was confined beneath it. Somehow the arrangement of the linen hid even her ears and neck from prying eyes. *Severe*, that was what it was, with no ornamentation to pretty it up and no glimpse of what was underneath.

It was the sort of garb that older women wore, or widows, who wanted to escape attention rather than draw the eye. She *was* a widow, of course. Or had been. Was that why she wore it so plain and unadorned? Well, she was a wife now and should start to dress accordingly, he reflected as he swung back into the saddle. It was not as though she was shy or retiring by nature; so why should she dress as though she wanted to fade into the background? It did not make any sense to Jeffree. Maybe he should ask her about it?

Parts of the pass were too narrow for two horses to ride abreast of each other with comfort, so he steered Radax behind Sabina for the next hour, noting the confident way she handled Blitha. He had been right. She had a good seat on a horse. She rode directly behind the cart, so Jasper and Crispin kept up a steady

172

flow of conversation with her, mostly about the two hounds which seemed to have completely won his brothers' hearts.

Jasper and Brisis lay side by side on a blanket, his brother's head propped up by his hand as he stroked the dog's sleek belly and aimed a flow of chatter in Sabina's direction. How old was Brisis? What was her favorite meat? Had she ever whelped any pups?

As for Crispin, he was sat up in the corner, hugging the white dog, an expression of dreamy bliss on his freckled face as Feste rested his head on the boy's shoulder and occasionally swiped his cheek with a lolling tongue. When this happened, Crispin giggled and fondled Feste's ears. Jeffree congratulated himself that combining the hounds with the boys had been one of his better ideas.

The rest of the day's journey passed without incident. They paused at one point to don cloaks, for the night air had turned cold. Like the rest of her wardrobe, Sabina's cloak was old and worn and of an indeterminate shade of brown. Jeffree did not think it could have been a handsome garment even when it was new. She seemed warm enough though, swathed in its folds, so he shrugged the matter off for now.

They reached The Nimble Goat at about half past nine as it was starting to turn dark. Hadley and Osborn took the horses and cart into the stable, and Jeffree led the way inside to procure rooms. Sir Dudley took one for himself and Maud and another for the boys and Githa. Hadley and Osborn would sleep in the communal room.

After the smallest hesitation, Jeffree reserved one room only for himself and Sabina. Anything else would look odd, he reasoned, when they were so recently wedded. He listened to Sir Dudley ordering their supper and suffered the nasty realization they would all have to dine together tonight. The look of long-suffering on his mother's face as this occurred to her too cheered him up considerably.

Supper turned out to be a relatively subdued affair. The boys were so busily occupied with passing their meat surreptitiously to the dogs lurking under the table that they had no time for their usual clamor. The food was good, plain fare, and Jeffree made a hearty supper. He noticed his wife did too, though his mother and stepfather only picked at theirs.

Lady Maud and Sir Dudley rose from the table first. "We will send down Githa to collect the boys," his mother pronounced and made a moue of distaste when she saw how eagerly her sons scrabbled to throw the scraps left on her plate to the dogs.

"Wait until your mother has left the table, boys!" Sir Dudley remonstrated as his own plate was similarly seized and appropriated. "We wish you a good night's sleep," he directed at Sabina courteously.

"I wonder, Sir Dudley, if you would permit the dogs to sleep in with the boys and Githa tonight?" Sabina asked, earning eager gasps from his half brothers.

"Oh, please, Father!" Crispin said, turning his large blue eyes upon his sire.

Jasper added his own pleas, going as far as to seize his father's tunic in supplication.

"It is up to your mother," Sir Dudley sighed. Lady Maud's eyes met Sabina's a moment and then she gave an inclination of her head which had the boys whooping. "Not so loud!" their father begged. "Many weary travelers will be wishing to get their heads down this night."

174

"Thank you, Mother!" both boys caroled, hushing their voices at once.

When Githa came down, she did not seem as pleased to be sharing a bedchamber with two large hounds, but the boys joyously led them up the stairs after a hurried "good night" and she followed behind resignedly.

"If you put half as much effort into pleasing me as you do my brothers," Jeffree said caustically as he lowered his tankard, "then I would be a fortunate man indeed!"

Sabina looked startled at his words, though he could not fathom why. Then she seemed to collect herself. "That was for our benefit, as much as theirs," she assured him with an uneasy laugh. "I have shared a bedchamber before with Feste and Brisis. They hog the bed, twitch, and snore. They also smell," she added darkly. "A thing boys will not mind as much."

He considered this a moment. It did lend a rather different perspective onto matters. "It may be that their second owner instilled rather better etiquette into them," he suggested.

"After observing the way they slobbered all over your brothers' fingers throughout supper, I think that unlikely."

Privately, Jeffree agreed with her. He let the matter drop and drained his cup. "Are you finished?" She nodded and they rose. "You go up and wash first. I want to go and check the horses and have one last word with Osborn before I follow you."

He did not tarry over these tasks, and when he knocked on their bedchamber door ten minutes later, she drew back the bolt and let him in clad in her shift with a gray mantle thrown over it for decency's sake. Once he was inside, she hurried straight for the bed and climbed in, turning her back to him, flinging her long braids over her shoulders. Jeffree made at once for the basin

175

and set about his wash. The water was only tepid, but he did not concern himself about that overmuch. There were soap flakes and cloths which were more important.

Once he had lathered and scrubbed himself clean, he stepped back into his braies and made his way over to the bed. It was narrower even than the one she called her own at Tipton Hall. After easing his way in, he realized there was no way he could distribute his limbs so that they were not touching hers, and after a moment, he stopped trying. Sabina shifted about a bit, and he realized she was attempting the same impossible feat.

"It is just as well the dogs did not sleep in with us. There is scarcely room enough in this bed for the both of us," he commented dryly. She gave a murmur of agreement. Jeffree stared up at the ceiling. He felt acutely aware of where his thigh rested against hers. The last time they had shared a bed, he had woken up covering her backside in a most undignified manner.

Annoyingly, even the thought of it made parts of his anatomy stir in a disturbing fashion. For such an abrasive woman, she was a soft and pleasing armful. And those fucking braids. He had no notion why they affected him like they did. All through his wash, he had been stealing glances at them where they hung down from the bed. He wanted to touch them, to close his fingers about them and squeeze them tight in his fist.

The thought made his breath quicken. He imagined wrapping the honey-colored ropes of her hair about his hand. That thought made him groan faintly. He heard a rustle and guessed Sabina's head had turned or lifted from her pillow bearer. She said nothing though, and he heard another rustle as though she had lowered it again.

"Was your first husband really gored to death by a boar?" he heard himself ask gruffly.

176

"Yes," she answered after a faint pause. "I would not make up such a tale just to amuse your brothers."

"But you were already living apart by that point?"

"Yes."

"He never…tried to reclaim you from your father's house?"

She sighed. "The first two times I left he did, but not the third."

Instead of thinking the man demeaned himself to chase after her even once, he found himself asking, "Why not the third time?"

Again, she paused before answering. "You do not think twice was enough for any reasonable man?" Her light, evasive tone caused him to turn his head sharply.

Of course, he could make nothing out in the dark. "Why did he not come for you the third time, Sabina?" he persisted, and he heard her give an audible swallow.

"Because…he knew I would not forgive him the third time," she answered at last.

"Why?"

She huffed again and the blankets moved as her knees rose and then fell as she changed positions. "I do not want to talk about it."

Jeffree pondered this a moment. Now that he thought about it, it struck him as strange that Wilfred Burrell should have allowed his married daughter to return under his roof. From the way he had strongarmed Sabina into remarrying for respectability's sake, Jeffree would not have said his father-in-law was the sort to go against public opinion. That meant there had to have been a good reason for him to fly in the face of the judgment of his neighbors.

"Did Hendry beat you?" he hazarded, feeling his throat grow unaccountably tight. Some would say this was still a husbandly prerogative, of course, but a fond father might not agree.

"No," Sabina answered. "I told you Miles's faults already. He was no wife-beater."

"Then why did your father allow your return?"

She moved again and he felt her foot brush his before she drew it hastily back. "My father did not precisely agree with my turning up on his doorstep," she admitted grudgingly. "But, well…the third time was sort of different."

"And why was that?"

She didn't speak for a long moment, long enough for him to nudge her foot with his own. That startled her into speech alright.

"It was our maidservant, Delia Selwyn," Sabina began reluctantly. "She…disappeared one summer evening. Miles said she must have run off with her swain. He said she was flighty and a few other things that struck me as odd. She had always been such a firm favorite of his. Then when I was in the village some weeks later…" Her words trailed off.

"Yes?" he asked sharply. "You saw her?" For a moment, he had envisaged Hendry drowning the wretched maid in the duckpond. But no, that was absurd. If Sabina's first husband had been a murderer, Osborn would surely have uncovered the fact in the local tavern.

"Not her, but her aunt, Mistress Selwyn, the blacksmith's wife. She apologized for approaching me, but they were desperate. It took me a moment to understand what she was telling me. Delia was expecting a child, you see, and Miles had thrown her out. It was his child, of course. He had refused to provide for it, had

178

threatened to deny it was his, but I knew the truth as soon as I heard it. It made perfect sense that he would have seduced the girl. I should have known." Her voice sounded removed and cool, as though it was something that had happened a hundred years ago instead of two.

"Then what happened?" he asked. "What did you say to this Selwyn woman?"

"I promised her that provision would be made for the girl, of course, and then I confronted Miles and told him he must discharge his debt honorably. My family had held their heads high for generations in this part of the country and it was not for him to destroy our good name.

"Miles did not see it the same way. He sneered at my notions of honor, and said my father was an old dotard and I could return to him for good this time as he'd had enough of me. I told him my father was a greater man than he could ever hope to be. Then I packed my things and left for the third and final time. I never looked back."

"You told your father of Hendry's conduct?"

"I did. My father was forced to provide for the girl and her babe, as to my shame, Miles would not. My mother was far from happy, of course. She was inclined to make excuses for 'poor Miles' and was convinced he would ride over the next day with his tail between his legs. She said that not all men can keep their passions in check and that we women should be understanding of their weakness. I was forced to tell her the things Miles had said about my father to finally harden her heart against him."

Jeffree was silent for a long time. He almost jumped when Sabina spoke again; this time her voice was small and there was a thread of emotion running through her words. "Later, Isemay

179

told me that Miles had cornered her once when they were alone in a room together. She had been terrified. She had confided in my mother, but Mother had advised her not to tell another soul and simply never to let herself be alone with Miles in the future."

Jeffree was appalled. "Hendry attacked her?"

The pillow rustled and he guessed she was nodding. "She assured me it did not go far before a servant interrupted them and he was forced to release her. He kissed and pawed her and tore her neckline. But I think he gave my sister a disgust of men which has lasted with her to this very day. I think that the reason she has only ever consented to marrying a man as old as the Duke of Bethencourt."

Jeffree was silent as he digested this. He had thought Isemay's acceptance of his uncle had been for purely mercenary reasons. He had done her a disservice it seemed. "And after that?" he asked, unable to stop himself.

Sabina sighed. "After I returned to Tipton Hall, Miles spent the next twelve months drinking and carousing to excess. His reputation started to suffer, and people started to talk darkly about him in the village. In a way, his carrying on so blatantly did me a favour, as less folk were willing to call me an unnatural wife or an undutiful woman because of it."

She gave a bitter laugh. "If he had only provided for the child, then he would not have been judged so harshly. Delia is a pretty girl and I...I have only ever been passable at best. The Selwyns have lived in Little Ganford longer even than the Burrells. Miles was an outsider, a latecomer to the district. He was bound to be viewed askance, at least locally.

"Also," she continued evenly. "Everyone knew it was my father who had been forced to provide coin to the Selwyns and not

Miles. That told against him, however much he might claim to all and sundry that I was a wayward shrew."

Jeffree felt an almost overwhelming impulse to go and haul Osborn out of his makeshift bed and kick the wretch in the seat of his pants for the piss-poor job he had done uncovering gossip on his new mistress. Had Osborn received his hearsay straight from the spiteful mouth of Alfred Hendry himself?

"I suppose that must have been when Miles started drinking his wine cellar dry and shooting arrows into his wall hangings," she concluded matter-of-factly.

Jeffree grunted in agreement. Well, he did not have much to live up to. There was that. No wonder Sabina dreamed of living at Morecotte without the hindrance of a husband.

She was the first out of them to fall asleep, and Jeffree lay quietly listening to her breathing. Something uncomfortable tickled away at the edge of his consciousness.

Sabina had told him the most painful and humiliating thing that had ever happened to her in her life. She had been the source of gossip and scandal in her small community through no actual fault of her own. Her first husband had been a disgusting and unprincipled lecher.

Jeffree frowned. He had listened and asked questions, but perhaps—a dim suspicion dawned in a vague recess of his mind—his response had been inadequate. Should his role have been to attempt to console her somehow? He rolled onto his side and pondered this. How did one comfort a woman? He imagined patting her head. That might be tricky with her bareheaded as she had been at the time. His hand would have been perilously close to her glossy braids. Suppose he had not been able to avoid the temptation to touch them?

181

It was not just her braids that was a temptation in her current state, he thought, disgracefully aware of the proximity of her warm body lying close to his own. He realized, with embarrassing certainty, that as soon as he fell into sleep, he would be all over her again. It felt like his body was already straining toward hers and resisting the impulse was giving him an almost physical ache. An ache that concentrated in one prominent and suddenly ungovernable part of his body.

Jeffree had always considered himself a disciplined man of reason with a cool head. He had lived his life ruthlessly suppressing any wayward or ignoble inclinations. He went to bed early and rose punctually, practiced his drills without fail, bathed frequently in cold water and avoided intoxication, overindulgence, and lewdness at all costs.

It was true that every once in a while, he had to take himself in hand to assuage certain physical urges, but he did so with a ruthless efficiency, never dallying inordinately over the business but exercising as much speed as possible to reach the desired endpoint.

He absolutely did not close his eyes and allow himself to dwell on things like Sabina Burrell telling all and sundry that she had played the whore for him and warmed his bed. A certain part of him was doing more than stirring now. He almost groaned again. Why, oh why had he allowed such a thought to pop into his head? Now he could not stop thinking of it!

In his mind's eye, she was not wearing her confining headdress when she said it. No, she was bare-headed with her long braids hanging down to her waist and gleaming in the candlelight. She walked toward him as she said her inflammatory words, and she reached right down between Jeffree's legs and—*damn it*. He half sat up, stifling an exclamation. What the hells was he thinking?

182

He blinked into the darkness, drawing ragged breaths in and out. *My gods.* If he was not careful, he was going to spill his seed all over the sheets in a shameful display of unbridled lust. Jeffree collapsed back against the mattress and lay there like a stunned fish.

There was no question of seeking relief from the almost painful throbbing between his thighs. He could scarcely lie here beside her and stroke himself to completion. It would be disrespectful to her and was frankly beneath him.

He wished something else was beneath him…namely his wife.

The realization was startling in its clarity and knocked the wind right out of him. He drew in another shocked breath. He wanted that? His mind immediately flooded with a hundred images of Sabina Burrell that he had not even registered noticing. The defiant tilt of her jaw, the way she narrowed her eyes, that mole above her top lip, the *feel* of her.

Because his traitorous mind chose to remind him at this point that he knew *exactly* how she felt. Not only had he woken hard, pressed up against her full, round backside that morning, but she had fallen forward the night before and he had felt her sprawled across him. For one moment, he had felt her cushiony soft body pressed right up against his corresponding parts. And it had been glorious. For one terrible moment, he had been unable to release her.

Jeffree was wholly unable to resist reliving the moment now in his head, only this time he did not release her. This time, he took her mouth with his and… *Oh gods, not again.* He shut his eyes and squeezed them tightly together as he strove to get his rampaging thoughts back under control.

Because apparently, yes, he wanted her like that. On her back. On top of him. On all fours, gods help him. He wanted her any way he could get her. Despite the fact Sabina had, not half an hour ago, poured out her bitterest disappointment in life, he, Jeffree, was lying next to her now, rampant and unsatisfied, and prey to licentious thoughts, all featuring his wife in the role of his seductress.

Gods. Every time he touched himself from now on, he would think of her, he thought with horror, swallowing with a suddenly dry throat. And that was wrong… He had never imagined a *particular* person before, just the vague idea of it. Surely it was an unpardonable liberty to take, picturing a certain person while you sought release?

Then he remembered…she *was* his wife after all. Surely that put a different complexion on things? For the first time in his life, Jeffree considered what it meant to have a wife in his bed. The wheels turned in his mind and something clicked into place. Men were supposed to slake their lust on their wives after all. He was just pondering this monumental point when Sabina started softly to snore.

Of course, there was the added complication of his vow. He frowned ferociously. How was he to navigate his way around that? His whole life, Jeffree had prided himself on the strength of his will. His word was his bond. At the age of eighteen, he had pledged himself to a life of chastity, duty, and knightly pursuits. The wife he had deemed worthy of the honor of the de Crecy name had been denied to him; therefore, he had renounced all women.

Perhaps he had been a little hasty, he now acknowledged; but at that time, he had not expected the fates to saddle him with a spouse like Sabina Burrell. No one could have foreseen such a thing.

184

There had to be some way around it; there just had to be. Otherwise…he would end up disgracing himself by failing his vow in spectacular fashion. His mouth drawing into a grim line, Jeffree contemplated the only decent way out of his predicament. There was nothing else for it. He would have to appeal to be released from his vow by the Lady Meliora herself, or whatever name she now went by.

He did not look forward to the interview. He would appear weak and ridiculous, but under present circumstances, he had little option. A sudden silence fell over the room, unnerving him. As abruptly as Sabina had started snoring, she stopped again, shifting onto her side, and pressing back against him with a sigh. Jeffree stiffened. *My gods, this is torture!* They would need to have some serious discussion on the morrow about the new direction he had decided their marriage was taking.

12

Sabina was woken from her slumber by a sharp rap on the door. By the time she had struggled onto her elbows and gazed bleary-eyed about the room, she realized Jeffree was getting up from a chair by the window. Had he not slept? She glanced in sleepy confusion at the empty spot next to her in the bed before turning back to watch him accept a jug of hot water from a servant.

"You rose early," she commented huskily and then cleared her throat. "Could you not sleep?"

"I slept sufficiently for my needs," he answered shortly, setting the jug down.

Which was strange, Sabina thought; she had not formed the impression he was such an early riser. She rubbed her eyes, then noticed he was staring at her. "What is it?"

"Naught!" he snapped. "I just thought you might want to wash first."

"Oh, thank you." It was the first time he had done that too, she thought with mild surprise as she sat up.

"Have some modesty, madam!" Jeffree scowled, turning his back to her.

Sabina glanced down, expecting to find she was somehow exposed, but found all was as it should be. She looked back at him in bafflement. To be sure her shift was thin, but it was unlikely he would be so flustered by that. Shrugging to herself, Sabina slid out of the bed and pattered over to the cracked bowl, sloshing some water into it.

She hurried through her wash, and after throwing her water out of the window, she left the other half of the jug for Jeffree. Once Sabina had moved to the opposite side of the room to dress, he shuffled sideways to take her place, careful to keep his back to her. She shook out her dress, which was fine for a second day's travel, and selected a clean shift. She found herself humming as she dressed. Jeffree may have found the bed uncomfortable, but she had partaken of an excellent night's sleep.

Doubtless, he would find her morning cheer and chatter extremely annoying, she reflected, which was exactly why she should give her natural inclination free rein. If he was determined to drag her to this tournament then he should suffer the consequences and find out just how much having a wife in tow would inconvenience him! Biting her lip, Sabina determined to let him have it.

"I wonder how your family spent the night," she began sanguinely, lacing her cuffs. "I expect the boys slept just fine, but I imagine your mother is like you and fussier about where she lays her head. It's funny," she mused aloud, "but I did not pick up immediately on your mother and stepfather's affection for one another."

He made no answer to this, and she shot him a speculative look before tilting her head and separating the fall of hair on the left side of her head into three strands. "Doubtless it is not the easiest time for Sir Dudley," she guessed as she started weaving her hair into a braid. "Visiting Ganford Chase and being surrounded on all sides by his wife's first husband's family, I mean."

Jeffree straightened up at this and shot her an odd look over his shoulder. He cleared his throat. "Yes, I suppose it would not be," he said in the manner of someone who had never considered such a thing before. She listened to the sound of him splashing water around as she braided the other side of her head. She was just tying the end when she realized he had turned from the washstand and was stood silently watching her.

She lifted her head. "What is it?"

He gave a guilty start. "Do you do that every morn?" To her surprise, he sounded genuinely curious.

Sabina glanced down at the braid between her fingers. "Yes." Suddenly, she remembered that Miles had often bade her to wear it loose when they were alone together. "Do you dislike them? The braids, I mean?"

He blinked. "No," he said shortly and flung down his drying cloth, making for the chair over which the rest of his clothes were slung. Sabina gazed after him in bemusement. Then she shrugged. This was all proving much easier than she had imagined. He would likely be thoroughly fed up with her long before they even reached his wretched tournament!

Subsequently, Sabina was in a cheerful mood as they broke their fast belowstairs along with the yawning boys and a pallid-looking Lady Maud. She and Sir Dudley ate sparingly of the food on offer and rebuked the boys on their slovenly manners.

"Lord, Mother, we're not at Ganford Chase now!" Crispin grumbled as he removed his elbows from the table.

"Do not speak to your mother in that tone!" Sir Dudley chastised him, and Jasper took the opportunity of his father's distraction to tip the contents of his plate under the table to the waiting dogs. Sabina resolutely turned a blind eye.

Feeling Jeffree's gaze on her, she met it, expecting to see censure in those blue depths, but strangely enough, he seemed to be staring at her headdress. Sabina lifted a hand to check all was in place, but everything seemed to be as it should be. She shrugged and returned her attention to her plate.

It was strange, Sabina thought, but all that morning Jeffree seemed to be constantly appearing at her elbow. On leaving the inn, she had found Jeffree waiting to mount her up on Blitha. He had done so, she realized dimly, the previous day, but today the attention seemed more pointed somehow.

On their ride, he frequently dropped back to ride beside her for long stretches, looking like he had something to say, but after casting a quick glance around at their company, not saying it. What on earth ailed him? she wondered distractedly as Crispin quizzed her on her opinion of fishing methods.

Around midday, they stopped for a rest, and when Sabina would have followed the Vyses to sit in the shade of a nearby oak, Jeffree caught her arm and led her instead toward another smaller tree. Casting a quick glance at his face, Sabina deduced he meant to speak whatever it was that was weighing on his mind.

After passing her the water, he watched her drink it and then cleared his throat. Sabina lowered the water and looked at him quizzically.

"After Areley Kings, there's a place I want us to visit," he started, looking grim.

"Is it nearby?"

"A day's ride."

"Oh." When nothing else was forthcoming, she prompted, "You have an acquaintance there?" He reddened at her question, piquing her curiosity.

"It is the holy order we spoke of yesterday," he answered, glancing away.

Sabina gazed back at him blankly, for it took a moment for her to comprehend. "You mean…the holy order your former betrothed joined?" she asked slowly.

"Yes."

"Why would you want to go there?" she asked, rather louder than she had intended.

"I would have thought it would be obvious. I need to be released from my vow," he answered, practically grinding his teeth.

"You need to be—?" Sabina repeated before sucking in her breath and staring at him with a heavy frown. "Is it not rather late for that? You have already wed another, Sir Jeffree," she pointed out. "I think you will find you have already broken your promise."

"Not quite," he answered with meaning, and Sabina flushed.

She took a step toward him and lowered her voice. "I assure you I am perfectly content for you to keep your vow privately if that is what we are speaking of."

"Well, I am *not* content!" he flung at her. "Far from it."

Sabina's mouth fell open. "You aren't? Since when?" she spluttered.

"Since we…started sharing a bed together," he answered frustratedly and stepped in so close they were practically touching.

"But this will not be a long-term situation," she pointed out, trying to sound reasonable. Instead, to her annoyance, she

190

sounded merely short of breath. Sabina tried to take a step back but came up against the tree trunk. "Once we have concluded this excursion to Areley Kings—"

"Who says it is not?" Jeffree interrupted her rudely, showing no sign of retreat.

Sabina swallowed. "Well, surely you will be back competing in your tournaments by then?" she hazarded. "Traveling from one place to another, whereas I will be back at Morecotte."

"Yes," he agreed. "What of it? Do you imagine I am the only married knight in Karadok?"

Sabina's mind flailed around. "Well…no," she admitted.

"Several of them manage to maintain a household and to travel the tournaments."

Maintain a household? "Do you…? Is it possible you mean to make Morecotte your…your home too?" Sabina stammered, aghast.

"Where else?"

She gazed up at him, completely lost for words.

"Are you two kissing?" asked a disapproving voice, making them both jump. Jeffree took a step back, and Sabina found she could finally catch her breath. She sagged against the tree trunk feeling wrung out by the encounter.

"What do you want, Crispin?" Jeffree asked his younger brother irritably. Not even slightly daunted, Crispin drew closer and started twittering on about what poor specimens the trees in this neighborhood were and how much taller they were in their own neck of the woods.

191

Sabina scarcely took in the child's words, so scattered were her own wits as she tottered her way back to her horse. Jeffree wanted to make their marriage a real functioning marriage. She could not quite wrap her head around the fact. *Why in the name of all that was holy?* She knew full well he had been as horrified by the necessity of their marriage as she.

Why then now had he suddenly decided she was worthy of the role in deed as well as in name? The only nice thing he had ever said to her was concerning her horsemanship, she reflected in disbelief. Was that enough to make one worthy of the dubious honor in his eyes?

By the time she had reached Blitha, Jeffree had once more appeared at her side. He lifted her up into the saddle, his hands lingering at her waist for a moment longer than she felt was strictly necessary. Sabina felt unaccustomedly flustered by the time he backed away, his eyes still on her till the last minute when he swung around to climb his own horse.

He could not possibly be in earnest about this, could he? His heated gaze disconcerted her. He had wanted things different since they had shared a bed, he'd said. Which was odd as Miles had always complained she was an awful bedfellow, hogging the sheets and even snoring on occasion.

She and Jeffree had only shared a bed twice. The first time, admittedly, there had been a couple of embarrassing mishaps. Her cheeks burned as she remembered the indignity of falling on top of him. Last night, though, had passed without event. She shifted in her saddle, remembering how she had woken wrapped in his arms, her cheek resting against the blond hair of his chest. Mercifully, he had been unaware, as she had managed to disentangle herself before he awoke.

192

As for his arousal, it was her understanding that men were often in that state first thing in the morning. As such, it meant nothing. *Nothing at all.*

Her mind was in turmoil all afternoon as they rode down the slopes at the other side of the pass. She simply could not believe that a sudden and unaccountable desire for her person had brought about this change of heart. For one horrible moment, she even considered that he might feel sorry her after her revelations about her first unsatisfactory marriage. The thought made her feel hot, then cold all over. To be an object of pity to Sir Jeffree would be truly awful.

Having said that, one did not usually feel inflamed toward an object of pity. No, that could not be what motivated him. It must be something else. It could not be material gain, for she had no fortune, and the only thing she brought to the marriage was an extremely modest property. No, that could have nothing to do with this reversal in his attitude.

It was not even as though Morecotte was impressive, she reflected. She was fiercely attached to the house, but even she, fond as she was, knew full well that to the likes of Sir Jeffree, it was little more than a hunting box for a weekend's sport.

Sabina glanced sideways at him cautiously. He was still riding beside her for long stretches at a time, though he seemed to have precious little to say now he had imparted the shocking news he wanted to consummate their marriage.

And so much for his lifetime devotion to his saintly beloved! What did he expect her to do while he groveled for forgiveness to his former betrothed? Was she supposed to kneel beside him and beg for the bestowal of his lordly penis? Her face twisted into a grimace. As far as she was concerned, it could remain off-limits. She had no use for it. No thank you!

193

As for the peerless lady herself, Sabina had no desire to meet her. Why should she be dragged along on such a humiliating errand?

She had gone over the matter forward and backward and wound herself into knots by the time evening came around. They stopped once again to don cloaks for the last leg of the journey, and Sabina stayed close to the boys rather than getting stuck with Jeffree for another secluded conversation with just the two of them.

It was bad enough they would be sharing a room again shortly. She snuck another look at him as he saw to the horses. This latest development was all nonsense, of course. He only *thought* he wanted a real marriage with her. Sir Jeffree was no doubt one of those contrary types who was no sooner told he could not have something than he determined that nothing else would do but that he must have it. The thought cheered her considerably.

Yes, that was probably it. *She* had shown herself disinclined for intimacy, so *he* immediately thought he wanted just that. Her mind ticked over. Mayhap she could work with that? Knowing how easily they irritated each other, she could only imagine his displeased reaction if she were to suddenly start clamoring for his attention.

If she were now to show a cloying attitude toward him, surely that would snap him out of this latest inclination. She recalled how annoyed Jeffree had been the only time she had ever praised his actions, telling his uncle of how he had reclaimed her home. A little voice whispered in her ear that maybe she should try to be clinging and affectionate to him now before Lady Maud and Sir Dudley? Doubtless, he would dislike it very much and would speedily reject her advances. She sat up straighter in her saddle.

194

The more she thought about it, the more convinced she grew that the idea had merit. She would just have to bolster her nerve and be willing to make herself look a fool. It would be embarrassing, of course, to be spurned in front of her in-laws, but hopefully, the boys would not really understand what was happening. And doubtless, their parents would think it only natural that he would harbor resentment toward her.

Nodding to herself, Sabina made her resolve. She would do it. Turning in her saddle, she found him drawing his horse alongside her again. Before her courage could fail her, she threw him an encouraging smile. Sabina was not really sure it would count as a *come hither* look, for she had never knowingly bestowed one before, but given Jeffree's startled reaction, she had disconcerted him at the very least.

She faced front with a triumphant smile curving her lips this time. Well, well, Sir Jeffree was *not* going to get everything his own way for once, Sabina thought with satisfaction. She had no doubt that after a bit of fawning over him, he would not be able to bundle her off to Morecotte alone fast enough. And serve him right too!

By the time they reached the inn that had been settled on for their next night's sleep, Sabina had decided on her plan of action. There was not much opportunity to play the smitten maiden at supper, for Crispin was in a plaintive mood and Jasper turned his nose up at the rabbit stew on offer. Sir Dudley delivered them all a crisp lecture on due gratitude which left them all avoiding each other's gazes.

They had no sooner climbed the stairs to their new bedchamber than the Vyses' maidservant, Githa, delivered the two dogs, explaining that as punishment Lady Maud had determined the boys were not allowed to keep Feste and Brisis in their bedchamber that night. Jeffree rolled his eyes and went back downstairs to demand an extra blanket for their room.

Sabina hurried to get washed and undressed while ordering the dogs to get down off the bed every time one of them made a spring for it. She was feeling thoroughly harassed by the time Jeffree reappeared. He spread the blanket down in front of the fire and ordered the dogs to lie down on it. They slunk over to it and, after casting many soulful glances over their shoulders, finally stopped pawing and circling and collapsed onto it.

Sabina clambered into the bed and drew the covers up to her chin. She felt stupidly nervous and unsure of herself, feelings she was ill accustomed to, and they annoyed her. Forcing herself to breathe evenly, she stared up at the ceiling, trying to remember her strategy. She was to be clinging and ingratiating, she reminded herself sternly. And thoroughly get on her husband's nerves. Jeffree went about his wash, oblivious to her schemes.

"Er," she started unpromisingly. "Who of your acquaintance may we see at Areley Kings?" When he did not immediately speak, she pressed on brightly. "No doubt you have many cronies on the tournament circle."

Something clattered which might have been his razor blade against the basin. When he spoke, she could almost *hear* the frown in his voice. "The company of knights varies from tournament to tournament," he said grudgingly. "There is no guarantee of any particular knight attending, save at the royal tournaments."

"But among them, whom do you number as your particular acquaintance?" she persisted.

"All and none," he answered at once. "We are competitors in the field."

"And off the field?"

"Off the field?" He seemed to consider this a moment. "Off the field, they are nothing to me."

"Oh." She did not know why she was startled. Had she imagined he would have moved in some merry band of friends? Now she thought about it, she could not even imagine what manner of man would be a true friend to the likes of Sir Jeffree. An extremely patient one, she concluded after a moment or two. Indeed, any friend of Jeffree's would have to be practically a saint!

Thinking of saints made her think of his former betrothed, Meliora, which immediately brought a frown to her face. She plucked at her covers. Mayhap that was why he was so attached to the lady, if she had been his only friend in life. "And what of this holy place we must visit after the tournament?" she heard herself ask.

"What of it?" he muttered in a muffled voice.

When she glanced his way, he was wiping his face with a drying cloth. "Well," she ventured, "where did you make this vow of yours? Was it at some nearby shrine, or on the actual steps of the convent your beloved entered? Must we revisit the site of the oath you made, or"—she paused heavily a moment— "did you make the vow to the lady herself? Is it Meliora in person to whom you must apply to be released?"

Jeffree flung down his cloth and turned to face her with a scowl on his face. "Must we discuss this now?" he asked. "I find the subject distasteful."

"Distasteful?" Sabina gasped, sitting up. *Pompous ass!* For one minute she seriously considered throwing a pillow bearer at his head. "I am trying to…to promote some understanding between us!" she stammered angrily. "Which you are making *impossible* with your...your insufferable rudeness and condescension! How dare you tell me you want to...to...with me! When you cannot even be bothered to tell me *anything*!"

Jeffree stared at her as she started to struggle furiously with the bedsheets. "What are you doing?" he barked out as she swung her legs off the mattress.

"I am sleeping with the dogs on the blanket!" she choked out, flinging the blankets from her.

"Like hells you are!"

She had no sooner set her foot to the floorboards than she felt herself seized about the waist and hoisted back onto the bed. Sabina found all the breath squeezed out of her as he followed her down onto the mattress, practically on top of her, pinning her beneath his much bigger body.

Sabina gave a muffled squeak and lay stunned beneath his encroaching bulk. Jeffree blinked down at her as though similarly taken aback by their position. He did not move away though, just remained very still, the only sound in the room their mingled, labored breathing. Sabina was just steeling herself to say something, *anything*, when he broke the silence.

"Tell me what you want to know and have done!"

Sabina considered him with wide eyes as she lay panting on her back beneath him. Both of them were breathing hard. She felt acutely aware of the fact she was clad only in her thin shift and he had stripped down to his braies. "Pray, don't put yourself out on my account!" she huffed and would have tossed her head if not for the confining circumstances. She should tell him to get the hells off her. Why wasn't she?

198

Jeffree continued to stare down at her, his eyes very blue, his gaze hot and intense. "I told you I am under a vow," he ground out. "I want to be released from it. I want to—to move on from the past. To concentrate on the future." His gaze suddenly turned evasive. "With you," he added raggedly, a flush mounting his cheek.

"The future with me?" she repeated blankly as a hot flush climbed up her neck. Of course he did not want to build a future with her! she scoffed inwardly. All he wanted to do was scratch a momentary itch. She could hardly blame him at this point in truth, her own limbs feeling strangely languorous against the press of his. There were a couple of places where no clothing separated them, and those spots tingled with new awareness.

Sabina shivered, though not with the cold. She had the strangest impulse to lift her arms and circle them about him. How would Jeffree react if she did just that? she wondered, half thrilled and half horrified by the notion. Would he try to break free from her embrace? Or would he succumb to her seduction? Seduction? Sabina swallowed. Wait, what was her plan again?

Her thoughts had scattered to the four winds at the feel of all his hard, bunched muscle against her. Had the plan been to seduce him? Was she even capable of such a thing? Looking at the way he was gazing down at her now made her feel strangely capable of such a task.

"I did not make the vow to the lady herself," he said at last. His voice was terse. "It was a…private matter between myself and my god, but…" He hesitated.

"But?"

"I did make the vow in her presence," he admitted, looking shamefaced.

199

Sabina's mind scrambled over this. Was he splitting hairs now? Strange to say, she did not think Jeffree *would* lie to let himself off the hook. "How did it happen?" she wheezed. "Will you tell me that at least?"

He sighed heavily and then rolled off her to lie at her side. Sabina quelled the strange disappointment that overwhelmed her. He was silent a moment, and when his voice did come, it was scratchy and hoarse. "Meliora requested a meeting betwixt us, and at this meeting, she told me of her growing religious conviction that she must enter holy orders. She expressed her regret at disappointing me but begged that I would release her from our betrothal contract."

Sabina digested this. "And you not only released her but felt compelled to make a holy vow of your own?" she asked slowly. "You must have been very disappointed."

Jeffree turned his head to look at her. "I was young," he said awkwardly. "I *was* very disappointed and…somewhat rash."

Sabina caught her breath. She thought this might be the first time she had heard him express anything remotely self-critical. "I suppose youth is the time for such wild conviction," she murmured. "No doubt you thought your heart would never recover from the blow."

He frowned, opened his mouth, and then closed it again. "What of you?" he asked, his voice still gruff.

"Me?"

Again, he hesitated. "You also made a vow," he pointed out. "Did your…heart"—he almost choked over the word—"recover from the blow?"

Sabina narrowed her eyes. From his glacial tone, she would imagine he was baiting her, but the expression in his eyes told a different story. Strangely, it seemed he wanted to know the answer.

She considered a moment before making a reply. "Any affection I thought I bore for Miles died a thousand deaths over the short span of our marriage. Our circumstances are very different, Sir Jeffree. My vow was not made from admiration like yours but from a wealth of bitterness."

Her throat closed over the last word, and she tried to turn her head away, but suddenly, his hand was at her jaw, preventing her from breaking eye contact. "Those tears in your eyes had better be of self-pity," he said grimly, "and not for him."

Sabina could not catch her breath for an instant. "I—I assure you they are," she replied at length, half choked. "I mislike being so…full of burning regret and self-reproach. It is no way to live."

He released her face, shrugging a muscular shoulder. "From what you told me, it is your father who should bear the weight of regret, not you. He arranged the match, did he not?"

Sabina nodded. "Yes."

"So, then it is his burden to bear. Not yours."

Sabina could do no more than stare at him. After a heavy pause, she cleared her throat. "Very well," she answered lightly. "I will try to think of it that way." They lay silent, side by side, for a moment. Collecting herself, Sabina reached for the covers, pulling them up to make herself decent. After the briefest of hesitations, she tugged them up about Jeffree's waist too, feeling ridiculously self-conscious about it.

"I have decided," Jeffree said heavily, "to forgive you."

Sabina dropped the blankets like they burned her fingers. "Forgive me? For what?"

"Your role incriminating me that day." Sabina's breath came fast, but she was too surprised to make a reply. "I accept you acted to spare your sister," he continued, "and with no actual intent of snaring me in matrimony."

Sabina flopped back onto the bed, her head reeling. "I hardly know what to say," she admitted.

"You are not required to say anything. I merely tell you in the spirit of…promoting this new understanding between us."

Sabina lay feeling stunned for a long time, well after Jeffree's breathing had evened out into sleep. She was surprised he managed to drop off so quickly. It almost seemed as though unburdening his mind to her had relieved him. She envied his peace of mind. In the dark, she heard the patter of canine footfalls. The bed dipped and Sabina felt a weight settle against her legs. She reached down a hand in the dark, felt a lick to her fingers, and sighed. Strangely enough, it comforted her a little.

Moments later the second dog joined the first, crawling up the bed on his belly to insert itself between herself and Jeffree. Sabina could not help but smile wryly. She reached down to pat a sleek head. This one nosed her hand insistently, demanding more fuss. Sabina fondled the velvety ears as her head crowded with the many astonishing things her new husband had said to her tonight.

She felt extremely conflicted. Jeffree had been…not nice, she told herself. *Nice* was not the word. Reasonable, maybe. And *reasonable* was not a word she would have ever dreamed she would have associated with Sir Jeffree's behavior. He had also been somewhat kind in laying the blame for her disastrous first marriage at her father's door instead of her own. Something her parents, though fond, had never done.

It seemed that he also no longer blamed her for what had happened on Isemay's wedding day. *Their* wedding day, she ought to call it, but the idea still grated. He wanted them to reach an "understanding" of sorts over their marriage. Which was all well and good, but she was sure this idea of consummating their union was a bad one.

Her thoughts shied away from her own strange reaction to his physical closeness. That had been a momentary confusion, nothing more. Once upon a time, Sabina had been open and affectionate. Resentment and cruel experience had soon closed off that side of her nature.

She petted her dogs and cudgeled her brains on how she could only convince *him* that they should keep things out of the bedchamber. An annoying little voice in her head piped up, reminding her that Jeffree had said he wanted a future with her.

She blushed in the darkness. Of course, that was all nonsense.

Maybe, after all, Sir Jeffree was mercurial of nature instead of staid? Maybe she had gained altogether the wrong impression about his being stuffy. She bit her lip, debating asking his mother on the morrow. Then again, Lady Maud had not had the raising of her son. That office had fallen to Sir Charles Ellis, who had tried to raise him in his own grave image. Tried and failed, she decided, for Jeffree had definite bursts of heat to offset his chilly disapproval.

Sometimes, she reflected, Jeffree grew so heated, even the tips of his ears burned. She suspected his nature was not really cold at all, not deep down. He burned hot and struggled to contain it. Against her better judgment, she recalled the feel and weight of him on top of her. It had not been unpleasant at all. *Oh gods.* What was she thinking?

When she finally drifted off to sleep, it was after telling herself that mayhap the Lady Meliora would refuse after all to release him from his vow of chastity. For some strange reason, the thought did not make her feel one whit better. *Who is being contrary now, my girl?* she asked herself wryly as her eyelids drooped down over her tired eyes.

*

Jeffree awoke to the sensation of dog breath on his face. He recoiled and almost tumbled off the edge of the bed. Hearing a smothered laugh, he sat up and found his wife was already washing. Noticing how her shift had slipped off one shoulder, he cleared his throat. "I did not hear them bring water."

"I know," Sabina answered him. "You were too occupied in cuddling with Brisis."

Jeffree glanced down at the gray dog who was curled into his side. The white one was lying shamelessly across his legs, displaying his belly. Jeffree sighed and scrubbed his face with his hand. "They have certainly made themselves at home," he commented wryly. "It is to be hoped that the boys behave themselves today." At Sabina's quizzical look, he added, "So they can sleep back in with them tonight."

Again, she laughed. "They were not so very disruptive. They waited until you were asleep at least."

"Humph." Absently he reached out to stroke the sleek hound's gray coat while his eyes dwelt on Sabina's shift-clad form. By the time he managed to tear his gaze away, his composure was decidedly ruffled. Previous to his marriage, for some reason, he had thought he admired women built along slender lines with cultured, refined manners. Now he knew that was not the case.

Hearing her fiddling with the window, he looked up to find her emptying out the bowl of water. The action caused her shift to pull tight across her ample thighs and backside. Jeffree was forced to close his eyes against the sight, for he did not have the strength to look away.

"The water left in the jug is still somewhat warm," she said, turning from the window. He made a rumbling sound in his throat. "You are tired today," she commented, retreating to the far side of the room to dress.

Jeffree opened his eyes again. He did not have it in him to point out she was quite wrong on that score. All his energy was concentrated instead on bringing order to his rioting libido. Hearing the rustle of her dress, he emerged gingerly from the bedsheets and, eyes strictly averted, made his way to the basin and ewer.

They met the others belowstairs and a haphazard meal was partaken of. The boys were particularly rapturous at being reunited with the dogs.

"Poor Feste," Crispin lamented, shooting an accusing glance at his father. "Having to sleep on the hard floor all night."

"Not so, I assure you," Sabina corrected him. "Feste spent the night sprawled across your brother's legs with his tongue hanging out."

Jeffree felt his face color as his brothers pinned him with incredulous stares. "Not by invitation!" He scowled. "The wretched animals waited until I was asleep to make themselves comfortable."

"Don't you believe him," Sabina said, reaching for the toasted bread. "While I washed this morning, he lolled abed with them both. Brisis was practically curled up on his chest."

Jeffree retreated into dignified silence, though he could feel his stepfather's startled gaze upon him.

Jasper chuckled. "That's her favorite spot," he agreed.

It occurred to Jeffree that if it had not been for the hounds, he likely would have embarrassed himself again by waking up plastered to Sabina. For some reason, he did not feel remotely grateful. "Well, if you behave yourselves today, mayhap she will occupy that spot with you again tonight, Jasper," he commented coolly.

His brother's face brightened at this prospect, though his mother rolled her eyes. "Poor Githa has my heartfelt sympathies," she murmured but did not forbid the suggested sleeping arrangement.

Their morning's progress was uneventful, and they made good time traveling through the neighboring county of Halfordshire. "If we were to travel south from this point," Jeffree found himself informing the party at large, "we would reach Rogets Ford."

"And what, pray, is at Rogets Ford?" his mother asked.

"A tournament."

"Why do you not journey to this one, if 'tis closer?" his wife asked with a frown.

"It's held in March," he explained. "It's an annual event."

"Who won it this year?" Crispin asked with interest. "You?"

Jeffree frowned. "Lord Kentigern," he admitted grudgingly after a moment.

"I have heard tell of him," Jasper piped up irritatingly. "He is a fearsome warrior, is he not?"

Jeffree ignored him.

"What tournament was after that?" Crispin asked.

"The Spring Tournament," Jeffree replied, starting to wish he had not raised the subject.

"And who won that?"

"Sir Garman Orde," he growled with a fearsome scowl. Even Crispin seemed to realize the subject was not a good one to pursue.

"And after that?" Sabina persisted.

"Tranton Vale at the beginning of this month."

"And who triumphed there?" she enquired with an arched brow.

His displeasure dissolved at the memory. "Me," he answered, earning a cheer from his brothers. He turned in his saddle to frown at them, but they looked entirely unabashed. He glanced back to Sabina to gauge her reaction and found her looking at him appraisingly. "What?" he asked before he could stop himself.

"I am just glad to hear there is some basis for your monumental pride," she answered sweetly.

Sir Dudley gave a choked cough, but Jeffree held her gaze. "Well, you shall soon be able to judge that for yourself, wife," he answered pointedly.

Sabina just laughed. "Is there only one tournament held each month?" she asked with interest. "It seems very well coordinated."

"In general, there is only one major tournament, but there are lesser ones held here or there."

"So, if one wished it, a knight could spend a full twelvemonth on the road?"

"Practically the whole year," he admitted. "None are held in December or January due to the harsher weather and the shorter daylight hours."

Sabina nodded thoughtfully at this, but before she could make a reply, his mother chimed in. "Was there not some impromptu May Day tournament held at the palace this year?" she asked. "Your cousin Hugo was telling me of it."

"Oh, that." Jeffree pulled a face. "I did not attend. It was all some royal ploy to marry off the northern princess."

"The Princess Una?" Sabina asked, whipping her head around. "Poor thing! Surely the King did not marry her off to the winner of a joust?"

"I believe that was the plan," Jeffree answered.

"What a rotten prize!" exclaimed Crispin.

"Most knights would surely prefer a pot of gold!" his brother agreed.

"As to that," Sabina cut in darkly, "I am sure the princess would have infinitely preferred it also. That and her liberty."

Sir Dudley shook his head. "It's a difficult situation for the King," he said, sucking in his cheeks. "Whether a willing pawn or not, she remains a rallying point for the northern rebels and as such constitutes a problem for King Wymer."

"Well, I had no taste for such a bride," Jeffree said, wishing to bring the subject to a close. Politics as a subject was fraught with difficulty, and though his stepfather was a cautious man, he did not think Sabina would hold back on expressing her own opinions. Seeing the expressions on everyone's faces though, he seemed to have blundered anyway. An air of awkward constraint hovered over the party. "What did I say?" he demanded, glancing around.

"Hugo also told me that the King's current favorite has been awarded his mother's estate at Kinerton. Apparently, she has been retired there for her *lying in*," said Lady Maud, sotto voce.

Jeffree, who disapproved of royal gossip, frowned. It was not like his mother to be so indiscreet. His stepfather cleared his throat and directed a pointed look at the cart where the boys were sat. Sabina said nothing at all. She dropped back and was seemingly suddenly occupied in patting Blitha's neck and murmuring to her soothingly. Jeffree felt annoyed. He had intended no slight to her and it irritated him that everyone plainly thought he had been tactless.

He steered his horse until it was abreast of her own. "Tired?" he asked awkwardly.

She shook her head. "No."

"Why so quiet, then?"

"I do not have any palace gossip to contribute," she answered lightly. "We do not hear much of court in Little Ganford." She hesitated. "Your cousin Hugo is a courtier?"

Jeffree's lip curled. "He is, yes."

"You do not approve?"

"He is a frivolous fellow with little to recommend him."

"Your mother seemed to find him entertaining enough."

"Even the best of women have failings." Sabina pursed her lips. "You disagree?" he pressed, though he was not sure why.

"I do not think that is only true of women, Sir Jeffree," she retorted heavily.

"I never claimed it was."

She turned in her saddle to direct a stare at him. "And what would say is your own besetting sin?" she asked. "If it is not a propensity for gossip?"

"You think me a gossip?" he demanded incredulously.

"You have certainly turned your ear toward it at some time," she muttered, bringing him up short. Well, that was true in any event. Osborn had told him she was known locally for a shrew. He had thoughtlessly repeated as much the morning after they were married.

"I have already apologized for that," he pointed out.

"Have you?" She sounded surprised. "When?"

Jeffree thought about it. "Well, if I did not precisely apologize, then I showed by my actions that I regretted it." Again, she looked blank. "When I came and fetched you back from your parents' house," he elaborated.

"That was in lieu of an apology, was it?" she asked. "I had not realized."

Jeffree regarded her moodily. "After you explained the true state of affairs to me, I realized that I had believed a falsehood."

He struggled a moment to put what he wanted to say into words. "When I said—what I said last night—it stemmed from that realization."

"I see."

The coolness of her tone was not lost on him. "You want the words, then? I am not too proud to say them if that is what you think." When she said nothing, he leaned forward in his saddle. "Sabina?"

Her eyes flew to meet his. "I do not need them," she said quickly.

Too quickly. He gazed at her in exasperation. "I want to move past this…these…preconceived notions we had of one another," he said stiffly. "But in order to do that, both of us need to show willing."

To his surprise, a flush mounted her cheeks. "I am not sure I am ready yet," she admitted with surprising frankness. "And I do not believe you can be either."

"Why do you say that?"

She cast a quick glance in the direction of the others riding ahead. "You say you have forgiven me, Sir Jeffree, for what I did that day, in the Great Hall at Ganford Chase." Her voice cracked slightly, making him feel strangely ill at ease. "But experience has taught me that you will fling it in my face every time I incur your displeasure."

"What experience?" he demanded. "Experience with me, or with another who came before me?"

When she looked strangely stricken by his words, he almost stopped. Then, suddenly the necessity of being understood

211

seemed overwhelming. "I ask you, wife, is this fair? You are quick to judge me on the standards of another."

The color in Sabina's cheeks seemed to deepen. She swallowed. "You may be right," she answered at last. "If you say all is forgotten, then I will take you at your word."

He had not actually said it was *forgotten*, but for the moment, he allowed this to pass. "I meant no allusion to our marriage when I spoke of the May Day tournament," he continued tersely.

"I knew that already," she replied at once. "You are not so subtle in your methods."

Jeffree huffed out a breath. "It is a good thing that I have a strong sense of self-worth," he said caustically, "or it would surely lie in tatters at my feet, thanks to you."

She smiled slightly at that. "I hardly think your self-worth is in any jeopardy from me, Sir Jeffree."

Jeffree was not so sure. "I think you should address me by my name alone now, wife," he answered with a frown. "Do you not agree?"

"And will you use my given name?" she asked. "Or continue to call me *madam* in that odious manner of yours?"

Instead of pointing out there were worse things he could call her in perfect truth, he held his tongue. So far, she had a way of making him regret any venting he'd ever partaken in at her expense. "Tell me about the time we were introduced at the Bishop's Palace," he said instead, surprising them both.

As soon as she had recovered from it, Sabina pulled a face. "Alas, there is not much to tell."

"Who were you with?" Even he could hear the thread of tension running through his voice. For some reason, he did *not* want it to have been her late husband.

"My aunt Mabel," she answered, and his shoulders relaxed at once.

"And who is that?" he asked after the tiniest pause. She had not mentioned an aunt before, had she?

Sabina looked amused by his sudden curiosity. "My mother's sister. She lives some five miles from Tipton Hall with her husband, whose name is Jessop."

"And what do they do, these Jessops?" he pressed when she seemed disinclined to continue.

"Uncle Jessop is a master builder. He designed the new hall for the Bishop's Palace, which is why we were invited that day to mix in such lofty company."

Jeffree ignored her faintly mocking tone. "And you say we were introduced?"

"That we were."

Jeffree shot a quick glance at her. He could vaguely remember visiting the new wing of the Bishop of Ganford's residence a couple of years ago, but little else. "What were you wearing?" he asked in a vague effort to spark some remembrance of the occasion.

Sabina opened her mouth and then closed it again. "I do not remember," she said at last, unconvincingly.

Jeffree found himself suddenly convinced it would have been that shabby red gown she had married him in. It must have been her best gown for at least five years. "What was I wearing?" he tested her.

213

She laughed. "Something very peacocky, I have no doubt. My aunt said you were the handsomest man she had ever met; I remember that much."

"And what reply made you?"

She darted a quick look at him. "That, too, I forget," she lied so smartly that he could not check the reluctant smile that sprang to his lips.

"I just bet you do." Sabina laughed again, looking completely unabashed. Suddenly, he was annoyed that the memory eluded him. He *should* remember her, godsdamn it. He had never met anyone else quite like her.

He continued to gaze at her in bafflement until her laughter abated. "You must have been unaccustomedly well-behaved that day," he said, sounding vaguely accusatory, "else I would have noticed you, to be sure."

Sabina shook her head. "You have the oddest notions about me, Sir Jeffree. First, you say I am *dangerously reckless* and then you are convinced I am in some way memorable. I am sure you must have been introduced to dozens of women of my ilk. I am wholly unremarkable, I assure you."

"That is not so."

She sighed. "Very well. I will own, I have been outspoken these past few days, but even you will admit they have been littered with peculiar circumstances outside the realm of norm." She paused before continuing. "In the general way of things, I am a woman who creates little stir in her day-to-day life. You gave me a cursory nod at the Bishop's Palace and carried on your way. I neither stopped you in your tracks nor haunted your dreams," she concluded drolly. "In short, you scarce noticed me, and I am sure I do not wonder at it."

Her answer had him frowning heavily and strongly disposed to argue with her. "If I did not notice you at the Bishop's Palace it must have been because you were acting out of character," he said stubbornly. "You are not a woman to be overlooked."

She gave a splutter, but whatever reply she had been about to make was quashed by Jasper calling over. "If you two have finished *flirting*, then mayhap Sabina can come and ride behind the cart with us again. It's growing devilishly dull up here without her."

Jeffree directed a glare toward his younger brother but found Sabina moving in that direction anyway, her vacated spot swiftly taken by his mother.

"She is very good-natured, I will say that much," his mother murmured, shooting him a significant look. Jeffree made no reply, a mistake with his mother as she tended to take this as tacit agreement. "You seem to amuse her at all events. Whenever I happen to look your way, she is laughing."

Jeffree glanced over to where Sabina was being regaled by his eager brothers. "She finds amusement in any situation," he said sourly.

"I expect, given her circumstances, she has learned to take her amusement where she can find it."

"What do you mean by that?" he asked sharply.

His mother's eyebrows rose. "I intended no slight, Jeffree. Merely that life as a young widow can be wearisome and exacting. I speak from personal experience, remember?"

Jeffree grudgingly nodded, though he did not think his mother's and his wife's circumstances had been so similar.

"What do you intend to do with her?" his mother persisted in a low voice. "You surely do not mean to drag her around the tournament circuit throughout the year. Such a life would be a punishment to most women." When he did not answer, her brows rose again. "Or is that your intent? *Do* you mean to punish her, Jeffree?"

"No," he answered shortly. "I was as much to blame for our predicament as she." He meant, of course, that neither of them was to blame for what had occurred, but his mother seemed embarrassed by his words, taking them as an admission of guilt.

"Yes, well," she said, shifting in her saddle and clearing her throat. "Let us not dwell on the more sordid aspect of your courting," she said primly. "If only Sir Charles had not encouraged you to live like some sort of monk, then your flesh would not have been so ripe for corruption."

Jeffree felt himself turn purple. "Mother!" he objected in a strangled tone, casting a look over his shoulder.

"Well, well," she said. "I know your godfather is a great man, but your father would have handled things differently, I assure you!"

"This subject is highly—"

"We will say no more about it," Lady Maud agreed hurriedly. "I only wished to explain that—well, never mind. Let us speak no more of it. What is done is done."

"Exactly."

"You are married now and must make the best of things." His mother took a deep breath and faced forward. "I only meant to say that things could have turned out a good deal worse than they have. Physical attraction, though it should never be the primary consideration in such unions, is not to be wholly despised. It can bring certain things to the table. Fruitfulness for instance."

Jeffree almost groaned. "We are not having this discussion, Mother."

His mother jutted out her chin determinedly. "All I meant was that you should not punish Sabina for your attraction to her."

"I have no intention of doing so."

"I am heartily glad to hear it, my son."

"If you must know," he replied, feeling goaded, "I told her only last evening that I bear her no ill will for what occurred and that I…I want us to put the whole manner of our…courtship"—he stumbled over the word choice—"behind us."

His mother looked impressed. "That was handsomely done," she said with approval. "I am sure she appreciates your willingness to reach an understanding."

Jeffree struggled a moment with his response. Sabina had not been markedly grateful. Then again, she had bitter experiences of her own to move past, which he did not. In the end, he made do with a noncommittal grunt.

"There is some jewelry," his mother continued calmly. "A necklace your father gave me and a matching ring. I have not worn either of them for years. I will fetch them from Longacre and bring them to Lord Blandivar's tournament so that you may give them to her. I have noticed she does not own any ornamentation of her own."

The idea of giving Sabina gifts had not even occurred to him. Jeffree flushed, thinking of her plain manner of dress. "Thank you, but I believe I can buy my wife trinkets aplenty."

"These are de Crecy heirlooms, and as such, you really ought to give them to your wife." Jeffree gave a stiff nod and his mother sighed. "Do you have any friend that you give your confidences to, Jeffree? I do not believe for one minute that you and Sir Charles speak freely with one another. You are both far too reserved." When he made no immediate reply, she gave him a frank look. "Mayhap you will be the kind of man who shares his innermost thoughts with his wife." Jeffree blinked. "Your stepfather is that kind, you know."

"He is?" Jeffree seriously considered Sir Dudley's character, perhaps for the first time in his life.

His mother threw him a quick, rare smile. "Oh yes. That is why I married him."

13

Sabina felt tired by the time they reached the village of Halterstappe that evening. To Jeffree's chagrin, the inn he usually made for was naught but a burned-out shell after a fire had broken out the previous spring. They were forced instead to head for the nearby monastery which locals assured them offered accommodation for traveling pilgrims.

The monks welcomed them amiably enough, and they were led to a long low building with white walls and very spare furnishings. They all sat to their supper together, the Vyses, their servants, Jeffree, herself, and her husband's manservant, Osborn.

Sabina was not altogether surprised to find they were expected to split into male and female groups for the night once they had partaken of a frugal supper of soup and bread.

"The beasts will have to sleep in the stable," Brother Michael informed them, eyeing the dogs doubtfully. His words were met by an immediate clamor of protests from the boys.

"The dogs will stay with my wife," Jeffree said firmly, cutting across all heated debate. When Brother Michael opened his mouth to disagree, Jeffree simply dropped a purse of monies into his hand, causing the monk's objections to cease at once.

"Very well, good sir," Brother Michael conceded with a small cough. "Your donation is much appreciated." He directed a bow toward Lady Maud, who sat at the head of the table. "If your stomachs are full, I will now show the ladies to their quarters." Sabina, Maud, and Githa all stood at once.

"Just one moment," Jeffree said, also coming to his feet. "I will have a word first with my wife."

Sabina, feeling very conscious of the eyes turned on her, rounded the table and followed Jeffree to the far end of the timbered room. "What is it?" she asked in hushed tones, turning her back resolutely on the others.

Jeffree frowned. "You have not said, but am I to understand this is your first time out of Ganfordshire?" he asked slowly.

Sabina's eyebrows rose. "Yes," she admitted.

"You have never left your home county before?"

"I have not," she agreed.

His frown deepened and he lifted his head. "Brother Michael," he said, raising his voice. "I would speak with you alone."

Sabina's mouth dropped, and she watched Jeffree stride out of the room with the cleric. What was he doing? She turned to face her in-laws, who were all eyeing her curiously. "Really, I have not the faintest notion what he is about," she started to utter feebly. Jeffree reappeared and beckoned to her. Cheeks aflame, Sabina hurried to his side.

"Change of plan," he said briefly. "We are staying in their visiting guests' suite up at the priory."

Sabina blinked at him. "But—?"

"It's all settled," he said, looking over the top of her head to address his family. "We will join you in the morning and bid you good night."

"What of the dogs?" Crispin's voice piped up.

"They can sleep with you and Jasper," Jeffree replied without consulting Brother Michael. Considering how many coins he had likely spent, Sabina did not altogether blame him for his high-handedness on this occasion. The monk beamed at her and indicated she should precede them out of the door.

"Good night," Sabina called waveringly over her shoulder. The Vyses bade them a good night, and Jeffree and Sabina crossed the torchlit courtyard behind Brother Michael, who led the way.

"But why are we sleeping separately to the others?" Sabina asked in an annoyed undertone. She had a horrible suspicion that everyone thought it had been at her instigation.

"It does not suit me to be parted from you so soon," Jeffree replied, sounding unconcerned.

"*Why?*" Sabina persisted. "It must look so strange to your family!"

"You think so?" He sounded skeptical. "We are newlywed after all."

"Yes, but—"

Her objections were cut short as they approached the looming priory. Brother Michael turned around to indicate they should enter a studded double door. A flight of stone steps followed, and then they were led into a large chamber sumptuously decorated with dark wooden furniture and beautifully painted tiles. A large bed was set upon a raised platform, hung about with golden curtains, and littered with tasseled cushions. It was so far from what Sabina would expect to find within monastery walls that she stared at it.

"The rooms were outfitted when the bishop came to stay with us last winter," Brother Michael explained, setting down a candle on a table. "We use it for visiting dignitaries now. Please, make yourselves at home. I will send some of my brothers to light the fire and bring you hot water and refreshment at once."

221

He hurried away and Sabina drifted about the shadowy room, examining the gleaming plate and polished glass as Jeffree sat in a chair and started pulling off his boots.

"They certainly saw to the bishop's comfort," she murmured. "Why, it is fit for a lord in here."

Jeffree grunted. "Oh, they don't stint themselves at the top," he commented wryly. "Not in my experience."

"I do not remember the Bishop of Ganford's residence being quite so richly furnished as this."

Jeffree frowned. "I doubt you saw the inside of his bedchamber."

Sabina flushed. "Of course not!"

"Well, there you go, then. For all you know, old Risdale sleeps on satin sheets and eats off gold plates."

Sabina thought of the watery-eyed bishop with his bony hands and thinning hair and could not quite believe he lived so luxuriously behind closed doors. She was just trying to imagine him lying atop six feather ticks like a prince when the door creaked open. Half a dozen monks glided in and started industriously building the fire, pouring wine, and lighting the candlesticks.

None of them would meet Sabina's eyes or even draw down their hoods. Seeing her puzzled gaze, Jeffree beckoned to her. She hastened to his side. "Brother Michael is the only one permitted to speak," he murmured in her ear.

"Truly?"

He nodded. "This is a silent order."

Unsure what else to do, and feeling vastly out of place, Sabina plunked herself down into the chair beside her husband's. He poured her wine and she sipped at the goblet. It was not long before the fire was lit and the monks once more melted away.

"Do you suppose I am the first woman to sleep in this bedchamber?" she asked as the thought occurred to her.

"Most likely," Jeffree concurred, unfastening his cuffs. "Wash now, while the water is hot."

Sabina stood up and made her way to the carved table where the steaming basin and ewer stood. "This room is even fancier than your own at Ganford Chase," she commented, drawing out the pins to remove her headdress. Hearing a rustle and realizing he was stripping down to his braies, she held her tongue, removing her wimple and setting it to one side.

Her mind raced as she reached for the soap flakes. For some reason, it appeared Sir Jeffree wanted to keep her close. *Why?* Could it really be concern for her first time out of her home county? Or was this another aspect of his pursuing their supposed future together? She scrubbed her neck with the washcloth and ventured a glance over her shoulder. He had his back to her and was rolling the chausses down his muscular legs.

Sabina turned hastily back to the washbowl, her face hot. She needed to remember how she had determined to deal with him. What was her strategy? This was the problem, she thought as she dunked the cloth in the soapy bowl and wrung it out. He kept wrong-footing her and her plan kept flying out of the window.

Something about using Jeffree's contrariness against him, she recalled as she scrubbed her face. That was it. She would turn the tables on him, initiating intimacy and he would back away

223

in alarm. She flung down the cloth and squared her shoulders. Now was probably a good time to try it, before he started getting carried away with this idea that their marriage could...function.

Taking a deep breath, Sabina pivoted around. To her surprise, she found herself faced with the broad expanse of Jeffree's chest. "Oh!" She jumped back, slamming into the table and almost upsetting the bowl. "I did not—had not realized you were there," she blurted, sounding like a flustered idiot.

"Are you finished?" he asked coolly, lifting a blond brow at her. Sabina practically gnashed her teeth at his infuriating calm.

"Quite. I was going to empty out the water for you..." She trailed off.

"I can do it." He stepped up to the table, and Sabina scampered off like a scared rabbit to undress. Internally, she cursed herself. *Why, oh why do I keep getting discomposed?* She wasn't usually so timid. It was infuriating! She unlaced her boots and then her wrists and bodice as she took steadying breaths, reminding herself that she needed to stay calm and focused. Jeffree was the one who was going to be unsettled, not her!

By the time she had stepped out of her gown and draped it on the nearest chair, she had reined in her nerves once more. Blowing out the majority of the candles, she sat on the bed in her shift, unpinning her coiled braids. It was not until she had removed the very last pin that she realized Jeffree's eyes were on her. Turning her head, she saw that he was leaning his hip against the table and watching her as he rubbed a drying cloth over his head.

Did he dunk his whole head in the bowl? she wondered distractedly. And wasn't he cold stood there clad only in his braies? Giving herself a slight shake, she threw back the sumptuous bedcovers and slid under them. "Aren't you coming to bed?" she asked, sounding more challenging than seductive. Inwardly, she winced. She was useless at this. Hopefully, Jeffree was too inexperienced to notice.

Instead of answering, Jeffree discarded the cloth and crossed the floor, climbing into the opposite side. This time, the mattress was so vast there was no need for their limbs to touch. Typical, thought Sabina. The one time a small bed would have been useful and there was not one to be found. Turning her head on the pillow bearer, she found Jeffree already steadily contemplating her.

"Wh-what is it?" she croaked, sounding about as far from a siren as was possible.

"I want to…" Jeffree's words were gruff, his eyes studiously avoiding hers. "I want to touch your hair. Can I?"

Oh. "You want me to let it loose, you mean?" she asked. To her surprise, he shook his head. "You want to touch my braids?" Sabina tried not to show her surprise, but from his embarrassed expression, she guessed she had not entirely succeeded. "Of course, if you want to," she said quickly.

The words were barely out of her mouth before he slid across the mattress to her side. Sabina found herself holding her breath as he reached out a hand toward her, his fingers closing about one of her thick braids, gliding lightly over the pattern of woven strands. The look on his face was of total absorption as he followed the length of her braid from her ear to her waist. When he reached the end, he seemed to hesitate before wrapping it about his hand three times. He gave a light tug. "You have good hair. Strong," he added, still gazing at the braid looped about his hand.

Sabina stared at him. *Strong?* "Thank you?" she ventured.

225

"You could make a good rope out of it."

"A good rope?" Sabina echoed, incredulous. Really, she could make no meaningful response to that.

"The color too…is pleasing to my eye."

As the light brown shade of her hair was entirely commonplace, Sabina's mind scrambled to make sense of this. That was when a sudden suspicion dawned. Was he trying to pay her a compliment? She was so astonished by the notion that she simply lay there while he turned his fist about, seemingly admiring the way her hair looked wrapped around it.

"I can plait hair," he said suddenly. "I learned the trick from a groom." When she continued to look blank, he added, "In the stable."

"You mean," she ventured cautiously, "you have plaited a horse's tail or two in your time?" He nodded. "Well," she answered lightly. "Mayhap that skill will come in useful sometime if I should ever sprain my wrist and need assistance."

She had meant to be humorous, but Jeffree nodded in all solemnity. "You should let me weave a ribbon through it. To match your gown."

As Sabina's gowns were all faded and entirely lacking in ornamentation, she cast a quick, suspicious glance at him. Was he making sport of her? There was not so much as a glint in his eye. "Th-thank you," she stammered and, to her own horror, felt her cheeks start to grow red. She was not used to compliments, if that's what this even was.

"So will you?" he persisted.

"Will I what?"

He tugged her hair again, drawing her face closer to his own. "Will you let me plait your hair, Sabina?" Their faces were so close now, she could feel his breath mingling with her own. *Oh, my gods.* What was happening? She felt her expression waver. Was he seducing her now? Her throat grew dry. Seeing his interrogative look, she recalled he had asked something of her.

"If you wish it," she quavered, sounding half strangled to her own ear. His firm grip on her braid prevented her from pulling back even if she wanted to. Her every instinct was warning her this man was about to kiss her. His expression was so…intense, and the blue of his eyes so very, very blue. Sabina swallowed and Jeffree blinked, jerking his head back and unwinding her hair from his hand.

Sabina felt a ridiculous wave of crushing disappointment wash over her as he dropped back onto the mattress. He *had* been about to kiss her; she just knew it! Then at the last moment, he had pulled back. *Why?*

"Jeffree," she said before she could grow chicken-hearted. "Do you want to kiss me?"

"Yes," he growled at once.

"Why don't you, then?"

"My vow," he reminded her tersely, and she could *hear* the frown in his voice.

"Your vow?" she repeated blankly. "Your vow to remain chaste?"

"Aye."

"That includes kissing also?" she asked incredulously. He closed his eyes and huffed out a breath before nodding. "You

227

mean you have *never* kissed a woman in your twenty-eight years?"

"Of course not!" he answered crossly. "I am a man of my word."

Sabina considered this a moment in stunned silence. "You kissed the Lady Meliora though," she ventured uncertainly, "before committing yourself to lifelong chastity in her honor." When he said nothing, she fidgeted with the edge of the bedspread. "I suppose if you could not have her kisses, then you wanted no one else's."

The forlorn sound to her own words appalled her. Of course, she was meant to be *acting* as though she hankered for Jeffree's affection, but it was quite another thing to be getting wistful over the man!

He gave an exasperated huff. "Of course I did not kiss her! We were formally betrothed, and she was nobly born, not some…some *village girl*." He spoke the last two words with such a wealth of contempt that Sabina felt winded. Had she managed to forget for one moment what an arrogant pig he was? Averting her gaze from his affronted profile, she stared up at the ceiling instead.

Anywhere was better to direct her gaze at than the handsome swine lay in her bed. He was such an ass, she seethed. She felt more like kicking him than kissing him. Perhaps that was a good thing after all. She was blatantly ill-equipped to put him in his place; she must have been mad to have such a notion. Hitching the covers up to her neck, she rolled onto her side away from him, rapidly blinking.

"Good night," she muttered darkly, squeezing her eyes shut. He made no reply for a full minute and then he rolled into her back, making her eyes spring open.

228

"I was not comparing you to a village girl!" he said in a furious undertone that tickled her ear. "For gods' sakes! You are a Burrell of Tipton Hall. Why must you always be so…so prickly?"

Sabina struggled a moment to catch her breath. It was odd how his physical proximity affected her. "I am sure I have more in common with a village girl than your former betrothed!" she hissed, sucking in a breath when his hand covered her hip. For some reason, the fact he deigned to remember the name of her father's house had affected her strangely.

The clasp on her hip went from tentative to firm. "Oh really?" His voice was low and tense. "What does that mean?"

"It means that we Burrells are nothing like the high and mighty de Crecys!" she burst out, then paused suspiciously. "What did you think it meant? That I had spent my life sporting on the village green with all the lads and lasses?" When he did not answer immediately, she snorted. "You have already shown yourself to be well acquainted with parish gossip. You know full well that I am considered naught but an ill-tempered shrew!"

"And what of my local reputation?" he asked in gravelly tones. To Sabina's surprise, he sounded genuinely curious.

"Do you really want to know?" She turned her head to look up at him. He nodded at her, his eyes gleaming in the candlelight. "Very well, then, locally you are thought to be haughty, disagreeable, and proud as a devil."

He gave a short laugh. "Well, then, I suppose that makes us a matched pair."

Sabina caught her breath, but before she could voice a denial, he rolled her onto her back and swiftly covered her body with his own.

"Jeffree!" Her squeak made his eyes flash, but his big body pressing down on hers made her flesh feel terribly weak.

"You can give me the benefit of your experience," he growled. "You can give it to me now."

"What?" Sabina gazed up at him, half appalled and half something she did not even want to name.

"Show me what it is I should have experienced before renouncing it," he suggested, his eyes drifting from her face to contemplate her thick braids flung out on either side of her. He certainly liked her braids, she thought dazedly. More than liked. Something was pressing very insistently against her stomach. Something that both alarmed and astonished her.

"Wh-what of your vow?" she reminded him, wishing to gods she did not sound so nervous. When she licked her dry lips, he growled and leaned down into her. "Wait! W-wait!" Sabina whimpered like the biggest pea goose in existence.

"I'm tired of waiting," he said simply, and the next thing she knew his mouth was against hers, his lips soft, though exerting a steady pressure. Sabina's eyes drifted shut and her hands slid up the front of his chest. His warm and lightly furred chest. Jeffree made a strangled noise in his throat and jerked his head back to stare at her. "Well?" he huffed.

"Well?" Sabina echoed, gazing up at him. The fact the color had crept into his cheeks, and he sounded out of breath reassured her. *She* had the upper hand here, not Jeffree! At least she knew what she was doing. *Well, sort of.*

"Is that it?" he asked, his eyes dropping to her lips. "Is that what I've been missing?" Sabina almost rolled her eyes at his dismissive tone. Did he really think she would be taken in by this show of disinterest when the evidence of his arousal pressed so blatantly against her belly?

"Well…" she said contemplatively, lifting her hand from his chest to tap her finger to her chin. Jeffree made an involuntary sound of displeasure in his throat. She ignored it. If he had liked her hands where they were, he should not have pretended otherwise. "It was fairly typical as first kisses go," she answered with a shrug.

Jeffree's face froze. "First kisses?"

"You are a novice in the art after all."

"There's an art to kissing?" His words were pronounced with scorn, but Sabina was not fooled. There was too much heat in his gaze, and rather than retreating, if anything, he crowded closer to her.

She stifled a whimper in her throat. "Indeed," she continued coolly.

"Tutor me, then, wife."

Sabina caught her breath. "I am not sure that is a good idea," she admitted in a wobbly voice. "These things should proceed by increments. You have already skipped several stages."

Jeffree looked instantly affronted. "What stages?"

"You have not kissed my hand or even my cheek!" she pointed out with alacrity. "You have never paid me a compliment—"

"Yes, I have!" he interrupted swiftly.

231

Sabina halted. Oh yes, there had been that business about her hair being strong and pleasing to his eye. "Oh. Well, mayhap you have paid me a compliment," she admitted grudgingly. *Of sorts.* "But you have not praised me to my family or general acquaintance or made it known that you admire me."

Jeffree scowled. "Our courtship was not conducted along those lines," he reminded her needlessly and rolled off her with a suddenness that left Sabina blinking. "Is that what Hendry did?" he asked moodily.

Sabina concentrated on breathing steadily in and out. "Yes," she admitted lightly and bit her bottom lip to steady the wobbling.

"If I am not to contrast you unfavorably with Meliora, then I think the least you can do is spare me the comparison to Hendry."

Sabina swallowed past the lump in her throat. "I am sorry," she said stiffly. "But you asked me to give you the benefit of my experience, and the only experience I have is with my first husband."

They both lay there a moment, breathing loudly. Finally, Jeffree rolled out of the bed and blew out the remainder of the candles. Not another word was spoken betwixt them until morning.

*

"I have been considering the matter," Jeffree said without preamble, drawing his horse alongside her own. They had been riding now for two hours since leaving the priory, and this was the first time he had addressed her.

"Yes?" she replied cautiously.

"I want you to carry on to Longacre with the Vyses and give this tournament a miss."

232

Sabina gasped, turning in her saddle to stare at him. "What? But why?" she demanded, as though attending one of his miserable tournaments was the dearest wish of her heart!

He was silent, and Sabina noticed his ears turning red. "I would have thought it obvious," he answered grudgingly. "Sharing a bed with you, before I've been absolved of my vow, is not a good idea any longer." Sabina opened her mouth to say she was perfectly fine with separate beds when he added gruffly, "I'm struggling. Why do you suppose I left our bed at the crack of dawn the last two days?"

"We could have slept in separate beds last night without anyone raising an eyebrow!" she pointed out. "You were the one who insisted we shared."

Jeffree's jaw worked a moment. "I don't like being separated from you. This will be hard on me. Can you not try and be a little understanding?"

Sabina's mouth snapped shut with astonishment. He was struggling? He did not like being separated from her? He wanted her *understanding*? She shifted in her saddle as she took this in.

"Besides," he added with a return to his usual arrogance, "having thought about it, I have already fulfilled all but two of the terms of courtship you spoke of last night. I can complete my tournament, fetch you from Longacre, and journey to Fulford Abbey with a clear conscience."

Sabina drew in a sharp breath and turned to give him her full attention. What was he about now? "How ever did you come to that conclusion?" she asked, stunned.

"I have paid you a compliment; you agree on that score."

233

Sabina pulled a face. "Aye, you paid me a compliment of such rarity I doubt any woman has heard its like before."

He ignored her sardonic tone, lowering his voice. "When I did not contradict your outrageous claims in my uncle's Great Hall, that could be taken as a public acknowledgment of my admiration," he continued.

Sabina gasped at this brazenness. "It was no such thing!" she protested.

"I allowed everyone to think I had been sneaking around and climbing through windows to receive your favors," he pointed out coolly. "Rest assured, among my family and acquaintances, that would be taken as extremely aberrant behavior."

"I am sure it would!" Sabina spluttered. "Such behavior would not necessarily stem from admiration though!" Her irritated expression gave way to one of sudden curiosity. "Out of interest, why was it you did not immediately refute Sir Leland's claims? Was it really outrage that tied your tongue so tightly?"

She watched the color climb in his cheeks. "We have already discussed this," he said in clipped tones. "I was too shocked to react with speed to what was happening. I readily admit my wits are not as sharp as your own." From his curled lip, he made her quick wit sound more like an insult.

"Probably from all your years of being a stuffed shirt," Sabina murmured, just loud enough for him to hear.

Other than a swift frown, this, too, he disregarded with a wave of his hand. "As for the praise to your family, the fact I married you is the highest praise a man can bestow on a woman. Your mother at least seemed sensible of the great honor done to your family."

234

Words failing her at this point, Sabina had to console herself by glaring at him in disbelief and clasping the reins so tight in her hands that her palms would likely wear their mark. Perhaps being separated from Jeffree for two whole days would not be such a bad thing. "Have you asked your mother if she is willing to forego the tournament and instead play hostess to me for its duration?" she enquired coldly.

"Not yet. I doubt she will be much disappointed. She has never shown any enthusiasm to see me compete before."

Sabina, remembering Lady Maud's true objective in attending the tournament, felt her heart sink. She had not yet secured Jeffree's word that he would train his brothers for squirehood. How was she supposed to bring that about now? She glanced over to the cart where the boys were once more intertwined with the dogs.

"It seems almost a shame they must be parted," Sabina murmured.

Jeffree followed her gaze and huffed. "Do you have any idea how much money I spent reclaiming those dogs for you?" he demanded testily.

"No," she admitted, "though I suspect it was a good deal. They are beautiful dogs. It's just…I feel they do belong with the boys." As soon as she had said it aloud, she realized it was true. Taking a deep breath, Sabina took a reckless plunge. "What if we were to gift the dogs to your brothers and I took the gesture in lieu of your show of public admiration?" she suggested, avoiding his eye.

"Say that again?"

"Then, if you were to agree to take both boys as your squires within the next twelve months or so, the dogs would be residing with us for the most part in any case."

Jeffree made a choked sound. "I will agree to no such thing! Take the pair of them as squires? I have never wanted one squire, let alone two! As for my brothers…" Words seemed to fail him.

"I think it is the least you can do," Sabina answered truthfully. "They are your close kin, and Crispin is clearly unsuited for the priesthood, whatever Sir Dudley may think."

Jeffree spluttered. "They are still too young to leave home anyway. Crispin is practically an infant!" he objected. "And in any case, Osborn sees to my needs adequately. I have never felt the need of a squire."

Sabina glanced toward his manservant, Osborn, who was sat in his saddle like a sack of turnips. Thus far she had not been terribly impressed with Osborn. To her mind, he had a shifty eye and a disobliging manner. "Is not the training of a squire seen as a noble duty?" she persisted. "The passing on the mantle of knighthood to another generation? I would have thought you would have leaped at the chance."

Jeffree bristled and stared stonily straight ahead. "You know very little of the matter, madam."

"I freely admit as much," she replied. "So why don't you explain to me how you are *not* beholden to pass the torch on to your younger brothers?"

Jeffree snorted. "As always, you express yourself with great vigor; however, this line of argument will not catch your quarry. Instead, I suggest you set your snare with the other bait you mentioned."

236

Sabina's ears pricked up. "What other bait?" she asked, even as his meaning dawned on her. *Oh.* She glanced about uneasily. For a moment, she had wondered if they were quite out of everyone's earshot. Lady Maud had cast a quick look over her shoulder that had put Sabina on her guard. "You mean…your meeting the terms of courtship?" she all but hissed at him.

He gave a short nod. "We need to be in agreement as to which point we have reached, wife. Apparently, I believe myself further along the path than you do."

Sabina felt herself turn a little pink. She cleared her throat. "If you were to make this gesture," she said slowly, "then I would accept that you have shown me public admiration and"—she added with only the smallest choke in her voice—"praised me in front of my family." When his eyebrows rose at this, she added self-consciously, "After all, the Vyses are my family now by marriage, are they not?"

Jeffree made no immediate reply. Instead, he frowned down at his horse's mane a moment. "If I agree to the undertaking in principle, it will still be some time before the boys are of an appropriate age to come under my custodianship." Sabina nodded, considering that, very likely, Jeffree knew more about the common age of squires than she. "You would trust me to keep to my word?"

She gave him a long, hard stare before nodding warily again. "If you declared your intent to your mother and stepfather now…" She trailed off. "After all, you have given me no reason to doubt your word."

He looked across quickly at that, their gazes meeting. He gave a nod and spurred on his horse to move up front to where Lady Maud and Sir Dudley were riding. Sabina let out her breath before dropping back to ride beside Githa's cart. She made no mention of the matter but conversed with the boys, who were inclined to be mournful about the impending parting of ways.

"There now, Master Jasper, Master Crispin, don't 'ee tell me you ain't going to be glad to see your own home!" Githa chided. "Why, I've never heard the like!"

"I thought we were going straight to Areley Kings," Jasper mumbled, tightening his arm about Brisis.

Sabina noticed the glitter of tears in Crispin's eyes which he wiped surreptitiously against Feste's neck. Her heart went out to them. "If it is any consolation, I do not think I am going to Areley Kings either," she told them.

"What do you mean?" they clamored.

"Your brother has just informed me I am to go to Longacre with you."

"Come to Longacre?" Crispin cried joyfully.

"We will make you right welcome there," Jasper vowed, his mood lifting instantly. "We can show you all the places we have made mention of."

"Have you told them?" Jeffree's voice broke through the babble as he steered his mighty horse beside her own.

Sabina shook her head. "Only about Areley Kings. I thought I should wait until you had struck the bargain with their parents."

"Told us what?" Jasper asked, shooting a glance at his brother and sitting up straighter.

"What bargain?" asked Crispin.

"Your sister-in-law is gifting you her dogs," Jeffree said without preamble. "As a precursor to both of you training as my squires within the next twelvemonth."

Crispin let out a yell as Jasper's mouth dropped open. Within moments they were hanging over the side of the cart and grasping for Sabina's hand.

"Feste is to be mine?" Crispin cried, squeezing her fingers.

Sabina smiled. "Feste is to be yours and Brisis is to be Jasper's."

"And we are to be squires?" Jasper demanded, his brown eyes shining. "Both of us? Crispin doesn't have to join the seminary?"

Crispin's expression was painful in its intensity. "Father has agreed?"

Sabina turned to look at Jeffree for confirmation. "It is all agreed," he said with solid reassurance.

Sabina's wrung hand was released, her shoulders relaxed, and she let the boys' happy prattle wash over her. At one point, her mother-in-law looked back over her shoulder and their eyes met. Lady Maud nodded ever so faintly and gave one of her thin-lipped smiles.

Sabina nodded back in acknowledgment but wondered at the wisdom of the bargain she had struck. Very likely she had won Jasper's and Crispin's unswerving loyalty for life, but Jeffree was quite a different matter. With him, she really had no idea where she stood.

They reached Lanyan's Cross by midday and an awkward leave-taking followed whereby Jeffree insisted on drawing her to one side from the others. "I will come for you in three days, wife," he said, clearing his throat. Sabina nodded. "Have you nothing else to say to me?"

Sabina thought a moment. "I wish you joy in your jousting?" she ventured. His annoyed face told her she had not hit on the correct sentiment. "A safe journey, then." He continued to glare balefully at her. "Well, then, I hope you sleep better contented without me there to discompose you, Sir Jeffree," she suggested instead with a barbed tongue and saw his eyes narrow.

"Careful, wife. Three days is not a long time," he cautioned her gruffly and took her by surprise by reaching out, seizing hold of her wrist, and dragging her hand to his face. Sabina's breath caught in her throat as Jeffree pressed his lips to her fingers and seemed in no hurry to get the gesture over with.

"That's another of your conditions met," he reminded her as he finally released her hand, not quite meeting her eyes.

"Yes," Sabina agreed dazedly, still feeling the tickle of his short beard against her tingling hand.

"I will kiss your cheek when I collect you," he promised.

Sabina practically whimpered. There would be no conditions left he had not met after that, and once he was finally released from his vow... Well, then there would no longer be any obstacles to their wedded lives.

She cast a quick glance around at the Vyses, who were all calmly watching them with interest. "We need to part," she reminded him unsteadily. She had a horrible feeling her face was scarlet by this point. Jeffree made a rumbling noise, but whether it was of agreement or displeasure she had no notion. Instead, she turned and stumbled back toward her in-laws' party. Hadley, their manservant, helped her back up into her saddle, but she could feel Jeffree's eyes on her the whole time, right up until they disappeared from his view.

14

Three days is not a long time, that was what he had told her, but the time that followed had seemed interminable to Jeffree. The tournament could not hold his interest. His biggest rivals did not even trouble to show.

Vawdrey, the so-called King's Champion, had chosen instead to celebrate the birth of his first child to garnering glory in the ring. Lord Kentigern was apparently otherwise engaged, preparing for marriage to some rich merchant's daughter.

Orde was there, brash as ever, and brandishing some new northern title, but he seemed more interested in squiring his pregnant wife about than squaring up to his opposition. It seemed no one could be depended on to show the proper dedication to the sport, apart from him. Not that was until Armand de Bussell showed up with the late northern princess on his arm.

De Bussell was unaccustomedly steadfast for once in his lackadaisical life, disturbingly so. If Jeffree had ever been asked for epithets to describe Sir Armand, he would have used words like *lax*, *blasé*, and *apathetic*. De Bussell swaggered through life with seemingly little effort, using his charm and easy manners to get what he wanted and rarely exerting himself to make it to the final of anything.

Jeffree wasn't sure what the hell was going on with de Bussell these days; he only knew that he barely recognized him in the competitor who turned up that year at Areley Kings. After three days of a damned hard slog, Jeffree managed to make it to the final two in the main event. He was not even surprised to find it was de Bussell facing him down the length of the field. It seemed practically an inevitability by this point.

As did his ignominious defeat. He could not even feel particularly robbed as he lay rolling in the dust, gasping for breath. He had lost to the better man on the day. He limped back to his pavilion, extricated himself from his battered armor, and ordered Osborn to pack their things without delay. If he left now, he could be at Longacre by nightfall. Sabina had spent three nights without him, and he had no intention of making it four.

True, he had thought sleeping in the same bed was torture, but in truth, he was not now sure that sleeping in a bed without her was any better. When sleep finally had taken him each night, his thoughts had been a confused jumble of unaccustomed longings and honey-colored braids. He would not stand for one more miserable minute of it.

Osborn grumbled and griped, but Jeffree had refused to tarry. Indeed, an emissary of Lord Blandivar's had had to chase him down the road, brandishing his winnings as first runner-up. He had forgotten the purse, forgotten everything other than his urgent need to reclaim his wife.

Luckily, everyone knew he frequently skipped the crowning banquet of these events, so no one would remark on his hasty exit. At least he hoped not. His reputation was something he did prize after all. Funny how he thought of it only now that Osborn was regarding him doubtfully and shaking his head.

"Something to say, Osborn?" he snapped.

His servant huffed out a great sigh. "Things isn't what they used to be, Sir Jeffree."

Jeffree bit back his instinctive retort as beneath him. Perhaps replacing Osborn with a squire would not be such a bad thing after all.

243

They reached Longacre long after a decent hour for visitors. Still, Jeffree reflected, he could be considered family by some small stretch. He was let in by a servant, who appeared to know he was expected, and led him into a narrow gallery room where Sir Dudley was sat poring over an account ledger.

He looked up at Jeffree with some surprise. "Ah, Jeffree," he exclaimed. "We did not expect you until the morrow."

For a moment, Jeffree considered voicing his most pressing concern, namely the whereabouts of his wife. Then better manners prevailed, and he grudgingly asked after his mother and responded that yes, he had fared well enough at his tournament. To his surprise, Sir Dudley seemed disinclined to be rid of him, but instead, stepped out into the corridor to call a servant for some wine.

"If you don't mind, I'd like a few words about Jasper and Crispin," his stepfather said, coming back into the room, and with a sigh, Jeffree took a seat and listened to half an hour of lecturing about the care and instruction of boys. At the conclusion of it, Sir Dudley stopped pacing and sat back in his seat. "You look surprised, Jeffree, by my parental anxieties."

Jeffree set his empty goblet back down. "I admit, I am a little taken aback," he admitted. "But then I have no sons."

"And you had no father to worry over you," Sir Dudley agreed. "It was made perfectly clear to me that I was to exercise little influence over you in that regard."

"Who made that plain?" Jeffree asked, startled. "My mother?"

"Gods no," his stepfather answered. "She found it hard enough to make her own voice heard where your upbringing was concerned!" He paused. "Your uncle, Bevis, and your

244

godfather, Sir Charles, made it very plain that they were to be the ones to steer you on your path in life."

Jeffree brooded over this a moment. "I do not recall their being much involved in the five years I spent with Sir Hereward," he said dryly.

"You did not enjoy your own training?" Sir Dudley asked, looking concerned.

"I learned all the skills necessary," Jeffree said, clearing his throat. "Including precisely what kind of knight I did *not* want to be." The last part slipped out. He had not intended to say it.

Sir Dudley looked troubled. "I am not familiar with Sir Hereward Acker," he confessed. "I understand the Ackers are an old family with a respected lineage." When Jeffree said nothing, his expression of concern deepened. "He was not a congenial master?"

"He was a drunkard, a womanizer, and a bully," Jeffree answered truthfully. After all, what was the point in tiptoeing around it? He had thought as much for years.

Sir Dudley's hand froze in the act of refilling Jeffree's cup. "Did you not tell your guardians as such?"

Jeffree shrugged. "I may have intimated my disgust of Sir Hereward to my godfather," he admitted. "But Charles was never in ignorance of Acker's personal morals. He believed I needed to learn how to exist alongside such men. In the event of battle, of war, you will need to exist cheek by jowl with them. As for Uncle Bevis"—Jeffree shrugged again—"he leads a very sheltered life. The fact that Acker's great-great-grandmother was sister to a duke was all that concerned him."

"Good gods. You never complained to your mother?"

245

"Certainly not. We both know there was little she could have done in the situation. It would only have worried her."

Sir Dudley sat back in his chair and rubbed his brow. "I cannot imagine Jasper dealing with a bullying master. I should not wish to imagine it."

"Well, Jasper will not have to. I am many things, but I do not think—"

"I never thought that of you," Dudley interrupted him swiftly. "Only that, you are not…not"—he floundered a moment and Jeffree watched him with interest—"the most tolerant of boisterous high spirits when it comes to young people," he said carefully.

"Well, I have not much experience in that field."

Dudley gave him a considering look. "Your wife is very good with them," he said at last.

"Yes."

"It was a kind gesture, giving them the dogs."

Jeffree almost snorted. "And how have you found them these past few days?"

"Disruptive," his stepfather answered heavily, and Jeffree stretched out his legs before him and hid his answering smile behind his hand. "The boys expect them to be fed the best cuts of meat," Sir Dudley complained, "and for them to sleep upon their beds every night."

"I expect they do."

"You will let them sleep thus when they live with you, I expect."

246

"Most likely. So long as I do not have to suffer the dogs upon my own bed, I will not care."

His stepfather nodded resignedly. "I think Crispin is too young to come to you next year, but he will be the very devil to appease if left here without Jasper."

"Then let him come. Ten is young for a squire, but not unheard of."

Sir Dudley did not say anything for a moment, but finally, he nodded. "I believe I will," he sighed at last. "But unlike *your* guardians, I will expect to be kept well-informed and will drop in to check on their progress," he warned.

Jeffree nodded. "I would expect nothing less."

"And I will want them home with us on high feast days."

"That was customary even in my day."

Dudley rose to his feet. "Shall we shake hands on the bargain?" he suggested. Jeffree grasped his hand and Sir Dudley cleared his throat. "I will have you shown abovestairs; you must want to change out of your traveling clothes. Sabina is in the yellow bedchamber, but perhaps you should not wish to disturb her at this advanced hour…?"

"I will be disturbing her," Jeffree answered without hesitation.

His father-in-law's eyebrows rose. "In that case, perhaps you should wash first. There is a small room opposite. I will have a servant fetch you hot water to wash and then lead you up to her."

Sir Dudley was as good as his word, and by the time Jeffree stood outside Sabina's bedchamber, he was clean and divested of his outer garments, candlestick in hand. He opened the door carefully and found the glow from the fireplace and two

247

guttered candlesticks above it still reasonably illuminated the room.

Sabina was lying in the middle of the bed on her side with her face turned into the pillow bearer. Quickly, Jeffree blew out the candle and set it down on a convenient table and stripped down to his braies. It was a matter of mere moments before he joined her beneath the sheets, wrapping an arm about her waist. She stirred and turned her head toward him making a sleepy sound of interrogation.

"It's me."

She sighed and lowered her head again. "What time is it?"

"Late. Almost midnight. Go back to sleep."

To his surprise, she complied almost immediately. Sleep took much longer to come for Jeffree, but as he had spent the last three nights staring at the ceiling of his pavilion with unaccustomed need gnawing at his gut, he felt strangely content to lie where he was. As he lay there, feeling the warmth of her body seeping into his own, he contemplated a future which held restoring a glorified hunting lodge to some semblance of order and taking his troublesome brothers under his wing. He faced both eventualities with surprising equanimity. Strange, it was all...very...strange.

Even the chilling prospect of having to get his vow rescinded failed to disturb the sense of calm that overtook him as he finally drifted to sleep at Sabina's side.

*

The previous night's serenity was shattered the next morning when Jeffree was wakened abruptly by the combined efforts of boys and dogs leaping on the bed with loud yells and whooping

cries. It was small consolation to see how both his brothers'
faces fell to find him in the bed beside their sister-in-law.

"My gods, was this how they wakened you every morning?" he
groaned as the chastened boys hurried off to break their fast,
their dogs following on behind, wholly unrepentant.

"No." Sabina shook her head and yawned. "I think it was only
because today is my last day here. They meant it for a special
send-off. After breakfast, they intend to lead me on a farewell
tour of Longacre."

Jeffree's displeasure deepened. "We need to set out directly for
Fulford Abbey this morn."

"I thought you said it was not far?"

"A day's ride only," he agreed. "But we want to reach there
before nightfall."

"Oh." Sabina looked thoughtful. "You do not think it would be
more expedient if you approached the Lady Meliora without me
in tow?"

"That would be most improper. Besides, the *Mother Abbess*"—
he made sure to stress the change of Meliora's title—"does not
receive male visitors alone."

Sabina formed a soundless *oh* with her lips and turned back to
fastening the laces at her bodice.

Over the course of their morning meal, Jeffree witnessed just
how effortlessly his wife appeared to have fitted into life at
Longacre in a mere three days. His mother, who rarely rose
before ten, deigned to appear a whole hour before that, and
what's more, asked if he might not leave "dear Sabina" with
them while he competed in his "nasty tournaments" over the
summer.

249

"For she would not be any bother here," Lady Maud continued graciously. "Indeed, Dudley and I are growing most accustomed to having her about the place. She is quite one of the family."

Sir Dudley, perhaps deducing Jeffree's answer was about to be forcefully given, interrupted hastily here to draw his wife's attention to some pressing household matter.

"You have exactly one hour for your farewell tour," Jeffree growled at Sabina. "And not one minute longer."

"Oh no, Jeffree de Crecy, you do not get off the hook that easily!" she assured him. "You are coming with us."

"I am?"

"He is?" He fancied his brothers' cries held as much dismay as his own.

Sabina unfurled a grubby and smudged-looking map. "The boys have been so kind as to make me a treasure map to complete along the way," she said. "And if you think I can decipher clues and map-read at the same time as trudging the grounds of Longacre, all within limiting time constraints, then you have a touching faith in my abilities which I do not share."

Jasper and Crispin exchanged smug looks. "He can help you if he wants," said Jasper with a shrug.

"Much good may he do you!" Crispin gurgled with mirth.

Jeffree sent them a quelling look. "Give it here," he said, taking the ink-splattered map from Sabina. "Perilous Lake," he read, then lowered the map. "Have you a lake?"

"We have a fishpond," his stepfather answered doubtfully. A bout of furious whispers passed between his brothers.

250

Sabina leaned forward. "You have to view their estate through the eyes of a boy," she murmured in his ear. "A fishpond becomes a lake. A dovecote, an impenetrable fortress, and an orchard, a vast forest."

Instead of asking her what she knew about the imaginings of small boys, Jeffree lifted the map again and scanned it. "Seems straightforward enough," he announced with insouciance. He had never lacked for confidence. At this, his brothers leaped up from their seats with battle cries and ran from the room, practically tripping over their own feet in their haste.

"Jasper! Crispin!" their father called sternly after them as the dogs bolted from under the table to chase them out.

Consequently, it was not until midday that they finally managed to take their leave of the Vyses. The boys were jubilant after leading them on a merry chase over field and down dale, culminating finally in a digging contest. Jasper was muddied after overbalancing on a ditch, and Crispin's tunic was torn after an impromptu bout of wrestling.

Sabina was now the proud possessor of a broken buckle in the shape of a lion's head, which had turned out to be the hidden treasure. "I shall have it mended," she announced to their satisfaction. "For it is a very fine buckle and would handsomely adorn any belt." Jeffree regarded it doubtfully but refrained from comment as she tucked it into one of his saddlebags.

To his surprise, Sabina was hugged about the waist by both boys, who then turned expectantly to him. He tousled Crispin's curly head and clapped Jasper on the shoulder as his mother and stepfather hovered nearby.

"We shall expect an invitation," his mother called, "once you have your household in order."

251

Jeffree darted a glance at Sabina, but as she was bidding a farewell to the dogs, it was possible she had not heard the alarming remark. He lifted her up onto her saddle and they were off, with Osborn following on behind.

They made good progress, and by early evening were within a mile or so of the abbey.

"It is lucky we left when we did," Jeffree remarked. "Or we should never have got here before nightfall."

"You were having far too much fun to tear yourself away any earlier," Sabina responded.

Jeffree cleared his throat. "Nonsense, we could not leave until we had found the prize."

"Oh, of course not!" she agreed gravely, though her eyes twinkled. "That would not have been sportsmanlike."

"Do you really mean to have that ugly thing mounted on a belt? The boys must surely have found it somewhere discarded." He threw her a disparaging look. "It looks more like a gargoyle than a lion."

Sabina smiled. "I like unusual things," she answered lightly.

"Is that why you dress the way you do?" He realized he had made a mistake as soon as he said it.

She stiffened and the laughter died right out of her eyes. "I suppose it must be," she answered flatly.

Inwardly he cursed himself for shattering the momentary goodwill betwixt them. "I only meant—" He flailed a moment, suddenly loath to say the wrong thing. "Those dresses no longer fit your station," he settled on uneasily. She said nothing, though Jeffree waited longer than he usually would for someone to respond.

"You must allow me to provide you suitable clothing," he concluded finally. "My mother has given me a de Crecy family necklace and ring. If you were to wear them with your present garb, they would look incongruous."

"I agree," she said finally. "You should save them."

"Save them?"

"For someone more appropriate."

"What does that mean?" he asked sharply. "They are for you, no one else." She shook her head but remained stubbornly mute. "What do you mean, no? 'Tis you are my wife, none other."

When she simply sat like a stone, he reined in his horse, wheeling it about and blocking her path. "Sabina?"

She huffed. "I don't want any dresses from you, Jeffree, nor jewels neither!"

"And why not?"

"Because," she flung at him, "we were wed under duress and there is little point in my trying and failing to play the grand lady! You need to simply accept that your wife is a perfect nobody and abandon her in the country. That is where she belongs and where she is happiest and that is all there is to be said on that score!" She sat a moment, trying to catch her breath after her outburst, and he stared at her.

"I am never going to match up to you as some paragon or perfect beauty, Jeffree," she continued in a calmer voice. "And what is more, I refuse to even try! I would look *ridiculous* trying to be something I patently am not!" Suddenly the fight seemed to go out of her, and she slumped in her saddle. "As for the jewels… Mayhap you should donate them to the abbey?"

she suggested. "'Tis Lady Meliora should have been the true recipient in any case."

That last rejoinder was the one that made him finally lose his temper. "Lady Meliora was *never* a de Crecy as you are!" he flung back hotly.

"Well, neither am I a de Crecy!"

"Yes, you are! Damn it, stop testing me!"

"In name only…" she persisted and broke off when they both heard a hoof fall behind them and realized the trailing manservant had caught up with them.

"Osborn, I want you to ride now into the town and secure a room for us at the nearest inn," he said in clipped tones.

Osborn's habitually injured air deepened. "I fort we was headed for that there abbey?" he objected, raising a pudgy finger to point at the distant silhouette of the towered convent, for it was now dusk.

"Well, obviously there has been a change of plan!" Jeffree snapped back, wondering for the thousandth time why he had never thrown Osborn out on his ear. "*We* are going now to the abbey. *You* are going to the nearby town. I seem to remember an inn near a bakery when I stayed five years ago." He reached below his saddle and threw a purse of money at him. "Take two rooms and order supper and a bath for one hour's time."

Osborn caught the purse and sniffed. Sabina would not look at him at all. With a muttered curse, Jeffree once more wheeled Radax's large and bulky form around and spurred him onto a brisker pace. After a moment or two, Blitha matched it and they headed with a new urgency toward the looming spire of the convent.

254

Radax was not built for anything but short bursts of speed, not with his bulk, but he was built for endurance. Neither Jeffree nor Sabina spoke a word for the next quarter of an hour as they drew closer and closer to their destination.

As they rode, Jeffree's mood continued to simmer on a steady boil. She would not permit him to dress her appropriately; she did not consider herself his wife in truth, though she might be in fact. Well, all that nonsense would be at an end shortly.

He would be released from the vow, which had grown so cumbersome of late, and there would be no impediment standing in the way of his—words failed him—*happiness*? Startled, he turned the word over in his mind suspiciously. Nay, that could not be the word he'd intended. He would ne'er believe he could be precisely *happy* with such a wife. He just knew he would be miserable as hell without her. The last three days had convinced him of that.

He cast a quick look at her stony expression, nose in the air as she rode along beside him. What the hells did she mean by claiming she was no grand lady? She was the proudest woman he knew, only look at her now, daring to flout him to his face! He bit back a curse and focused on the approaching stone walls.

There was a stout door on the east wall, and he made for that now in the failing light, dismounting when he saw it and banging on it hard. When this brought about no immediate action, he banged on it again, so hard he was not surprised to hear approaching footsteps. A small section of wood shot back and a wimpled face appeared behind it.

"The hour is late," the voice scolded. "This place closes its doors to pilgrims at dusk."

"It is dusk now," Jeffree insisted, though when he glanced up at the sky, night was indeed falling fast.

The holy sister grumbled something and then he heard the clank of heavy keys. As soon as the door swung open, he led both Radax and Blitha into the courtyard.

The elderly nun looked him up and down with disfavor. "You are seeking a roof for the night?"

"We are not. We seek an immediate audience with the abbess."

The old woman looked shocked. "The Reverend Mother? You could never hope to see her on such short notice. You must return in the morning."

"Certainly not. We will see her now," Jeffree assured her coolly. "I have made several large donations to this establishment over the years and could be reasonably be seen in the light of a long-standing patron."

This made the nun pause. She cast another look over Jeffree's costly raiment. "May I take our kind benefactor's name?" she enquired.

"Certainly, I am Sir Jeffree de Crecy."

If the name meant anything to her, she did not show it. Instead, she inclined her head. "Will your servant remain here with the horses?" she asked, glancing up at Sabina, who had remained silent and seated on her horse during the exchange.

"My *wife* will accompany me," Jeffree corrected her sharply. "Where is your stable?"

The old nun gestured vaguely in the direction of an outbuilding not far away. Reaching up, Jeffree caught Blitha's halter and led both horses toward the stable. On arriving, Sabina hurriedly dismounted, not waiting for his aid as she usually did. Wordlessly, he led both horses inside and saw them into stalls before rejoining her.

256

The old nun ushered them up the path to the abbey and ushered them inside.

15

Sabina sat on the hard bench and seethed as she waited for Jeffree to emerge from his private interview with his former betrothed. So much for her essential presence, she thought crossly. The Reverend Mother had requested Sir Jeffree's presence alone in her inner sanctum.

Not that she cared one bit, she told herself, folding her arms across her chest and shifting on the uncomfortable seat. She had *never* wanted to come on this fool's errand, she reminded herself grimly. Listening to Jeffree grovel to the woman who had a prior claim on him was not likely to afford her any pleasure. Stupid man. *Infuriating* man.

Her sense of injury grew. How dare he put her through this? He knew her background full well, for she had told him of it herself. Yet *still*, he expected her to sit here and wait for him while he fawned over this precious Meliora woman. It was too much.

It was one thing for a man to have a first love, but for her then to be practically *sanctified* in his memory… She broke off her thoughts impatiently. She had never been going to match up in any case; it was foolish of her to be sat here fizzing with indignation. Still, part of her had expected Jeffree to drag her in there with him, displaying his customary ill grace, loudly proclaiming her as his wife.

Instead, there had been that awkward look he had bestowed on her, looking so *sheepish* and irresolute. How dare he look like that? Like he was torn between the two of them. Her cheeks heated. *Was he not married to me now?* Had he not made vows in her presence too?

The thought almost sent her shooting off the bench. What were they doing? *Reminiscing?* He had been gone at least five minutes now. She stared at the door as though she could fling it open by sheer force of will alone. She wanted to march in there, grab him by the ear, and drag him back out again. Her chest rose and fell.

What if they were in an embrace? Her breath froze in her lungs. She had walked into such scenes before with her first husband. Would Jeffree spring guiltily apart and start talking boisterously and loudly with a false booming laugh and then grow angry at her refusal to play along with his game of appearances? Her spirits plummeted, and at that precise moment, Jeffree came barreling out of the door.

"She wants to see you now," he pronounced, looking thunderous. Oh, she did, did she? Sabina's chest rose and fell again. She stood up from the bench and stalked over to the door. "Sabina…" Jeffree started, but she did not wait to hear whatever it was he had to say. Instead, she flung the door open, then slammed it shut after her.

She might as well see what the saintly Meliora was made of. To her astonishment, instead of an ethereal beauty sat behind the desk, she found instead a tall and dark woman with a hawklike nose and very cold eyes.

The other woman placed down her pen and sat back in her chair. She wore a heavy wimple of starched white linen which revealed a dark widow's peak and a high forehead. Her intelligent gaze scrutinized Sabina a moment in silence.

"Sir Jeffree hath requested that I free him from his vow." Her voice was deep and commanding but not unattractive. "It seems rather a moot point as he has already married you," she added

259

dryly. "But then, I find it entirely typical of the male point of view."

Sabina opened her mouth and then closed it again on whatever retort she had been about to make. "Did you free him?" she heard herself ask with grudging curiosity.

Meliora's brows rose. "Tell me what difference would it make, either way?"

"None to me," Sabina responded before she could stop herself. "But Jeffree, like many men, loves a grand gesture."

The other woman gave a rich, deep laugh, and suddenly Sabina found herself imagining the Lady Meliora in clothes other than her plain black habit. In velvets and jewels, she would cut an equally impressive figure. She would have been a handsome girl at eighteen, Sabina thought. Especially to a boy of fifteen. Handsome, rather than pretty.

A wry smile curved up one side of the Reverend Mother's mouth. "You are weighing me up, Lady de Crecy," she said slowly.

"That must be a novel experience for you. I don't imagine many people have the nerve to do that in your presence," Sabina replied and earned another husky laugh in response. Meliora was attractive still, Sabina realized with a pang. Maybe Jeffree's devotion was not so hard to understand after all.

"Hmmm." The other woman nodded, picking up a paperweight and turning it over in her hands. She had elegant hands, long and white. "Jeffree said you were a widow I think?" she ruminated.

"Yes," Sabina admitted.

"That must have given you some advantage. Some experience of married life to draw upon."

"I suppose so," Sabina agreed, though privately, she doubted it.

"Even so, I cannot imagine you find Sir Jeffree an easy spouse to manage."

Sabina's chin rose. *Manage?* "You speak of him rather as though he were a horse, Reverend Mother."

"I suppose I do," the other agreed musingly. "I am a good horsewoman," she said, rising from her seat and making her way toward the window. "But I never could brook any disobedience or deviation from my will." She stood looking out over the fields a moment before looking back over her shoulder.

"On my seventeenth birthday, my father bought me a very fine stallion, of purest blood and pedigree. I was the envy of the neighborhood." For a moment Sabina actually thought she was talking about Jeffree.

Then Meliora continued, "Anaska was his name. He balked once at jumping a hedge I put him to and sent me in a fury with him. Three times I turned him back and urged him on, and finally he threw me, rather than take it." Meliora paused heavily before continuing. "That horse saved my life, for later it turned out that the river had burst its banks, and if he had jumped, we would have ended in a flooded ditch."

She turned about to face Sabina. "But I still insisted my father sell him, for I could not forgive his disobedience. Every time I looked at that horse, I remembered how he had dared to defy me. Tell me, do you think that was contrary of me?"

"I think it was absolutely ridiculous behavior!" Sabina answered with spirit.

261

Meliora looked contemptuously amused. "Yes, I imagine someone like you would struggle to understand such a thing," she conceded.

"Do you know," Sabina said, leaning forward in her seat. "Until this moment, I thought Jeffree was the most ludicrously proud person I had ever met." She looked the other woman over impassively. "You would have made a truly *terrible* couple," she said wonderingly as the realization dawned. "Beautiful," she admitted, imagining a portrait of the two of them, both so tall and handsome. "But I'll wager you would have been estranged within a twelvemonth."

Again, Meliora's eyes flashed with humor, and she gave a dry laugh. "More than likely," she concurred. "Dear me, you are not at all what I had imagined when Sir Jeffree came in here all rampaging emotion." She rose and crossed to a small refectory table where she decanted a gold filigree bottle and poured out two glasses of dark red fluid. "You will take a glass with me, Lady Sabina?" As she had already poured, it was not so much a question as a statement.

When Meliora placed the glass beside her, Sabina found herself murmuring her thanks.

Meliora resumed her seat and gazed at her over the top of her glass. "When I imagined Jeffree's matrimonial future, I had pictured him succumbing to someone quite different."

Sabina lifted her own glass to her lips, hoping to forestall her own comment. So, it seemed Meloria had not in fact expected Jeffree would live out his days a bachelor. Clearly, she had set but scant score on his word. Sabina hated herself, but could not forbear from asking, "Who did you imagine?"

"I thought either some celebrated beauty," Meliora answered with a contemptuous curl of her lip, "who would have a main

262

eye to his prospects, or some little doe-eyed schemer who would flatter and cajole him into marriage." She regarded Sabina steadily. "I suppose his uncle's title compelled him to marry at last."

"Oh, did Jeffree not tell you?" Sabina was inordinately pleased to have one up on the all-knowing Meliora. "His Grace, the Earl of Bethencourt, is betrothed to my younger sister." She did not actually know if this was still true, but she said it anyway to give the other woman pause.

Meliora lowered her glass. She regarded Sabina through enigmatic eyes. "Is that so?"

"Have you ever told Jeffree that story about Anaska?" Sabina asked abruptly, for suddenly she had to know.

Meliora looked taken aback. "No," she answered after a moment's pause. "No, I don't believe I ever have."

"I think you were wise."

Meliora looked amused. "You think love would have withered in his bosom?" she asked dryly.

"I know it would have!" Sabina retorted. "It would for any sensible man."

"Dear me, you think your husband sensible, do you? Not the word I would have used for him."

Sabina felt herself bristle all over at this implied criticism of Jeffree. The gods alone knew why, but it seemed she did not like anyone to criticize him but her! She finished her glass and rose to her feet. "Thank you for the interview," she said politely. "I believe I must be on my way now."

Meliora blinked. "You do not wish to know if I release him?" she asked archly.

263

"No, you were right. It does not make a scrap of difference."
She gazed at Meliora for a long moment. "I am pleased to have
met you though," she admitted, for Sabina had been harboring
wholly the wrong impression of her in her mind's eye. She
nodded, then she made resolutely for the door.

"And I, you," Meliora called after her, still sounding mildly
entertained. "Send him back into me and—"

Sabina slammed the door shut behind her, cutting off the other
woman's request. Jeffree was awaiting her on a bench in the
outer sanctum. He leaped to his feet as she walked briskly past
him.

"Sabina? Where are you—?"

She did not answer but instead hastened her steps toward the
large, studded door which she knew to be the way out of the
abbey. When she struggled with the unfamiliar latch, he reached
around her to pull back the bolt and together they emerged into
the night air. Sabina marched straight-backed across the
courtyard.

She was a jumble of emotions, all of which needed to be
brought back under control or she would make a fool of herself.
Jeffree's gaze was heavy upon her as they made their way back
to the stable and reclaimed their horses and afterward during
their ride to the village. Though neither one of them spoke, their
unsaid words seemed to hang heavy in the air.

Sabina rode blindly; it did not matter in any case since Blitha
was clearly being led by the larger horse's direction and Jeffree
obviously knew where he was going. Sabina bit her lip. He had
mentioned a previous visit to Fulford Abbey. Was it a regular
pilgrimage, then? She had no notion why that thought should
make her eyes sting.

264

She thought of Meliora's rich, deep laughter and felt her stomach turn over. Such a woman would not have suited him as a wife, she told herself again, swallowing. They would have been the most loathed couple in Ganfordshire with their insufferably arrogant ways. Then again, Jeffree did not exactly care that other folk thought him proud and arrogant. Likely he would not care if his wife suffered from the same conceit. Maybe she would have suited him after all. There was an acrid feeling in the pit of her stomach.

In vain, she told herself that Jasper and Crispin would not have liked Meliora for a sister-in-law. Lady Maud would likely have approved of someone so majestic and Sir Dudley, she suspected, generally just agreed with his wife. What of Jeffree's uncle? she wondered. Doubtless, someone as proper and dignified as Lady Meliora would have been duly deferential of the duke and would never dream of criticizing his fussy ways.

Sir Charles, of course, would have loved for his godson to marry a human glacier. He thought the Burrell females wholly beneath him.

"Sabina!" Jeffree barked her name, and she realized they had come to a halt beside a tall shadowy building. "We are here."

She glanced up and down at the building and then saw Osborn had slouched into the yard to greet them. He looked sulky as always and avoided her eye. She did not care. Jeffree handed the reins to his manservant and reached up for her. She did not want his help. It was true that climbing down from his charger was well-nigh impossible, but Blitha was quite a different matter.

"I can manage," she told him stiffly and was ignored, seized, and set down on her feet. Once there, he grabbed her arm above the elbow and held her anchored to his side as he exchanged a few words with Osborn. Sabina did not listen, and once he was done, Jeffree propelled her into the dimly lit building and dragged her up two flights of stairs and down a dark corridor where he flung open the door to their room.

Someone squawked and two serving maids looked up in alarm from the supper they were setting out on a small square table. Jeffree ignored them and jostled her into the room. Sabina flung his arm off as soon as they were inside and moved toward the window.

"Leave now!" Jeffree barked at the servants, who were eyeing her with open curiosity. Sabina rolled her eyes. He really was insufferable.

One of the maids curtseyed. "If you please, sir, your bath lies in yonder corner." She and Jeffree turned to glance at the tub that had been set up in the far corner of the room. "Will your own servant see to your needs?" she asked with a quick look at Sabina. "Or will ye be needing any assistance with it?"

Sabina closed her eyes briefly and braced herself for the sharp words of correction that would surely follow, but Jeffree said nothing and there was a heavy pause. For some reason, Sabina felt a hot color climbing up her neck. Good thing her wimple was so severe no one would see it. He was going to demean her, she realized at once, to teach her a lesson for going about in her own shabby clothes. He would let them think she was his servant to teach her a lesson.

Sabina tightened her fingers in her skirts and let her face go perfectly blank. She had faced worse humiliation than this in her life; why then did it send such a scalding sensation all down her spine?

Jeffree turned toward her slowly. "Will you require any assistance with your bath, my lady?" he asked with a heavy formality that made her blink and forget to breathe.

Oh. He did not mean to humble her. Quite the opposite.

She struggled a moment with her reply, then shook her head. "Thank you, no," she managed.

"That will be all," Jeffree added, and both maids scurried from the room. "You had better get in the tub while the water is still warm," he suggested without looking at her. "We don't know how long it has sat there." He moved to stand in front of the fire, gazing down into the flames.

Sabina crossed the room and dipped her fingers in the tub. It was warm but would not be for long. She had taken a bath the previous night and performed the arduous task of washing and drying her waist-length hair. Then again, she had spent a few hours in the saddle since then.

Glancing up at the ceiling, she saw there was no hook to hang a sheet from and preserve her modesty. Was she supposed to sit naked in the tub while Jeffree partook of his supper? She wanted to point out the lack of a curtain or screen, but that would make her sound timid. She was not, nor never had been, timid.

Inspiration struck. "You should take the tub," she said instead. "I had a very thorough bath last night at Longacre. You have been living in a pavilion for three days, have you not? And competing in the hot sun."

Jeffree turned to look at her. "I will take a bath later," he said shortly, then he looked away. "I have to return to the convent," he muttered.

Sabina sucked in her breath. "Over my dead body!" she flung at him angrily before she could stop herself.

He blinked, then seemed to weigh his next words carefully. "I have to go back," he said simply.

"*Why?*"

"Because Meliora did not absolve me from my vow," he said through gritted teeth. "She wanted to meet you first."

Sabina's chest rose and fell indignantly. "That's outrageous! She had no right to demand such a thing! She has sworn herself in service to her god and worldly matters should be nothing whatsoever to do with her anymore!"

Jeffree narrowed his eyes at her. "You think I don't know she was being damnably awkward?" he asked angrily.

"If you go scurrying back to her now…" She ran out of breath before she could think of retribution dire enough.

"What?" he asked roughly. "You will what?"

Sabina shook her head again. She knew she was being ridiculous. It was not as though she held any leverage with him. Why should he care about her feelings? She lifted her chin. "Go, then!" she said instead tightly. "Go hurrying back to her and beg her for her favors!" He stiffened perceptibly at her words. "Though for the life of me I cannot think why you are making two wasted journeys," she added bitterly. "Why did you not simply tarry and receive her permission before you left?"

"How could I?" He scowled. "You had no mind to wait when you finally emerged from her study. I dared not turn my back on you in case you took off!" His tone was extremely belligerent. For some reason, his anger went some way toward soothing Sabina's raw feelings.

"How do you know I won't now?" she asked coolly. "As soon as you go to prostrate yourself at Meliora's feet?"

He let out an incredulous huff at that. "I have never prostrated myself at a woman's feet and I never will. Stop being intentionally difficult."

"Oh," said Sabina, placing her hands on her hips. "Are you not enjoying it? I thought your taste must run to haughty bitches after meeting your former betrothed!" As soon as the snide words flew out of her mouth, Sabina gasped and clapped a hand to her mouth.

Where had that come from? She had not disliked Meliora precisely, for she had shown herself to be a woman of strong character and indomitable will. In a way, Sabina had been vastly relieved she had not turned out to be some saintly, classical beauty. So why was she saying such mean things about her now?

Jealousy, she realized with dismay. A prickly heat ran all through her body and she felt shame wash over her. She was acting like the jealous, unreasonable wife everyone had always said she was. Her throat closed painfully, and she clutched a chair back so hard she would not have been surprised if the wood had not splintered between her fingers.

Jeffree was staring at her, most likely with disgust. She shut her eyes and drew a couple of steadying breaths. When she opened them again, he was stood directly in front of her.

"No words of love were ever spoken between us," he said in a furious undertone. "I did not love her! I barely knew her in truth. I simply believed that she was the most praiseworthy woman in the land and that made her the best."

"And you have always believed that you deserve the best, have you not, Sir Jeffree?" she hissed back, matching his own tone. "My, however have you borne the disappointment of winding up with me?"

"I have borne it just fine!" he flung back. "I am fully reconciled!"

"How good of you!" she responded sarcastically. "Well, I am not!"

"If I am satisfied, madam, then I fail to see why you have reason for complaint!"

Sabina gasped. "You *pig*!" she fumed. "You know how I hate it when you call me madam!"

He gave a short laugh. "How fortunate that I do not mind your own dubious manner of addressing me."

"Unspeakable toad!" Sabina added with feeling.

"Anything else?"

"Loathsome wretch!"

"Never at a loss for words, are you?" he murmured, and for one astonishing moment, she thought he was about to smile. "I did not know what my tastes ran to," he said suddenly in a low, gravelly voice that robbed Sabina of all breath again. "Not until I met you."

"What?" she gasped.

"Meliora was my guardian's choice, not mine! I was too young to know what I liked then." This last part was muttered gruffly, his eyes sweeping over her with a boldness that made her breath catch. He did not hide the fact his eyes tarried on her breasts, waist, and hips.

Sabina made a strangled noise in her throat. She needed to regain control of this conversation *and* her breathing. She gave a short, mirthless laugh. "And you expect me to believe that *what you like* is a dowdy widow with a reputation for shrewishness, Sir Jeffree?" she scoffed. "Is that what you really expect me to believe?"

His eyes snapped back to her face, then the next thing she knew she was being jostled into his arms and Jeffree's mouth was crushed to hers, one hand at her nape, holding her clamped in place and the other squeezing convulsively at her waist. She knew not if his kiss was meant to punish or placate, so unrestrained was it and lacking in finesse.

His lips dragged roughly over hers, their teeth clashing. When he did not fling her away after the first suffocating minute, it dawned on her that he must be kissing her because he wanted to, no other reason. The thought made her head spin. Reaching up her arms, she circled them about his shoulders, returning the embrace in the hopes it would make him relax the strength of his grip. To be honest, she was not even sure he noticed.

Her hip pressed almost painfully into the chair back. What could she do? Mustering her nerve, she shifted her hands up and pressed them gently to his face. He halted, resting his brow heavily against hers and breathing raggedly against her lips. Sabina ran her thumbs over his cheekbones in a tender caress. The clutching fingers at her waist relaxed.

"*Sabina...*" he breathed, and she felt it right the way through her, coursing through her veins like a potent wine. Instead of taking the opportunity to slip away, she wrapped her arms about his neck and brushed her lips against his, gently sipping. Jeffree shuddered and stilled, his hand dropping from her waist and simply resting at her nape, letting her do as she willed.

271

"Kiss me back like this, Jeffree," she whispered against his lips. He gave a muffled groan, then his mouth moved against hers, slow and tentative, reverent almost. Sabina swayed against him, barely noticing him tugging at her headdress until she felt the linen tumbling down her shoulders and falling to the ground. Then his fingers were sliding into the coiled braids, drawing out the hair pins and scattering them at her feet.

She felt her heavy braids unfurl, the ends brushing at her waist, then his fingers clutching and gathering them into his hands which moved fitfully over her back. Boldly, Sabina licked her tongue along Jeffree's bottom lip. He froze, so she did it again, and this time when he drew in a ragged breath, she snaked her tongue right into his mouth and back out again before he could react. He made a choked sound, his hands stilling on her back,

"Again?" she murmured against his lips. Maybe he did not like it. The first time Miles had done it to her she had secretly thought it disgusting. It had taken her time to come around to such kisses.

"Again," Jeffree repeated hoarsely, his hands urging her closer still. *Then again, maybe not.* She did it slower this time, savoring the sensation of his hot, welcoming mouth. He did not taste at all of honeyed mead. Mayhap Meliora had not offered him any refreshment as she had her? She wondered if he could taste it lingering on her tongue.

This time as she retreated, she sucked gently on his bottom lip, and he made a low, rumbling noise which seemed to come from his chest, pressing his face closer to hers. He wanted her to do it again. She gave a muffled laugh. "Your turn," she uttered against his mouth. She felt his hesitation, his uncertainty, and parted her lips against his expectantly.

272

He did not respond at once, instead altering his stance slightly, the placement of his hands sliding down to her lower back. When she finally felt the tentative foray of his tongue into her mouth, Sabina gave an embarrassing moan of mingled relief and satisfaction. Why had he made her wait for it when she wanted him so badly?

There was a clatter in the background. She rather thought the chair she had been standing next to had mysteriously overturned. Suddenly, there was a cold flat surface at her back. What was happening? She didn't really care, because for some reason, she was sucking on Jeffree's tongue and rubbing herself against him like an abandoned creature making whimpers and sounds she had never dreamt would come from her own lips.

In the back of her mind, she was astonished by herself. She had never been like this with Miles. So wanton and wild. During their betrothal and the early days of their marriage, she had been the shy pursued. Then had come disillusionment and she had retreated rapidly, revolted by his disloyal touch.

But Jeffree was not like Miles. He ground his hips against hers as she sucked his tongue, and Sabina moaned into his mouth, feeling half-crazed with…what? Lust? She tightened her arms about his shoulders, wanting him close, needing him closer. He obliged, practically crushing her with his strength and she welcomed it.

"*Jeffree!*" Instead of the reproachful tone she should adopt, her voice was naught but a breathy gasp which spurred him on, rather than discouraging him. The gentle kiss she had sought to teach him had somehow become a hot slide of mouths. With a sense of bewilderment, Sabina realized her hands were now in his hair, sifting and tugging. Far from being horrified at his manhandling, she was instead wrapping herself around him with unbecoming enthusiasm. What was she doing?

273

It was the fact it was Jeffree de Crecy breathing so raggedly against her mouth that excited her. His big chest heaving against her own. When their tongues tangled, Jeffree groaned, and she felt that groan in the oddest places!

She was against the wall, she realized dimly, when he finally jerked back his head to catch his breath. Jeffree had picked her up and pinned her against it, pressing his body up as close to her own as it would go. She blinked back at him as he stared at her mouth, a wild look in his eye.

"I did tell you there was a knack to it," she joked weakly.

His eyes snapped to hers, but her words seemed barely to have registered. He closed his eyes and drew a shuddery breath as though trying to strengthen himself to some resolve. He was still trying to resist her, she realized. He was trying to step back, but could not quite wrench himself away from her. He was still trying to return to the convent, she reflected incredulously. Her bosom heaved. She would not stand for such treatment!

"Stay," she urged taking a deep breath and trying to ignore how the action caused her breasts to brush against his chest. "My vow is already broken after all," she continued striving for an even tone.

"Your vow?" he echoed hoarsely.

"Ne'er to remarry. You swept that one before you," she reminded him and with great daring, arched her back, bringing her lower body into closer contact with him. He made a choked sound. "Maybe I should treat your vow with a similar contempt?" she suggested sweetly.

"*Gods*… Sabina," he groaned.

"It is vain to struggle against it," Sabina insisted. "Fate, it seems, had something different in mind for us." His tortured

274

gaze bore into hers, but he said nothing, neither did he pull away. "Take me to bed, Jeffree," she ordered, aiming for wifely authority, but to her embarrassment, sounding more a breathless wanton. "Now."

He shuddered again. "Sabina…" he groaned.

"As a husband, you have certain duties," she added desperately, then almost smacked herself on the forehead with frustration. *My gods, this was not the time to speak of duty!* Husbands hated that kind of talk. She was fast losing all the ground she had gained!

To her surprise, she found herself hauled up into his arms and carried over to the bed. Instead of dropping her like a stone and striding from the room, Jeffree laid her on the bed and stood staring down at her with a look of open frustration.

Words bubbled up that she had to clamp her lips together to stop herself from saying. *Don't go. If you leave me now, I will never forgive you.* Somehow she managed to choke them back, only to blurt out something even worse. "You need her blessing to bed me, then?"

Her audacious question seemed to rob him of speech for a full minute before he let out a ragged breath.

"*Sabina*, that is not—! Woman, you misunderstand me."

"You know I hate it when you address me thus!"

He raked a hand through his hair. "I thought it was *madam* you did not like."

Oh yes, so it was. She turned her face aside. "Perhaps you should just go," she muttered bitterly. She would not cry. No matter what it cost her.

Jeffree said something; she paid it no heed. Then he spoke her name again. Sabina shook her head to clear it. "What?"

"I said I need to wash. I can't put my filthy hands all over you like this."

Oh. She opened her eyes tentatively and found he had not moved from the side of the bed. She glanced toward the corner of the room and flapped her arm in that direction. "The bath," she reminded him.

He swallowed, avoiding her eye. "You take it first. I need…a few minutes."

She had just opened her mouth to ask why, when he turned his back on her and she saw him adjusting his braies. Oh. He needed the minute to calm himself.

Sabina rolled off the bed and tottered toward the bath. She was still faintly shocked that Jeffree de Crecy, the proudest man in Ganfordshire, was happy to climb into her used bathwater. Snatching up her long braids, she wrapped them about her head, using a couple of pins still dangling from her hair to secure them again.

Then she set about tugging the laces loose on her bodice, dropping her gown to the floor and stepping out of it. By the time she had divested herself of her shift and lowered herself into the tub, Jeffree had flung himself down into a chair in front of the fire.

Cloths and soap leaves had been left at the side of the tub, and Sabina soaped and scrubbed herself with a thorough single-mindedness that acted as a defense against the rapidly cooling water. At Jeffree, she did not dare direct a single glance.

If he watched, he would find no titillation in the sight of her practical ablutions. It was only when she climbed out and

276

wrapped a large drying cloth about herself that she noticed she was covered all over in gooseflesh.

"Come and sit before the fire," Jeffree's voice rumbled from the seat he had taken. She turned her head and looked at him, but he was still gazing into the flames, not at her.

"The water is lukewarm at best," she told him apologetically. He stood up with a muffled sigh and moved toward the bath. Sabina shut out the sounds of his disrobing by concentrating on patting her arms, neck, and face with the corners of the large cloth.

Glancing about the room, she saw their things had been placed just inside the door and padded over to fetch a clean shift. Jeffree was in the tub now and splashing about but she kept her eyes averted, right until the moment she was about to slip her shift over her head. Then she took a quick look, just to check he was not looking. Their eyes met. He *was* looking! Sabina almost dropped the flimsy garment in surprise.

Jeffree scowled. "Why are you putting clothes *on*?" he asked, standing suddenly up out of the water.

Sabina's eyes almost popped out of her head. Only the utmost exertion of will allowed her to avert her eyes from his impressive physique. She had caught mere glimpses of it before and never in its entirety. Her heart beating so fast she thought he must surely hear it, she dropped the shift and instead bent her footsteps toward the bed. Drawing back the covers, she slid underneath them and dragged the drying cloth out from under her body.

Listening to Jeffree moving about over by the tub, presumably getting dry, Sabina steadied her breathing and reminded herself that she was the one with, as Meliora had put it, *some experience of married life to draw upon.* The drying sheet dropped to the floor, and she forced herself to relax back against the pillow bearer.

Why wasn't he shy about his nudity? She snuck another glance at him as he stalked toward the bed and could only suppose that, possessing such a body, he rightly thought he had nothing to be embarrassed about. She took a deep gulp of air as Jeffree stretched out beside her on the bed looking unaccustomedly ill at ease.

Of course, she thought after a couple of heartbeats, he would expect her to take the lead in this, would he not?

"Will you take your braids down?" Jeffree asked, breaking the silence.

Sabina hesitated. "And by that you mean—?"

"Just unpin them from your head," he clarified. "Not undo them."

"I wonder what it is that you like about them so much," she wondered aloud. Oddly enough, his request seemed to have dispelled a good deal of her anxiety. "Do you want to pull my braids, Jeffree?" she guessed shrewdly.

His face turned red. "No," he said at once, but his averted eyes and sharply indrawn breath betrayed him.

"Oh, yes you do," she contradicted him.

"I just like to touch them."

"You have not imagined it? Pulling them? Tugging on them?" she asked as she reached up to pluck out the pins. He did not answer, and Sabina had to bite back her smile. "I'll wager there were not many women or young girls in Sir Charles's home during your upbringing. What happened to Sir Charles's wife?" She stretched to place the pins on a small bedside table.

"She died," Jeffree answered, "but she was barely noticeable when she was around. She was a meek, colorless woman with little to say for herself."

Sabina turned back to survey him. "Likely that is how Sir Charles prefers his women."

A look of faint impatience crossed over Jeffree's face. "I don't want to talk about other women right now," he said shortly. "Or my godfather."

"That's good," Sabina assured him, arranging her long braids on either side of her head. "There. How is that?"

Jeffree's gaze roamed over her face and hair at once, his blue eyes heating. He cleared his throat. "Good," he admitted. "Pleasing."

Sabina nodded and made no move to grab the sheet that was fast slipping down and exposing her cleavage. Jeffree's startled gaze dipped, then returned hurriedly to her face. He cleared his throat.

Strange to say, she liked the fact he had no polished phrases to trot out at this point. Miles's repertoire, she was now convinced, was most likely spouted to all his conquests. "You can touch them," she offered lightly.

Jeffree's face turned even redder. "And by them, you mean...?"

Sabina gave a faint splutter. "Well, I meant my braids, but...whatever you will." He shifted closer, one hand reaching and clasping her left braid where it started behind her ear. Sabina watched his face as he lightly squeezed and ran his thumb over the woven sections of her hair. He looked so absorbed in his task, it quite took her breath away.

Really, she thought, the Duke of Bethencourt's heir must not have been allowed to mix with any young girls in his youth. And did old Sir Hereward never have a daughter to throw smiles Jeffree's way? All she recalled was Jeffree saying he was a drunkard who passed out face-first in a wineskin of an evening. Was Jeffree raised like a monk, deprived of all female company? It was a puzzle to be sure.

Impulsively, she reached over and ran her hand tentatively down the intriguing blond fuzz covering his chest. Jeffree caught his breath, his eyes seeking her own. She gave him an encouraging half smile and he exhaled noisily, his other hand mirroring hers by reaching for her almost bared bosom.

When it hovered there uncertainly, Sabina reached out and captured it, pressing it to the softness of her breast. Jeffree froze, one hand wrapped around her braid, the other resting on her bosom. For a minute she thought he had forgotten to breathe.

Sabina cleared her throat. "Perhaps we should kiss?" she suggested quietly, and his eyes widened as though she had asked some impossible feat of him. "Or not," she said quickly, interpreting his silence as disinclination.

"I want to," he said at once, licking his lips. "It's just…can you permit me a moment to savor this much?" She felt his hand tighten convulsively on her braid.

"Yes, of course. I did not mean to rush you." Slowly she moved her hand to stroke gently through the blond hair on his chest. Even that careful movement made him hiss through his teeth. He was not relaxed at all. Mayhap they just needed to get this over with, Sabina thought suddenly.

After all, her mother had warned her the first time was not pleasurable and she had been right. Likely, however hard she tried, Jeffree would find it a strange and embarrassing experience. Swiftly, Sabina slid her hand down his stomach, wincing when he sucked in his breath. "You should tell me if I do anything you do not like," she said, striving for a confident tone.

She let her hand rest a moment on his muscular stomach, and when he pointedly said nothing, she slid her fingers down further. He uttered a faint sound and she halted at once.

"I did not say to stop," he said quickly.

Sabina gave a short nod before reaching down to tentatively cup his manhood.

"Oh gods," Jeffree groaned, biting his lip.

As she had suspected from her previous brushes with his appendage, it was of a surprising size and girth. Sabina's eyes widened as she made out its substantial shape. "Oh my," she murmured, feeling slightly alarmed at the way it was hardening and lengthening in her grasp. "Does it always—um—" Words failed her. Was it always so big?

Pushing the sheet out of the way, she glanced down in some apprehension to see how eagerly it was spilling out of her clasp. "*Oh.*" Mayhap it was because she had always been far too embarrassed to really take a look at Miles down there, but she found she could barely tear her eyes away from the fat tip of Jeffree's cockhead. It looked so rosy red and glistening, as though it was on the point of exploding.

When she could do no more than gape, Jeffree made an impatient huffing sound, straining toward her. Why was it so slippery? She pressed a curious thumb to the slit at the top where it seemed to be leaking a copious fluid. Jeffree let out a surprised yelp. "Sorry!" she said guiltily. She was making far too free with his body, she thought distractedly, even as her fingers closed gently about the head. Was it only a product of her fevered imaginings or did the thing practically have its own heartbeat by this point?

Jeffree's eyes closed and he moaned. When she felt his full-body shiver, she knew she must be doing something right at least. Grasping her courage along with his cock, she slid her hand firmly down the shaft to his ballocks. "Unnngh!" Jeffree grunted, thrusting into her grasp. "*Fuck*, madam, have a care!"

"Sorry!" Sabina blurted, drawing back her hand in alarm.

Jeffree looked pained. "That is not what I—" He broke off with a huff. "I do not think I can take much more of this. "Can you not simply…" He glanced away, refusing to meet her eye. "Put me out of my misery."

"You mean…" Sabina stared at him, her mind a jumble of confusion. Then she realized, of course, he meant for her just to roll onto her back and part her legs for him. The thought brought her up short, but after all, that had been what Miles had expected on their wedding night. However, the thought of Jeffree's large appendage forcing its way between her legs made her wince.

She took a steadying breath. "You are a large man, Jeffree," she made herself explain. "'Tis a good thing I'm not a nervous virgin or I would be hiding under the bed. Your size is… daunting. We need to—" She broke off frustratedly. *Oh, my gods, why did men think everything was about them when it came to beddings?*

"What?" he demanded.

"It is not all about you! We need to do those other things for me!"

282

His brows snapped together. "What other things?"

"The kissing! The touching!" she burst out frustratedly. Her cheeks were hot as flames by this point. "In order to—to ready me for you."

"Oh." To give him credit, Jeffree did look somewhat shamefaced. He drew up the sheet, concealing his rampant manhood and eased himself back against the headboard. "I am not used to"—he made a rolling gesture with his hand— "spinning it out. Usually, I try to get it over with as quickly as possible."

Sabina's eyebrows rose so high she thought they must have disappeared into her hair. "Usually?" she echoed, mystified.

"By my own hand." When she turned to look at him, he held up his hand to show it to her. The gesture was so absurd, it surprised a gurgle of laughter from her. His own lips quirked briefly upward, but he looked too tortured to join her.

Sabina bit her lip, noticing the way his eyes kept falling on her breasts. He kept averting them, but his gaze seemed drawn almost against his will. She should probably draw the sheet up over them, but strange to say, his hot, devouring gaze was not displeasing. In truth, the way he looked at her almost made her feel…

An idea occurred to her, so audacious she almost gasped aloud. "Perhaps, I could…" She rolled onto her back and, keeping the sheets at her waist, reached down between her legs, petting herself there.

"What are you doing?" Jeffree's choked words made her glance his way.

"Touching myself," she admitted. "Your words gave me the idea. This way, *I* can make myself ready."

283

He stared at her, and for some reason, Sabina found herself suddenly unable to look away, even though touching herself, while Jeffree de Crecy watched, felt more than a little wrong. The rush of wetness between her legs shocked her. She gasped, her eyes fluttering closed. The harsh noise Jeffree made had her opening her eyes again, only to find him sat up and edging closer toward her.

"That readies you?" he asked, his voice low and guttural. She nodded and he swallowed audibly, his gaze riveted between her legs though he could see nothing. "Your hand scarcely moves."

"Oh well." Sabina licked her lips. "It is mostly my fingers I employ. It's a little different from, well, what you do." She gestured toward his own lap area, also obscured by blankets, though she suspected his own grip was for comfort at this point, rather than stimulation.

"Can I see?" he uttered, and Sabina's eyes flew wide.

"Umm…" She hesitated.

"Please," Jeffree added tightly.

Sabina contemplated him a moment under her lowered lids, then, instead of answering, shoved down the bedsheets to midthigh, exposing her body to him.

Jeffree dragged in a ragged breath, and rather than look for his reaction to her wholly unremarkable body, Sabina concentrated instead on circling the pleasure point between her thighs. She could almost feel Jeffree's stare burning into her as she touched herself.

Again, she found his attention oddly invigorating more than anything. She bit her lip; likely he wasn't gaining much from the experience though. She snuck a glance at him from under

284

her lashes and found him still staring between her legs with rapt attention. Emboldened, Sabina drew her knees up to let him see.

She kept her eyes on his for the next minute or so while her fingertips made her dig her heels into the mattress and gasp. While her breathing quieted, she rested her hand on her stomach and contemplated Jeffree's flushed face. He really was very beautiful—her eyes drifted downward—and *very* aroused.

When he finally managed to drag his eyes up to meet hers, she opened her arms to him. "Come here, Jeffree." Her voice was husky. She felt more than ready for him. As though her words broke a spell, he made haste to clamber over her, giving a muffled groan when their bodies came into contact with one another.

Feeling too sated for nervousness, Sabina took his shaft in hand and guided him between her legs. He needed no further stimulation. Indeed, she was privately of the opinion he was perilously close to spilling his seed.

"Fuck," Jeffree wheezed as she placed him where he needed to go.

"*Have a care, madam?*" Sabina ventured, but he was past caring about being teased. Sweat was beading at his brow. Seeing his half-agonized expression, she took pity on him. "All is now prepared," she assured him, sliding one arm about his neck. "You can come inside me."

He gave a shaky moan and shifted forward. The very tip of him lodged in her cleft, but she was forced to move her hips to encourage the rest of him to follow suit. "Jeffree," she breathed. "You—you need to…"

As though in answer to her hesitant promptings, he gave an upward thrust of his hips.

285

"Oh!" Sabina's eyes watered and he immediately stilled with a swift curse. "No, no, do not stop," she assured him, squeezing his shoulder. He ventured another cautious dip of his hips, but it was a good deal shallower this time.

It just made her all the more anxious to have him all the way inside. "Jeffree!" she keened, arching her back. His nostrils flared, his eyes on her breasts, and he thrust in earnest this time.

"Oh!" yelled Sabina, tears once more springing to her eyes as he filled her up to the hilt.

"Is that—?"

"No, that's good. That's very good," she told him breathlessly, patting his shoulder. To her surprise, she was not lying. It *did* feel surprisingly good. In the past, Sabina had always enjoyed the preliminaries far more than the act itself. He muttered something above her, and Sabina squeezed his sides with her knees. "Why have you stopped?"

He huffed out a breath. "Madam, I'm *trying* to—to gather my wits," he replied through gritted teeth. "I am barely holding myself together here!"

He did sound very strained, she realized, as he held himself rigid above her. "Just let yourself go," she recommended warmly. "Really, you deserve it at this point. You have done very well for your first foray."

He gave her the oddest look. "What is it you expect me to—?"

Sabina slid her hand up his shoulder to his neck. "Don't you want that, Jeffree?" she asked with as much sweetness as she could muster. He shuddered, then stopped trying to hold himself in check. He drove his hips forward, forging into her.

286

Sabina muffled her surprised groan of pleasure by slapping the back of her hand over her mouth. Jeffree glowered down at her. "Put it back. Hold on to me," he demanded, and only when she replaced her hand at his neck would he move again.

"Jeffree," Sabina moaned, arching her back to meet his increasingly forceful strokes. He swore again. Really, he had a surprisingly foul mouth when it came to lovemaking. Sabina wondered at the fact she was not offended. Miles had certainly tempered his language when the two of them were alone together. Jeffree seemed to be the opposite way around. Still, that did *not* explain why she found the filthy curses so stimulating when they fell from his lips.

"Yes, Jeffree," she gasped. "Like that." He obliged with another firm buck of his hips but was disappointingly silent. "Keep talking to me. I want to hear your voice."

His grunts punctuated his thrusts. "What do you expect me to say to you?"

"Whatever you will," Sabina gasped. "I care not, save that I hear it."

Jeffree groaned. "I cannot think straight," he admitted in a choked voice. "I can barely string two thoughts together, not when..."

"When what?" she pressed breathlessly.

He swallowed. "When we are *one* like this," he groaned, falling forward and resting his weight on his forearms. "I do not want to finish and yet..." He gasped and closed his eyes. "I cannot stave it off any longer." He shuddered and lowered his head so that his brow rested against hers, and she realized what his low, harsh moan betokened. Jeffree de Crecy had come apart in her arms.

287

Sabina lay still beneath him as she caught her breath again. For a moment she had almost thought she was going to reach a second peak which would be unprecedented in her experience. It had been surprisingly enjoyable being swived by Jeffree, she marveled silently. Perhaps there were some perks to being Lady de Crecy after all.

After a moment of heavy panting, Jeffree bestirred himself to roll off her and onto his side. He did so with an almost flattering expression of reluctance on his face and lay contemplating her in stunned silence. Sabina made shift to muster some modesty and cover her flushed body with the bedcovers. "I think you are always going to call me madam, on occasions," she remarked to cover any awkwardness. Jeffree's head moved slightly, but he did not answer.

Sabina turned her head to look at where he lay panting. Of course, he would hardly know that this was where he was supposed to praise and reassure her. Not with his having never partaken in bed-sport before. If anything, she thought, struck by the notion, she supposed she must be the one to adopt that role now.

He must have become aware of her scrutiny, for he lifted his eyes from her cleavage to look at her, a slightly self-conscious look on his face. "What is it?" he mumbled abruptly. "Tell me."

Sabina hesitated. "Usually, in the aftermath, bedpartners will have some speech between them," she admitted.

"Speech?"

"Such as…attempting to comfort one another."

"Comfort?" He sounded bewildered.

"Or…praise," Sabina suggested. She remembered her late husband's easy caresses and empty words. Bedpartners must

288

have been interchangeable to him, she thought. Likely he gave them all the same compliments.

"Such as?"

As usual, thoughts of Miles had already soured her to the topic, so she shook her head. "It was just a notion. Forget I said anything." She shut her eyes to enjoy a pleasant doze.

"Are you in need of comfort?" Jeffree asked after a moment's tense silence.

"No," she replied truthfully.

"Very well, then I will hear your words of praise now," he decided, robbing Sabina of speech.

She opened her eyes and looked at him. "You want my praise?"

He shrugged a tanned shoulder, his blue gaze scrupulously avoiding her own. "Did I not say so?"

For a moment, the crazy idea crossed Sabina's mind that his nonchalance might mask something else. She regarded him with a faint pucker between her brows. Nay, that could not be the case. For when was Sir Jeffree de Crecy ever insecure about himself? "What about *my* praise?" she asked, feeling suddenly irritable.

He snorted. "Have you forgotten, woman? I have naught to compare you with, good or bad."

There it was. The customary arrogance. It was never far away when it came to this husband of hers. Still, in her current relaxed state, it did not irritate her as much as it should. Sabina sighed and considered their frenzied coupling impartially. "You are well equipped to please a woman," she admitted. "And with time I am sure you will do so."

Jeffree's face turned a dull red. "*That* is your praise?" He sounded stung. "Gods, if that's the case, madam, then I would hate to receive your criticism!" He scowled and rolled away from her, showing her his back.

Sabina bit the side of her mouth. Had she hurt his feelings? "Nay, husband, I intended no criticism…" Her words trailed off. "You are handsome of face and well-formed of limb and full pleasing to look upon. I am sure you are well aware of this."

His shoulder shrugged irritably, and he let out an irritated huff.

Sabina sighed and steeled herself to drag her body out of bed to wash between her legs. The moment her feet hit the floor, he turned to look back over his shoulder.

"Where are you going?" he demanded.

"Just to wash." She gestured to her lower half.

"Oh." He laid his head back down on the pillow bearer, and Sabina lifted her shift and used the tepid water from the jug for her ablutions. Jeffree cleared his throat. "Do women always do that?" he asked after a moment's heavy pause.

Sabina looked up. "Wash?"

"No! I mean…" He hesitated. "Prepare themselves as you did."

"Oh, I see. Well"—she thought about it a moment—"I suppose it depends on whether the man wishes to play an active role in readying her or not."

This seemed to strike him into silence, and Sabina wondered if she had shocked him with the idea of his fingers between her legs. Feeling herself grow flushed at the thought, she ducked her head and dabbed her thighs with a drying cloth.

"Should you like that?" Jeffree asked in a gruff voice.

Sabina straightened up. "Only if you wanted to," she answered lightly. "I know where I like to be touched so it seems more efficient for me to just do it." She made her way back to the bed, blowing out the bedside candle before clambering under the sheets.

She was just drifting off to sleep when she heard Jeffree's voice beside her. Her eyes blinked back open again. "I beg your pardon?"

"I said I should like to do it," he repeated testily.

"Oh. Well, mayhap next time," she suggested sleepily and let her heavy eyelids droop until they closed.

16

"I wonder how the older nuns feel having to address Meliora as *Reverend Mother*," Sabina mused as they broke their fast the next day.

Jeffree regarded her moodily across the rough-hewn table. They were sat outside the inn they had hit upon to eat their noon-day meal. The sun was shining and the sky was blue and they had now put a good four hours between themselves and Fulford Abbey. Why the hells was she raising the specter of his former betrothed between them now?

Picking up on his unspoken dissatisfaction, she added, "I was just thinking it must feel strange addressing someone as that when you are old enough to be their grandmother."

"It is a title," Jeffree pointed out irritably. "Nothing more." She relapsed into silence and he heard himself ask grudgingly, "Why are we still speaking of her anyway?"

"The thought just occurred to me." Sabina shrugged. "I suppose her parents must have used her dowry to buy her such an important rank."

He eyed her impatiently. "Doubtless," he said shortly. He had more important things to think about right now. He had realized that under her unbecoming apparel, Sabina Burrell was a siren. Mayhap that was why she had to dress so unassumingly, to keep away the hordes of men who would fall at her feet as willing victims.

He wanted to fall at her feet himself. Then kiss all the way up to those plump thighs and beyond. His thoughts halted. He gave his head a small shake. The oddest thoughts kept popping into his head these days.

He wanted to kiss her mound. He wanted to kiss her pretty round breasts. He was almost sure respectable men did not fill their heads with such thoughts. This way led to a life of self-indulgence and ruination. He knew that full well, but still, he did not think it would stop him from wanting those things. He feared he was already a lost cause.

Sabina fiddled with her napkin, as though mustering the courage to frame the question she really wanted to ask. "Will you visit the convent again next year do you suppose?" she asked and met his gaze squarely. Jeffree had just opened his mouth on a sharp retort when she plunged recklessly on. "If so, I shall expect to be at your side, as is my rightful place."

Her words robbed him of all speech, giving him the oddest sensation. Was she jealous, then? He felt oddly gratified by the thought, though, of course, she should trust him more. "No," he answered before noticing the expectant look on her face.

"No, you will not visit or no, I may not accompany you?" she asked, squaring her shoulders as though about to sail into battle.

"No, I will not be visiting the convent again," he said quickly before she seized hold of the wrong end of the stick.

"Oh." Her shoulders relaxed. "Well, I cannot pretend I am not relieved. I realize it has become something of a tradition for you to make the journey, but—"

"There are other charities just as worthy," he interrupted her, "and I think they have done well enough from my coffers over the years. Though"—he frowned—"I would not call it a tradition for me to travel there. I have only visited on one occasion prior to this and that only because I was in the area."

Sabina exhaled softly. "Thank you for explaining," she said, lowering her gaze to her plate which now contained naught but breadcrumbs.

Jeffree felt the strangest impulse to reach across and touch her. *Absurd.* He was not sure what strange mood had inhabited him all morn, but he could not seem to keep either his eyes or his thoughts from dwelling on her.

When she fell silent, he wanted to ask her what she was thinking about. The problem was, then she would tell him, and it was doubtful her pretty head was full of thoughts of him. His mood would doubtless take an inevitable turn for the worse.

She *should* be thinking of him, damn it. It was only fair.

A terrible presentiment fell over him as they made their way back out again to their horses, that he would *never* be rid of these strange feelings that churned through his stomach and fluttered in his chest whenever it came to his wife. That he would be like this forever. Always longing for her, his thirst never quenched.

He had never really paid heed to talk about such things in the past, but he had heard men talk about conquering such hankerings. His old master, Sir Hereward, had kept many mistresses in the four years Jeffree had been in his service. *Women, my boy,* he had frequently opined, *are like thorns that embed themselves in your flesh. There's only one way you can work them back out again.* Then he had roared with laughter at his own jest and disappeared for an afternoon or an evening, or sometimes even a full day, to spend in a woman's embrace.

Jeffree did not think that would work in this instance. Joining his body with Sabina's seemed to have made the pull he felt toward her stronger, rather than purging it from his body. The thought of locking her in a room with him for a few hours and attempting to cure himself by fully immersing himself in her charms made a light sweat break out on his brow which he did not think could be wholly accounted for by the midday sun.

He had a horrible suspicion he would end up completely bewitched with her if he did not ration himself severely. Besides, he reflected uneasily, mopping his brow, it was not just the lures of her admittedly beautiful body he felt. He wanted other things from her almost as badly. This odd dissatisfying yearning was *not* just to get her back underneath him again.

He felt the strange conviction that, if she would only turn her eyes upon him favorably, he could bask content in them all day. *That* was what would satisfy him, he realized in astonishment, and that alone. Mayhap that was what really broke him out in a cold sweat for he was almost certain his wife did not feel the same way about him.

The thought made him feel slightly sick at heart. *Heartsick.* The word formed in his mind and brought him up short. Where had that come from? What the fuck was wrong with him? Half the time the little wretch was barely polite to him! She certainly did not strive to keep him happy. He stared at her back in frustrated bafflement as they headed on horseback for the foothills.

He had surely met many more distinguished ladies than Sabina Hendry in his time and the fact was not one of them had ever made much of an impression on him. Take Meliora for instance. He had faced her with perfect indifference the previous day. Now that he knew what genuine attraction felt like, he knew that he had felt naught for his former betrothed, not even a passing fancy. Duty was what had prompted their former association and duty alone.

The only thing that caused even a flicker of hopefulness in his breast this day was the fact Sabina had not wanted him to return to the convent without her. Even a show of possessiveness would hearten him at this juncture, so far gone was he. Then, as the rays of the sun flashed out from behind Midsummer Mount, he was struck with fresh inspiration. He needed to make his wife fall in love with him. Then she would hang on his every word and seek him out as he desired.

How hard could it be to sway a woman's feelings in your favor? Jeffree frowned over this a moment, having never considered such a thing before. Women fell in love all the time, did they not? He glanced Sabina's way again. *Any affection I thought I bore for Miles died a thousand deaths over the short span of our marriage.* That was what she had said previously about her first husband.

The trouble was, she had not had any affection in her bosom when she had been forced to wed Jeffree. How was he supposed to inspire her with any now? He shifted in his saddle uneasily. Then it came to him. Undoubtedly, he appeared at his best in his own arena of knightly pursuits. When she saw him at his best and most laudable, then her flinty heart would soften.

In two weeks' time, it was the Summer Tournament. He would take her to Caer-Lyoness to watch him compete against the best Karadok had to offer. Then Sabina would know that Sir Jeffree de Crecy was indeed worthy of her love.

They passed from the lower slopes, following the winding pathways until they were steadily ascending the upper climbs of the first ridge. The homeward journey meant taking a different route, as they were approaching Ganfordshire in a different direction after their detour to Fulford. This way was steeper and, to Jeffree's eye, rather more perilous.

"Halt!" he called loudly and reined in Radax, coming to a standstill. He glanced to where Sabina and Osborn were looking at him enquiringly. "You," he said, pointing to Sabina, "dismount. Osborn, tie the horses together." He did not look for their reactions, but instead, swung down himself, making for Blitha.

"Why am I dismounting?" Sabina asked when he reached her side. She had already slid down to the ground and had a faint pucker between her brows.

"I want you up before me," he answered shortly, taking her arm and leading her back to his own horse. Sabina looked puzzled but voiced no argument which he felt profoundly grateful for. He was not so sure it would look much steeper to her untutored eye, though for his part, he felt sure it was.

He passed her a waterskin and watched as she drank from it before boosting her up onto Radax's back, swinging himself up behind her. It was wrong to feel a thrill from their proximity, the press of her back against his front, but it suddenly *felt* intimate with her sat between his thighs, and his heartbeat picked up, nonetheless.

On the previous occasion she had been on his horse before him, he did not think it had made his pulse race. Or at least, not this much. He found himself squeezing the hand that rested at her waist and wanting to say something. He cleared his throat. "Does this not remind you of the time we journeyed from your father's house to Morecotte?" he asked, lowering his voice so Osborn should not hear their private speech.

Once again, he wished her headdress was not so all-encompassing. He should like to see the turn of her cheek from here, a glimpse of ear. Anything really, other than flapping white linen.

Sabina was silent a moment. "How so?" she asked blankly.

"You were sat up before me on that occasion too," he replied.

"Oh. Then yes."

Her answer seemed distinctly lacking to Jeffree. He frowned. "You are the first woman I have had up on Radax's back," he pointed out. Clearly, she was not fully aware of the honor he did her.

"Oh really?"

She sounded polite, nothing more, and Jeffree felt irritated. Clearly, there was more to this wooing business than he had ever realized. It was foolish to be courting one's wife at this late point. He wanted to tell her so but bit his tongue. "Why are you so quiet?" he asked instead.

"Am I? I suppose I just thought you would prefer that. You seemed a little…testy at midday."

Testy? "Did I?"

"I thought perhaps a little quiet might be your preference when traveling."

"No such thing!" he protested.

"Very well, it seems I was mistaken." She patted his hand which held the reins. Was she placating him? Jeffree was not sure if that was a good sign or not. "It will be good to look upon Morecotte again," she sighed. "I cannot wait to set the place to rights. It is sorely in need of my attention."

Jeffree pondered this but could not think of a rejoinder. The place was a disaster, but clearly, she was fond of it. "You will have to take me to visit that mill pond," he reminded her.

"What?" She half turned her head, sounding startled.

298

"The one at the village."

"Oh."

"Have you forgotten our conversation so soon?"

"No, no, I just…I suppose I thought you said that in jest."

"I was in deadly earnest."

His words seemed to flummox her. She gave an uneasy laugh. "I hope I have not led you to believe it something it is not. If so, you will certainly be disappointed."

"A smithy, a mill, and a duckpond was all you promised me," he reminded her. Again, she seemed struck dumb by his words. "Sabina?"

"It is naught; I just did not think…"

"What?"

"That you were paying such close attention to me. To my words, I mean."

"Certainly I am." A silence rose between them that could only be described as awkward. Jeffree did not think he had ever thought that about a silence before. "You will be pleased to return…home?" he ventured.

"Yes, yes I will. I will certainly be keen to see—" She broke off from whatever she had been about to say abruptly.

"What?"

"How my sister has fared in our absence," she said carefully.

He supposed she meant if Isemay Burrell had been reconciled to his uncle but had then decided that was impolitic to admit that to his heir. "Do you suppose they will have been married?"

he asked without much interest. It had been ten days after all and time enough.

Sabina gave a faint splutter. "Would you think me very terrible if I answered I hope not?"

"Terrible? No," he answered. "In truth, you would be unwise to think otherwise."

"Unwise?"

"If your sister should marry my uncle and provide him with an heir, then you will never be Duchess of Bethencourt." Once again, his words seemed to stun her. "I know, unlike your sister, you have never aspired to the title," he began calmly, but an impatient gesture from Sabina halted him.

"You misjudge her entirely. If you knew her then you would not think—" She broke off frustratedly. "Isemay is a talented musician," she started again. "Your uncle admired her excessively and she was, of course, wonderfully flattered by his offer. He was kind and attentive in his wooing, and she truly thought she could make him happy. Of course," she added awkwardly, "she knew he would also aid our father with his financial woes, and that was a consideration, but I assure you—"

"There is no need to assure me," he cut across her words. "I will accept your word on it."

She half turned in the saddle again to look at his face, subjecting him to a searching gaze. "Thank you, Jeffree," she said a little stiltedly after a moment's pause. "I appreciate that."

He scarcely noticed, so much was his mind working over her words. *Kind and attentive in his wooing?* No one had ever described him thus in his life, and it galled him no end that his uncle Bevis should show more aptitude in this than he. He coughed to cover his chagrin. "If you believe their attachment to be sincere, why then do you no longer desire it?"

"I don't know that I ever desired it," Sabina admitted with a sigh. "Even if you put aside the disparity in their ages and station, I still could not see that... well, that they would not be rather tired of one another within a sixmonth. Isemay looks like an angel and plays divinely on her harp, but she can be very impetuous at times, and I think the duke really has no idea of it. He seems a man quite...er...timid in his outlook and easily shocked." Jeffree maintained a tactful silence in the face of this accurate reading of his uncle's character. "Then, too, I had also lost faith in my parents' judgment when it came to such things. After my own wretched experience of matrimony, I mean."

Jeffree cleared his throat. "It is only natural you should feel thus."

"You think so?" She sounded gratified, if a little surprised.

"I do."

"I am sure the rest of your family will be terribly shocked if Isemay does not accept His Grace's suit, should he renew it." Again, Jeffree found himself unable to refute this claim. The de Crecy clan had pronounced the Burrells naught but a pack of fortune hunters. His relations would be both shocked and incredulous if Isemay were to reject the duke.

In the face of his silence, Sabina asked suddenly, "Does inheriting Bethencourt's title mean so very much to you?"

"Of course," Jeffree answered aloud. "I was raised as my uncle's heir after all." But inwardly he wondered a little, remembering his godfather's words to him on the subject. How Sir Charles had urged him to guard against the designing Burrells and how little Jeffree had heeded his warnings.

It had not even occurred to him to eschew Areley Kings and remain at his uncle's side counseling him against any possible reconcilement with Isemay. "Ganford Chase is the most impressive estate in all of Southern Karadok," he added more for his own benefit than anyone else's. "I would be a fool not to covet it."

"Yes, but what I mean is, you spend most of your year touring to compete. It is not as though you are following in your uncle's footsteps or helping to run his vast estates. You are forging your own path in life."

"My uncle's land stewards manage his estate," he pointed out, though he liked that she saw he was his own man. He hesitated a moment. "Let us talk now of the restoration of Morecotte," he suggested cunningly. That would be a subject after her own heart, and he fancied would distract her from wanting to return too soon to Blitha's back.

"Truly?" Sabina perked right up at that suggestion. No wonder she did not think he really cared for Ganford Chase. He would wager he did not hold it in even one-tenth the regard she held her former home, and he marveled at it. Morecotte was a pretty spot, but little more than a picturesque hunting box that had been left to go to ruin.

"The approach is quite choked up with weeds," Sabina began enthusiastically. "They must all be cleared away so that delivery carts may approach with their wares for we need to restock the cellars." She paused as though expecting him to concur.

He cleared his throat. "Certainly. The unsightly holes in the walls of the Great Chamber must also be plugged up."

"Yes," she agreed, "and some attempt made to clean and mend the wall hangings if that is even possible. There was also a

302

broken window in one of the bedrooms which must be considered a priority in case of rain."

"Aye," he agreed. "What else?"

The next half hour passed in the closest thing they had ever reached to accord in their lives together thus far. Jeffree trod carefully, agreed with everything she suggested, and when considerations such as economy encroached on her plan-making, he dismissed them. "I have plenty of money for the refurbishment," he pointed out absently, for his mind was considering the vast stash of costly fabrics he had accumulated in his dressing room. They could be purposed for bed hangings, draperies, and even, if she would only permit it, to clothe his wife's delectable body.

These past few days he had learned better than to simply voice his opinion on this subject. He wondered how he could even broach the matter once again without incurring her displeasure. Now he had made it clear he intended to live at Morecotte, it seemed she accepted the use of his purse in its restoration.

Would the consummation of their marriage make his offer of replenishing her inadequate wardrobe any more acceptable? He was strangely loath to raise it and find out. What if such talk shattered the temporary harmony betwixt the two of them?

The afternoon passed swiftly, and they soon left the rocky summit behind them as they descended through a more navigable pass leading to the remote inn where they would spend the night. The evening was a fine one in June and, though they did not reach their destination until late, night was only just falling.

They were served with a simple supper of bread and pottage and a wine so sour that Jeffree left his share to Osborn before retiring for the night. Sabina yawned several times as she disrobed and was quick to jump under the covers after her wash. Jeffree made haste to follow, and they lay side by side in the failing light provided by the small casement window.

"I felt so tired during supper, but now I lay my head down, sleep will not come," Sabina remarked companionably.

Jeffree cleared his throat. How did one respond to such remarks? As a rule, he coldly ignored such empty chatter. Then again, he'd never shared a bed with anyone before. Surely a different etiquette would come into play here. "Indeed," he settled on after a moment's hesitation. He did not feel remotely tired.

"Why do you suppose he did it?" she asked suddenly.

"Who?" Jeffree blinked, bewildered by the turn in conversation.

"Leland Ellis. Why do you suppose he came up with such a fantastical plot against you and Isemay?" she asked, turning toward him.

Jeffree could not speak for a moment; had she been long pondering this matter? It had hardly been uppermost in his thoughts. He shifted uncomfortably. "Leland has ever been a troublemaker," he said grudgingly. "And long resented me."

"Was it always that way?" she asked curiously. "After all, you were raised together almost like foster brothers."

"Always," he agreed shortly.

"I suppose," she debated slowly, "looking at it from his point of view, you were rather a cuckoo in their nest. And I daresay that father of his did not pass the opportunity to use you as a stick to beat Leland with."

"What do you mean?" His tone was sharp. He had not realized her opinion of his mentor and guardian was so scathing.

"Well, if Leland was always wild and you the studious, 'perfect' son, then it was only natural he would resent you." The silence between them stretched as Jeffree frowningly considered this. "Leland must have wanted his father's approbation on some level," she persisted. "Perhaps he thought this way he could kill two birds with one stone."

He did not want to ask, but he heard himself do so anyway. "How so?"

"By both preventing the marriage which Sir Charles so abhorred and besmirching your name in one fell swoop. It makes a sort of horrible sense if you think about it," she continued. "For doubtless he thought his father would forgive him eventually, for he would have preserved your inheritance by his actions, would he not?"

Jeffree breathed out. This was not a subject he wished to dwell on and neither did he want to encourage her criticism of his godfather. "I would not put anything past Leland," he admitted grudgingly. "Though it little matters now."

She nodded. "I suppose we will never know the twisted workings of his mind." She shrugged. "Tell me, when you came to Longacre, did you notice Sir Dudley was a little quiet?" Sabina mused. She was awfully chatty for someone who had been yawning her head off all through their meal. He angled his head to make out her profile, so taken with the slope of her nose that he forgot to answer. "Jeffree?"

Her use of his name almost startled him. "He's always quiet," he said belatedly when she cocked her head to look his way. "He's a quiet man."

"Only until you get to know him," she answered lightly. "Then he has plenty to say for himself."

Jeffree considered this a moment, recalling the night he had fetched her from Longacre. "I suppose that is true," he conceded slowly. He had never really considered Dudley Vyse's character before.

"I like him," Sabina said blithely. "I hope he does not feel we have trampled all over his aspirations."

Jeffree felt instantly soured at this praise of his stepfather. "What aspirations?" he asked grudgingly. Vyse had aspirations?

"Having a son enter the church, I mean."

Jeffree snorted. "My mother seems satisfied at all events."

"Yes, and the seminary spared from a most unruly pupil," she agreed with a smile in her voice.

"I suspect he will also make a most unruly squire," Jeffree pointed out.

"More than likely, I would say," his wife agreed with a sanguinity Jeffree thought wholly inappropriate.

"You need not sound so unconcerned," he replied, extending his foot to nudge her calf. Sabina gave a muffled yelp at the unexpected contact. "As my squire, he will reside wherever I go," Jeffree added. "Much like my wife."

She turned her head sharply at that. There was a heavy pause. "Surely you jest, husband," she replied uneasily. "For now I come to think of it, you must surely have rooms at court?"

"Yes," he agreed, thinking of the cramped palace quarters with no great fondness. Then it came to him how fortuitous the turn in the conversation had taken. "You have ambitions to be presented at court?" he asked. If so, he could certainly grant that wish with the greatest of ease at the upcoming royal tournament.

306

"What? Certainly not!" Sabina practically recoiled at the suggestion. "I just thought… Well, that you must reside there for a good deal of your time," she finished lamely.

"I rarely stay at court," he retorted. "Only during the royal tournaments as a rule."

"Oh. That sounds rather wasteful. Of the palace resources, I mean."

"The rooms are not exclusively mine," he explained. "My cousin Hugo uses them and also my godfather, Sir Charles, and his son." The bed rustled as though she had stiffened at this indirect mention of Leland and he couldn't say as he blamed her. "The royal summer event is the next major tournament to be held next month. That is always held at the King's summer palace in Caer-Lyoness."

Sabina held her tongue for a minute, then she said evasively, "I will surely be very busy at Morecotte for the rest of the summer. As we discussed earlier, there is so much to be done."

Jeffree's brows snapped together. It was on the tip of his tongue to tell her she would damned well attend whatever he deemed fit, but something held him back. After all, what was the point of introducing a discordant note, when things were finally starting on an even keel between them?

He had already made such huge concessions to secure her cooperation. Had he not saddled himself with the mammoth task of transforming his bratty younger brothers into squires? He had only agreed to such a preposterous thing to get into Sabina's good books.

If someone, anyone, had told him he would willingly take charge of his siblings, he would have thought them mad. They would be in his charge for at least four years, if not longer. It suddenly struck him that it would likely have been far less painful to simply perform those pitiful courtship steps she had thought so essential.

What were they again? Praise her in front of her family? Make some public show of admiration? He cast a sidelong look in her direction. Would it have been so difficult, after all, to do those things? He was starting to think he had overcomplicated everything when it came to this woman.

"Jeffree?"

"Yes?"

"If neither of us are tired, mayhap we could practice that matter from before," she suggested tentatively.

His ears pricked up at once. "What matter?" When she did not answer at once, he could not wait. "Kissing?" he rasped. "Is that what you mean?"

"Indeed, it was" was all she managed to get out before Jeffree had turned and taken a firm hold of her. He fancied she gave a spurt of laughter, which he stopped with his lips. He had recalled the feel of her lips a thousand times already that day, but as soon as their mouths touched, he realized his memories had done her scant justice.

Sabina's arms wound around his neck, and he groaned with pleasure. *Oh, my gods.* It was at this moment that Jeffree realized he had not been wasting his time all day, tiptoeing around this woman. When she was in his arms everything seemed to fall into place and make a strange sort of sense. Why was that?

"You have been so nice today, Jeffree," Sabina murmured against his mouth. *What?* "Really, you have been almost a pleasure to be around." He had? Wait, what did she mean "almost"?

"Hrrrrmmm" was all he could manage by way of response. She sighed, and the contented sound made his half-hard cock stand to full attention. He wanted her to make that sound when he was deep inside her. He wanted her to tell him how nice his cock was. He wanted her to demand he give her pleasure. Such thoughts astonished him. Where the hells was this coming from?

Before he was even aware, he had rolled atop of her and was palming her plump backside like it was his perfect right. She shifted against him. "Jeffree?" She had to feel how hard he was, but she made no attempt to wriggle away from his lusty embrace. "Is all well? Why have you stopped?"

Unable to make a reply, Jeffree simply bent his neck and took her mouth again, this time with a slow thoroughness that made his head reel. Gods, he could not get enough of the teasing slide of her tongue. He was barely aware of the fact he was grinding into her until he felt her thighs squeeze against his hips.

"Jeffree," she panted against his mouth.

"Can I touch you?" he practically begged, a ridiculous request considering how they were bodily intertwined.

"Yes." She grabbed his hand and pressed it to her soft bosom. He had meant between her legs, but her generous breasts distracted him sufficiently from saying so. His face flamed hot and his breathing was ragged as he made out the shape of her through her thin shift and felt the weight of her full, round breasts in his hands.

"Gods," he whispered, and shifting down her body, he brushed a kiss atop each sweet swell of flesh above her neckline, feeling his face heat as he did so. His fingers twitched with the impulse to yank the flimsy material down and out of the way, but likely Sabina would not care for such rude treatment of her undergarment. The thing was likely to rend in two between his hands.

Instead, he sought comfort by rubbing his face over and around her glorious breasts, wishing he had left a candle burning when he had climbed into bed, but the light had seemed sufficient then. Little had he known at that point how desperately he would want to see what color his wife's nipples were.

"Jeffree?" Sabina squirmed and he halted at once. Was this not as pleasurable for her? She struggled to sit, and Jeffree backed up, feeling suddenly glad it was dark. It would hide his mortification. Then he heard a rustle and realized she was divesting herself of her shift. She collapsed back onto the cushions. "Where are you?" He felt her fingertips graze his shoulder. "Come back here."

He was back on top of her in a trice. "Tell me what to do," he muttered into the valley between her breasts as he kissed his way down. "Tell me what feels good."

Her fingers sifted through his hair. "Everything you're doing right now feels *so* nice," she sighed, and once again, he felt it almost as though she had sighed directly against his ballocks. It was strange how potently the idea of giving her pleasure seemed to affect him. He had never guessed he possessed an altruistic bone in his body before now.

Surrendering to his baser impulses, he ran the slope of his nose over one nipple, and the noise she made in her throat had him breathing hard. "That feels nice?" he pressed as he repeated the action on the other nipple. She shivered, and when he would have returned to kissing around her glorious breasts, her fingers tightened in his hair, holding him in place.

Guessing she had anchored him there for a purpose, Jeffree nuzzled against the pointy nipple wondering what it might be. "Tell me," he urged.

"In your mouth," she whimpered.

Oh. Tentatively, he opened his lips over her pouting nipple and sucked it into his mouth.

"Oh, *Jeffree!*" She practically arched up off the pillow.

His nostrils flared. So, she liked that, did she? He licked his lips. Well, so did he. He set about sucking her pretty nipples in earnest. Her reception of his attentions was more than gratifying, and he was forced to flex his hips against the mattress in search of relief for his aching cock.

"Yes, Jeffree," she gasped as he released her nipple after a good hard suck. He kissed across to the other and teased it gently with his tongue. The fact she liked it all the ways he could think of made his chest swell.

"Tell me what else," he murmured, kissing the undersides of her bosom and absently down to her belly button.

She gave a soundless shriek and caught hold of his ears. "N-not that, Jeffree!" she squeaked, half sitting up. "I've never had that."

Had what? Jeffree narrowed his eyes in the dark. Why was she sounding so suddenly nervous? "I won't do anything you don't like," he said needlessly. He was not remotely interested in doing anything she did not enjoy. Except…he didn't think she sounded like he had done aught amiss. He extended his tongue and touched it tentatively to her belly button. Sabina gave a muffled squawk.

"It's sensitive here?" he asked.

"A little," she said in a stifled voice, but it did not seem terribly sensitive now as he carefully licked around it, and she relaxed and released his ears.

He shrugged it off. There was some mystery here he would revisit later. "Can I make you ready?" he asked huskily against her soft stomach.

Sabina gulped. "You already have."

He frowned. "I have not yet touched you between your legs though."

She gave a soft dissenting murmur. Why did she sound embarrassed?

"I want to," he insisted. "Let me."

She was silent a moment and then drew back from him, letting her legs fall apart. Jeffree's breathing hitched and he stared in the darkness, wishing he could see her clearly. Her hand sought his own, drawing it between her legs. He felt the hair of her most private place brush against the backs of his fingers and felt a rush of blood to his head.

"I'll show you," she whispered, and the next thing he knew she was pressing his thumb to her wet slit, and he was feeling her exquisite trembling flesh against his questing fingers.

"Do you feel that?" she asked so quietly he could scarce hear her over his labored breathing.

Jeffree nodded, then realizing she would likely not see it, growled "Yes" aloud.

"This is my bud. It is where I touch myself when I wish to make myself ready. It is very sensitive."

Carefully, Jeffree pressed the pad of his thumb to the delicate bud. Sabina gave a muffled sob.

"Too hard?" he asked quickly, relaxing the pressure, though he could not bring himself to withdraw his hand from where it rested so intimately against her, feeling her nether hair tickling his fingers.

"Nay, 'tis not that." He felt the brush of her own hand against his and then she guided his thumb to touch her over and over with varying touches. Some featherlight, others firmer. Sometimes she had him circle his thumb, others he had to drag it over the bud, teasing and tormenting. Sabina gasped and moaned beneath their joint ministrations until he felt almost light-headed himself from the contact.

Suddenly, he felt her hips jolt and she gave a choked cry and held his hand in a viselike grip. He was not *completely* ignorant. He had heard a few moans and groans over the years when staying at rough and ready inns and had even walked in on a couple once who had been making use of an empty chamber. Apparently, women could reach the point of pleasurable oblivion as well as men, despite the fact they spilled no seed.

Clearly, Sabina had just reached hers. She breathed raggedly for a minute and then plucked his hand away. "My bud's too sensitive for touching now," she explained. "You can just put it in."

"Put it in?" he repeated blankly.

"And seek your own pleasure," she explained. If he had not been ridiculously overstimulated, he was pretty sure this would have dampened his ardor. As it was, nothing was likely to do

313

that now. Still, when he made no immediate move, she reached for him and encouraged him to position his cock at her cleft.

Still, he paused before thrusting home. She gave a choked gasp beneath him, and Jeffree stilled, despite his loins clamoring for him to lose himself in her body's tight clasp. "You take no pleasure in this part, then?" he heard himself wheeze. Despite his mind closing down from sheer delight, the thought was oddly disquieting to him.

Sabina hesitated before replying. "I did not say that precisely." She sounded flustered as she slid her arms about his shoulders. "'Tis only that, for me, the kissing and touching is the part where I feel the moment of rapture, not when you"—her words faltered a moment—"er…give me your seed," she concluded in a stifled voice.

Jeffree frowned furiously as he strove to take this new information on board. Still, he could not resist a firm buck of his hips. The attendant jolt of exaltation almost made him shout aloud. Instead, he buried his face in her neck to muffle his groan. He did not notice when he started kissing along her jaw. Not until she whispered his name and ran a hand up his neck and into his hair. Then the scrape of her fingertips against his scalp made him groan again.

Suddenly, inexplicably, it became of the utmost importance that he captured her lips with his own and that he made her feel the same wild urgency that consumed him in this moment. She liked kissing and touching? Well, they were already kissing, but what if he touched her now, even as his hips shifted restlessly over her own?

She had said her bud was too sensitive, but what about her glorious breasts? He cupped them beneath his hands and squeezed. Sabina gave a gasp which went straight to his groin.

"Too sensitive?" he asked huskily and scarcely recognized his own voice.

Sabina let out a shuddering breath. "N-no," she stammered. "I just did not think… I mean, you are already…that is—*oh!*"

He had no idea what she was babbling about, but from the way she was catching her breath and whimpering, guessed she liked his fingers which were now plucking at her delightful nipples. He wondered if he could stand to suck them into his mouth or if it would all be too much and send him hurtling off the precipice he was climbing until he felt as though he was poised on a perilous ledge.

"Jeffree?" she said breathlessly, and he belatedly remembered that she liked speech during the act. But what to regale her with? he wondered a little wildly. He was never exactly smooth of speech and the current social etiquette defeated him altogether. What did you say to a woman when your finger and thumb were squeezing her nipple and she was accommodating your cock between her sumptuous thighs?

Praise her. He was not sure where the notion originated, but he was too far gone to fight it. "You're magnificent," he heard himself utter hoarsely. "Incredible, *exquisite,* I can't stop—I never want to—don't you dare expect me to—" He had no idea what the fuck he was saying.

"I won't," she moaned beneath him. "I would never."

He was so relieved; he took her mouth again, her beautiful, impertinent mouth. The stroke of her tongue against his own made him fear he was in danger of losing his wits. What were they even talking about?

Sabina writhed beneath him, and for a moment, he almost pitched over the side. He wanted them to go off the edge together. Was that too much to ask? Maybe so, he realized as another groan was wrenched from deep in his chest. She felt so good he was going to lose his mind. He never wanted to be parted from her, he realized, half incredulous, half elated. She was his and he would never let her go. Not ever.

He sent up a prayer of fervent thanks to whatever god of mischief had led Leland and Alfred Hendry to accuse him of trysting with her. He *should* have been climbing through her godsdamned window if he'd had known what was good for him. He chased her lips again in the effort to distract himself from the increasing urgency of his thrusts, his almost overwhelming urge to spill deep inside her.

Sabina's thighs squeezed his sides; she wrenched her mouth from his. "Oh, Jeffree, *Jeffree*—" she keened. Then she gasped and arched her back, and he felt her shudder and clench all around him. "*Oh!*"

She was there again and the *feel* of it, when he was inside her, made his eyes roll back and his entire body convulse. Jeffree bellowed like a maddened bull, and then he was pounding into her, all rhyme and reason gone. He could not get close enough or deep enough. Words fell from his lips, disjointed words, curses, he was not sure he did not implore for the moment to never ever end.

He wanted to lose himself within her without any hope of ever being found. He had never been a religious man, but he had heard of ecstasies overtaking the holy. If they were anything like this then he did not blame them for renouncing all other ways of life. Then he was spurting so long and hard that he would have been alarmed if he had not been quickly overtaken with a sweet bliss that rolled through his limbs like a potent, drugging wine and he collapsed like a dead man, oblivious to everything.

When next he came to his senses, he was slumped over her like a dead weight and all he could hear was harsh, labored breathing. It took him a moment to realize the one panting was him. He reared back as quickly as his sluggish body would allow. Had he crushed her to death? Sabina let out a faint moan of protest. "Wife?"

"Mmmph," she mumbled, gently pushing on his chest. "Let me up. I need to wash." He rolled off her, though in truth, it was the last thing he wanted to do. Sabina shuffled out of bed and made for the basin, where she started pouring water and splashing about. He listened to the sound of her squeezing out the washcloth and yawning as she cleaned herself up.

"Did you want me to pour you some water?" she asked with a yawn. With a flicker of surprise, Jeffree realized his impulse was to refuse it and stay where he was. "Too tired?" she added, sounding amused.

Not caring for the implication that she had exhausted him, he grudgingly dragged himself across the room and took her place at the basin as Sabina made her way back to the bed. When they passed each other, he had to quell the impulse to catch her in his arms again. Jeffree gave his head a quick shake. He needed to nip these impulses in the bud.

Still, he rushed through the most perfunctory of washes and hurried back to take his place beside her in the bed. After the briefest of hesitations, he curled his arm around her, drawing her in close to his side.

Sabina sighed. "That's nice," she uttered sleepily before lapsing once more into silence.

Nice? Not the word Jeffree would have chosen. "Sabina?" He paused, but there was no response. "Aren't we supposed to

317

exchange some words now?" he asked uncertainly. She had said so last time, though it had not gone well.

He heard a rustle and felt a vehement shake of her head. "Gods no," she murmured. "Let us not go down that route again. It will spoil the moment." He opened his mouth to protest when he felt her reach up to pat his arm. "All is well. Let us sleep now, husband." She yawned again, and he was not surprised when a few minutes later he heard the faint snore in the darkness.

He really ought to roll her off onto her side, Jeffree reflected. If memory served, that prevented the phenomena. He had always barged into his old master's room and shoved a boot against Sir Hereward's shoulder to turn the old sot when his snores grew loud enough to disturb the rest of his household.

To Jeffree's surprise, he found he did not have the heart to disturb Sabina's slumber. In any case, despite everything that had passed between them, he still did not have words he was confident would please her. Instead, he listened to her snuffles awhile, realizing they were actually a source of comfort to him. He lay there, thinking over everything they had shared in the hope it could shed some light on what he was supposed to say to a wife who pleased you inordinately in your bed.

There had been that odd business about her belly button, he thought, frowning into the darkness as he reviewed it in his mind. He had not led a sheltered life exactly, despite his godfather's strict sobriety and his uncle's fastidiousness. It was not as if he had been raised exclusively in their households.

It was more that he had chosen to turn a deaf ear to ribald talk and the many lewd jokes that had been spoken around him over the years. He had chosen a different path to most of his fellow knights, one of abstinence. He had curled his lip and risen

318

above their baseness when they were drunk and frequently coarse at table.

Now his brain groped and actively sought out the bits and pieces he had stopped his ears against for so long. Slowly, he recalled the many boasts of old Sir Hereward about his many conquests and the tales of the low company he had kept as they bragged about their amorous escapades. Something clicked into place.

She had never had a tongue in her cunny. That was what she had meant. When his chest began to burn, Jeffree realized he needed to start breathing again. He gulped in the sweet night air and tried to quiet his racing heart, which was thudding so loud in his breast, she would surely hear it.

He glanced down in the darkness but had to make do with the feel of her beneath his arm, all curvy and warm. *He* wanted to do that for her, with his mouth between her legs. What would she taste like? What noises would she make for him? Would she sigh or gasp and moan? When she said his name, would she cry it with a scream or choke it brokenly as he sought out her precious bud with the tip of his tongue?

He had to swallow and take a deep breath to quiet his rampant thoughts and cease the tumult they caused in his rapidly stiffening cock, the throb in his ballocks. It was strange, for as a squire, hearing of such things, he had thought they sounded lewd and depraved. Of course, he had not known intimacy then, the pleasures of the marriage bed. Just as well, or his self-imposed chastity would have been well-nigh impossible.

Or would it though? He could not imagine salivating at the idea of paying such attentions to any other woman save Sabina. The vague and faceless female forms he had always imagined at dead of night when he had stroked himself to completion had never made him shout aloud or pass out from sheer mind-numbing satisfaction.

Never before had he felt that intense physical longing for another person. He had certainly never wanted to please a woman and win her good opinion. Was this…? He balked at the realization looming before him. He wanted *her* to love *him*, but *his* feelings needed to remain aloof from such things. Feminine weakness was permissible in certain spheres of life, whereas a man was wise to rise above such things.

It was not becoming for Jeffree de Crecy to become some lovesick churl, trailing around after his wife like some prating fool, begging for her favor. He felt himself turn hot then cold all over. If he was not careful, he would become a figure of ridicule instead of admiration. All he had strived for in life, his noble reputation, spotless and without flaw, crushed beneath her heel.

People would laugh behind their hands at him. *There goes de Crecy*, they would say. *Oh, how the mighty have fallen! See how his wife flouts and cusses him, and all he can do is clutch at her skirts, poor wretch!*

Gods, he needed to make her love him before he made a complete ass out of himself!

17

Sabina woke suddenly in the early hours and found she was lying on her stomach next to Jeffree, her hand resting with great familiarity on his chest. She was not terribly surprised by this, for her new husband was an uneasy sleeper, frequently flinging blankets around and turning over. At some point in the night, presumably, she had decided to try pinning him in place.

In truth, she could not complain about his restlessness for a bedpartner. She had startled herself awake not long after midnight, mid-snore. For a moment, she had lain disoriented and horrified that she could have made such a noise, then she had hurriedly rolled onto her side and hoped Jeffree had not realized his wife was so uncouth.

She lay a moment now, making out his relaxed profile in the dim light before carefully moving to lift her hand away. To her astonishment, her hand was firmly captured by his and replaced on his lightly furred chest. Sabina swallowed her instinctive exclamation, her gaze flying to Jeffree's face, but his eyes remained closed.

Was he asleep or merely resting his eyes? He kept his own hand atop of her own to hold it where it lay. After a moment, Sabina set her head back on the pillow bearer and closed her own eyes. It could not be much after five in the morning, and clearly, he was in no hurry for them to be on their way.

When next she woke it was to birdsong, and light was streaming through the window. Quickly turning her head, she found Jeffree propped up on one elbow, gazing down at her with a furrowed brow. Had she been snoring again? She sat up hastily, clearing her throat. "Did I oversleep?" She fussed with the neckline of her shift to check it was decent and spare his blushes.

"No," he answered grudgingly. "I would have woken you if you had."

Thinking he sounded a little surly, she swung her legs out of the bed, then almost jumped out of her skin at the knock on the door. It proved only to be a servant with hot water for them, and Sabina made haste to get washed and dressed.

She felt skittish around him this morning and strangely apprehensive. Would he attempt to be agreeable again today or would he revert once more to haughty disdain? Yesterday he had certainly been on his best behavior, and she had appreciated his efforts. For a while, they had even made her feel optimistic about the future they faced.

If Jeffree could find it in him to be agreeable, then these early days of marriage would certainly pass much easier. Then, when he inevitably grew tired of her, their lives could separate smoothly and without resentment. The process had been difficult with Miles because she had imagined an initial affection there that had not existed. She had thought he owed her things like loyalty and faithfulness, and he had not agreed.

With Jeffree it was different, she told herself firmly. They did not like each other. Well… She cast a sidelong look at him as he buttoned his tunic. Perhaps that was not strictly true. She had started to think of him with a sort of…wry affection, she realized uneasily. Was that something she should be worried about? Petting his chest in her sleep was likely not a habit she should indulge herself in. Then again, she had not knowingly done it. She pinned the swathes of her wimple in place and examined herself in front of the tiny mirrored glass before letting her gaze slide over her shoulder to where Jeffree was sat pulling on his boots.

If she did not actively dislike him, at least she did not imagine herself to be in love with him. Such a course of action would be disastrous. Imagine falling in love with an arrogant beast like Sir Jeffree de Crecy! A woman would have to be an absolute fool to succumb to such an impulse. She did not imagine for one moment that Meliora had nurtured any such tender feelings in her bosom.

Why then had she insisted he could not visit his former betrothed again, without her by his side? She flushed at the memory. That had been both foolish and nonsensical. Then again, Jeffree had not seemed to resent the condition she had demanded. He had acquiesced quite willingly; indeed, he had reassured her no further visit would e'er take place. Was it possible he had been lying?

It was always a possibility, but somehow she did not think so. She did not think Jeffree the kind of man who would lie for convenience. He did not shrink from argument or possess a lying tongue. Likely he had never troubled himself enough to tell anything but the blunt truth.

She considered this a moment as Jeffree threw his effects into a saddlebag and looked up at her expectantly. Sabina nodded, but when she turned to fetch her own pack from the bed, he picked that up too and opened the door open for her. She could not really accuse him of being ill-mannered toward her anymore, she reflected as she preceded him down the narrow passageway.

She was not sure when, but he certainly now showed her the attentions a wife might expect from her spouse. Her cheeks heated. Certainly, he was a fast learner when it came to the bedchamber. She could have no complaint in that respect. She

323

blinked as memories from the previous night flooded into her mind, making her breathing fast and her step on the stairs falter. Her new husband was certainly proving no slouch between the sheets.

He had brought her to that pleasure precipice not once but twice and sent her shooting over the edge. The second time had really astonished her. She had not disliked the act in the early days of her first marriage when conjugal relations had still existed betwixt herself and Miles, but certainly, she had not over-relished it.

Never had she reacted like *that*, not even when she had thought herself fond of her bedpartner. With Jeffree it was different. Mayhap it was because he was so *intense*.

His hand clasped on her shoulder, steadying her as she reached the bottom step. "Watch your step."

Sabina nodded, glancing over her shoulder at him. She thought his eyes narrowed, seeing her flushed face. "Will we break our fast here or find somewhere else at midday?" she asked hurriedly to distract him.

"Let us see what is on offer," he answered, looking about for a servant.

He must have had quite an appetite, for despite the place offering only a dark maslin bread and some cold leftover mutton, Jeffree elected to partake of this fare. Osborn joined them at table, and Sabina resolved to think no more disquieting thoughts as she helped herself sparingly to the food on offer. She was only making herself needlessly flustered.

Still, she started violently when seeing the paucity of food on her plate. Jeffree touched her hand. "I will find you better food later," he muttered.

Sabina cursed herself for an idiot when her color rose at his words. "That really is not necessary," she assured him and forced down another mouthful of the rye bread. "This will do very well." He made no reply, though Sabina was careful to avoid his eye when she pushed away the rest of her slice uneaten.

"It's good bread is this!" Osborn objected.

"You have it, then," Jeffree told him sharply. "And do not attempt to reproach your mistress again or you will suffer for it."

Sabina felt embarrassed when Jeffree offered her his hand for her to rise from the table and led her out of the hostelry like she was some grand lady. "I can mount by myself," she pointed out feebly when he helped her into her saddle with the same amount of attendant ceremony.

She was not sure he paid much heed to her words, but she could feel Osborn's sour gaze between her shoulder blades from where he brought up the rear. She shrugged this off when she felt the sun warm on her back. There was barely a cloud in the sky, and it was hard not to be cheerful when she was homeward bound and well-slept and in good company.

The last thought brought her up short. *Good company?* Where had that unbidden notion sprung from? Osborn was certainly not good company with his sulks and mutterings and as for Jeffree… Well, he had faults a-plenty, even if none sprang immediately to mind when she looked now at his handsome face and regal bearing in the saddle.

He was proud and haughty, she reminded herself hastily. He had a nasty tongue. True, it had not seemed so nasty the night before when she had welcomed it into her own mouth and sucked on it like it was the most delicious comfit she had e'er

325

been offered. Sabina gulped. There she went again, letting her thoughts wander. What was she thinking of?

Self-preservation seemed to be flying out of the window. She snuck another glance at him and felt her heart quail. This would never do. She was getting distracted by his beauteous face and form, that was all. It was small wonder that a provincial nobody like herself should be dazzled by the high and mighty Jeffree de Crecy.

The surprise of it was that she had not felt the full effect of his appearance from the outset. His manner back then had been so distasteful that it had blighted his beauty in her eye. Now, his manner toward her had...what? Not *softened* exactly, and it was not as though he was trying to exercise charm on her either, for she did not believe he had any.

It was more that he was trying *not* to antagonize her, that was all. After all, they had decided, had they not, that they must try to rub along together while they navigated these early stages in their marriage?

At least, she thought that was what they had decided. Uneasy remembrances rose in her mind. Of Jeffree speaking of a future together. But when he had said that, she reminded herself, he had been prompted by man's most basic of urges. Men could convince themselves of anything when lust raked at their backs.

He had surely meant that their lives would forever be entwined now, even if only by name. Sabina nodded. Yes, assuredly, that was what he had meant. She would be his wife now until death did them part. Even if he spent his days pursuing tournament glory and she spent hers bustling about Morecotte making her old home comfortable once more.

For some reason, the thought did not comfort her as she would once have imagined it would. Why was that? She reminded

326

herself that Jeffree had agreed without hesitation to all her suggestions for renovation. He had swept away all her considerations of thrift and economy, pledging his considerable coffers to the cause.

Why, then, did she feel so discomposed? She was worried about her sister, it was true. Their father and mother must surely be pushing for such a reconciliation between Isemay and the duke. Sabina's absence would make very little difference to what happened. After all, her sister had entered into her engagement with Bethencourt the first time without Sabina's counsel, and if she did so a second time, then it would not be so very surprising. An older sister's word held very little sway compared to that of a parent's.

No, this current strange mood must be solely because of things growing complicated with Jeffree, she thought with a sigh, nibbling at her bottom lip. Then it struck her. She no longer disliked him! With a gasp, Sabina sat up in her saddle and stared ahead of her with shock and consternation. She could no longer in all honesty say she did not like Jeffree de Crecy. The realization left her disquieted, and she had to make a hurried grab for the reins which had slackened in her grasp.

She needed to have a care, she thought, breathing hard through her nose, or ridiculous as it sounded, the next thing she knew she would be growing overly attached to Jeffree and dependent on his company. Then, when her novelty wore off, as it inevitably would, where would she be? Jeffree would start finding her irksome exactly as Miles had done, and Sabina would be left all alone and despised for a second time.

This time, she would not even have her own hatred for company as she could not imagine Jeffree betraying her as Miles had. After all, he had never pretended to care for her as her first husband had done. No, it would be different, she decided, different but still…oddly painful.

Sabina was in a grave mood by the time they stopped for a break at midday. After pacing about a bit to stretch out her legs, she dropped down onto a convenient grassy bank. Jeffree joined her moments later after seeing to the horses. He glanced at her a little warily, then cleared his throat.

"Why so stony-faced?" he asked, passing her the waterskin.

"I don't know what you mean," Sabina answered briskly and took a swig of water.

"You look solemn."

"Don't I always?"

"No," he answered promptly. "Not usually."

"You have not known me very long," she pointed out, lowering the waterskin with a frown. He gave a shrug but did not deign to argue with her. For some reason, this made her feel even worse. "Would you say you tire of people rather quickly as a rule?" she asked impulsively, passing back the waterskin.

"People?"

"You know." She shrugged. "Family, friends, acquaintances."

"I tire of my family all the time," he answered, sounding unconcerned.

"Yes, but…" She fidgeted where she sat. "Well, I suppose family is not really the same," she muttered half to herself. When she looked up, Jeffree was eyeing her curiously.

"The same as what?"

"Who would you say is your closest friend in all the world, Jeffree?"

His brows lowered, and he seemed rather puzzled by the question. "I don't think I have one," he admitted at last, gazing into the distance. "Who would you say is yours?"

His turning the question back on her was surprising. "My sister," she answered absently.

He nodded. "What is the age difference between the two of you?"

Again, his curiosity startled her. "I was six when Isemay was born."

"And where is it that you get your brains from?" he asked, as though he had been puzzling over the question.

"What do you mean?"

"Clearly, you do not follow your parents in that regard." Sabina spluttered, but before she could take umbrage, he added, "Neither you nor your sister lack for wits."

Deciding to overlook the insult to her parents, Sabina turned a thoughtful look upon him. "What was *your* father like?" she asked. "Was he like you?"

Jeffree's shoulders rose and fell. "I do not know," he admitted. "I have no memory of him."

"I wonder if he was a hothead like you," she mused. "Your aloof manner you could have learned from your mother, or Sir Charles, I suppose, but that hot temper…"

"I don't have a hot temper." He sounded annoyed.

329

"Oh yes you do, Jeffree de Crecy! A hot temper and a hot, lusty nature."

He snorted. "You taught me that," he growled. "I did not have that before you."

"I expect you did. I just uncovered it." Noticing the look in his eye, Sabina clamped her mouth shut. Somehow she had gone haring off down a completely different track than the one she had intended. She cleared her throat. "Well, that's neither here nor there," she said, rising swiftly to her feet. "It looks like Osborn has finished watering the horses."

For one minute, she thought it was touch and go if he would pounce on her with scant regard for their surroundings. Hurrying down the bank, she did not dare to look back over her shoulder, though she could hear him moving behind her. Sailing past Osborn, she made straight for Blitha and soothed herself more than the horse by stroking her velvety nose. Footsteps followed close behind, so she was not surprised when she heard Jeffree's growl in her ear.

"Why are you running away from me?"

"I am not."

"That is what it looked like from where I was standing." She turned her head to frown at him and dart her eyes meaningfully toward where Osborn stood nearby. Jeffree's eyebrows rose.

"Shall we reach Morecotte before ere long taking this route?" she asked loudly.

He did not answer at once. "By tomorrow eve," he admitted at last, grudgingly.

"So soon?"

He nodded. "This pleases you?"

330

"Of course! It is always good to arrive home." She wondered at his expression. "You do not agree?"

He shrugged. "I am used to travel."

The way his eyes dwelt on her face made her feel strangely shy. Usually, in her frumpy headdress, she felt impervious to the scrutiny of others. With Jeffree, she almost felt like he could see beneath it now. She touched the crisp linen folds distractedly to assure herself it was still in place. "I suppose you must be," she murmured, avoiding his eyes.

*

Hearing Osborn's cough close by, Jeffree swiveled in his saddle. His servant had passed by Sabina and drawn his horse alongside Jeffree's own which rode in front.

"If I might be permitted a word, sir?" Osborn said dolefully, spearing him with a reproachful eye.

"Yes? What is it, Osborn?"

"I thought the other morn I heard tell of you taking on a couple of squires, Sir Jeffree, but maybe my ears deceived me," Osborn began, sounding injured.

"They did not deceive you," Jeffree answered briskly. "I will be taking on both of my brothers as squires, may the gods help me." Osborn looked so disapproving that Jeffree felt stung into further speech. "Not immediately, though some time in the next year."

Osborn sniffed. "Lot of changes," he muttered, shaking his head. "Always served households with bachelors, I have, not with womenfolk nor children neither."

331

Jeffree gave him a hard stare. "You are not bound to me, Osborn," he said stiffly. "If the position no longer suits, then you must feel free to explore pastures new."

Osborn's look of wounded dignity grew more marked. "I wasn't saying of that, Sir Jeffree. Not after these past five years of faithful service I have given thee."

"Then what *were* you saying?"

"Just pointing out how circumstances has changed," said Osborn mournfully, rolling his eyes.

Jeffree, who knew himself to pay a generous wage, sighed irritably. As if he did not know his own circumstances had changed of late. *Drastically.* "Very well, now you have pointed it out. Consider yourself heard."

Osborn sniffed again but let his horse fall back so he was once again bringing up the rear.

Unable to help himself, Jeffree followed suit so he dropped back to ride abreast with Sabina.

"Is aught amiss?" she asked.

"Naught. Just Osborn thinking he deserves recompense for serving an expanding household." That brought a reluctant smile to her lips, he thought irritably, if nothing else did.

"And will you? Raise his wages, I mean."

Jeffree shrugged. "Possibly. It would be a vast inconvenience to train up a new man."

"Don't forget we have Penny and Lancer back at Morecotte," she reminded him. "It is not as though we are expecting him to chop firewood and tend to the hens."

"Do we have hens?"

Sabina laughed and he felt it right down to his toes. "Not presently," she admitted, "but back in my day we did. They are good for fresh eggs."

"You should get more, then," he heard himself assert. "Now you are mistress of Morecotte once more."

She smiled at that and Jeffree examined his reaction. There was no denying that her smile gave him a warm feeling in the pit of his stomach. He wanted to see more of it. He wanted to see more of *her*. "Have you always...?" He gestured first toward his face, then his whole head.

"Worn a wimple?" she asked after a moment's hesitation.

"Yes. Such a heavy one with a double veil," he elaborated. "Encompassing everything."

There was a pause, then she shook her head. "N-no," she admitted. "At least, not until my first husband and I were estranged. Then my mother thought it might be advisable."

"Why?"

"Such a headdress is considered the epitome of respectability," she pointed out. "Even the holy sisters at Fulford Abbey were not swathed any more thoroughly than I."

"I cannot argue with that," he admitted. "Though I might wonder at the necessity."

She shrugged. "My mother did not want my respectability to be called into question," she answered lightly. "I was living apart from my husband and she did not want me to fall prey to vicious gossip or speculation."

Perhaps Thora Burrell was not so vapid as she had appeared. "That shows good sense," he conceded, "but why now do you continue with such garb?"

Her face turned blank. "Well, then, I was widowed so suddenly..." She let her words trail off.

"But now you are a married woman who is *not* separated from her husband," he pointed out.

Sabina flushed. "I have not yet had time to adjust my attire," she said defensively. "You will admit the change happened so fast that neither one of us was prepared for the change in our circumstances."

"I will admit that much," he acknowledged. "If you will agree that I have ample resources to clothe you as befits my station." When she made no answer, he fixed her with a stern eye. "You saw the quantities of fabrics I already own in my store at Ganford Chase."

"Those are for your own wardrobe," she protested.

"If you liked none of them, then I can obtain more."

"It is not that!"

"What, then? What possible objection can you have dressing as befits my wife?"

She huffed out a breath. "All those fabrics were extremely sumptuous—so sumptuous that I—I could not possibly swan about Ganfordshire clad in them! Not in front of people who have known me all my life!"

He snorted. "Your sister and mother did not seem to feel the same way."

"That was Isemay's wedding day! It was only fitting—" She broke off, narrowing her gaze at him. "Do you find my manner of dress displeasing?" she asked outright.

"It neither does you justice nor reflects well on me that you should dress thus."

"I see." Her chin came up and her words were clipped.

Jeffree regarded her frankly. "It is good you are proud," he commented, nodding. "De Crecys are always proud."

Sabina gasped and seemed to struggle with a response before electing for stony silence. Jeffree waited a few moments, feeling oddly disappointed nothing else was forthcoming, not even barbed words. He could not be annoyed the subject had been raised, for it needing broaching; however, he was strangely sorry to be in her bad books again so soon. In the face of such a straightforward question though, he could never tell her a bald-faced lie.

She deserved always the truth from him, and the truth was he wanted her in silks and satins and the costliest raiment his purse could afford. He wanted her to acknowledge she was a de Crecy, that she was his wife. He wanted others to be in no doubt of the fact. This current state of affairs could not be allowed to continue, where others could mistake her for his servant, so meanly was she attired.

Jeffree stole another look at her and was forced to conclude she was ignoring him. With some reluctance, he maneuvered Radax back into the lead position again and resigned himself to the fact Sabina was unlikely to welcome his embrace in the privacy of their inn room later. This thought made him feel oddly depressed in spirit.

For someone who had never much valued the society of others, this newfound clamor for the good opinion and company of another was a strange one to him. Doubtless, a good deal of it was grounded in his desire for her, he reflected, but not all of it. No, not all of it. He was shocked by the strength of his ardor, he would admit that much to himself.

Previously his idea of admiring women was of a vague, idealistic sort, not earthy or sensual. He had curled a lip at ribald talk, despised those who seemed weak to the lures of the flesh, thinking himself above such coarse and debased pleasures.

Now, he found himself contemplating things he had previously dismissed as completely beneath his dignity. If he had entertained lewd thoughts, they had been in the privacy of his own bedchamber and his own hand had brought him the temporary relief he had sought. Afterward, he had felt mildly disgusted with himself. He did not feel disgusted after joining his body with Sabina's though; he felt exhilarant. Elated even.

These strange new urges to kiss and embrace her were a little alarming. If they were confined to the bedchamber he could understand it, but today he'd had random promptings at the oddest of times. Just now on that grassy hillock, the urge had been almost overwhelming. If she had not fled, he would certainly have succumbed to temptation.

He wished someone would tell him the words he was supposed to say in the aftermath of their lovemaking. *Words of comfort or praise*, that was what she had said. He took those words out and puzzled over them for the hundredth time as the afternoon wore on. Now that he came to consider it, he could not actually think of a time he had praised anyone. In Jeffree's world, if someone did well, you gave them a curt nod and held off on the scathing comments for a while.

A curt nod would not really cut it when acknowledging your wife's magnificence between the sheets. *You're magnificent.* He had some recollection of gasping out those words the last time, though the vague memory made him squirm slightly. In any case, that had not been after the act but during. He was not sure those counted. Why did he have such a problem with it? Such words tripped off the tongues of others with ease.

Wheels creaked and turned in the dark recesses of his mind. Mayhap because no one had ever praised him? He dismissed this almost at once. No, that was not true. As heir to the Duke of Bethencourt he had been held to the highest standards, that was all. Their whole family knew the de Crecys were one of the first and most venerated in the land. Still…that was not exactly the same as being praised for your own sake, was it?

He chewed the side of his mouth as he considered this. His mother had not been permitted to raise a child with such high expectations as a dukedom. When he *had* seen her, they had always been rather formal with one another. No, it was Sir Charles who had molded him, but he could barely remember his guardian's spouse, so insignificant she had seemed. He tried and failed to remember a single interaction between them.

His godfather was a stern and exacting man who expected absolute perfection. *That* was who he had learned the curt nod from. When Jeffree met Sir Charles's expectations, he received a curt nod. When Jeffree did *not* meet Sir Charles's standards, he had received icy disapproval and disdain. Neither occasion had called for much by way of outward expression.

Sir Hereward, the old knight he had served for four years, had been such a braggart that Jeffree's achievements had been met only with rivaling tales of his own feats and prowess. Jeffree frowned over this. He should not like to do the same to Jasper and Crispin. Mayhap he *should* learn how to throw out a word or two of approval?

As for his uncle… Bethencourt had always been rather self-involved. Perhaps most dukes were. Everyone around them sought to please them after all, so it was hardly surprising. Still, he should not like to think of himself being so coddled and detached from the world around him as his uncle Bevis was.

Darkness was falling by the time Jeffree emerged from his thoughts to see the flickering lights of a hostelry ahead. This time tomorrow they would be home. *Home?* He meant Morecotte, of course, which was Sabina's home. As for himself, he had never really had one.

First had been his guardian's home, then Sir Hereward's dilapidated hall, then his rooms at Ganford Chase. Even Ganford Chase was more of a stopgap than anything else, a future home, perhaps, though that was no longer guaranteed. Who knew what his uncle might get up to in the next twenty years?

Jeffree certainly could not be hovering around corners in the hope of preventing pretty girls from catching Bethencourt's fancy, whatever his mother and Sir Charles might think! He had his own life to live.

Casting an eye over the approaching inn, he was dismayed to see it was a good deal larger than he recalled. Had they extended the property since last year? Suppose Sabina demanded separate rooms?

As it happened, Sabina did not demand separate rooms, but she was inordinately quiet, insisting she was just tired when he commented on it. They supped on cheese and pickled vegetables with crusty bread, a broth of cabbage and leeks with bacon bits, and a creamed haddock. Sabina picked at the food again, much to Jeffree's displeasure, though Osborn managed to hold his tongue this time.

"You have not eaten enough to hold body and soul together," he told her sternly as she pushed away the fish dish.

He summoned the landlord and asked what else was on offer before she could tell him not to. Eventually, a custard tart was fetched, and that she deigned to eat. Jeffree sat and watched her eat a large slice of it.

"Satisfied?" she asked pointedly after clearing her plate.

Jeffree, who had been looking at the mole above her top lip, flushed. *Hardly.* Satisfied was the last thing he felt. He was ravenous, ravenous for his wife. He lowered his guilty gaze and wondered if *he* should have been the one to request separate rooms. How was he supposed to lie next to her now for ten hours like a starved man at a feast? It was insupportable.

Suddenly, it came to him, a way to get past all this bullshit about praising and courting, things that were beyond his ken. He could simply stop pussy-footing around her and tell the truth, both to himself *and* Sabina. He was in love with her. She was his wife, so she would simply have to take this fact and deal with it. His shoulders relaxed. Yes, that was the way forward, and he was tired of overcomplicating things.

18

Sabina straightened up and moved away from the chair she had been folding her clothes over. "What did you say?" she asked, astonished by the words she thought had just passed her husband's lips.

"I love you," Jeffree repeated through gritted teeth, staring at some point past her left shoulder. Sabina could not help but send a fleeting glance over her shoulder at the bare patch of wall, just to check. Finding nothing there to inspire such devotion, she turned back to the irritated man confronting her.

What possible response could she make to such an impossible statement, especially when it was uttered by someone who looked like they would rather pitch her out of the window than kiss her hand? "Perhaps with time, you might find some outward expression of your love that did not involve your penis?" she suggested tartly.

To her surprise, instead of blowing up at this, he frowned and placed his hands on his hips, seemingly considering her words. "Have you any suggestions as to how?" he asked after a moment.

She flung her arms wide. "Oh, I don't know, Jeffree. Maybe look a little less murderous whenever your eye falls on me? You speak now of love, but in truth, you seem barely to tolerate my presence most of the time!"

"That's a lie!" He scowled.

"Very well, then, you make it plain I am welcome in your bed," she amended.

His face was immediately suffused with hot color. "I—you—" He broke off, shaking his head. "Since we have been wed, I…have not wanted us to part," he pointed out defensively. "I missed your presence at Areley Kings. I may not have told you so, but you must have seen I was relieved to reunite with you."

Sabina frowned. Where was all this coming from? "I thought being dragged in your wake was all part of your elaborate plan of being revenged on me."

"*My* being revenged?" he retorted indignantly. "What of *your* revenge on me? You will accept none of my gifts. Will scarcely allow me to provide for you! How am I supposed to show my regard when you prevent me at every turn? I have not even seen you wear that family heirloom my mother gave you, not once."

"Giving me jewels or gowns is hardly proof of regard, Jeffree!" Sabina retorted. "You are extremely wealthy. You can spend a purse of gold and scarcely give it a thought! Such things are mere trifles to you. I am talking of…affection, consideration, regard. Things which are nothing to do with mere passion!"

He stared at her uncomprehendingly. "You are a passionate man, Jeffree de Crecy," she continued wearily. "But when passion flares as fiercely as yours it burns itself out. It consumes itself like a great ball of fire and then nothing is left behind. You burn brightly for me now, but…" She shrugged. "That won't last, and then what is to become of me?"

"Is that what you think?" he burst out hotly. "My gods, you really are the most—" He tilted his head back, staring up at the ceiling a moment. Sabina steeled herself and waited for him to lambast her. "I am only a passionate man since I met you," he said at last, flummoxing her completely. When she opened her mouth, he cut her off. "And I am not just talking about in the bedchamber. Gods, since I met you, I have *no* self-restraint left to me! In any area of my life!"

Sabina stared as he struggled to get himself under some semblance of calm. "I might have known you would not make this easy for me," he muttered bitterly before pinning her with his bright blue gaze. "Is that what he did?" he asked sharply. "Tell me now."

"Who?"

"The one who came before me!" he bit out with loathing. "Hendry."

He was asking her if Miles had courted her with a passion that burned out? "Hardly!" Sabina spluttered. "Miles married me for convenience, and I found out afterward I was not even his first choice. He courted me with empty words, which I have no doubt he used a dozen times before me *and* after me. He did not think me anything special and, given time, neither will you!" The last few words choked her, and she turned away to gaze unseeingly out of the window.

"Those tears had better be of self-pity and not for that bastard," Jeffree said grimly.

If she weren't so churned up and exhausted, Sabina would almost marvel at his unfortunate choice of words. Truly, if this was Jeffree de Crecy trying to make himself agreeable, she dreaded to think what his idea of disagreeable would be!

"It seems obvious that my method of wooing is nothing like Hendry's," he continued in a surly tone. "So, it is hardly right that you should punish me for his missteps."

His method of wooing? The gods preserve her! Only by the greatest of efforts did Sabina prevent herself from retorting. She took a deep breath. "I should think your 'method of wooing' is unlike anyone else's in existence," she said quite honestly.

He narrowed his eyes at her. "So, tell me, then, what it is you want from me?" he persisted stubbornly.

Sabina passed a hand over her face. "Did I not just say? I want you to treat me with civility and consideration, Jeffree, both in front of others and when we are alone!"

He frowned over this as though the notion of being called inconsiderate was a foreign one to him, which was absurd as up to this point Sabina was sure the man had lived only to please himself.

"I have been raised with impeccable manners," he said in a surly tone as he moved away from the washbasin toward the bed. When she threw a speaking look at him, he had the grace to turn a little red. "Very well," he conceded as he climbed under the covers. "I was angry and accusatory in the early days of our marriage, but I have not repeated any of those things in a long time. I told you early on I no longer believed you were in league with Alfred Hendry."

She nodded. "Oh yes," she agreed dryly. "You told me you forgave me for snaring you into holy matrimony."

Jeffree's mouth opened and closed again as she joined him under the covers. "My early misconceptions about you were soon dispelled," he insisted, rolling on his side toward her. "I quickly realized the gossip about your reputation was unfounded."

Sabina rolled her eyes. "So you no longer believe me shrewish, despite the fact you think I deliberately make things awkward for you?" Catching sight of his confused expression, she felt a strange flash of compassion for him. "Jeffree..."

343

"I am ill-accustomed to…this kind of talk," he admitted. "My address is clumsy when it comes to…lovemaking." Sabina's eyes widened. *Lovemaking?* "You said yourself that I am nothing like Hendry," he continued stiffly. "Will you not give me the benefit of the doubt and forget your prior experience, however bitter it proved?"

Sabina felt oddly touched by his words. "I did not mean to tar you with the same brush as Miles," she said after a heavy pause. "That would hardly be fair. It is just…" She plucked at the covers. "I also am not accustomed to…such things." She stole a look at him and found him still regarding her closely.

"My declaration of love, you mean?" he asked with a faint frown.

Sabina spluttered. "Jeffree…"

"What?"

Was he really going to bandy that word about from now on? It flustered her and made her skittish, but after all, it was just a word and she had a notion Jeffree was as clueless about it as she. Maybe she was worrying about this too much. Mayhap Jeffree thought words of love were just her due as his wedded wife?

She felt something almost akin to affection well up inside her for this awkward, trying man. Before she could change her mind, she leaned across the space between them and pressed a hurried kiss to his cheek. When she would have retreated, he reached out and caught her upper arm, holding her where she was.

"You accept it, then?" he asked gruffly. "My love, I mean?" Sabina felt her face grow hot and she almost tutted. *There he went again!* What response could she possibly make? That she

344

did not think he even knew what love meant? It was all so difficult, and truth to say, she did not wish to wound the man.

When she opened her mouth, he threw up his hand. "Do not make your reply. I already know I will not like whatever words tremble on those lips." He turned his face away from hers, and from the tension in his jaw, she suspected he was grinding his teeth.

"Jeffree." She softened her voice and shuffled closer, patting his chest. "We will be home tomorrow and—and—we—are becoming *accustomed* to one another's ways. That is a very good thing," she added soothingly. "I am growing fond of you too, in a strange sort of way." She could not help the bewildered tone that had crept into her voice, and she felt him stiffen at her words.

Damn it. She had made things worse. He shrugged off her hand and rolled onto his side away from her, drawing the blankets up to his chin. Sabina sat hopelessly gazing at his back a moment, hoping better words would spring to mind. After a few minutes of nothing occuring to her, she, too, lay down and consoled herself with thoughts of returning home on the morrow.

*

They both woke early the next morning, but Sabina had to feign sleep for a few moments while Jeffree released her from his sleepy embrace and made haste to put some space between them. After hurriedly washing and dressing, they were on their way. This time they did not tarry to break their fast. It seemed as though Jeffree could not get out of the place fast enough.

The rest of the day he barely looked at her. He barked out orders to Osborn and rode way out in front of them as though the mere sight of them sickened him. Osborn flashed her a resentful look which seemed to ask, *What have you done now?* As for Sabina, she ignored them both.

She could not *wait* to be home to Ganfordshire. Being at the mercy of a husband was the worst fate that could befall a woman. Jeffree was a petulant *child*! She quietly seethed as she watched his figure in the distance. How dare he speak words of love to her, when he could not even treat her with common decency?

It was stupid of her to feel lingering guilt over his obvious disappointment that she had not responded in kind. Of course he did not love her. He only *thought* that, as she was the first woman he had ever been intimate with. She chewed her lip. Mayhap now he would kiss every one of his uncle's many servant girls and realize she was nothing special whatsoever.

The thought had her sucking in her breath and sitting up straight in her saddle. *Ridiculous.* She was being ridiculous. Jeffree was not the kind to kiss servant girls. He thought himself far too superior to mix with his social inferiors. No, when he had fallen, it had been for a flinty-faced harpy like the Lady Meliora. Sabina breathed out again in a huff.

In any case, she did not care. Once she was safely ensconced in her own home, she would be finally free from the absurd whims of men and she could concentrate on the life she had always dreamed of. A life where she relied on herself for her day-to-day happiness and no one else.

The day wore on. Sabina grew weary. Jeffree did not halt until late afternoon, when he exchanged some brief words with Osborn, and the shambling servant brought her the waterskin and a handful of dry biscuits. Sabina accepted them and left her complaints unvoiced. Osborn was not her ally and would very likely delight in carrying tales to his master.

She felt stiff and sore from the saddle and bruised of spirit. As night fell, nameless dreads started filling her head that Alfred Hendry could have reinfested Morecotte in their absence or even burned it to the ground in revenge. She imagined having to return once more a despised bride to Ganford Chase and her heart quailed. She could not bear to go through all that again! She would rather return to her parents at Tipton Hall and that prospect was bad enough.

When she finally saw Morecotte's shadow rising up out of the darkness, with a light showing at the window, no less, she could have cried aloud with happiness. Jeffree was so far ahead, that by the time she and Osborn reached the end of the lane, he had already roused the occupants and the Lancers were rallying around.

"I'll take your horse, milady," Lancer offered in his gruff way, and Sabina dismounted, gratefully passing Blitha into his care.

"Welcome home, milady," Penny called out of the darkness.

"I am very glad to *be* home," Sabina answered and allowed herself to be led inside. She was so tired by this point that she cast no more than a cursory look about at the freshly scrubbed interior before she was led to the supper table where a hasty meal had been thrown together for them of bread and pottage.

Hearing Jeffree's voice in the hallway, Sabina craned her ears, trying to make out his words. Was he not joining her now?

She raised her own voice. "It is looking a good deal better," she commented to Penny, who was pouring her a cup of ale. The place certainly looked cleaner, though it looked somewhat bare now the damaged hangings had been removed, along with the battered-looking furniture.

347

"Oh yes, milady. Four of the servants from Ganford Chase come over and helped us to strip the place back and scour the walls and floors. Been right through the place we have."

A cleared throat in the doorway had Sabina looking up. Jeffree stood there, and she noticed at once that he had not removed his boots or cloak. "I make now for Ganford Chase," he said coolly.

Sabina lowered her spoon. "Ganford Chase?" she repeated.

"I will carry your regards to my uncle."

Sabina stared at him. "Good of you," she managed to force past her lips, seeing how curiously the Lancers were watching them both.

Jeffree nodded at her, then spun on his heel and was gone.

Well, thought Sabina. *That was that.* She was glad, she told herself a half an hour later as she climbed the stairs to bed. *Glad.* This was what she had wanted after all. To live at Morecotte as her own mistress. What need had she of a husband? Mayhap having one in name alone would be the best bargain of all.

This way she need not fear her parents marrying her off again, but she would not actually have a spouse underfoot to plague her life. She managed to keep up a bright patter of conversation with Penny as the excited maidservant led her through the house and up to the main bedchamber. Sabina was not surprised to find it only contained a narrow cot at present and one chair, for all the rooms were now but sparsely furnished.

"If you remember, your ladyship, you bade us up and burn the old 'un," Penny pointed out.

Sabina shuddered, slightly remembering the foul pit Hendry had slept in. "Quite right," she agreed. "This is ample for my needs." She smiled tightly. "You have been very busy, Penny. Thank you for all your hard work."

"Not at all, milady. There's a jug of hot water here," Penny continued, gesturing toward the chair. "No doubt, now you and the master are returned you will be ordering new furniture for the place."

Sabina hesitated. "I am sure," she replied insincerely, for it now seemed obvious to her that Jeffree would go his separate way and return to the luxury of his quarters. For the first time, it occurred to her that living apart from a second husband would likely make her even more of a gossip's target than she was before.

Suddenly Sabina felt fit to drop. Waving away Penny's offer to help her disrobe, she stripped down to her shift for a thorough wash, though all she really wanted to do was crawl under the covers and close her eyes. Typically, once she was there, having blown out her candle, she lay wide awake, her eyes burning.

I love you, that was what he had said. Well, his feelings of love had certainly been fleeting! She should have been scathing, really told him what she thought of his supposed love. Instead, she had been worried about hurting his feelings. *His feelings!* As though he had any. She made a suppressed noise of irritation. Jeffree de Crecy was a selfish monster!

At least she could sleep this night without him flinging out his arms and legs and disordering the bedcovers, she thought, rolling onto her side. She would sleep like a babe tonight. She could snore her head off without worrying she would give him a disgust of her. Then, tomorrow, she would wake fresh and carefree without a muscular male encroaching on her space.

349

When she woke the next morning, Sabina did so with heavy eyelids and itchy eyes. She doubted she had snatched more than a couple of hours at most. It beggared belief that she had slept in a procession of strange beds better than she did in her own home.

She sat up, rubbing her face and groaning. She felt tired and irritable. Today was the first day in July; the birds were singing and the sky looked hazy with the promise of sunshine. Her spirits ought to be soaring, but instead, they were limp and leaden. She dragged herself out of bed, heavy of heart.

The next couple of hours did not improve her mood, though the Lancers gave her a painstaking tour of everything that had been done to her house and grounds.

"You have both done very well," she muttered for the umpteenth time as they showed her the freshly scrubbed pantry. "Where did all these new provisions come from?" she asked with surprise, seeing the sacks and barrels stacked in one corner.

"They were sent over from Ganford Chase," Lancer told her, scratching his neck. "Grain and salted meat and fish. They's sent ale and wine too which I put in the buttery. A quantity of things. One of His Grace's stewards come over to do an inventory and went away with a long list."

"I see," Sabina murmured. "Well, that was very good of His Grace." She hesitated. "Have you seen anything of my family in my absence?"

"Your sister, Mistress Isemay, has been over most days to enquire if there had been any word as to your return," Penny put in, closing the pantry door behind them.

Sabina felt a pang of guilt that she had not managed to write, but indeed the only chance she would have had was during her four days at Longacre, and those had passed very quickly. "She seemed well?" she asked.

"Oh, a most lively and agreeable young lady," Penny enthused. "Several times she's had me make her up some provisions for her to take into the woods."

"Provisions?" Sabina asked, startled.

"Bread and cheese and such like."

This seemed odd to Sabina, as Tipton Hall had its own farm down the road with plenty of cheeses. If anything, it would have made more sense if her sister had brought *them* a wheel of cheese, for currently Morecotte had no livestock.

"Isemay has taken to walking in Langley Woods?" Sabina repeated slowly. "Surely not alone?"

"Nay, for most days she brings that hulking brute Samuel Johns with her," Lancer assured her. "There is none would tangle with the maid when she has him at her side."

Sabina relaxed. Samuel was an old family retainer of many years. "I am surprised my father can spare Samuel from the farm," she murmured aloud. It seemed strange but sometimes Isemay got these peculiar whims. Perhaps wandering in the forest was the latest one and her parents were indulging her after her horrible wedding ordeal.

Shrugging off her momentary unease, Sabina expressed a desire to see the buttery. The Lancers obliged, and Sabina surveyed the many casks and flagons with astonishment. The duke at least must have thought Jeffree would be spending the lion's share of his time at Morecotte, for there was an impressive selection of wines and some of the smaller flasks looked to be

351

honeyed mead and brandy-wine as well as three large casks of ale.

"Most generous," she murmured distractedly. She hoped His Grace would not request it all to be returned when he realized his heir had no intention of living under Morecotte's roof. "We are fortunate indeed."

"If I might ask when Sir Jeffree will return?" Lancer ventured. "Only I've a few questions to put to him and…"

Sabina was not able to hide her reaction to this question, and she saw the glance the Lancers exchanged. "You may put any question you have to me, Lancer," she told him, recovering quickly. "I am mistress here of old."

Lancer scratched his ear, and Penny elbowed him in the side. "I just wondered where them hounds of your'n might be, mistress," he admitted. "Feste and Brisis, I mean."

"Milady!" his wife hissed out of the corner of her mouth.

"Milady," he corrected himself hurriedly.

"The hounds were gifted to my husband's brothers," she told Lancer, who looked frankly crestfallen. "But you will see them again soon, Lancer, never fear. Both Jasper and Crispin will be joining our household in a few months' time as my husband's squires."

As soon as she said it, she felt a lurch in her stomach. Was that even the case now? What if Jeffree went back on his word? What would the Lady Maud think? How disappointed Jasper and Crispin would be if the plan fell through. Mercifully, she found herself distracted by how disconsolate Lancer looked by this news and busied herself telling him all about her brothers-in-law and their instant bond with both dogs.

352

"They are absolutely devoted to their care and were taking instruction from an old countryman in their father's employ. Mullins is his name, and the last I saw of him, he was passing them a recipe for the making of a salve to give the dogs strong paws."

Lancer was just commenting he would like to see such a recipe himself, when they heard the sound of a horse and cart outside. Penny ran eagerly to the window to peer out. Sabina followed at a more sedate pace. After all, she thought, Jeffree would hardly ride in a cart, now would he?

"Lord save us!" Penny exclaimed. "Would you look at how high that wagon is piled!"

"There's two more following on behind," Lancer commented, heading quickly for the door to lend a hand.

Sabina gazed out of the window, trying to make out the bulky objects loading up the cart. She screwed up her eyes. It looked like…furniture, she realized with stupefaction. Cabinets, cupboards, and…chairs. Yes, chairs.

Penny gave a squawk. "It's the master!" she exclaimed.

Sabina's heart lurched. "Where?" She whipped her head around and saw Jeffree swinging down from Radax's broad back. Before she could stop herself she was rushing toward the door and hurrying out to the front of the house. Words clamored on her lips, which she was determined would remain unspoken. *Where have you been? How dare you leave me?* Stupid words that had no right to be spoken, except by a termagant wife.

She was halfway down the path when she almost ran straight into him. Mercifully, she managed to pull herself up short just in time.

He glowered down at her. "Wife," he greeted her coolly.

353

"Husband." She managed to add a little more ice to her greeting. She waved a hand toward the carts which were now being unloaded by the men who had driven them. "What is all this?"

"What does it look like?" he growled back.

She noticed the first of the large carved trunks being heaved out the back of the nearest wagon. "Well, it *looks* rather like your furniture from Ganford Chase," she said slowly. "But..." She whipped around to gaze at the second cart. "Is that a bed frame?" she gasped. "Jeffree, if that is your bed, it will *never* fit."

He ignored her, carrying on into the house, and Sabina turned smartly on her heel to follow him inside.

"My uncle is visiting us on the morrow," he said to her over his shoulder. "You will have to offer him some sort of refreshment."

"The duke? Here?" Sabina heard a gasp and turned to see Penny hovering nearby, wide-eyed with excitement. "Penny, do you suppose you could bake some tarts in his honor?"

"Oh yes, milady!" Penny bobbed up and down and fled from the room, no doubt to get started on perfecting her recipe.

Jeffree had already started up the stairs, so Sabina followed hot on his heels. He made straight for the master bedroom and stood just inside the doorway, his hands on his hips.

"What are you looking at?" she demanded.

He did not answer for a moment, then he turned and looked at her hard. "It will fit," he asserted.

"Your bed?" she snorted, catching his meaning. "It will not. An entire family could fit in that thing without touching. Three generations!"

But he was already striding back down the corridor, having made up his mind. Sabina threw her hands up in the air. He was impossible, truly. If he was sending that monstrous oversize bed up her stairs, then she supposed she would have to tidy the narrow cot away that she had used the night before. She started stripping off the covers and folding them into a tidy pile.

"What are you doing?" His voice made her jump, for he had reappeared in the doorway.

Sabina looked up. "I thought—"

"Leave that," he said abruptly. "I've brought others to do that." She straightened up. "Come. And stick close to me." He frowned. "We have much to organize this day."

Sabina nodded, trailing after him and feeling rather dazed. Down in the courtyard, the first of the wagons was still only partway unpacked. "What are all these?" Sabina asked, gesturing toward a pile of rolled-up textiles.

Jeffree glanced at them without much interest. "Naseby packed those," he said. "They are tapestries and such which are not currently being used at Ganford Chase. If you do not like them, we can send them back."

Sabina's eyes widened. "I am sure they will be most useful," she said, thinking of the newly patched walls in the dining chamber which needed covering up. She made at once to start sifting through the heavy canvases, looking for the largest and most vibrant colored. When she had picked out four that she thought would be large enough to cover the entirety of the Great Chamber walls, she had them carried inside.

355

"I might have to interrupt Penny's kitchen work," she murmured as two men unfurled the first tapestry and held it up against the wall for her approval.

"Why?" Jeffree asked.

"To garner her opinion," Sabina answered, tapping her chin. "I do not know if these tapestries look well together. This one seems to depict an allegory of sorts, in a theme of greens and blues. Does it not contrast rather ill with the one we placed on the opposite wall?"

Jeffree turned to face the other wall now covered in a hanging predominantly of bold reds and yellows, showing a group of lions prancing around a striped pole. "Does it matter?" he asked.

"As to that, I would have supposed you more of a judge than I," Sabina admitted. "My taste is not considered anything special. In such matters, I usually defer to Isemay's opinion."

"Is your sister considered such an arbiter of taste?" He sounded skeptical.

"In our family, yes."

He shrugged. "In your own house, I say the only question should be whether you like to look upon it or no."

Sabina turned back to the allegorical tapestry and considered it. Four women stood under three blossoming trees holding caskets in their hands. "Do you know the fable it illustrates?" she asked with sudden misgiving. Jeffree shook his head; he was already moving toward the door.

"So long as it is not anything irritating like 'How to measure the true worth of a woman' or something of that nature," Sabina murmured darkly as she hurried after him back outside.

"You need to direct them where everything is to go in the house," he said, coming to a halt before the first cart.

"This cannot all have fitted into your own two rooms," she commented, glancing over the vast array of carved wooden furniture being unloaded from the carts. There seemed even more of it, now it was not neatly piled on top of each other.

He crossed his arms. "I thought I said Naseby had some of it taken out of storage."

They gazed in silence at the scene of activity in front of them as men staggered under the weight of the heavy pieces.

"Perhaps the best thing to do would be to make groups of furniture for the different rooms," Sabina suggested, feeling rather daunted by the task in front of her.

Jeffree gave a nod and lifted his voice. "Listen, men!" he began. "This is how we are going to do this."

It took hours getting everything organized and even longer getting it all set up. Sabina was convinced up until the very end that Jeffree's huge bed was not going to fit even into the largest of the bedrooms. As it was, they did manage to wedge it in there, though there were scraped walls on both sides, and the only way to get into it was to climb over the bottom of it.

"I told you it would fit," Jeffree said.

"Whoever has to make it up will not thank you," Sabina replied. He shrugged. Clearly, as it would not be him, he hardly cared. "A trunk at the foot of the bed is not a good idea. It will just be an obstacle to climb over," she added.

"The room next door will have to suffice for a dressing room. Put the trunks in there," he answered and, seeing Sabina's hesitation, asked, "What?"

357

"The room next door was originally mine."

He said nothing for a moment, and Sabina felt her face grow warm. "Where did you sleep last night?" he asked at last. Clearly, he had seen the cot set up in the main bedroom.

"Where did *you*?" Sabina retorted before she could stop herself.

He narrowed his eyes. "You know where. I told you when I left."

Sabina shrugged a shoulder and scuffling feet in the hallway heralded the arrival of the first of the large carved chests.

"Take it in the room next door," Jeffree directed loudly. "Along with the large mirrored glass and the two matching cabinets. That room will be our dressing room." He lifted a challenging brow at her, but Sabina averted her gaze.

Our *dressing room?* Her heart thudded. So, he did mean to make Morecotte his home?

At midday, Penny set out a hearty pottage with beans and peas, four fresh loaves, and a large game pie. Everyone sat around the oak trestle table which had arrived that morning. On either end, it bore the de Crecy crest with its black tree on a white field. The benches they drew up to it did not match, for they were painted green and a little scuffed, though still handsomely made.

Once the trenchers had been emptied, Sabina was borne off to the kitchen to examine the strawberry pies Penny had made for the duke's impending visit. They were excellent, the pastry flaky and flavored with thyme. Penny had also added a curd of lemons to the fruit filling which Sabina felt was sure to go down well with the duke who she had noticed had a small and fussy appetite, quite different to his nephew's.

358

Indeed, when Jeffree tried a small bite of one, he pulled such a face that Sabina hurried him out of the kitchen before he could wound Penny's feelings. "Do not, for goodness' sake, say anything derogatory about those excellent tarts, Jeffree!"

She swept him back into the now-empty dining chamber for the workers had returned to fetch the few remaining items from the carts. These consisted of smaller items that had not been assigned to a room, such as individual carved tables and straight-back chairs covered in leather and a quantity of rugs and cushions.

"There was a strange aftertaste to those small pies," he complained. "Though the pottage and bread she cooked were very flavorful."

Sabina rolled her eyes. "Has anyone ever told you that you lack self-awareness to an almost alarming degree?"

He looked affronted. "What do you mean by that?"

"I do not know how to tell you this tactfully, but the fact is that you, Sir Jeffree de Crecy, have unrefined tastes!"

"What are you talking about?"

"That deep down, under all that posturing and swank, you prefer plain, honest food on your tongue and plain, honest women in your bed!"

He gazed at her a moment, his eyes bright and fierce, and then he was crowding into her. "What the hells are you talking about now?" he demanded. "I know what I like and there's nothing plain or honest about it! And there's no 'women' to speak of either! There's only one woman in my bed and she's a sharp-tongued scold that I cannot get enough of!"

Sabina huffed indignantly but had no chance to make a reply for he had seized her and claimed her mouth in a possessive and all-consuming kiss of teeth and tongue.

"A scold?" Sabina panted in outrage, at last tearing her mouth from his. "I am no such thing!"

He backed her against the wall. "Beautiful, then."

"I am not that either!" Sabina objected, twisting her head to escape his seeking mouth.

"To me you are," he growled. Sabina was so disconcerted by this claim that she forgot to struggle for the next minute or so, and Jeffree used that to his full advantage. By the time a knock on the door disturbed them moments later, she was a disordered mess, her veil wrenched crooked and her braids half unraveled by Jeffree's questing fingers.

As for he, one hand was clamped at the back of her neck and the other was squeezing her breast through her dress. Sabina gasped as Jeffree flung back his head to roar, "Who is it?"

The door pushed open, and Sabina gave a low moan of distress. She could not so much as retreat a single step, for her back was pressed flat to the wall. Jeffree's only concession to decency was to slide his hand from her bosom to her waist. He turned to look back irritably over his shoulder.

"Osborn, is that you? Go to the devil, you plaguey nuisance! Can't you see your master is otherwise occupied?"

"Osborn told me where to find you, it is true" came back the clipped reply that was certainly not Osborn. "If my business here could be avoided, I assure you I would do so assiduously."

Sabina gasped. It was Sir Charles Ellis. She tried to wrench herself out of Jeffree's embrace, but he was having none of it.

Instead, he practically dragged her to a chair beside the fireplace and thrust her into it. "Do not move," he growled at her before lifting his voice to invite his godfather to come in. "Charles, you are welcome here; come take a seat."

Sir Charles advanced into the room, distaste clear upon on his pale, shaken face. Sabina could see a hot flush climbing up his neck, even from where she was sat. He seemed incapable of even looking in her direction.

"You have not greeted my wife," Jeffree pointed out.

Sir Charles turned her way and swallowed. Sabina took pity on him. After all, he did believe her to be the worst kind of trollop, ensnaring his godson and forcing him into marriage. "It is good to see you again, Sir Charles," she lied. He made some murmured reply and Jeffree bade him take a seat.

"Well and how fares it with you, Charles?" Jeffree asked. "Can I send for some refreshment?"

Sir Charles made an impatient gesture with his hand. "Never mind with that. Have you heard from my son?" he asked hoarsely.

"Leland?" Jeffree's tone was surprised. "Never tell me he is still missing!"

Sir Charles closed his eyes briefly. "I have not discovered hide nor hair of him for nearly three weeks."

Jeffree seemed taken aback by this news. He walked to the chair opposite his godfather and sat down. "You wrote to Mallenby as I suggested?" he asked slowly.

"Mallenby, Spencer, the whole pack of his friends, past and present. None of them will own to having heard so much as a peep from the boy." Sir Charles opened and closed one bony fist convulsively. "I fear the worst." He covered his eyes abruptly, his words ending with something approaching a sob.

"Charles…" Jeffree darted a panicked look in Sabina's direction. She rose reluctantly to her feet.

"I will fetch some brandy-wine," she suggested and, when Jeffree looked as though to argue, added quickly, "I think Sir Charles will speak easier without me here."

The older man said nothing, though she thought his shoulders relaxed slightly. She darted her eyes at Jeffree, but he seemed entirely clueless of how to proceed.

Quickly, Sabina crossed the room and hurried out to the kitchen. She was not the right person to console Sir Charles. She had no sympathy for his missing son. Leland Ellis was a villain as far as she was concerned, and whatever fate had befallen him, he likely deserved.

She tarried in the kitchen as long as she dared, resecuring her headdress before fetching a flagon of brandy-wine from the buttery along with two of Jeffree's own fancy goblets from his stores. On the threshold, she paused to steel herself to withstand the older man's blast of dislike.

"And you *believed* her?" she heard Sir Charles hiss.

"I did. I do," Jeffree answered. "She has given me her word that she was no part of the plot. Any action she took that day was purely to mitigate her sister's plight."

"I cannot believe you would simply accept the word of a woman like that—" Sir Charles began hotly, then broke off his incensed words when Sabina took a step through the doorway.

"Here we are," she said loudly and walked to the table, plunking her tray down noisily.

"Sabina," Jeffree beckoned to her. "Come here." She obeyed though she dragged her feet. Jeffree pulled up a chair beside his own and patted the leather-lined seat. "I would consult with you on this matter."

Sir Charles made a choked sound, which Jeffree ignored.

"Yes?" Sabina asked warily, sitting herself down.

"My godfather's son is still not found, despite the enquiries that have been made hereabouts." He paused heavily, his eyes boring into hers. "I ask you plainly, can you think of any avenue we have left unexplored when it comes to recovering him?"

The hairs on the back of Sabina's neck started to rise. What was this? She darted a glance at Sir Charles Ellis, and what she saw there gave her small comfort, for his eyes were full of unspoken accusation. *Did they think her family had some hand in Leland Ellis's disappearance?* Sabina's throat turned suddenly dry.

"How should I?" she asked. "I am barely acquainted with Sir Leland and his habits." She could not forbear a curl of her lip at the mention of the last.

Jeffree paused, but when Sir Charles started to angry speech, he shot him a quelling glance. "As you have said before, we inhabitants of Ganford Chase do not mix much with the local populace. It could be that you have some ideas that have not occurred to those there."

Sabina stared back at him, her fingers curling until her nails bit into her palms. She took several deep breaths before making a reply. "Perhaps they should make enquiries at The Blue Boar," she suggested bitterly. "That is an old haunt of his and where he met with his coconspirator, Alfred Hendry, is it not?"

"Hendry?" Jeffree echoed thoughtfully.

363

"That miscreant has naught to do with my son! I would take an oath on it!" Sir Charles exclaimed angrily.

"Has anyone made enquiry as to Hendry's whereabouts, Charles?" Jeffree interjected swiftly.

"Of course not!" the older man spat. "Such a suggestion is an insult!"

"They were in league together, were they not?" Sabina pointed out, her hackles truly up.

Jeffree shot her an exasperated look as Sir Charles shot to his feet. "Sabina." Her husband's murmured tone was reproachful. He, too, climbed to his feet before addressing the older man. "It is worth investigating, Charles," he pointed out.

Sir Charles was practically vibrating with affront by this point. "That *you* could think such a thing, Jeffree!" he choked out. "Could even entertain such a suggestion!"

"Charles—" Jeffree said as the older man went rushing toward the door. He swung around to look at Sabina. "Could you not have employed even a modicum of tact?" he demanded in a low voice.

"Oh? As Sir Charles did to me, you mean? Should I have waited until he had left the room before I made my insinuations?" Jeffree's gaze grew flinty. "I have no doubt that he did not hesitate to implicate my own family as soon as I left!"

Jeffree's heightened color told her she had hit the mark, and he glowered at her a moment before stalking after Sir Charles.

Sabina sat fuming she knew not how long until she heard the sound of horse's hooves outside. That was more than one horse, she thought, starting impulsively for the window. Surely he had not gone again? She had been steeling herself for their inevitable row, one which would hopefully clear the air.

Instead, her disbelieving eyes saw both men disappearing down the lane together. She stood there, gazing out, a strangely numb feeling creeping over her. He had not even told her he was leaving. She rubbed her arms, feeling suddenly rather chilled.

"Shall I have the fire lit in here, milady?" Penny's voice from the doorway made her start.

"Did your master send any word for me when he left?" Sabina could not help herself from asking.

"No, milady." Penny sounded apologetic.

Well, thought Sabina, that was that. It was obvious where Jeffree's loyalties lay. It was also obvious where her husband's true home lay, Ganford Chase. Whatever amount of cast-off furniture he threw her way, that would remain his true home.

Now that she came to think of it, he had bidden her to direct where every stick of furniture in the house was to be laid. Perhaps he had not cared about the tapestries in the Great Chamber because he never intended to be sat there much. "I do not require a fire down here, Penny," she heard herself say through numbed lips. "It has been a long day and I am rather tired. I believe I will retire early to bed."

"Yes, milady. Will you be wanting the fire lit in the master chamber?"

"The back bedchamber, if you please," Sabina corrected her, for she knew the cot she had used the night before had been set up in there. "That is the room I shall be taking for my own."

19

Jeffree felt unaccountably irritable the next morn as he waited for his uncle to be ready to set forth for Morecotte. They had tarried long enough in his opinion. He had risen early and ridden over to Tipton Hall for an uncomfortable conversation with his father-in-law two hours before. Charles had wanted to accompany him, but Jeffree had put his foot down about that. "You will simply set their backs up, Charles, as you did my wife's," he had stated, and his godfather had retreated into affronted silence at that.

As soon as Jeffree crossed the threshold of Tipton Hall, he had known Sir Charles's suspicions were unfounded. Thora and Wilfred Burrell were delighted he had "condescended to visit with them" and insisted on plying him with various refreshments and tidbits of local news they seemed to think he would appreciate.

As he sat there, being bombarded with roasted fish and "those thin, fried cheese crackers you enjoyed so much last time, Sir Jeffree," he reflected that the only Burrell with backbone and spleen enough to exact a revenge plan was Sabina herself. And she had not had the opportunity.

"My daughter is well, I trust, Sir Jeffree?" Thora Burrell twittered and then accepted his stony-faced assertion that she was entirely at face value.

Jeffree cleared his throat and brought himself to make mention Sabina's short stay at his mother's house. Her own mother was instantly wreathed in smiles at this show of generosity from his family, welcoming her into their open arms. Jeffree had stirred uncomfortably in his chair, but really, the woman could not do enough to put him at his ease. He had to remind himself that, unlike her daughter, she was happy to view his every move in a good light.

After they had broken their fast together, he had walked outside with Wilfred Burrell in the early morning sunshine. He was less voluble than his wife, but his open, honest gaze could not be feigned. When Jeffree made cautious allusion to preceding events or bad blood between their families, the older man had seemed keen to put all that had occurred behind them. "For what is done is done," his father-in-law opined. "Isemay no longer wishes to marry Bethencourt, it is true," her father lamented, "but I do not think even her sternest critic could fault her for that."

Which reminded Jeffree that he had not seen his sister-in-law that morn. "No," Wilfred Burrell had replied easily. "She has taken to rising extremely early of late. The child takes these odd starts. We are indulging her for the moment until she has fully recovered from the… er"—the older man had averted his eyes—"all that unpleasant business."

And with that Jeffree found he was content to let the matter lie. Their conversation turned to other things. Jeffree found himself suggesting they discuss the financial aid his uncle had pledged as part of Isemay's marriage settlement. It did not take much for Burrell to pour out his monetary woes. Jeffree listened and made a few suggestions of his own. His father-in-law seemed more than happy to embrace them, and at the close of conversation, they exchanged a hearty handshake.

Which brought him back to current events, kicking his heels while his uncle delayed his own return to Morecotte. Would the tiresome old fool ne'er make ready? He had some doubt that his wife's welcome would be anything more than sadly tepid after yesterday's events. She was not one to mask her feelings in politeness. In truth, her tongue could hold a decided sting.

That brought back memories of yesterday's tussle before Charles's unwelcome interruption. He groaned faintly. Doubtless, she would still be seething about his espousal of his godfather's cause. Of course, a reasonable woman would own he owed as much to his former guardian, but Sabina was *not* a reasonable woman. She was fiery and lion-hearted, and no doubt she would expect to haul him over hot coals for entertaining suspicions about her family's possible involvement.

Well, she would have to learn that he was not a man to be led around by the nose however much he…craved her. His thoughts shied away from the declaration he had made, the declaration she had spurned. His ears burned with the humiliation of the memory.

There was a place for a wife in his life, he had come to realize, but that place was not ruling over him from some kind of throne. There was only one place she could ride him roughshod, he thought, before his own thoughts brought him up short. *Gods.* It did not do for him to dwell on such things, though he could not forbear for a moment from thinking of her sleeping in his massive bed alone.

Had she waited up for his return? He had been strongly tempted to head back to her after the council of war with Charles. If he was not mistaken, his godfather was heading for some kind of breakdown if Leland was not found soon. Besides, he thought sourly, she had told him to find other ways of expressing his love, had she not? Ways that did not involve his penis. He was uncomfortably aware that if he had climbed under the covers with her, his ways would have been sadly predictable.

Jeffree scowled. What other ways were there? Well, for one, he had now taken some steps to prevent her father from being dragged down by his debts. Would that make her smile upon him again? What else could he do? He cast about him. He had returned Morecotte to her; that had pleased her. What other wrongs had she left to be righted?

A moment's deep reflection brought the business of that blacksmith's niece or daughter, whatever she was, to mind. The one that had borne Hendry a bastard brat. Mayhap he could pay for that family to relocate, so Sabina should not fear running into them whenever she ventured into the village.

Yes, that was an idea. He resolved to find out the direction of the forge and the present circumstances of the wretched female. Had Sabina not said her own father had been forced to provide for them? He cursed softly under his breath. He should have broached the subject with Burrell that morning and he could have dealt with it in one fell swoop.

At this point, Naseby came hurrying in to tell him that the duke was finally ready to depart. About damned time, he thought, springing from his seat. Naturally, his uncle was accompanied by one of his under-stewards and rode at a snail's pace, exclaiming all the while how shocked he was that Sir Charles did not mean to accompany them, for this visit was to "pay a compliment to Mistress Sabina."

Jeffree ground his teeth for it was the third time he had heard his uncle address her as such. "Her name," he burst forth, no longer able to swallow the insult, "is Lady Sabina."

"Upon my word, you are in the right of it, nephew," his uncle replied with a sad smile. "'Tis just that I was used to addressing her this way on our previous acquaintance, and I find I am not good with change."

It was odd, but Jeffree found he bitterly resented the fact his uncle had a prior acquaintanceship to boast of, even if it was only in passing. Though it might be truth in point of fact, he

369

thought it bad taste for his uncle to flout it like that in his face. The duke had been engaged to her sister, nothing more. Likely Sabina had not met with him above a half dozen times and then in mixed company.

Noticing the way his uncle's under-steward was cringing in his saddle, Jeffree realized his murderous feelings must be showing in his expression and stopped fantasizing about dragging his uncle off his horse and wringing his scrawny neck.

"I hope you do not think it rash to have moved all your personal belongings from your chambers at The Chase," his uncle rambled on. "You are my heir, Jeffree, and as such, it is only right that you should maintain rooms in my house."

"Rash?" Jeffree echoed. "How can it be considered rash? No sooner had I emptied my rooms than you had Naseby refill them with replacement furniture."

"Never let it be said that my heir shall not be welcome in the halls of Ganford Chase," his uncle answered grandly. "And it is just as well that Naseby is so efficient. If he had not been, then you would have had to sleep upon the floor last night, for none of us expected you to return so soon."

Jeffree felt his eye twitch with irritation. "Sir Charles had some matter he wished to discuss with me—" he started.

"Nay, Jeffree!" His uncle raised an embroidered glove. "No explanation need ever be given for you to sleep under my roof. You are always welcome therein."

"Most generous," Jeffree ground out.

The Duke of Bethencourt inclined his head. "I know what is due unto my heir," he said. "Never let it be said that I am in dereliction of duty."

Jeffree pursed his lips but forbore to comment on his precarious status as heir. After all, had not his uncle planned on marrying only a few short weeks ago?

"I shall ne'er wed now," his uncle sighed, jolting Jeffree out of his thoughts. A heavy silence lay between them for a few moments.

"There is still time," Jeffree heard himself say gruffly.

His uncle waved this aside. "No, no, I am an old bachelor and set in my ways. Mistress Isemay was like a breath of spring to the autumn of my life, but it was naught but a fleeting dream." The expression on his uncle's face was pleasurably melancholic and it struck Jeffree forcibly that the old fool had no idea of the bumpy ride marriage involved.

"She is a most estimable maiden," the duke continued, "but since that debacle that was our ill-fated wedding day, not one slender foot has she put through my door, despite repeated invitations. The prettiest note she sent to me could not disguise that she was releasing me entirely from my obligation toward her."

Jeffree did not know how to reply to this, but he saw the under-steward's eyes were wide as saucers. No doubt it would be all around Ganfordshire before long that Mistress Isemay Burrell had refused a duke.

"I will never love again," the duke said with another tragic smile.

That was not love, Jeffree thought with scorn. He might not know much, but he knew that much. If Sabina ever tried to wriggle out of her obligations to him, he would tighten about her like a trap and refuse to let go. Such a thing would be untenable, abhorrent even. Anyone who truly loved another would not speak of losing or relinquishing that person with such complaisance.

The visit itself proved a test of his patience in ways he could never have anticipated. Sabina was cool with him, so cool that he seemed almost invisible to her. By contrast, she was cautiously welcoming to his uncle which annoyed him. Such deference was the duke's due, of course, but in Jeffree's opinion, his uncle encroached on her hospitality.

Firstly, Bethencourt was shown around the house, a tour which had annoyed Jeffree greatly after Sabina described the main bedchamber as "Sir Jeffree's room" and the second bedchamber as "Sir Jeffree's dressing room." The smallest and most meanly furnished room she described as her own province, a thing he had no intention of tolerating and so he would tell her later.

Following the tour, the duke was seated in the dining chamber, and after he had made several pointed comments about draughts, Sabina bade a fire be lit despite the clement weather. When Jeffree reminded all present that it was now July, no one paid him the slightest heed. Sabina had then served the duke mead and the peculiar strawberry tarts which Jeffree had not approved of.

His uncle exclaimed over the tarts repeatedly, and when told the cook had created them in his honor, nothing would please him but that Penny was fetched from the kitchen and presented to him. The blushing woman had then had to repeat three times the process she had undergone to produce such "excellent" tarts. When asked what she called her creation, she had replied promptly, "Why to be sure, Bethencourt tarts." And the duke had then bade his under-steward to write down every step for it to be emulated in his own kitchens and had praised the woman until she was giddy.

His uncle's appreciation had gone down so well with Sabina that she had unbent her scrupulous politeness and deigned to bestow a good deal of sincerer smiles upon the duke, a thing which made Jeffree inwardly fume.

They then sat for a good hour before the fire while Bethencourt cautioned her against a whole host of household mistakes, as though she had never run a home before and numbered fifteen in years rather than twenty-five.

Instead of bridling at his strictures as Jeffree might have expected, Sabina seemed amenable to his advice, gravely listening and nodding as the duke covered a whole host of subjects which Jeffree was damned sure his uncle knew nothing about. She even agreed to rearrange the pantry at his whim, for Bethencourt was certain that the salted fish would spoil if they were not moved to the other side of the room and the barrels kept scrupulously separated from the sacks.

The whole time, Jeffree alternated between pacing about impatiently or leaning against the mantel and glaring in their direction with ill-concealed annoyance. After the first hour, his uncle's under-steward had felt unequal to the atmosphere in the room and had begged to be excused to await his master outside.

In the end, Jeffree followed his example and escaped outside to the sunshine. It was damnably stuffy inside. Lighting a fire at midday on such a day was madness. Seeing the under-steward was wandering through the herb garden, Jeffree headed for the stables instead, where he found Lancer forking hay and having a one-sided conversation with two small unkempt-looking hounds who were lolling near the stalls.

"—and that's what I said to her, not that she listened," the manservant griped. Hearing Jeffree's footfall, he whipped his head around looking rather sheepish. "Sir Jeffree." He nodded.

373

"Where are the horses?" Jeffree asked, glancing at the empty stalls.

"I put 'em in the field. Too nice a day for them to be cooped up inside."

Jeffree grunted and let his critical eye fall on the dogs, who had climbed to their feet and made their way over to him to say hello. He let them sniff his hand and realized their coats were curly rather than uncared for. "These your dogs?" he asked when they seemed friendly enough.

"That they are," Lancer affirmed. "They're good beasts, though I do say so myself, and right good guard dogs when they's let loose at night, for all they're on the small side. They'll bark up a storm if they spot a stranger about the place, b'aint no one getting past them," he finished with satisfaction.

Jeffree lowered himself onto an upturned bucket and bestowed some head pats on the shaggy dog heads. "What if Hendry were to show up at the property?" Jeffree asked. "Would they not recognize him and allow him entrance?"

Lancer snorted. "Not they! They never tolerated him above half. He never could abide dogs, and that's a bad sign, my grandfather used to say. Why, one time he aimed such a kick at Amos—" Lancer broke off his wrathful words to shake his head. "Well, it's not my place to criticize an old master," he muttered, casting a sidelong look at Jeffree.

"The man was a villain," Jeffree agreed as it suddenly occurred to him that Lancer might be a good source of information when it came to the enquiries over Leland's disappearance. "Is Hendry still in the vicinity or hereabouts?" he asked slowly, making sure to keep his tone casual.

374

Lancer gave a chuckle. "Lord, you don't need to worry about him daring to show his face round 'ere, Sir Jeffree. Not after you pitched him in the horse trough." He curled his lip. "Hendry was ever a craven little swine."

So much for not criticizing a former employer, Jeffree thought wryly. Then he recalled that he had also pitched Lancer into the horse trough and wondered if the hulking countryman held him in any higher esteem when all was said and done.

"That may well be," Jeffree agreed, "but I have a friend who would fain like a word or two with Alfred Hendry."

Lancer's gaze sharpened, and he paused in his work, lowering his pitchfork to lean on it. "A friend?" he repeated quizzically.

Jeffree considered. It was unlikely Sir Charles would know how to deal with a weaselly fellow like Alfred Hendry. "Myself," he clarified. "The one who would like a word with him is me."

Lancer frowned. "Well, I hear he's not been seen at The Blue Boar in a two-week. Still owes them money and Wat Begley is spittin' mad about it. Not that I would know," Lancer added quickly. "For I've been trying not to run afoul of the wife, since we've been given this new start, so to speak, so I have been avoiding the tavern."

Jeffree nodded but did not speak, for he was sure Lancer knew more than he was letting on. Lancer shot him a quick, appraising look. "A course," he began awkwardly, "our loyalties have changed now, so to speak. The missus has been a lot happier since Lady Sabina took over the running of the place." He scratched his neck.

"My wife is very satisfied with your services," Jeffree replied without intonation.

Lancer looked uneasy and tugged on his curly beard. "Hendry did have a friend of sorts," he admitted at last. "Think he was a childhood companion of his or at least he knowed him of old. Owns a mill he does in Flyford Parvell."

Jeffree's ears pricked up. "Flyford Parvell? Where is that? I have never heard of it."

"Why should you?" Lancer shrugged. "It's a little coastal town about twenty miles from here. Sometimes when Hendry's debtors grew too pressing, he would retreat there to lay low awhile until this fellow Gordon grew tired of him too."

"Gordon?"

"Gordon were his name. James or mebbe it was Jacob Gordon; I forget which."

Jeffree nodded his thanks and stood up from his impromptu seat. It should not be hard to find the fellow with his hometown, surname, and occupation. Mayhap this Gordon could shed some light on Hendry's whereabouts and then Hendry could reveal what had happened to Leland?

Lancer hesitated. "And maybe by the by you will forget 'twas me gave you his direction, Sir Jeffree?" he asked hopefully. Seeing his unease, Jeffree nodded again, and Lancer relaxed. "Only I promised the wife I'd put all that business behind me," he confessed. "I don't want to be riling her up now she's finally agreed to give me another chance."

Lancer seemed an odd candidate for henpecked husband, Jeffree reflected as he walked slowly back across the yard. Penny was plump and round of face, with a pleasant manner and beaming smile. Her husband was a rough-hewn brute you would not like to meet in a dark alley. Still, it seemed he went in fear of incurring his wife's displeasure.

This no longer seemed as baffling to Jeffree as it would once have done. Wives were a complicated business, he thought darkly. As for his own, he was frankly unsure of his next step. He knew himself well enough to know that if he stayed under Morecotte's roof this night, the row that had been brewing all day would blow up, not disperse.

If he returned to Ganford Chase this eve, to confer with Sir Charles about this new development, he would avoid this disaster. Then tomorrow he could devote to riding to Flyford Parvell and seeking out this confederate of Hendry's. After that, he would have breathing space to consider anew what next should be done. Did they not say, after all, that absence made the heart grow fonder? Mayhap if he absented himself, then this wife of his would realize his love was not to be despised after all. It was worth a shot in any case.

20

Sabina had finally relaxed when the Duke of Bethencourt departed, for all he had been so affable a guest. Then her relief had quickly turned to ire when she realized that Jeffree had left with the others.

"He definitely left?" she echoed as Penny nodded. *Well!* Sabina plunked her hands on her hips. What a *hypocrite*! She had seen how he had bridled when he realized she had not been sleeping in his ridiculously large bed. If he had no intention of using it either, then pray, what cause did he have to be so put out about it?

Sabina had pursed her lips and started up the stairs when the sound of more cartwheels in the courtyard had sent her wheeling about and rushing back down them again. Her disappointment on realizing it was her family and not her recalcitrant husband had been palpable.

"I'll fetch more of those Bethencourt tarts," Penny had said, hurrying back toward the kitchen as Sabina had composed herself to receive a second lot of visitors.

Luckily, her mother was voluble enough to make up for Sabina's lack of spirits. Thora Burrell hurried from room to room exclaiming over the new furnishings with delight and excitement. "Such excellent material," she said, feeling the fabric of a wall hanging between her fingers. "And there's still a good deal of wear left to it. How good of His Grace to let you have it and what a shame we only just missed him!" She sighed gustily and sent a meaningful look at Isemay. "I daresay he is still quite cast down by your sister's refusal."

Sabina glanced at Isemay, who was unusually quiet. "The duke seemed in excellent spirits," she said repressively. Isemay flashed her a grateful smile, but their mother could not let this stand.

"Nonsense! He must be broken-hearted, poor man! And *so* generous always. You know"—she lowered her voice conspiratorially—"he did not demand the return of the monies he paid over to your father before the wedding day, though he would have been quite within his rights to do so. I do not say that your father was not expecting more assistance in that quarter, but it stands to reason. It is such a relief now that your own husband has stepped into the breach. We are apparently out of harm's way."

"My own husband?" Sabina echoed, lowering her strawberry tart.

Thora Burrell tipped her head to one side. "I will own, he does not have that easiness of manner to immediately draw one in. In truth, he can seem a little...aloof at times, but I assure you he has been kindness itself to your father."

Sabina blinked. "He has?"

"Yes, indeed." Her mother colored faintly. "But do not press me for more details, for that is men's business and not for us to know about."

"Men's business?" Sabina echoed. "What are you speaking of?"

"Well, if you must know," her mother said, avoiding her eye and drifting about the room, picking up a carved wooden box to examine it, "I refer to money matters."

Not one word more could Sabina extract from her mother about it, but when her father finally came in from the stable, she was a little more successful. She waited until her mother and sister

379

were on the far side of the room, examining some finely wrought silver candlesticks Jeffree had brought over from Ganford Chase, before broaching the subject.

Wilfred Burrell wiped the foam from his ale that had caught in his moustache and lowered his voice. "I will admit," he confided in a quiet voice that did not reach his wife. "It is not such a blow to lose Bethencourt's support now I have your husband's. He has been most generous though." He mopped his brow. "I do not think he will be the disinterested benefactor his uncle would have been."

"What makes you say that?" Sabina asked, still reeling from the news that Jeffree was her family's benefactor at all.

Her father winced. "He expects to be kept fully updated and supplied with rationales for how I spend the money when it comes to the farm and the planting."

Instead of wondering aloud if Jeffree knew much of such things, Sabina held her tongue. She supposed he could always confer with Bethencourt's steward and estate managers. Besides, Father had shown himself to throw good money after bad in the past. Likely it would not do him any harm to be held accountable now for his decisions.

"Sir Jeffree has pledged the money to hire workers for this autumn's harvest," her father added, stroking his fluffy whiskers. "A great relief, as Samuel could not have managed it alone, poor fellow, and I knew not where to look for the money once your sister made it plain she would no longer accept Bethencourt's suit."

Sabina shot another look at Isemay, who stood so meekly by their mother's side. "Isemay seems a little distracted. Is she quite well?"

Wilfred Burrell looked surprised by her words. "It is only natural her change in circumstances should make her grave. If you had not stepped in to save her…" He let his words trail off and cleared his throat. "She is aware of the risk you ran, daughter. The jeopardy in which you placed your own skin, and naturally, this weighs down on her. On all of us, save your mother, who remains in perfect ignorance on the matter."

Sabina nodded. Her mother had accepted things at face value however unlikely a clandestine relationship between herself and Sir Jeffree should appear to anyone who knew her.

"You have not lived to—er—rue the day as it were," her father continued uncomfortably, only able to meet her eyes for the briefest of moments. "He does not make you an unkind husband, I hope."

"No," Sabina answered at once, lifting her chin. "Indeed, he…" She hesitated. "He tells me that he loves me." She didn't know why she said it, and the note of wonder in her own voice was clear, for she spoke out far louder than she had intended.

"Of course he loves you!" her mother said, looking up sharply. "A proud man like Sir Jeffree would never have gone to such lengths as to climb through your window if 'twas not so. Why my own sister, you're aunt Mabel, said 'twas plain to see that Sir Jeffree admired you greatly when she took you to the Bishop's Palace last year."

Sabina lifted an incredulous brow, but before she could argue, her mother rattled on. "Doubtless, that was where you caught his fancy; we are both convinced of it, but there, you will not confide in your poor mother!" Thora Burrell sighed and shook her head. "I declare I have no notion why my daughters are so hard on their wooers. Was I not generosity itself when you courted me, Wilfred?" she demanded of her spouse.

381

Their father made some reply, and Sabina waited for her heated cheeks to cool as she realized she should have expected her mother and aunt to gossip. Indeed, it was quite natural they should have put their heads together and spun their own yarn about how her and Jeffree's liaison had started. Aunt Mabel had an imagination almost as vivid as her sister. Sabina almost laughed aloud at the notion Jeffree had been struck with her on that occasion, for he had nary given her a glance and did not even remember it!

Something was definitely amiss with Isemay though, she reflected, for by rights, such a subject would have had her fanciful sister instantly clamoring for more information. Instead, Isemay merely nodded and smiled, her eyes glazed and absent. What was going on with her? Sabina wondered uneasily. It was not like her.

When she informed them that Sir Jeffree was spending the night at Ganford Chase, her parents were disappointed, but accepted her invitation to sup and made an excellent meal of the various food stuffs donated to Sabina's cupboards by the duke.

As for Isemay, Sabina did not have the chance to get to the bottom of it, for their parents never left them alone together, and when Sabina tried to take her aside, her sister was evasive and hard to pin down. In the end, she simply had to accept her sister's assertions that naught was wrong.

Once everyone had gone, Sabina felt weary and partook of a bathtub in the back bedroom. Once she had washed her hair and scrubbed her body, she crawled once more into the narrow bed and fell into a light and troubled sleep. It was strange, for again, she felt tired. Her eyes burned, yet sleep continued to elude her.

All too soon, early light was breaking through the window, and Sabina watched it creep across the room, dispelling shadow.

She lay as long as she could abed, until she could stand her own clamoring thoughts no longer and climbed out, washing in the leftover cold water from the night before. Dressing and donning her wimple, she made her way downstairs, resolving to help herself to some of Penny's excellent bread. She doubted the Lancers would be up and about this early.

She was just reaching for a loaf when she noticed the two cloaked figures hurrying down her lane. Instead of coming right up to the house, they left the track a few yards away and furtively entered the wood. Sabina caught her breath, for she fancied she recognized the light step of the first figure and the heavy plodding of the second.

If she was not mistaken, it was her sister, Isemay, followed by faithful Samuel, their father's manservant. But where were they off to? Without even consciously deciding to follow, Sabina found she was helping herself to Penny's brown cloak and slipping out of the side door along the garden path. Her heart hammering against her ribs, Sabina entered Langley Woods and made her way tentatively through the trees.

It did not take her long to catch sight of Samuel's bulky figure, though she caught only glimpses of Isemay, who was far nimbler. They moved with purpose, and Sabina followed at a distance, her mystification growing. Samuel was carrying a sack over his shoulder, and it looked like Isemay had a basket under her cloak.

Sabina was just pondering if they could be on some harmless quest to gather herbs or mushrooms when they stopped abruptly outside an abandoned shack. Sabina frowned, for she knew it of old. No one had lived in it for years. Indeed as children, she and Isemay had sometimes played there, creeping into its empty tumbledown shell.

There had been a rumor a wicked wizard had once lived there and that kept most trespassers away, though whether this was fact or just story, Sabina did not know. She crept closer now, taking care to avoid any snapping branches or twigs as she made cautiously for the window.

Peering in, she heard Isemay's voice before she could make out the murky interior of the shack. Her sister was speaking in low, sweet tones, though Sabina could not make out the words. Samuel, she thought, was not in there. He must be posted outside the door on the other side. It was a shock then when she heard a male voice within respond to her sister.

"Yes, my love," he murmured. "I am well. All the better for seeing you."

Isemay stooped to stroke his brow, making small crooning noises over him. He caught her hand and pressed it to his lips.

Sabina reeled as her eyes picked over the long, recumbent figure lying on the makeshift pallet in the middle of the shack. He was very pale and covered in a gray woolen blanket, his head swathed in bandages. Even so, Sabina could make out those lean, hawklike features.

It was Leland Ellis.

*

Stifling a gasp, Sabina had stepped aside from the window and plastered herself against the mossy stone wall for the duration of her sister's visit. She could scarcely believe her eyes, but the buzz of low conversation in the hut convinced her that her sister was indeed involved in Sir Leland's disappearance. She could scarcely fathom it! *Why?* How had Leland Ellis ended up in this hovel being tended to by her sister of all people?

384

She was not sure how long she crouched there, but when she recognized a fond farewell was being made, she straightened up, stretching her cramped legs. She gave it a couple of minutes to give Isemay and Samuel time to leave the building and then skirted her way around to the other side before setting off in pursuit through the wood.

Only when Isemay and Samuel exited the wood to join the lane again did Sabina raise her voice to hail them and stop them in their tracks. "Halt!" she cried, and Samuel wheeled about as Isemay let out a startled cry.

"Sister!" Isemay recovered fast, plastering a bright smile to her face. "Well met! We were just coming to visit with you this fine morn, is that not so, Samuel?"

Her henchman was slower to recover. He gulped audibly before stammering, "Th-that's right, Miss Isemay, Miss Sabina."

Sabina folded her arms. "I *saw* you from my kitchen window and I followed you. I know what you have been up to!"

Isemay's color drained, then flooded her face in a hectic rush. "You sly thing!" she cried before a thought seemed to occur to her. She cast a rallying look at Samuel before fixing her sister with a searching look. "Did you really or are you simply bluffing? Do not try to deceive me, sister, for you know I know you better than anyone."

"Have you run *quite* mad, Isemay?" Sabina demanded, her patience running out. "How long have you been concealing Ellis there? Are you aware his father is searching for him most assiduously?"

Samuel gave a low moan and covered his face with one hand. "Your father will throw me out on my ear for this!"

"Nonsense!" Isemay stamped her foot. "He will do no such thing. Pull yourself together, Samuel! My sister will not betray us."

The two sisters glared at each other before Sabina made a frustrated sound and started back toward her home. "Follow me!" she flung back over her shoulder, not stopping to check that they obeyed her summons.

On reaching the Great Chamber, Sabina cast off Penny's cloak and sat down at the oak table, steepling her hands before her. Isemay and Samuel followed on behind, Isemay's nose in the air, Samuel looking rather like a chastised dog. "Take a seat," Sabina ordered.

Samuel dragged out the bench and plumped himself down at once, while Isemay made a great show of untying her cloak strings and then setting it neatly over a chair back before joining Samuel on his bench.

"Now tell me what you have been about," Sabina said in a low stern tone, "and be sure you start at the beginning."

Isemay darted a quick glance at Samuel. "Well, you were there at the beginning, sister. Samuel did not join until later, so I must relate this part." Samuel looked relieved and Isemay cleared her throat. "We shall skip over Leland Ellis's wicked actions at Ganford Chase and how he became my mortal enemy, for you already know that much."

Sabina opened her mouth to point out that Isemay had not addressed Leland as one would an enemy, but her sister held up an admonishing finger.

"Am I to tell this tale or am I not?" she asked with dignity.

Sabina closed her mouth and inclined her head. "You are."

"Very well, then. I am sure I do not need to describe to you my feelings on this occasion, how my bosom burned with impotent rage. How I hungered and thirsted for revenge, yet *knew*, just *knew* the villain would escape without punishment, despite the fact that you, my savior, would be forced to endure a lifetime of suffering being married to one such as Sir Jeffree!"

Sabina felt her face grow hot. "Nay, Isemay..." she protested, but again, her sister held up her hand.

"You will allow this is my tale to tell, sister." Sabina pressed her lips together and nodded her assent. "After the occasion of your visit to Tipton Hall with your new husband, I realized how hopeless the situation was. Up until that point I still clung to a desperate belief that you could somehow be freed from your predicament. That hope died in my bosom after seeing you together. I realized there would be no escape for you, sister. Sir Jeffree made it quite plain that he would not countenance any separation. How bitter were my reflections that *I* should be the cause of your downfall."

Isemay dashed a hand across her brimming eyes, and Sabina reached out a hand to her. Her sister glanced at it but did not take it. "I know how much you suffered under the yoke of your first marriage, Sabina." Her voice shook. "I could not forgive myself for being the cause of another period of such misery in your life. Not after your providential deliverance from the first."

Sabina shook her head, but Isemay was staring down at the tabletop. "The burden felt almost unbearable that morning after you left. I felt utter despair. Mother and Father simply did not understand my feelings on the matter. I had to get away from their inane comments." Her lip curled. "Mother would not stop speaking of the fine gowns and jewels that would now be yours. Father was almost as bad, saying it might have worked out *for the best*.

"Neither of them understood that your life stood in ruins! I ran out of doors. You know how I always feel comforted by wild places, and I am not really sure why, but I felt if I could only get to Langley Woods I could preserve my sanity. I could scream and rail at the cruel fates and the iniquity of men and none would hear me or judge me for my fury.

"I saddled up Top," she said, naming her father's gray mare, "and I rode like a fiend all the way, almost to Morecotte indeed, but I did not wish to see that knave Hendry or his henchmen, so I stopped instead at the Maiden's shrine at White Leaf Oak instead. I said a prayer there, then tethered Top in the grove before entering the wood to lose myself for a few hours."

Isemay fell into brooding silence a moment. "You may guess what I wished for," she said, directing a glance at Sabina then giving a short laugh. "Nay, not what they advise us women to pray for. Not for acceptance or strength to abide that which we cannot change, but for *vengeance*." Her eyes burned at the memory.

"I asked the Maiden to give me vengeance for the wrong done to me, but I did not really think she would grant me my wish," she admitted softly. "I should have had more faith."

"Vengeance?" Sabina echoed in alarm.

Isemay nodded. "I am not sure how long I wandered in the wood before I stumbled on it. Maybe an hour or so, my heart festering in poison, almost choking on it. I felt like I was drowning."

"It?" Sabina prompted when Isemay relapsed once more into silence.

"The body," Isemay answered.

"Whose body?"

388

"Hmmm?" Isemay looked up. "Oh, Leland Ellis's."

"He was *dead*?"

Isemay nodded. "Or so I thought. He was lying there, completely lifeless, crumpled and torn, his skin quite gray and splattered in blood."

Sabina raised a hand to her mouth. "But how…?"

Isemay shrugged. "I neither knew nor cared. In my dreamlike state, it seemed perfectly natural to find him there like that. An answer to prayer." Samuel gave a low moan and covered his eyes with his hands.

"Samuel was still not involved in this point?" Sabina asked sharply, nameless dread forming in the pit of her stomach.

"Not at all," Isemay answered simply, and Sabina was relieved to see Samuel's eyes peering through his fingers were guileless as ever.

He shook his head. "I was still in ignorance at this point and wish to gods I had remained so!"

"What did you do?" Sabina asked quickly, seeing the irritable look Isemay flashed at Samuel.

"What else?" her sister continued. "I gave my heartfelt thanks and started gathering wildflowers, leaves, and twigs to cover his broken body. I felt exultant, *ecstatic*. It was only as I was covering his face with dandelions that I noticed him draw in a ragged breath. That was when I realized he was still alive. You may imagine my feelings at *that* point."

Sabina found she did not want to imagine Isemay's feelings.

"The goddess was testing me to see if I was in earnest," Isemay sighed. "I stood there an age, just gazing down at him. His

389

breathing was shallow, so shallow. I knew that if I just did nothing, left him exposed to the elements for even one night, he would be dead upon the morrow."

Sabina covered her mouth with her hand, and Samuel interrupted at this point.

"But o' course she could do no such thing," he said with unconvincing heartiness. "Instead, Mistress Isemay, she came back to Tipton Hall and fetched me and a bunch of provisions to fortify him with."

Isemay hunched a shoulder and let it fall. "We set him up in the old shack with blankets, bandaged his hurts, and barricaded him in against any wild beasts for the night."

Sabina turned to the burly manservant. "And in your opinion, what ailed him, Samuel?"

"He had been beaten, milady, and beaten badly. Some might say to within an inch of his life."

Sabina shuddered. "And you did not tell anyone where he was?"

"I swore Samuel to secrecy," Isemay said quickly. "The responsibility was all mine."

"I see. And from that day, you have visited him, bringing him food and medicine?"

Isemay nodded. "His recovery has been slow and…my revenge has now taken a curious turn."

Sabina frowned. "And that is?" she asked when Isemay started wordlessly drawing patterns on the tabletop with her fingertip.

"He don't remember nothing," Samuel put in eagerly when his mistress did not speak, "for the beating emptied his head. He believes whatever Mistress Isemay sees fit to tell him."

Sabina's mouth fell open. "And what is it that you tell him, Isemay?" she asked with mounting alarm.

Isemay tossed her head. "Nothing that he does not deserve! Do I not hold him now in the palm of my hand? *I* chose to preserve his life. It is for me to mete out his punishment; that is my right."

Sabina regarded her gravely. "You have told him you are *lovers*? But why?"

Samuel shifted uncomfortably on the bench as Isemay's color heightened.

"I had to tell him something. This way he will mind me and do as I say."

"And what will you do if he recovers his memory, Isemay? This plan is foolhardy and ill-thought-out!" Sabina's voice rose with each word, and her sister shushed her, whipping around to check the door was still closed.

"I will have my revenge before that point," Isemay said, turning back hurriedly. "Only keep your voice down for surely your household must be up and about by now!"

"My household currently consists of two servants only," Sabina admitted. "Jeffree and his man, Osborn, are currently at Ganford Chase."

"Oh." Isemay relaxed. "Well, pray do not concern yourself, sister, I know what I am about. I will have my revenge forthwith, and until then, he is wholly at my mercy."

Sabina let her troubled gaze rest on Isemay's face a moment, searching her expression. "You are sure you know what you are about, Isemay?" she asked with misgiving. "I have a terrible presentiment of disaster."

"Quite sure!"

"Sir Charles is frantic about his son's fate…"

"He need not be," Isemay said serenely. "Once my revenge is secured, Sir Charles will learn his son yet lives. Thanks to me."

"And you are sure, are you not, of his recovery?"

"Quite sure," her sister repeated with supreme confidence.

"Only if his health was to take a turn for the worst…" She noticed Samuel turned an alarmed look upon his mistress, but Isemay was not fazed one whit.

"I have not the smallest doubt," Isemay insisted, rising from her seat. "Now, if that is all, sister, then Samuel and I must return to Tipton Hall before our absence is noted."

Sabina jumped up as well, but nothing she could say could convince her sister to delay their departure. "We have the wagon tethered further down the lane and must not leave it any longer lest anyone happen upon it," Isemay said, clinching the argument. Not long after, Sabina stood at the window, watching them hurrying back down the lane.

"Where the bloody hells have you been?" a furious voice asked from the doorway and Sabina whipped around with a gasp.

Jeffree stood there, a thunderous frown on his face. "I rode back early, and you were nowhere to be found!"

21

The row had been furious. At least on his half, it had been. It was only after he had finished thoroughly berating her that he noticed she seemed a little off-color. "Why are you so quiet?" he bit out, abandoning his tirade all at once.

"I have not slept well these past two nights," she answered, lifting a hand to her brow.

Jeffree felt an uncomfortable pang in the vicinity of his chest. Had she not? Neither had he. "Well, what do you expect?" he demanded crossly. "Squeezing yourself into that narrow cot in the back bedroom. Why must you always be so damnably stubborn?"

"It is my nature, I suppose," she answered wearily. "Are you going somewhere?"

"Flyford Parvell," he answered in clipped tones. "I have business there this day."

"Oh." It was just one word, but for some reason, it sounded oddly forlorn.

"Where were you anyway?" he asked sullenly, returning to the subject of his original displeasure.

She only hesitated for the briefest instant before making reply. "I met my sister for an early morning walk."

"A sensible woman would have informed her servants of the fact," he responded cuttingly. "And not sent her husband fruitlessly scouring the place for her." When Sabina only nodded in mute agreement, he realized something was definitely amiss. "What ails you?" he asked.

"Nothing; my health is always excellent."

Then why do you sound so listless and look so wan? Jeffree wanted to ask but bit his tongue. "You should not have risen so early if you got no sleep," he heard himself respond abruptly. "Why do you not return to bed for a couple of hours?" His solicitude embarrassed him, but in truth, she barely seemed to notice it.

Sabina made a dismissive gesture with her hand. "I would not sleep now; besides, I am perfectly well. Do not fuss."

Fuss? Jeffree was incensed. He never fussed. Still, something held him back from telling her as such. "Do you want me to tarry awhile? We could break our fast together." Hot color crept into his cheeks at these placating words, but his darting glance told him his wife had not even noticed his uncharacteristic behavior.

She was twisting her hands together and pacing now before the window. "What?" She turned to face him with surprise. "Oh…no. I am not hungry. Do not delay setting out on my account."

Jeffree bit back his instinctive retort. To add insult to injury, she had not even asked his purpose in riding out to Flyford Parvell! He brooded on the matter for the whole of the ride there. Since Sabina had been in residence once more in her old home, he had been relegated to a position of insignificance in her life, he thought wrathfully.

What he ought to do was leave her to stew in her rural obscurity. Then she would realize her mistake. Or would she? More than likely, she would forget about him altogether. It was no surprise that he was in quite a bad mood by the time he reached his destination of the little coastal town.

His errand proved a fruitless endeavor, for Hendry had already been and gone.

"I meant to send him away with a flea in his ear," James Gordon admitted. "But he seemed so hard-pressed that I ended up lending him my second-best mare and what little money I had to hand." He shrugged. "Some inheritance he'd wangled had come to naught, and he reckoned he might have the law on his heels."

"The law?" Jeffree repeated sharply. "Did he say why?"

Gordon shook his head. "There's always some reason with Alf," he admitted wearily. "He was ranting something about being done out of his rights, but he never has had a clear view of right and wrong and that's the truth."

"Was he alone or did he have company?"

Gordon shook his head. "When he's broke, I'm the only friend stands true to him, and he's known that these past ten years. And that's only for old time's sake. If my Polly knew I'd given him money again, well…" He shook his head. "She'd raise me a rare scolding."

"Did he make mention of anyone named Ellis? Leland Ellis? Think, man."

Gordon frowned. "I don't think so… Leastways, I'm not sure. That's a funny sort of name, and he did mention as how some fine gentleman with a funny name had tried to cheat him at cards, now I comes to think of it."

Jeffree narrowed his gaze, for he knew Leland's play to be not overscrupulous. He would not put cheating at cards past him. "Did he say what happened to this person who cheated him?"

"Said he broke his head and left him in a ditch," Gordon answered promptly. "But he's always talked big, has Alfred. He's never been a one for fighting, so if he did, he got someone else to do it for him. He had a couple of nasty brutes in his employ a while back, but they certainly wasn't with him on this visit."

Jeffree had not stayed above a half hour before deciding the fellow had nothing else useful to tell him. He would need to be careful when telling Charles what he had learned. Hearing his son and heir might have been "left in a ditch" would not sound reassuring. Jeffree headed back to Ganford with no clearer idea of Leland's location than when he had left.

On top of that, he had still not figured out how to make his own wife fall in love with him. It was galling that his own declaration had led nowhere, but on the whole, he did not think this current stratagem was working. Abandoning her at Morecotte, to realize the error of her ways, was failing miserably. He had felt closer to her when they were on the road. Mayhap that was just physical closeness, but he did not care. He was miserable without her.

Probably she did not love him, maybe she never would. Still, that did not mean he could not have her constant companionship. That was only her duty after all. He was her husband. In two days' time, he needed to leave for Caer-Lyoness and the Summer Tournament. Sabina's rightful place was by his side at such an event, admiring his knightly prowess. She was damned well going to attend, whether she wanted to or not. He would brook no argument, and so he would tell her on his return to Morecotte.

The more he thought about it, the less appeal another night under Ganford Chase's roof held. It was only early afternoon, he determined, glancing up at the sky. He would swing by the village on his return and meet with the blacksmith and his wife. There had to be a neater way of solving the issue than the way Burrell had gone about it.

He could not believe that Sabina's father had been able to pay more than a pittance for the child's upkeep. His own inclination was that the wretched woman needed to be found a husband to give her and the child his name. A husband with a trade who could be relied on to provide for his new family. Preferably in some village or town a good distance from this one. It was not fitting that his wife should be at risk of embarrassment every time she set foot in the village.

His course determined, Jeffree cheered up considerably. There would be no more of this tiptoeing around, this trying to curry favor with his own wife. He would simply *tell* her the way things would be between them going forward.

22

Five Days Later

The Summer Palace, Caer-Lyoness

Sabina gazed around the cramped quarters of the de Crecy rooms at the royal palace. Somehow it was not at all how she had expected it, for surely the de Crecys would have the very best, would they not? Yet these rooms seemed so small and airless.

"Where is my cousin?" Jeffree asked the smart-looking servant who had admitted them.

"Sir Hugo is attending the celebrations in the Grand Salon," the servant supplied. "There are troubadours and entertainers gathered there to celebrate the tournament's start on the morrow."

Jeffree snorted. "Is the second bedchamber free?" he asked, turning to survey the three doors leading off from the antechamber.

"Yes, Sir Jeffree," the servant replied. "Sir Hugo said you would likely be arriving for the tourney, so we made it ready."

"Osborn, set those things down and go back and collect the rest," Jeffree barked over his shoulder as he flung the door to the room open and unburdened himself of his saddlebags.

Sabina hovered a moment, feeling wretchedly sticky and dusty from the last leg of the journey. Belatedly, she noticed the superior-looking servant was frowning at her. "Yes?" she had no sooner asked than Jeffree stepped back out of the room.

"What's this?" he asked sharply. "Wilton, go and fetch my lady some refreshment and clean water for a bath."

Wilton's jaw dropped. "Y-yes, Sir Jeffree," he stammered and hurried away.

Oh, thought Sabina. She had been mistaken for a servant again. She rolled her eyes.

"Go and take your ease within," Jeffree instructed her, pushing open another door to a small-looking sitting room. He scanned her anxiously. "You—er—feel well?" He still had not recovered from her bleeding all over the bedsheets the night before they had left Morecotte.

"Nothing ails me, Jeffree," she reminded him tersely. "I have simply been on my monthly courses this past week." Of course, it had not made a four-day journey any easier, but that was neither here nor there, as she had been given precious little choice about making it.

He cleared his throat and colored faintly. "I am aware of that."

To give him credit, he had insisted she still share his bed every night since, despite the fact she had bled on his thigh. Squeamishness, it seemed, was not one of his many faults. Sabina ducked under his arm and walked across the stuffy room to fling a window open. It was noisy in the courtyard below. Sabina leaned out to see torches being lit and people milling around, laughing, and calling to one another.

"There will be a banquet tonight," he said. "We will be attending."

Sabina's hands tightened on the window ledge. It was one thing to be dragged around the tournaments but being presented at court was her idea of hell. "If we do," she warned without

399

turning, her voice shaking slightly, "then you may be sure I shall wear my meanest apparel."

Jeffree gave a short laugh. "Your meanest apparel?" he mocked. "It's hard to tell one from another they are all so—" He bit off his words, thinking better of what he had been about to say.

Sabina found her breath coming fast. "You might think I will be the one demeaned, but *you* will be the one judged for having a threadbare wife, Sir Jeffree de Crecy," she pointed out.

"Turn around and face me," he said harshly. Sabina was slow to turn but turn she did. Once they were facing one another, he looked her up and down with deliberation. "You are covered in travel dirt and sweat," he said with deliberation, "and it makes not one whit of difference to how I view you." Sabina swallowed. "I will not be ashamed to be seen with you, and in any case, I do not care about the judgment of others, my fellow knights included."

Sabina stared at him. "You are so—" She broke off and tried to muster her thoughts. "Can you please just stop"—she waved a hand to illustrate something—"all this."

"All this what?"

"All this newfound concern for my comfort!" she flung at him. "All this politeness you now show me. All this concern for my well-being! You are making things overcomplicated and…and confusing me! I want you to go back to how you were before."

Jeffree looked at her uncomprehendingly. "Before?" he asked cautiously.

"Before you…before you started all this!" she practically howled at him. "You know what I am speaking of."

"No, I do not," he replied testily. "I have not the faintest idea what you are speaking of."

"Before!" she yelled. "When you called me madam and—"

"I still call you madam."

"Yes, on occasion you do, but not all the time as you once did."

"Is that all?"

"No, that is not all!"

He crossed his arms. "What, then?"

"When you…when you did not give a damn about me and thought I was plain and impudent and not fit to even clean your shoes!"

Jeffree looked winded by her words. "I still think you're impudent," he managed at last.

"What about the rest?" she challenged.

He opened his mouth, but whatever he had been about to say, it seemed he could not bring himself to do it. Instead, he gave a slight shake of his head and tried again. "Because," he blustered hotly, "you told me to find other ways to show you…how I feel!" he ended frustratedly. When she looked blank, he started again, taking a deep breath. "You said I should show you proof of my regard in how I treat you outside of the bedchamber," he reminded her tightly. "That is what I have been trying to do."

"Oh." Sabina felt deflated. She *had* told him that. She gave an exasperated huff and plunked her hands on her hips. "Well, forget about that for now. I do not want you making a spectacle of me in front of the palace and all the courtiers with your attentions."

He was practically grinding his teeth at this point. "What do you mean?"

"I want you to be the old Sir Jeffree and largely ignore me."

He gave a harsh laugh. "When exactly did I ever do that?"

"At the Bishop's Palace," she responded quickly.

"The Bishop's—?"

"When I was there with my aunt."

He was silent a moment as her meaning sank in. "I was not even aware of your existence at that point!" he all but roared.

"Exactly. I see you have finally taken my meaning."

Once again, Jeffree seemed to find difficulty in drawing breath. "That is what you want?" he demanded furiously as soon as he had regained it. "My *indifference*?"

Sabina's chin rose. "It is," she said flatly. "Indeed, I am convinced it is the only way that I can get through this ordeal."

Jeffree was clearly fuming at this request, and he could not hide it over the next hour as he snapped and snarled at her in front of his cousin's servant. This was not indifference, Sabina thought with misgiving. It was more like blazing resentment and fury. Oh dear, now she had gone too far the other way. At this rate, everyone would think he *hated* her.

She had her bath and tarried over it, for every moment in the tub meant she was not spending it in the banqueting hall being stared at by all and sundry. Forty minutes later, they descended the spiral stone staircase together, and Sabina smoothed the brown linen skirts of her most unbecoming dress. She had teamed it up with a matching brown veil over the top of her head, though the one pinned under her chin was still the usual

402

crisp white. For a minute, pausing before the mirror, her vanity had rebelled.

I cannot do this, she had thought, gazing at her reflection, a light sweat breaking out on her top lip. It was too warm in this castle on this summer eve, and though no beauty, she had never thought herself outright ugly before. Tonight, she thought, she danced perilously close on the edge of it.

Oh gods, she thought as they paused on the threshold of the banqueting chamber. Why could he not just have left her in peace at Morecotte? She did not want to be paraded before all these fine folk as Sir Jeffree's bride!

Was it purely her imagination or did conversation indeed halt as they stepped into the large, cavernous hall? Sabina gazed straight ahead. That was one of the best features of her heavy wimple. It restricted both her view of others and their view of her.

"Jeffree!" startled accents rang out before an exquisitely dressed courtier appeared before them. "I thought I would see you here, well met, cousin."

"Hugo," Jeffree responded without enthusiasm. Sabina remembered Jeffree had said his cousin was frivolous.

An elegant bow was presented to Sabina. She bobbed a perfunctory curtsey in return. "Lady Sabina," Hugo greeted her cautiously. "It is good to see you again. I—er—did not anticipate Jeffree would bring you to court."

"Why not?" Jeffree asked coldly.

"Did we meet at Ganford Chase?" Sabina interrupted. "I don't remember." It was without a doubt the rudest thing she had ever said in polite company in her life. She cast a sidelong glance at Jeffree as she insulted his cousin, but he did not even flinch.

403

Hugo, however, was a different matter. He looked instantly affronted. "We did, madam," he answered stiffly.

"Don't call her that," Jeffree shot back. "Only I call her madam."

Hugo blinked. "Er…my lady," he corrected himself quickly.

Sabina inclined her head. "One gets introduced to so many people as a newlywed," she complained. "I can hardly be expected to remember everyone. And you de Crecys are so very *prolific*."

Hugo looked stunned. He gaped at her. Jeffree inclined his head and they moved on.

Sabina darted a sidelong glance at him, but to her disappointment, he looked entirely unruffled. This would not do. She had vowed, had she not, to make him regret dragging her to the summer palace. She would have to hit on some new way of annoying him.

A passing servant held up a tray of wine and Sabina accepted a goblet. "You do not drink?" she commented, seeing Jeffree wave the server away.

"I will take ale only this eve to keep a clear head for the morrow."

"Because of the joust?" Sabina asked, and he nodded as they approached a table. It looked perilously close to the raised central dais in Sabina's opinion, though it currently only housed the King, who was lolling on his throne with a bored expression. Jeffree halted next to a bench. "You sit here," he instructed.

"Could we not find a quieter corner?" Sabina asked, glancing up at the overhead circular chandelier suspended on a chain and illuminated with candles. "One that is not so well lit."

"No," Jeffree replied briefly. Catching sight of the look on her face, he added grudgingly, "The tables are allocated by rank. We sit here because it is our right."

Sabina pulled a face. She might have known the dubious honor was down to being a high and mighty de Crecy! She took a sip of wine and glanced about her. To her surprise, the hall was not packed to the rafters with nobles but instead looked rather sparsely attended. "Why are there not more attendees?" she asked Jeffree, who was sitting down next to her.

"It is only competitors who are invited this eve."

"What about your cousin?" She frowned.

"And the competitors' families," he added.

"So then, he attends courtesy of his connection to you?" Jeffree nodded. "Oh." Despite herself, she found she was interested in the various people grouped about the hall. There was a very elegant lady with black hair in blue satin and accompanied by a man cradling an infant in his large muscular arms.

"Who is that?" Sabina asked.

Jeffree turned his head to follow her gaze. "Sir Roland Vawdrey." He scowled.

"Oh, is he a prominent competitor of yours? He is very good-looking." Jeffree's glower grew more pronounced. "Is that his baby he carries?"

"How should I know?"

"Well, you would know if Sir Roland was usually accompanied by a gaggle of his offspring," she pointed out.

"I do not think he has been married long enough to produce more than one," he admitted after a heavy pause.

"Oh." Sabina's attention was snared next by a heavily pregnant lady accompanied by a knight with pale, rather cold eyes. "Who is that?" she asked in a low voice, leaning forward.

"Sir Garman Orde," Jeffree answered, his voice practically vibrating with hostility. "Do you think him good-looking too?"

Sabina thought about this a moment before replying. "I would say that strictly speaking, he is more attractive than good-looking. Another of your rivals?" Sabina guessed, seeing his irritation. Jeffree did not deign to answer this. "Is that his lady wife beside him?"

"Yes."

"She looks as though her babe could be born any day now. I wonder that she does not stay at home."

"Perhaps *some* wives like to support their spouses when they compete," Jeffree responded snidely.

Sabina ignored him. "I expect they're all wondering what you're doing with the likes of me," she mused.

"I'm sure they will hazard a guess."

Sabina bristled. "How so?"

"Because I have ne'er been accompanied by a woman before," he answered, sounding goaded.

"Oh, I see." Sabina's gaze next alighted on so striking a newcomer that she almost gasped. The scarring down the one

406

side of his face was extensive, and he looked very fearsome. "Who is *that*?" she asked out of the side of her mouth, as she did not want to appear rude.

Jeffree practically twitched with annoyance. "Lord Kentigern," he growled. "A northern baron."

"Is he really?" Sabina had not met many northerners, so she made sure to get a good look at him. "Do all northerners look as formidable as this one? And so tall?"

"Of course not," Jeffree snapped. "He was grievously wounded in the late war."

Sabina nodded hastily at this tragic explanation. "Poor man." Her sympathy did not seem to appease Jeffree one bit. "Is he a good jouster?"

"Yes, damn him."

Sabina had to bite her lip to stop a wayward smile at his grudging praise. At this point, a server approached to offer them a selection of courses from the stepped display in the center of the table. Sabina gave up on her crowd observation for a while and concentrated instead on an almond tart served with berries and a thick dollop of cream.

As for Jeffree, he grumbled and complained through his own dish of capon for he did not enjoy the rich sauce it was served in.

"It must be a great trial to you," she commented, "having such an unsophisticated palate when you are surrounded on all sides by such excellent cooking."

He sent her an exasperated look. "I do not agree with your pronouncement about my taste," he reminded her.

"We agree on *nothing*."

"Not true. There are places we are in accord."

"Oh? Pray, enlighten me, Sir Jeffree, where might that be?" He gave her a very level look, and Sabina felt her face grow hot. "On second thoughts, do not bother!"

It was little wonder that, by the time they retired, they were both tetchy and short with each other. They walked the five minutes back to the de Crecy palace rooms in silence, and Sabina was glad to retire to their room without catching so much of a glimpse of Jeffree's cousin.

Osborn was nowhere in sight, but Wilton was on hand to fetch them hot water, and Sabina was soon tucked in the rather small bed. It was at least half the size of Jeffree's one back in Ganfordshire, and in truth, she did not think it much bigger than her old one at Tipton Hall. It trembled on her lips to say so, but she bit the words back as Jeffree continued to wash in silence.

When he climbed in the bed, she pressed her lips together, rolling onto her side and facing away from him. Jeffree blew out the last remaining candle and silence ruled over the room for all of five minutes.

Jeffree cleared his throat. "Are you entirely healed now?" he asked in a lowered voice.

"Healed?" Sabina frowned into the darkness. There was an awkwardness to his tone which made realization dawn. *Oh.* "I was not injured, Jeffree," she told him matter-of-factly. "It was just my woman's time."

Silence greeted these words. Clearly, the idea of bleeding without injury made little sense to him. Still, when he spoke again, she was surprised. "Yet you wore bandages to staunch the flow," he said. "I saw them soaking in the bowl afterward."

Sabina lay silent a moment. Jeffree's ignorance on this subject was not surprising, but his curiosity was. "There is no staunching it, in truth," she answered carefully, "for 'tis a steady flow that lasts several days. We simply wear rags down there to…absorb it."

"Rags?"

"The strips of fabric you mistook for bandages."

"Ah," he said, and though she waited, disappointingly he did not follow this up with anything else.

"I suppose neither Sir Charles Ellis nor Sir Hereward Acker taught you of such things," she heard herself say.

"Never," he agreed. "My education was sadly incomplete until I met you." Sabina turned her head sharply but could not make out if his expression was earnest or sarcastic. "You did not answer my question," he prompted.

She ran back over the last few sentences. *Oh.* "It is now done," she admitted.

"Good."

She fidgeted with the blanket edge. For a minute then, she had thought he was hinting at the expectation of conjugal relations between them. Ridiculous, when she thought about it, as Jeffree was not really much of a one for hinting. "You were surprisingly unruffled by my woman's time," she admitted, remembering the fuss Miles had made on a couple of occasions. He could be easily nauseated considering his keenness for hunting.

"Oftentimes I have cuts and wounds and will bleed on the sheets," he said off-handedly. "It is the nature of combat."

Sabina considered this. "Even in a tournament?" she asked with mild surprise.

"Of course."

"Oh." It occurred to her that she had no notion of what to expect on the morrow, and suddenly this struck her as a little worrying. With a guilty start, she realized she had not even enquired if he had won at his last tournament at Areley Kings. Had he told her? She cast her mind back; she did not think he had. "Jeffree," she said suddenly.

"Yes."

"Did you win at Areley Kings?"

He breathed out noisily. "Nay. I reached the final, then lost to de Bussell."

De Bussell? Again, Sabina drew a blank. Should she know who that was? There were *so many* of these knights. "And will you win on the morrow?" she asked instead.

"There is always a good chance I will win," he answered, "but I am a strong competitor in a field of other strong competitors. There is never a sure winner."

"Oh."

*

The next morning dawned with a hazy blue sky that seemed to promise a hot July afternoon. Jeffree rose early, and he and Osborn disappeared off to the tourney field before even breaking their fast. Sabina washed and dressed at a more leisurely pace, in no hurry to emerge from their bedchamber and renew her acquaintance with Hugo.

When she did venture out into the cramped palace apartments, she found the three rooms completely empty apart from Wilton. He informed her in hushed tones that his master would likely not rise until noon, for he had not returned until the early hours from the festivities.

Wilton was not particularly friendly and seemed to expect her to wait for her husband's return before she could break her fast. On Jeffree's reappearance, they partook of roasted fish and finest pandemain, and Sabina was informed that a palace page would be sent to escort her to the arena in a half hour.

When the page duly arrived, a gangly boy of thirteen or thereabouts, he looked her over with frank surprise.

"Lady de Crecy?" he asked cautiously, and Sabina guessed he was checking lest he had her servant in her stead.

She nodded. "I am she. And what is your name?"

"'Tis Laurence, my lady. Laurence Everill."

"Well met, Laurence." Sabina joined him out in the corridor, closing the door resolutely behind her. "Do you usually attend the palace tournaments?" she asked as they made their way belowstairs.

"Yes, my lady," he responded promptly, his eyes gleaming. "For 'tis rare sport indeed."

"That is good to hear, Laurence, for this will be my first."

His eyes widened, and he came to a halt on the stair. "Are you truly Sir Jeffree's wife?" he blurted.

"I am, but that is a recent development." He nodded and Sabina could see he was a little disappointed by her dowdy appearance. She sought for something agreeable to say. "Do you suppose he stands much chance of winning today?"

411

"He is always a strong contender," Laurence answered thoughtfully, "but for my part, I put my money on Lord Kentigern."

"Your money?"

"I bet a ha'penny against Wilf Keenes," he said promptly.

Sabina could not forbear smiling at this artless confidence. "And who does Wilf back to win?"

"Sir Roland Vawdrey."

"Ah." She nodded. "I saw both of them at the banquet last night. They both seemed very capable-looking." Jeffree had tossed some coins onto the table by her plate that morning, for any expenses she might incur throughout the day, and Sabina tipped Laurence up front, asking him to lead her to a nice, sheltered spot.

The sheer number of people packed into the stands was a little overwhelming at first, and Sabina was not keen to be squeezed in among a press of spectators or exposed to the July sun which would no doubt be beating down fiercely later.

She had been, perhaps, a little naïve, she realized as Laurence led her up many flights of stairs to a large, elevated box filled with many pretty gowns and veils. Of course, she need not have been worried she would be crammed into the standing spaces. Despite her plain dress, she would be sat among the nobility.

Laurence gallantly saw her seated and then slipped to the side of the box where the other attendants were smartly lined up. Seeing him jostle another boy with his elbow, she wondered if that might be Wilf before looking about the box curiously in spite of herself.

412

The courtiers were certainly dressed to impress. She saw several hard stares leveled her way, and a few ladies speaking behind their hands before their companions looked her up and down in open surprise. Sabina was grateful for her concealing headdress. When asked, they would not even be able to comment on the color of Sir Jeffree's wife's hair, she told herself comfortingly.

For all they knew, she could be secretly dripping in jewels, for the wimple hid all of her neck and bosom. Of course, it would be unlikely, in such plain dress, but still, they could not know for *sure*. Fleetingly, she thought of the ruby and pearl necklace and matching ring which Jeffree's mother had passed on to her. Sabina had locked it in a cupboard at Morecotte without even trying them on. She wondered if she should have brought them with her. Too late now, of course.

Everyone shot to their feet, and Sabina followed suit without even realizing why, until she noticed movement in the royal box as two crowned figures accompanied by many attendants were seated. Sabina gazed her fill at the dark lovely Queen with her green-jeweled collar and the King beside her in a puffed sleeve tunic, who waved at the crowd by rotating his hand and nodding his head.

She would certainly have plenty to tell Mother and Aunt Mabel, she thought, making note of the royal blue backdrop in their stand. She had seen the Argent Lion himself, she thought dazedly, though King Wymer did not look particularly leonine, in her opinion. He was a little on the short side too, if she was not mistaken.

Down in the arena below, Wymer's colors and standard were paraded, and then the banners and pennants of all the competitors were displayed one by one to the expectant crowd. Some of them were so popular they caused a spontaneous cheer, such as the red banner with the black panther. Others caused a groan or a ripple of excitement, such as the black heart oozing three drops of red blood or the golden portcullis on a field of blue.

Sabina was not familiar with any of the heraldic devices, so none of them meant anything to her until she saw the black tree on white. Her heart leaped then, for she knew full well that was the de Crecy crest. The arena was deathly quiet, save for a few disgruntled murmurings, though she realized that in the noble's box, several faces had turned her way and a low buzz of speculation started to rise.

Sabina frowned, and for a minute, she could not think what the source of the conjecture could be. Then she heard a footfall to her right and Laurence's hurried whisper. "The Queen!" he hissed in her ear. *The Queen?* Sabina turned to look across at the royal box and found the Queen leaning forward and staring straight at her, her expression alight with interest.

Sabina gave a start and felt her face start to fill with color. How was she supposed to conduct herself now? And how in heaven did the Queen know who *she* was? At a complete loss, Sabina bobbed her head. "What do I do?" she asked Laurence in a strangled voice.

"Naught." He shrugged. "Just let her look her fill of you." A look of sympathy crept into his eyes. "Try not to fret; she's always interested in brides," he consoled her. "Shall I fetch you a drink?"

"Oh please, Laurence," she agreed gratefully, reaching for the alms purse suspended from her belt. "Take this and get whatever you like for you and your friend."

Laurence's expression brightened and he grinned. "I shan't be long, my lady," he promised and skipped away. Still feeling the

414

Queen's intent gaze, Sabina looked blankly ahead, hoping she looked more composed than she felt. She could only be grateful when activity down below distracted everyone from staring at her.

She had to sit up very straight-backed in her seat to see past the tall steeple headdresses of the three ladies in front of her, but she managed it after only a moment's shifting around. The first spectacle seemed to be a procession of small horse-drawn chariots which wheeled about as those driving them shot bows at targets that had been set up around the ring.

Despite the undoubted skill involved, Sabina found herself wholly uninterested in these proceedings. Resisting the impulse to check if the Queen watched her still, Sabina let her attention wander about the box. To her surprise, various well-dressed people were moving up and down the rows exchanging greetings and huddling in little groups to talk. It almost seemed like a social meeting place rather than a spectator event. Sabina was just noticing the arrival of a very pretty young woman in a heraldic gown of blue and yellow when Laurence arrived back at her elbow holding a cup of ale out to her.

"Tell me," she hissed as she accepted the drink, "who is that lady, for surely I have seen those colors already this day."

Laurence glanced across. "That is the new wife of Lord Kentigern," he answered discreetly, his mouth barely moving. "They all stare for her father is a rich merchant, and though lowborn, she is now a baroness by rights."

Sabina's eyes widened. *A merchant's daughter and a lord?* She had never heard of such a disparate match. Maybe it was partly because Lady Kentigern was flanked on both sides by such plain older women, but to Sabina, she looked almost radiant in beauty.

415

Such a lovely girl would surely present a cruel contrast to her heavily scarred spouse, Sabina pondered. Yet here she was practically flaunting her new husband's banner on her person. "Lord Kentigern is most fortunate in his wife," Sabina murmured, glancing about and noticing that Laurence spoke naught but the truth. Everyone was now staring raptly at Baroness Kentigern as she descended the steps.

"Aye, for their marriage hath restored to him the castle and all the lands he lost after the war," Laurence replied quietly. "But look out," he warned, "for she is sitting now on the bench directly behind you."

Sabina nodded and faced forward again. She drank her ale as the ring was made ready for the next event which seemed to be a sort of mock battle between two sides in different colored armbands of yellow and green. Sabina watched the lines form without much interest until she suddenly recognized Jeffree among their number wearing a yellow sash at his arm.

This did make her sit up. She had not realized there would be group events as well as jousting. Having said that, she could not see much evidence of camaraderie between Jeffree and the other participants even on his own team. To her surprise, it looked as though the battle would take the form of a mounted charge, despite the fact they all had swords drawn. Would not spears be more appropriate?

Acknowledging she was far from knowledgeable on such things, Sabina shrugged and simply settled in to watch the repeated charges. It was a hot, dry day, and between the dust kicked up by the horses, and the impact of various heavily armored bodies hitting the floor, proceedings were rather hard for her to follow.

Sabina rubbed her eyes as she watched the fallen half dragged, half carried out of the arena. As each knight was eliminated, their pennants were pulled down off the display to signify their exit from the competition. In truth, it was only by checking Jeffree's crest still remained on the board that Sabina could be sure he had not been knocked out already.

The sun blazed down, and the number of knights left on their horses dwindled considerably until there were so few remaining it was a good deal easier to see who was who. Sabina could now make out Jeffree's shield as an additional identifier, and she pinned her gaze to it as best she could. It was surely nearing the end of proceedings now, Sabina thought, realizing how dry her throat was and wondering how soon Laurence would return to fetch her another drink.

In that momentary distraction, disaster struck. Sabina's eyes widened as she saw both Jeffree and his direct opposite number unseated. Indeed, it looked to her eye as though Jeffree unbalanced himself by the fury of his sword swing. Both men rolled in the dust a moment until Sabina realized they were still trading blows, this time with their gauntleted fists.

Surely that was not permitted. She glanced about uneasily to make out what her neighbors made of such unruly conduct, but in truth, the various nobles did not seem to be paying much attention to the melee at all. She beckoned to Laurence, who came hurrying over. "What is happening?" she asked. "Why are they being allowed to fight on and no one putting a stop it?"

Laurence gave her a lopsided grin. "Oh, they will be separated alright, as soon as someone gets up the courage to step in," he assured her. "Listen to the crowd."

It was at that point that Sabina noticed the rest of the stands were jumping up down with excitement, and the air closer to

417

the arena was rent with shouts and bawls of encouragement as the two knights threw punches at each other. As they had only paused to tear off the bits of armor that hampered them, their fight seemed slow and unnecessarily jarring to Sabina. She almost fancied she could hear the crunch and clang of metal even above all the noise.

Sabina winced and again glanced about at the disinterested nobles around her. Laurence seemed to pick up on her confusion. "The joust is the event the court cares most about," he explained. "That is the one with the most prestige attached to it."

"Oh." Sabina nodded as enlightenment dawned. "I see." Finally, two officials managed to insert themselves between Jeffree and his quarry. Naturally, being Jeffree, he accepted neither their interruption nor their authority to do so with any grace. To be fair to him, Sabina acknowledged the other knight took it just as ill, for he immediately flung himself out of the arena in a high dudgeon.

As for Jeffree, he dragged his helmet off his head and started yelling at the officials in an excess of thwarted passion. Sabina fought a terrible impulse to laugh. He looked so incredibly angry with his face all streaked with dirt and his golden hair dark with sweat and plastered to his head. It was strange that none of these things served in any way to detract from his good looks, she reflected as he gestured furiously between both officials.

No wonder the crowd was incensed their sport had been cut off. They started booing loudly, and to Sabina, at least, it seemed obvious it was the officials they were mad at for preventing the fisticuffs.

"Who *is* that?" one of the older ladies sat behind Sabina wondered aloud. "He is exceedingly good-looking, is he not?"

Yes, he is, thought Sabina. The most handsome man in all Karadok and the most absurd.

"'Tis Sir Jeffree de Crecy," came the reply by a younger-sounding voice. Sabina wondered if it was the lovely Lady Kentigern who spoke now. She sounded very disapproving, whoever she was. "In my opinion," she continued, "handsome is as handsome does."

All of a sudden, Sabina had to know if it was Lady Kentigern speaking and she turned quickly around and saw that, yes, it was indeed the raven-tressed baroness. *Good for her*, Sabina thought. *She has a good head on her shoulders as well as fairness of face.*

At this point, Jeffree lost his temper altogether and flung his helmet on the ground with such force he surely dented it. Then abruptly, he turned on his heel and stormed out of the ring to the accompaniment of disappointed groans and jeers.

"Such conduct," the older companion tutted in shocked accents

"Most unbecoming in a knight," the baroness's voice agreed with youthful gravity.

Sabina almost choked on her spurt of laughter. She lifted a hand and Laurence hurried over again. "Could you fetch me something to drink, please, Laurence? I am s-so th-thirsty." Her eyes brimmed over, and her shoulders shook slightly. She saw the boy looked alarmed as though he could not tell if she was overcome with mirth or sorrow. She pulled herself together by the greatest of efforts and flashed him a reassuring smile.

"Yes, Lady de Crecy, at once." He hurried away.

Pull yourself together, Sabina, she scolded herself, though all she really wanted to do was hold her sides and indulge in a good belly laugh. *Jeffree's incensed face.* She wiped the corner of her eye with her sleeve. *Oh, my goodness, he was absolutely ridiculous!* She watched in amused good humor as Roland Vawdrey and Lord Kentigern were awarded the winners of the event.

This time, Laurence brought her wine instead of ale, as though he feared she needed something stronger to get her through the next event. How right that would prove, though as she sat politely clapping the early rounds of the joust, she could not have dreamt the terrible turn the afternoon would take.

For her part, Sabina did not enjoy the formality and order of the joust as much as she had the more chaotic melee. This required a lot of sitting still and waiting for two knights to thunder at one another on horseback down a marked-out straight with lance extended. She could not fathom why it was so much more popular with the courtiers than the melee. Then again, maybe she just had common tastes.

This time even their box joined in with the "ohhhhs" and "ahhhhs" of the crowd. Sabina stifled a yawn as the competitors were slowly whittled down. Would it never end? It seemed to take an age to get through all fifty men, and Sabina had drunk a second goblet of wine before they were down to the final ten.

To her surprise, it was only shortly after this that Jeffree went crashing out, defeated by a knight the announcer hailed as "Sir Edward Bevan of Knollesley." The crowd was both stunned by this exit and gratified for the victor, for this Sir Edward seemed a popular fellow.

Sabina watched Jeffree climb to his feet, looking stiff and disheartened. This time she did not feel like laughing at all. She

420

bit her lip when he touched hands with Sir Edward and raised his helmet aloft in acknowledgment of the crowd. *See now, he can be good*, she thought and could not help but glance back over her shoulder to see if his critics behind her would acknowledge this show of sportsmanlike behavior.

To her surprise, however, Lady Kentigern was nowhere in sight and only her two mature companions remained, neither of whom seemed to be remotely attending what was happening in the field.

So that was that, then, Sabina thought, looking about for Laurence. Surely she could now leave. Then she noticed just how deep in conversation the boy was with his fellow pages. Likely, Laurence would not wish to be dragged away before the end.

Sabina groaned inwardly and steeled herself for another hour of jousting. Her bottom hurt from the hard wooden bench, and she could feel a trickle of sweat between her shoulder blades, for she had now sat a good few hours in the stifling heat. At least her starched wimple would have spared her from the consequences of the hot sun burning her face and ears.

By some miracle, she actually recognized the four finalists. Sir Roland Vawdrey, Sir Garman Orde, Lord Kentigern, and finally the knight who had earlier defeated Jeffree. She was not terribly surprised when Sir Roland knocked out Sir Edward and then Lord Kentigern knocked out Sir Garman Orde.

This meant that for the final charge it was Sir Roland Vawdrey against Lord Kentigern. To Sabina, at least, there seemed an inevitability about the final outcome. The northern baron looked so very formidable in his horned helmet astride his huge charger that, though Sir Roland was substantially built himself, she was not remotely surprised when he was knocked to the ground and lay there inert for several minutes before his squire came running to throw a bucket of water in his face and he rolled painfully onto his side.

The cheer of the crowd when Sir Roland clambered to his feet was far louder than it had been when Lord Kentigern had knocked him to the ground. Though he had not triumphed this day, it was plain to see who held the crowd's heart in the palm of his hand. When Sir Roland tore off his helmet to show his good-natured grin as he congratulated the victor, Sabina found she was not surprised by his wild popularity.

Well, it was all over, at last, she thought gratefully, arching her back and pressing her fingers into the small of her back. She was exhausted and aching all over which was strange considering all she had done was sit in one spot for nigh on five hours. What she wanted now was a nice cooling bath and then to lie about in her shift and drink lots of cold water with the window wide open to allow a breeze. She hoped the wells could be depended on to be clean at the King's palace, even if hardly anywhere else was.

Looking across at Laurence, she saw him grinning with high glee and receiving many backslaps from his fellow pages for his successful wager. She was just idly wondering which of his companions was the unfortunate Wilf when she noticed Laurence's jaw drop and saw to her consternation that he was staring fixedly at her.

Suddenly, everyone in the crowd seemed to have gone extremely quiet, and Sabina could feel every ominous thud of her heart. When the boy beside Laurence lifted a hand to point at the area just above her head, Sabina slowly turned and found a circlet of flowers dangling just to the left of her brow.

Sabina blinked at it. Where had that come from? On closer inspection, she realized it was dangling from the tip of a long lance. Sabina's incredulous eyes traveled along the length of it until they alighted on the knight holding the other end. To her astonishment, it was none other than Lord Kentigern. Sabina swallowed past the lump in her throat. He must surely mean it for his lady wife, or another of his kinswomen sat behind her, she thought desperately.

However, when she turned to glance back in that direction, Lady Kentigern was still nowhere to be seen. Two pairs of hostile eyes glared into her, and Sabina turned hastily back, her face flushing with hot color.

The lance thrust at her impatiently, and she reached up just in time to catch the coronet which was now perilously close to slipping off the end. Even from her elevated position, Sabina could read Lord Kentigern's expression which plainly said, *Take the damn thing, woman.* As soon as her fingers closed over a handful of petals and leaves, he was wheeling his horse around and heading back into the center of the ring.

Belatedly, Sabina noticed all the heads in the audience were now swiveling to fix on a point at the top of the nobles' stand. With a sense of dread, Sabina, too, glanced up to the top of the box and found Lady Kentigern stood, frozen like a statue, staring with wounded eyes at the flower tribute in her hand. Sabina likewise turned to stone. It felt almost like the garland was scalding her fingers. She wanted to fling the cursed item away from her and beg Lady Kentigern's pardon, but of course, she could do neither of those things.

The poor girl lifted a hand to her bosom and pressed it there as though trying to comfort the ache in her own heart. It was borne home to Sabina in that instant what a wicked betrayal Lord Kentigern had performed of his tender young bride. He ought to

423

be flogged! If Lady Kentigern had dropped down dead on the spot, Sabina would have thought him a murderer, and she almost as bad.

She felt shame wash over her like a cold wave, submerging her wholly before receding to an icy trickle down her spine. Sinking down into her seat on heavy legs, she set the flowered crown upon the bench next to her with the utmost care. It was not hers and she would never wear it.

Sabina knew not how long she sat, perspiring profusely, despite the fact she was trembling and numb. Only when she dimly became aware that the crowd noise had faded back into her consciousness did she dart her eyes around and find that most people were now watching the award ceremony being performed by the King in the arena.

Then, and only then, did Sabina rise on shaky legs and make her way toward the steps which would lead her out of this ghastly place. She stumbled once, halfway up the steps, and gave a stifled sob. Luckily, a hurried grab at the partition spared her the ignominy of a tumble in front of all these fine folk and soon she was pushing through the crowds with increasing desperation.

One good thing about her humble dress was that she faded into the background, she thought as a hand caught her elbow. She wheeled around and found it was Laurence.

"You're going the wrong way, my lady," he told her and angled his thumb over his shoulder. "The palace is that way."

Her face crumpled. "Oh," she sobbed and covered her face with both hands.

Laurence looked alarmed but passed an arm about her waist and towed her in the direction he had indicated. "'Tis the heat," he said awkwardly. "It can take people strange." Sabina could manage no more than a muffled choke by this point. "Never fear, I can take you right back to your door."

Sabina nodded and let the lad tow her until they were once more entering the castle and headed for the courtiers' quarters. She managed to get a hold of herself by the second staircase, taking very deep breaths and clinging very hard to Laurence's hand. By the time Wilton opened the door to the de Crecy rooms, she was dry-eyed at least.

When she turned to Laurence, he handed her the alms purse he had taken charge of. Feeling the coins still within, Sabina loosed the strings and poured them into his hand. When Jeffree had given her the money that morning, she had thought she would never spend it all. "Thank you for your escort today, Laurence," Sabina said, forcing a smile to her lips. "You were truly invaluable to me."

"Thank you, my lady." He hesitated. "Perhaps you will send for me again, next time you are in the capital?"

"Oh, there is no doubt about it," she told him, and he bowed and turned with a whoop, clearly ecstatic with his handsome tip, and went skipping off to the staircase. Looking around, Sabina found Wilton had disappeared, so she dragged her weary feet along the corridor until she reached her bedroom door, then took a deep breath and whisked inside, slamming it shut and resting her brow against its wooden surface.

She gave one choked sob and then another, then before she knew it, she was sobbing so uncontrollably that she could not stop.

425

23

"Sabina?" Jeffree's shocked accents startled her so badly that she almost stumbled as she wheeled around and slammed straight into his dripping wet body.

"J-Jeffree!" she gasped as his hands came up to clasp her tight, just as well, or she would have collapsed into a heap on the floor.

He gripped her upper arms, peering into her face. "What has happened? Why are you crying?" His blue eyes blazed as he searched her swollen face.

"Nothing, I am entirely well," she gabbled, but could not stop her face from crumpling up, and then she was sobbing again like a perfect idiot.

"Is this because I lost?" Jeffree asked, frowning.

Sabina stared at him, stunned. "No, of *course* not!" she wailed.

"So, someone has upset you?" he clarified grimly. "Who?" When she started sobbing even harder, he gave her a slight shake. "Give me their name."

"Everyone h-hates me!" she wept. "You should have seen their faces!"

"What? Whose faces?" When Sabina would only shake her head as tears coursed down her cheeks, Jeffree scooped her up and carried her toward the bed.

"No!" she cried out. "Do not set me on the bed. I am sweaty and sticky and dirty," she wept. He changed direction, and Sabina realized they were headed toward a large tub. This must be why Jeffree was leaving puddles at every step, she realized dimly. He had been soaking in the tub.

When he set her down next to it and started unfastening her laces, Sabina tried to bat his hands away. "I can do it," she mumbled with embarrassment. She did not want him to see the unbecoming sweat patches under her armpits and at her back.

He scoffed, but did not speak, dragging her ugly brown gown up over her head and then casting it down into a puddle of water. Then he tackled her shift and pulled off her stockings and shoes. Sabina did not stop weeping the whole time.

The next thing she knew, she was submerged in water and still in Jeffree's arms. He had climbed in with her, she realized dimly. "This water must surely be very dirty," she hiccupped, remembering his grime-streaked face from earlier.

"I have already had two baths. This is my third and entirely clean. It is to help my muscles relax."

"Your third?" Sabina gasped, gazing at the vast tub. My gods, no wonder Wilton did not seem to like them. Even filling it once must have taken an age!

Feeling his hands in her hair, she realized he was unfastening her braids. She closed her eyes and allowed it. The fight had gone out of her completely, and she just wanted to close her eyes and drift away from the horror of her day.

When she felt the soaped washcloth along her shoulders, she opened her eyes. "What are you doing?"

"Washing you," he answered. "Take a deep breath."

"What?" Sabina drew in her breath and then found herself dunked under the water. When she emerged coughing and spluttering moments later, he started soaping her wet hair.

427

"Most people would simply wet my hair with a jug!" she informed him indignantly. "Not by half drowning me."

He frowned. "I have never washed anyone before."

"Oh," Sabina said lamely. "Well…" She trailed off as Jeffree's fingertips rubbed against her scalp. It was startlingly pleasant, and her eyes drifted shut again as she surrendered herself wholly to his ministrations.

"Are you going to tell me why you were crying?" he asked in a low voice some moments later as he wrung the last drop of moisture out of the length of her wet hair and dropped it over the edge of the tub.

Sabina sniffed. "It is…stupid," she admitted.

He cocked an eye at her. "Stand up."

Now it was Sabina's turn to frown. "I don't want to." Being in water up to her neck was comforting. Exposing her far from perfect body was not.

"Up," he said firmly. "I need to soap your limbs. You will feel better when it is done."

Sabina sighed, for this was true enough. Screwing her eyes shut, she straightened up from the water and stood entirely still as Jeffree ran the soapy cloth all over her body. He did not flinch from the more private areas of her breasts and between her legs, but neither did he tarry there. The cloth carried on its unhurried circular route, whether it was over her thighs and buttocks or her lower back and ribs.

Sabina felt herself relax at his light, comforting touch and swayed on her feet.

"Sit back down," he said gruffly, and Sabina sank down into the water, her eyes springing open at last to look at him. He had

428

sunk back down into the water beside her and was gazing intently at her. "Tell me now," he said insistently.

The words flew out of her mouth before Sabina could even check them. "I love you," she said and then clapped her hands over her own mouth in dismay. Why had she blurted that? What was she saying? That was not even what he had meant, she realized, her eyes widening with horror, for his stunned gaze informed her he had merely been asking why she was crying.

You stupid fool, she raged inwardly at herself. *Oh, my gods, could you be any more of an embarrassment this day?*

Jeffree's eyes bored into her. "Say that again." His voice sounded odd, husky, and sort of gravelly.

Sabina shook her head, her cheeks growing hot with embarrassment. He moved in closer, his body crowding hers against the side of the tub. Sabina whimpered as his hand pulled hers away from her mouth. "Say it again," he ordered, his gaze fixed on her mouth.

"I m-mistook your meaning," she stammered. Then when he did not draw back so much as an inch, she said, taking a deep, fortifying breath. "I love you," she said, closing her eyes tight. Oh gods, she thought as her stomach plummeted. It was true. She *did* love him. She loved the most arrogant, insufferable man in all Karadok! How could this have *happened*?

She felt Jeffree's breath against her face, then his lips were gently brushing kisses against her brow.

"Now say it with your eyes open," he said, drawing back.

Sabina opened her eyes to find his face right in front of hers. "I love you," she said wonderingly, before adding a panicked, "Oh gods, whatever is to become of me?"

"I will tell you, shall I?" he asked, catching her hand, and threading his fingers through hers. "I am going to take care of you, wife," he said, lowering his mouth and kissing her lingeringly. "And spoil you so thoroughly that you will never ever regret giving me your heart."

While Sabina reeled at these astonishing words, Jeffree stood up, pulled her to her feet, and then stepped out of the tub. He fetched a drying cloth and started patting it over her upper body. "I can dry myself, Jeffree," she protested weakly. "You are dripping water all over the floor."

He paid her words no heed, and once he had dried her off down as far as her thighs, he scooped her out of the wooden tub and carried her over to the bed. Then, when he had lain her down, he proceeded to dry her knees, calves, and feet before turning his attention back to his own body. She could not help but notice he dealt with it in the most perfunctory manner after his almost worshipful attitude toward Sabina's own.

"Will you let me braid your hair?" he asked, discarding the drying cloth.

"I half thought you were joking that time," she admitted with a smile.

He reached out and touched her hair. "'Tis still slightly damp," he commented. "Does that matter?"

She reached up to feel it. "No, for in this humidity, 'twill soon be dry enough."

He fetched a comb and hesitated next to the trunk where they had unpacked her clothes. "Do you want a shift?" he asked.

Sabina lifted her eyes to meet Jeffree's own heated gaze. He wanted her to sit there naked, she realized while he dressed her hair. "Will you be wearing anything?" she asked boldly, letting her gaze travel over his nude body. He had been aroused since the tub when she had blurted out her confession of love.

"I won't if you won't," he answered, a glint in his eye.

Sabina laughed softly. "Very well. It is so very warm after all."

Jeffree shivered slightly, and Sabina hid her smile, for she did not think he was remotely cold. She sat up, back straight as Jeffree brushed her hair a hundred times and then separated it into two sections on either side of her head.

He began the first braid with scrupulously deliberate passes of his hands, tugging each time in order to ensure the woven strands were secure. His progress was slow and steady, and he did not utter a single word.

Sabina could not see his face, but she imagined he was frowning in total concentration. "Is it looking ropelike?" she joked. He grunted distractedly, and Sabina thought she had better give him silence to work by. Once he had fastened the first, he tossed it over her shoulder and turned to the next.

For some reason, the second braid gave him problems and he had to start again twice, rebrushing it out and muttering under his breath.

"Do you want—?"

"I can do it," he cut her off. "I'm just getting a little distracted."

"Oh. Shall I put on my shift?" she asked, smiling to herself, but again, she just got the disgruntled noise.

"I want to put my mouth between your legs."

"What?" Her voice was practically a squeak.

"You heard me. Hendry never did that for you, did he?"

431

Sabina shook her head after a moment of stunned silence. "No…er…no," she repeated, her face aflame. He seemed satisfied with her answer.

"Good."

"But Jeffree," she asked as he secured the second braid, "what if I do not like it, or *you* do not?"

He considered this. "Then we tell the other, and we stop."

Sabina thought about this. "Very well." She nodded, and suddenly he was on the bed in front of her, his gaze roaming over her face.

"Such a pretty blush," he whispered, staring at her mouth. "Gods," he muttered, "that mole."

"My mole?" Her hand flew to touch the small black spot above her upper lip. *What about it?*

"You're so lovely," he groaned. "I can't believe you're mine." And with that he drew Sabina into his arms and kissed her so thoroughly that she melted right into him, any insecurities about her nudity entirely forgotten. *Lovely?*

"Tell me again." This time she knew exactly what he wanted her to say.

"I love you, Jeffree de Crecy." As before, she could not keep a slight note of wonderment out of her voice.

He gave a low, rumbling sound from his chest and lowered his head to kiss down her neck. "You have the most perfect bosom in Karadok," he murmured.

Sabina tangled her fingers in his hair. "Do you really think so? You are getting very good at the talking," she marveled. "Oh!"

She arched her back as he sucked first one, then her other nipple into his mouth.

"I spent a disgraceful amount of time wondering about their color," he admitted, before running his tongue around the hardened peaks.

"Jeffree!" she whimpered as he kissed down her stomach, gently cupping her mound.

"Open your legs for me, sweeting."

Sabina almost gasped at the endearment. He certainly had not addressed her as such before. She let her thighs fall apart and his breathing hitched. Sabina lifted her head off the pillow bearer to assure him that he did not have to do anything he was unsure about when she saw the rapt expression on his face as he settled between her legs, lying on his stomach. *Oh.* He *really* wanted to do this for her.

"Gods," he groaned. "I want to touch you with my tongue the way you showed me with your fingers." Sabina's eyes widened. "Do you think you would like that?"

"I—um, I—not sure," she panted. Why was she finding it so hard to draw breath?

"Just lie back and let me try it," he said, running a warm hand up her thigh.

"Yes, I will," she agreed, collapsing back against the cushions. The first nudge of his tongue against her bud had her lifting her head again with a gasp. She gazed down, scarcely able to believe her eyes which showed Jeffree's golden head between her thighs as he licked at her with increasing enthusiasm. It seemed there was no fear of his not liking it, she thought feeling dazed and incredulous.

"Ohhh!" she moaned, biting her lip.

He paused. "Good?"

"Oh yes!" She had to shut her eyes against the sight of his glistening mouth, but that just made her focus more on the wet sounds they were creating between them. Sabina's heart thundered in her chest. She could scarcely believe that the uptight Jeffree de Crecy was lapping at her like this. How could he be...so *abandoned*? she marveled, her ears burning as the sensations built low in her belly.

Suddenly he gave up teasing her alternatively with the tip and the flat of his tongue and started rubbing her bud with the pad of his thumb whilst running his tongue along either side of it. Sabina clapped her hands over her mouth to muffle her scream as she hurtled through a shuddering orgasm.

The next thing she knew, she was back in Jeffree's arms sobbing against his chest and he was murmuring against her brow as though he remembered how terribly sensitive she grew just after she reached her peak. "Well," she said weakly, once her breathing had evened out. "I never, never, never would have imagined such treatment from the heir of Ganford Chase."

Jeffree laughed softly. "Madam," he said, "I am just getting started."

Sabina chuckled, but she could feel the tension running all through his body, particularly his manhood, which pressed insistently against her hip. She twisted in his arms.

"Lie down on your back, Jeffree," she urged him, pushing on his solid bulk. For a moment, nothing moved, then he seemed to comprehend what she was asking and released her to lie back on the mattress. "Good, Jeffree," she praised him warmly, rolling onto her stomach and crowding against him.

434

He made that growling noise in his throat, and screwing her courage to the sticking place, Sabina swung one of her legs over his thighs and eased on top of him. A thrill ran through her as her soft, pliant body slid against his, for the contrast between them had never felt more glaringly obvious. She could feel his hard, unrelenting muscle pressed up against her.

Jeffree grunted as she forced herself to relax, ignoring the insistent press of hard flesh she had trapped now against her soft belly. Good grief, he was impressive. Almost alarmingly so. One of his hands grabbed the braid hanging down to her waist, wrapping it around his hand and lightly tugging it.

Lowering herself down over his upper body, Sabina swallowed, suppressing a whimper as her sensitive full breasts came into contact with the hair of his golden chest. She need not have bothered, for Jeffree's own groan was so loud he quite startled her and would have surely drowned out any noise she might have made.

"Is all well?" she whispered down at him, for Jeffree had squeezed his eyes shut. Resting her elbows on the mattress on either side of his neck, Sabina swallowed and tried by sheer will alone to slow the rapid beating of her heart. "Do you want me to get back off? Am I too heavy?" she ventured, glancing back at the spot she had vacated.

"No!" His eyes sprang open and they blazed bright blue. "Don't you dare." His low voice was so incensed it brought a half smile to Sabina's lips. His hand tightened about her braid as though to prevent her retreat.

Sabina gazed down, feeling a surge of warmth toward him again. She had felt it on a few occasions now, never even suspecting the true cause. "You are very beautiful, Jeffree," she murmured, tipping her head to one side as she contemplated his

435

face. He made a choked sound by way of reply. When he looked at her like that, she felt almost confident in her role. "Your muscles and sinews are well-formed indeed." She wiggled her hips. "And this part most particularly."

Up to this moment, he had been breathing noisily through his nose like a bull, but at this point, he stopped breathing altogether and just stared up at her as though transfixed. "*Gods*," he uttered. "Are you trying to—to make me humiliate myself?" he demanded in a strangled voice.

"I'm trying to seduce you," she admitted frankly. "Tell me what I'm doing wrong."

"What you're doing wrong?" he wheezed. "Absolutely naught, but I am in danger of spending against your belly at this moment." He squeezed his eyes shut.

"I do not think you will," she murmured, trailing fingers down his chest.

His hips thrust up and he groaned aloud. "Have mercy," he whispered. "Since last we lay together, I have thought of nothing else. I have…longed for this. For you."

She stared down at him in amazement. "Jeffree," she murmured, quite shaken, for he made her sound well-nigh irresistible.

"Take me inside you," he implored. As though unable to stop himself, his hands seized her hips and lifted her over him. Sabina felt a vague panic steal over her as lowered her over the insistent thrust of his cock. "Have a care with me, Jeffree!"

Hearing the panic in her voice, he halted at once. "Always," he vowed.

436

Sabina's fingers clutched at his shoulders. "I trust you," she panted. "'Tis just that you need to go slow with me. You are on the large side and—" To her surprise, even as she said this, her cleft yielded to the insistent press, and she engulfed the bulbous head before she was scarce aware of the fact. She had forgotten how wet he had gotten her, she realized with a shocked gasp as she slid a couple of inches down his thick shaft.

Jeffree groaned and muttered something. He did not thrust, but his whole body flexed hard, and Sabina sank another inch onto him. "Fuck," he groaned. "Fuck, you're so wet. Tell me when I can move."

"You can m-move!" Sabina gasped as Jeffree's hips drove up, driving his length and breadth into the very heart of her. "Ohhhh!" she groaned, her head dropping back. "Oh, Jeffree!"

Jeffree's eyes closed and he bit his tongue between his teeth. "Keep saying my name like that. I like it."

"Ohh, Jeffree," she obliged.

He grunted, grabbing her backside, giving her an encouraging bounce over his lap. Sabina gasped, her eyes flying wide.

"W-wait!" she panted. "Don't do that!"

"Why?" he asked gruffly. "It feels like you like it. You're gripping me so tight."

"It's too much, too soon." She sounded panicked. "I won't have any strength left to me."

"You don't need any strength," he pointed out. "I've enough for both of us."

"No!" Sabina knew for a fact if he kept doing that she would reach her peak too soon. "I want to do this for you."

A pucker appeared between his brows as though the idea of her moving in this position intrigued him. He fell back onto his elbows, his gaze raking over her body with a proprietary eye. "Move, then, wife. Show me."

Sabina tutted at the return of bossy Sir Jeffree and shifted over him, redistributing her weight as she tipped forward and placed her palms on the bed on either side of his shoulders.

"*Gods*," he uttered, his gaze riveted to her breasts as she started to propel herself, lifting up on her knees and then lowering herself back down onto him. She was not sure how many times she had managed to repeat this before she was panting and his gaze caught fire. Sabina could not look away from his devouring eyes. When he looked at her like that, she felt like the most desired woman in Karadok.

Suddenly he sat up, his hands gripping her hips tight, moulding her to him as he groaned and shook through his release. "Sabina…" he groaned. "*Sabina*, I cannot withstand you."

Sabina gasped as she felt his release set off her own. Pitching forward, she buried her face in his neck and sobbed as his arms slid up her back and wrapped tight around her.

*

She was not sure how long they lay together in contented silence, but eventually, they disentangled long enough for them both to wash again in the cold bathtub water. Jeffree threw on his braies and chausses. "I will go and see what has become of our supper," he said as Sabina donned a clean shift.

He returned not much later with some cold chicken, bread, and a herb salad on a tray. "We could go out and eat it in one of the other rooms, but it is already crowded out there with just Hugo, Wilton, and Osborn cluttering up the place."

438

"I had no idea the courtier quarters at the palace would be so small," Sabina commented, taking the plate he passed her and balancing it on her lap. Her ears still burned from the heated words Jeffree had given her. Why had she always thought he was terrible at praise? This moment of ease and comfort between them now soothed her, for it showed he could also be considerate of her feelings when passion was not ruling him.

He gave a murmured agreement and disappeared, only to reappear minutes later bearing two goblets of wine, shutting the door behind him with his foot.

Sabina made a good supper, for she found she was suddenly ravenous. It was only as Jeffree was piling up the plates on the side that she noticed the marks appearing down his right side. "My gods, Jeffree! What is that?" she gasped, pointing.

He glanced down at the large red welt spreading down his right side. "This is what happens when you get struck from your horse with a lance," he answered dryly.

"I thought the armor would protect you!"

"It does. To a certain degree."

She stared. "Well, I feel guilty now," she murmured, "for all the fuss I was making. Does it pain you?" A horrible thought occurred to her. "My sitting atop you did not contribute to it, did it?"

He gave a short laugh. "Of course not." He set the tray on the side and joined her on the bed. Sabina stretched out beside him with a contented sigh. "By the by," he said, turning toward her with a pucker between his brows, "you never did tell me what it was that set you crying."

"It was so silly," she confessed, "I am almost ashamed of reacting the way I did. I think the heat combined with how

439

sticky and overwarm I was just made everything worse. I felt totally overwhelmed."

He slipped an arm around her shoulders. "What happened?" he persisted curiously.

Sabina sighed and rolled into him, tucking her head under his chin. "Lord Kentigern gave me the tourney crown. I felt just dreadful for his wife, but very likely she—"

"*What?*"

His furious yell made Sabina jerk her head back so sharply it smacked him on the chin. She gasped and fell back as Jeffree scrambled to an upright position. "What did you just say?" he demanded, rubbing his jaw. "Lord Kentigern did what? Repeat that!" It was almost uncanny how the words echoed their earlier conversation but with a wealth of difference in the emotion behind it.

"I—well—Lord Kentigern," she repeated, "he gave me the tourney crown."

For a moment he seemed to struggle for words. Then they burst from him. "That *unspeakable piece* of…" He ground his teeth. "I'll kill him," Jeffree vowed, bounding back off the bed.

"Jeffree!" Sabina squawked in alarm. "Come back!" He was already struggling into a tunic. "Where are you going?"

"To have a word with Lord bloody Kentigern," he bit out.

"But why?" Sabina gasped. "What's done is done! You cannot change it now after the fact!"

"Oh, can't I?" he asked grimly. "Well, I can ram that damned crown down his throat now, can I not?"

"Actually, you can't, for I did not keep it! Did not even set it on my head," Sabina flung back desperately. "I left it in the stands." He wasn't even listening as he pulled on his boots so savagely that he snapped off one of the laces. "Jeffree, please!" She slipped off the mattress and was heading around the bed toward him, arm outstretched, when he went barging out of their bedroom door.

"Wait!" Sabina called, hurrying after him. "Jeffree, *please* do not do this!"

He did not even pause, barging past his bewildered-looking cousin and manservant. "Jeffree?" Hugo said blankly, looking from him to Sabina and back again. The door slammed after him and Sabina stared at it in despair. She could hardly pursue him down the corridor dressed like this, she realized, glancing down at her revealing shift.

"Well, what on earth—?" Hugo asked in bewilderment as Sabina ran back into their bedchamber.

"They're always like this," she heard Osborn say glumly before the door shut behind her. "You'd best get used to it, Master Hugo."

Sabina lay awake fretting she knew not how long. How Jeffree could deny he was a hothead, she had no notion! She had never known someone so impetuous and fiery-tempered in her life. She punched a cushion and rolled over for the umpteenth time. She could scream at him, honestly! Leaping out of their bed like that, and after they had been in *such* accord too. *Just* when they seemed to finally be on an even keel, he had to go upsetting the apple cart all over again! It beggared belief.

She finally fell asleep in the early hours of the morning and, when she woke, did so in Jeffree's arms. Taking pains to extricate herself without waking him, Sabina dressed in haste,

441

kicking the brown dress into one corner of the room, and donning her faded red one instead. The braids Jeffree had given her looked pristine, so she simply coiled and pinned them to the side of her head and then donned her heavy wimple.

As she dressed, she cast many backward glances at his sleeping figure, but from what she could tell, he looked none the worse though the red marks down his side were starting to turn purple.

Wilton looked relieved when she emerged from the room. "I did not like to knock and bring you hot water when you…er…when Master Jeffree returned so late last night," he said nervously.

"It is of no matter, Wilton. I used cold water."

"Yes, Lady Sabina. I will see to the tub's removal this morning." He hesitated. "Is there any other way in which I can be of service?"

Sabina noticed with surprise that his manner was a good deal more obliging toward her today. "If the brown dress I wore yesterday could be laundered, Wilton, I would be most grateful."

He bowed. "Of course, milady. I will convey it to the palace laundresses after you have broken your fast."

"Thank you." She walked into the adjoining room and found Jeffree's cousin sat at table.

"Come in, cousin, and welcome," he greeted her with enthusiasm. "I hope there is plenty at table to tempt you this morn." Sabina drew out a chair opposite him and sat down. "Will you take some of this sop in wine?" he asked, gesturing to a plate of breads which had been soaked in wine and toasted.

"Not for me, I thank you," Sabina answered, feeling surprised he was so friendly this morning. When his face fell, she added, "For I cannot eat such rich dishes at this early hour."

He cheered up at her explanation and urged her instead to try the toasted cheese, making haste to pour her a goblet of ale.

Sabina ate her fill as Hugo rattled on about yesterday's tournament. From what he said, it seemed he had attended only the first two events and then ducked out after the melee. From his disappointed expression, she could tell he wished now that he had remained for the main event.

"As for myself, I prefer the melee also," she admitted. "The joust takes so long to set up with everyone having to wait their turn."

Sir Hugo's expression relaxed into a beaming smile. "Why, then we are of one accord, Lady Sabina. In truth, I felt it too hot to sit there in the blazing sun all afternoon. Though if I had known what would transpire…" He sighed gustily. "The court is quite agog with it this morning," he said, lowering his voice. "Queen Armenal will speak of nothing else. It is rumored that she hath invited Baroness Kentigern to join her this day in her Court of Love and Beauty."

Sabina felt herself grow stiff and awkward again. "Has she?" she heard herself ask in a high, unnatural voice. "I am sure Lady Kentigern would grace any court, for she is so very beauteous."

Hugo nodded. "And yet, it seems there are some who *can* resist her charms," he said slyly.

Sabina's hand trembled where she held her toast. "Perhaps you are not aware that Lady Kentigern was not sat in the stands when Lord Kentigern was given the garland to bestow," she said, striving to keep her voice steady. "If she had been sat in her place then I am persuaded that her husband would have awarded the wreath to her."

Hugo's eyebrows rose. "Clearly you are not aware of how these Knights of Karadok often turn even so simple a gesture into a cause of contention and strife."

Sabina paused in the act of raising her goblet. "That does not sound very chivalric."

He snorted. "You have not heard the half of it!"

"Tell me, cousin," she said, addressing him airily in the manner he had extended to her. "Have you heard aught of...of what my husband got up to last night?"

Hugo looked gratified by her calling him thus and leaned forward confidingly. "I have not yet been abroad this morn," he admitted, "but Wilton has been down to the palace kitchens thrice to garner me all the latest news and intrigues."

Sabina nodded encouragingly. "How enterprising!"

"Apparently, Jeffree went tearing down to the banqueting hall in a warlike mood. He scoured the place in search of retribution but was denied for Lord Kentigern did not attend the celebratory feast. Indeed, if he had been thinking at all clearly, then he would have remembered how rarely Kentigern ever does attend court suppers and such. These northern nobles," Hugo sighed, "can be so very barbarous in their ways."

Sabina's shoulders slumped with relief. "Well, thank goodness for that!" she breathed before another worry assailed her. "Tell me, do the Kentigerns have rooms at the palace?"

Wilton shook his head. "Apparently, Lady Kentigern's sire bought them a monstrous townhouse in Caer-Lyoness." He

444

looked scandalized as though such a thing was in the worst possible taste, and Sabina wondered at his attitude, for surely a large townhouse must be preferable to such cramped rooms as the courtiers were forced to make do with. It must be a prestige thing, she supposed, for otherwise it scarcely made sense.

"That is good," she commented slowly, "so we are unlikely to bump into them about the palace."

"No," Hugo agreed, looking regretful about this. "Though," he said, cheering up a little, "Jeffree may still catch up with him in the tourney field, for no doubt they have to collect all their weapons and horses and such before all can be packed away. Then, too," he added, warming to his theme, "there is always a chance that Lord Kentigern may accompany his lady wife when she attends the Queen this morning." When Sabina looked alarmed, he added quickly, "Though that seems unlikely in so inattentive a spouse." He cleared his throat. "Lady Kentigern's husband is not so—er—*devoted* as yours, cousin."

Sabina felt a moment's horror that Hugo might have overheard their lovemaking from the previous day and almost choked on her mouthful of toasted bread. How thick were these walls?

"Everyone is speaking of it," Hugo rattled on, looking smug. "It is the talk of the palace. Poor, spurned Lady Kentigern and *you*, cousin, the unexpected Queen of the Tourney." A vaguely puzzled look passed over his countenance as he gazed at her. "Everyone is wondering what it is about you that inspires such strong feeling in these men."

It was lucky Sabina had swallowed her toast or another coughing fit would surely have been forthcoming. She remembered her mother-in-law saying something equally ludicrous once. "Lady Maud says men suffer from a strange fascination in my presence," she uttered hollowly.

445

Sir Hugo looked much struck by this. "A strange fascination," he echoed thoughtfully, looking her over with renewed interest. He pursed his lips. "I have always thought the Lady Maud a woman of shrewd understanding," he mused. "Yes, I suppose that *does* make a sort of sense when you consider why it was you were compelled to marry."

Sabina stiffened. She heartily hoped that Sir Hugo had not spread about court the scandalous story about being Jeffree's harlot before they were forced to wed. Remembering Hugo's glee earlier over court gossip, her heart suffered a sinking sensation. Then again, he was a de Crecy himself, she thought desperately. Surely he would not wish to blacken the family name?

"Apparently Jeffree was breathing fire last night," Hugo continued with relish. "He took violent exception to something Sir Horace Nash said, for he sent the poor fellow sprawling, and when his friends attempted to intervene, dispatched them in much the same manner. A whole table of sweetmeats was overturned, and between them, they made *quite* the spectacle."

Sabina gulped. "I don't suppose it is widely known what exactly Sir Horace said?" she asked faintly.

Sir Hugo looked evasive. "Sir Horace is known for something of a wit," he admitted. "It is possible he aimed for humorous and missed the mark entirely. Whatever it was, doubtless Jeffree found it vastly offensive."

"Jeffree found what offensive?" came a voice from the doorway, and both Hugo and Sabina started violently in their seats to find Jeffree regarding them with narrowed eyes.

"Oh—er—" Hugo stammered.

446

"Rich foods," Sabina interrupted hastily. "I was telling your cousin how offensive you find rich foods at table."

Jeffree snorted but threw himself down into the chair at Sabina's right and started piling food onto his plate.

Disaster averted, Hugo flashed her a look of gratitude and tried to engage Jeffree in conversation about some new title Sir Roland had recently acquired. "Those blasted Vawdreys are taking over at court," Hugo complained. "I tell you it is remarked upon how much favor they find with the King. Their father was naught but an obscure baron, and only look now how high his sons have risen! A duke, an earl, and now a viscount, all in one family! And a family with nothing like the rich lineage of *our* line, cousin."

Jeffree shrugged. "Cadwallader was not made a duke by the King but by his marriage," he pointed out, his gaze roaming unhurriedly over Sabina's face.

"If something is not done about it," Hugo continued plaintively, "then they will end up one of the premier families at court!"

Sabina set down her napkin, unable to bear Jeffree's frowning scrutiny a moment longer. "Is something amiss with my face?"

"Naught that I can see. Why do you ask?"

"Well, you are staring, and you look annoyed."

"This is the expression my face makes when my thoughts are not engaged."

Sabina made a derogatory noise and rested her chin on her hand. "I suppose you must be habitually disgruntled, then," she pronounced, "even when your head is empty. How exhausting that must be."

Jeffree sat back in his chair. "I have never found it so."

447

"And now you look superior and aloof," Sabina told him briskly. "You only seem to have two moods." Then she remembered his look of bliss as she had collapsed on top of him the previous night. *Well, maybe three*, she amended conscientiously.

When Hugo cleared his throat, they both turned their heads remembering his presence. "If you will excuse me now, cousins, I must be about some urgent business this morning." He stood and bowed to Sabina, then nodded at Jeffree, before sauntering forth with a merry tune on his lips.

Sabina found herself fervently hoping he was not off to spread more gossip about court.

24

Jeffree took himself off after their refreshment to oversee Osborn's progress packing up his armor and jousting equipment and Sabina spent an uneasy morning walking between the three reception rooms designated to the de Crecy family. They were cluttered and stuffy, and though Sabina flung the windows open, it did not much help, and she longed to escape outdoors.

From the glimpses she had of the cultivated gardens to the palace, however, she realized it differed vastly from her own beloved countryside. Gazing down at the groups of elegant ladies drifting about the winding paths, she realized that at court, even walking about the grounds was regarded as a public display of one's person. No one was unaccompanied, and Sabina got the impression that a solitary woman marching up and down the walkways would be considered an oddity.

Then, too, there was the concern she might be mistaken for a servant again. Sabina sighed. She ought not to have refused Jeffree's repeated offer of new clothing. That had been a mistake. How much easier things would have been for her if she had simply had a couple of elegant gowns made up for occasions such as this.

Lately, though, he had not renewed the offer, as though he had simply accepted that she preferred her shabby old dresses and would not be moved on the subject. She supposed she would have to steel herself to reopen the matter on their return home.

Jeffree did not return at midday, and Sabina was just trying to settle with a book of poems she had found when a knock on the door had her sitting up straight and craning for the sound of Wilton's soft tread as he answered it. She heard the murmur of voices and then Wilton was clearing his throat at the doorway to the sitting room she currently occupied.

"Milady, the Queen has sent for you."

Sabina blanched. "For me?"

"Indeed, milady. She hath sent an emissary to collect and escort you to where she is gathered with her ladies at the south arbor."

Sabina hesitated, but a royal page had appeared in the doorway and was making his bow, his fashionable scalloped sleeves almost scraping the ground. Given little choice, Sabina followed him along the corridor and out into the well-maintained gardens. They proceeded down a long walkway flanked with hedges that had been cut into all manner of shapes, mostly birds, skirted a fountain, and then came upon a lawn flanked with flowerbeds and a backdrop of trellises. This was where the Queen was set up in her outdoor court beneath a flowered archway, sat upon a luxuriously plush seat, and eating fruit.

All the other ladies were sat on much lower couches or footstools, or even blankets, and were grouped and bent industriously over what looked like shared needlework. The page twirled his sleeve. "Behold the Queen's Court of Love and Beauty," he intoned cheerfully.

Sabina quickly scanned the group but found she did not recognize a single soul present. Her shoulders relaxed, and she followed the page right up to the Queen and sank down into her lowest curtsey.

"Arise, Lady de Crecy," Queen Armenal said, looking her over with bright, curious eyes. "Will you take a seat at my court and perhaps some refreshment?" She gestured toward a low table covered with dishes of dainty-looking foods and goblets of wine.

Sabina looked the plump low seats over with surprise, for to her they resembled nothing so much as a large collection of satin-covered footstools. She made for the one that looked most in the shade from the afternoon sun, only for the Queen to throw up a hand in protest.

"Do not sit all the way over there, for I would have some speech with you," the Queen said, frowning. With some reluctance, Sabina moved closer. When she lowered herself onto the uncomfortably slippery couch, it occurred to her that perhaps the Queen liked to have the other ladies at court sat at a much lower level than her.

She gazed back at the Queen with a blank expression.

"I had Baroness Kentigern brought to my Court of Love and Beauty this morning, but sadly, the Lady Kentigern, she does not embroider, and her ambitions they all seem to center around her husband." Queen Armenal sighed. "Which was so disappointing to me as she was *such* a revelation after the jousting, such refreshing openness, such honesty!

"How she enchanted me, and I thought how amusing it would be to have such an artless creature in my retinue. But then today, when she attended me at court, she barely opened her mouth, and I could get nothing out of her. I was amazed to find her so quiet, so dull!"

"Mayhap she was overwhelmed to find herself among such exalted company, Your Majesty," Sabina ventured, realizing some response was expected of her. "I expect your ladies' needlework is, too, of the highest quality and she felt daunted by it."

451

The Queen shrugged. "Such a pity, but I suppose with her upbringing she has not been raised with all the accomplishments expected of a born lady. Now *you*, Lady de Crecy, I expect have many such arts at your disposal."

For some reason, Sabina felt herself flush at Queen Armenal's words. There was something about their intonation that discomforted her.

"You are fond of embroidery, Your Majesty?" she asked as colorlessly as she could manage.

"Me? No, for I am royalty," the Queen answered dismissively. "It is not expected that I should ply the needle. At least," she added thoughtfully, "it was not expected in my brother's court in the Western Isles. My husband's cousin, Lady Una, was raised in the northern court, and it was expected of her that she should do the sewing of the garments. But then…northerners!" She shrugged eloquently.

Sabina gazed about at the many ladies all so industrious sat around them. "I can embroider a little, Your Majesty," she confessed, "but my sister's skill is far superior to my own."

"Your sister?" The Queen's ears pricked up. "Now, pray tell me, is this the sister who was to marry the Duke of Ganfordshire?"

Sabina's heart sank. How on earth could the Queen know about Isemay's betrothal? Unless Cousin Hugo had been talking. "It was the Duke of Bethencourt," Sabina corrected her, "though it seems that will now come to naught."

"Your sister must be a great fool, I think," the Queen said impartially. "It is good she has some skill with a needle to fall back on as she has no intelligence."

Sabina bridled. "My sister is *not* a fool, Your Majesty!"

452

"No? Then why does she throw over a duke? Answer me that."
The Queen helped herself from a dish of almonds. "I understand
your father owns a small property in Ganfordshire and only a
paltry amount of lands."

Sabina thought of Tipton Hall and the attached farm. It was true
her father's lands were not anything to brag of compared to the
likes of the Duke of Bethencourt. "There have been Burrells at
Tipton Hall for many generations, Your Majesty."

The Queen nodded. "Oh yes, yes, I am sure, but still, none of
them were duchesses, now, were they?"

"No, Your Majesty."

The Queen cupped her chin. "I suppose, this duke, he is very
old and rather ugly. Apparently, he has attended court in the
past and made me his bow, but I do not remember him at all."

Sabina's eyes widened. "N-no," she denied. "He is fifty-nine
and not ugly precisely." Unable to think of anything flattering
to say about the duke's unremarkable features, she heard herself
add lamely, "He has a great dislike of draughty places."

The Queen blinked. "Oh, I *see*. He is a bore. Yes, that is much
worse than being ugly," she conceded. "But still, your sister
should have gritted her teeth. She is much younger than he, is
that not so? Then eventually, she could have been the very
merry widow."

Sabina could think of no reply to make of this, so she glanced
around uneasily to see if anyone could have overheard and then
report back to Hugo that she had claimed Jeffree's uncle was
both ugly and boring. The ladies were all bent so industriously
over their needlework that she could not tell if they were
listening or not.

"If you do not think your sister, she is a great fool, then it must be because she has someone else in reserve," the Queen pondered. "Perhaps someone young and virile, no?"

For some reason, Leland Ellis's mocking face flashed into Sabina's mind, and Isemay saying, *This way he will mind me and do as I say.* She gasped. "No, not at all!" Isemay was looking for revenge, not love!

"Ahah!" the Queen said triumphantly. "I can see that I am in the right of it. Very well, I will accept that your sister, she is not the little fool, but instead knows what she is about."

Sabina gazed at Queen Armenal in dazed horror. She had never met anyone like her before. She wished she could get up and walk out of this cultivated garden. It was like some horrible nightmare, even the potent scent of all the flowers was combined to make her head swim.

"Now let us put an end to all pretenses and be perfectly frank with one another," the Queen urged. "I wish to know how you exert this strange fascination of yours over the menfolk, for I have heard all about it and I must know!"

Sabina made a choking sound. "I—I—assure you, Your Majesty, that I do no such thing!"

The Queen wagged a finger at her. "This will not do, Lady Sabina. I have seen this husband of yours but many times. Always it is said about Jeffree de Crecy that he is of the most arrogant nature. Always I have seen him turn stiff with disapproval, even outrage at any imagined slight to his consequence. He is moreover always *immaculately* turned out. Until this past week, he would *never* have shown up to a banquet in an unfastened tunic and attacked someone like a rabid beast who dared to offer you some insult."

454

"Insult?" Sabina repeated quickly.

"But of course. I daresay you have not yet spoken to this Sir Horace Nash and exerted your famous charm over him. He just thought you were dowdy and plain and wearing an ugly old dress."

Sabina flushed. *Famous charm?* "I see," she said repressively and tried not to feel glad that Jeffree had punched Sir Horace and his cronies through a table.

"But you cannot see your way clear to sharing your secrets with me," the Queen sighed. "Which is too bad and not at all generous of you. Never mind, I shall observe you most closely for the duration of your visit at court with us. I am, above all else, a great observer of mankind."

Sabina shifted uncomfortably on the slippery seat and tried not to slide off it. "Indeed, Your Majesty?"

"It is a little hobby of mine. You observe these works all my ladies are so busily undertaking?"

"I do."

"They depict my observations of some of the foremost ladies of the land." Queen Armenal nodded with satisfaction. "Walk about," she added generously. "Let me know your thoughts."

Sabina rose to her feet with some reluctance. She felt wholly unequal to the task. Drifting from one industrious group of ladies to another, she peered dubiously at the large canvases being covered with so many tiny stitches.

Only one of them was entirely finished so far, and this showed a woman in a blue dress with red hair being weighed on a large scale against a pile of gold. Rather improbably the dainty-looking female depicted was weighing heavier than the coins.

455

To one side of her, a male figure in a suit of armor was pointing at her, presumably choosing her rather than the wealth.

"Very nice," Sabina commented, feeling quite at a loss. Was this some famous parable she did not know? She peered at the lettering which spelt out: "The Duke of Cadwallader chooses his wife, Linnet, over all her wealth and riches." Cadwallader? Had someone mentioned that name earlier?

And why pray would this duke need to choose one or the other? Sabina wondered. For surely on marrying her, he would gain both in any case. She shrugged to herself and paced around all the little groups, peering at the sketches hinting at what the final picture would resemble.

None of the images meant anything to her, but she supposed the stories behind them must be common knowledge at court. Not being a courtier herself, they conveyed precisely nothing to her. She returned to the Queen at the conclusion and was as polite as she could manage to be about the skill of the ladies and the scale of the endeavor.

Queen Armenal tutted. "Do you know, I thought perhaps we might dedicate a panel to you and Sir Jeffree," she admitted sadly, "but it seems I was mistaken."

Sabina was both shocked and alarmed. "To us?"

"But how can I convey to my ladies how to illustrate this elusive charm of yours when I have seen precious little evidence of it myself?"

Sabina swallowed down the lump in her throat. "That would indeed be difficult, Your Majesty," she agreed.

"Of course, you will feature on the Kentigern's panel," the Queen murmured, tapping her chin thoughtfully.

Sabina gave a little gasp. "I will?" she croaked.

"But yes."

"I thought you were disappointed in Lady Kentigern," Sabina heard herself point out before she could stop herself. "Yet you still intend to dedicate a panel to them?"

Queen Armenal nodded. "I do, for yesterday's entertainment was too delicious, even if the little baroness does not aspire to be one of my ladies-in-waiting. Anyone who can elevate a dull tournament in such a fashion will always occupy a place of favor with me."

In all, it was a most unsettling afternoon. Sabina returned to the de Crecy rooms in a dejected mood. It was not that she wanted the Queen to like her, or to imagine theirs was some epic love story, she told herself. It was only that it did hurt one's feelings somewhat to be told to one's face that you were a sad disappointment. It was unworthy of her to take comfort in the fact Lady Kentigern had similarly let down the Queen today in her expectations of amusement.

The slam of a door alerted her that someone had returned, and she whirled about from her spot by the window. Jeffree was stood in the doorway, looking grim.

"We attend the feast tonight for the closing of the tourney," he announced, looking as though he wanted to say more, but then changed his mind and turned away to order water for washing instead.

"Closing feast? Does that mean that we return home on the morrow?" Sabina asked, hurrying after him as he made for their bedchamber. He did not answer at once, so she followed him inside to find him unlacing his cuffs.

"Why are you in such a tearing hurry to go back?" he asked with a frown. "Things are settled at Morecotte. You have made things habitable. What is it there that has so urgent a claim on you?"

She clammed up at that. "My—my sister is not herself. She has still not recovered sufficiently from the great shock she suffered on her wedding day. Isemay needs my support now more than ever."

He snorted. "You said yourself that she is no shrinking maid in need of cossetting."

"It is not that, but—" She broke off, staring down at her hands.

"I was thinking we could go straight from here to Beres Caple," he suggested.

"What is Beres Caple? Another tournament?" She could not keep the dismay out of her voice.

"Yes, another tournament," he responded testily. "Why do you look like that?"

"Jeffree!" She averted her face.

"What?"

"Is it not obvious?"

"Not to me." She shook her head. "You hate the tournaments," he said flatly.

Sabina clenched her fists at her sides and steeled herself for the coming confrontation. Squeezing her eyes shut, she burst out a heartfelt, "Yes, I hate them. I feel horribly conspicuous and out of place and like everyone is staring at me and finding me wanting."

458

When he said nothing, she opened one eye to find him stood staring toward the window. Sabina fully opened her eyes to look at him. "Jeffree?" His silence unnerved her.

His gaze flickered briefly to her before returning to the window again. He shook his head slightly.

"I am not good at being gracious," she added desperately, thinking of the fine noblewomen in the gardens that day. "I have no winning ways to charm people or put them at their ease. I never know the right thing to say; I just turn stiff and awkward. I am fully aware that your wife should be some pearl of womanhood, but unfortunately, that is just not me! I have no discernible talent or charm."

"The tournaments are what I do and where I display at my best," he said grimly. "If you do not see me at my best then how am I to retain your love?"

Sabina stared at him, dropping her hands to her sides. What did he just say?

The knock at the door both startled and frustrated her, but it was only Wilton with two jugs of hot water. He set them down and, after gazing at them nervously, backed out of the room.

Jeffree turned to her without preamble. "I don't expect you to charm anyone but me," he said bluntly. "In fact, I would not like it if you started charming all and sundry."

Sabina's head jerked back. "What?"

"You seem to have completely the wrong idea of what I expect from my wife. I don't want you to have all of court fawning over you. I can't spare you for that."

"But—you—" Sabina stopped and took a deep breath. "Jeffree," she said carefully. "Do you not understand that your

459

wife is seen as a reflection of you? That everyone who sees me is judging me and wondering what the hells you saw in me? Today the Queen asked me to attend her at her garden court and I—I gave her an extremely poor impression of me. It was painfully obvious I did not fit in with all her fine ladies."

"I don't give a damn what anyone else thinks. Stop comparing yourself to inconsequential people."

"Inconsequential?"

He waved a hand. "Those other women you mentioned. Courtiers, the ladies at court."

Sabina eyed him incredulously. "The Queen?" she suggested.

"What about her?"

"She certainly had a lively interest in the state of our marriage. Will you own that her opinion is worth something?"

"Not to me," he admitted frankly. "I don't want someone who is constantly charming everyone and making friends of all she meets. Those sorts of people get on my nerves."

"Likeable people, you mean?" Sabina suggested in disbelief.

Jeffree huffed out a breath. "You are likeable. My mother likes you. My brothers adore you, but none of that matters. The only one whose opinion you need to worry about is mine. And let's face it, you can do no wrong in my eyes, so that's hardly a cause for concern now is it?"

"*No wrong?*" Sabina echoed. She held up her hand when he started to speak. "Just a minute, Jeffree. Allow me to just let some of these words sink in." He gazed back at her impatiently as she stared at her feet, before lifting her head again to face him full on. "The only tournament I have attended with you so far has been a complete unmitigated disaster," she said slowly. "Would you agree?"

"No," he answered without hesitation.

"*No?* Jeffree, you cannot be speaking in earnest!" she cried, throwing up her arms. He looked bewildered by her vehemence. *Bewildered. My gods…*

"Well, I did not win," he conceded, "but I do not always win. No one does."

"Jeffree," she answered weakly. "You—you really are *impossible!*"

He placed his hands on his hips and looked her up and down. "Just tell me what I need to do," he said at last gruffly.

"Do?"

"To continue in your favor," he added, flushing slightly and refusing to meet her eye.

Sabina swallowed. He had used a different term before. "You already have it," she admitted. "Did I not say so last night?" Her cheeks burned.

"Sabina—" he started with a groan.

Suddenly, it was imperative that she stop whatever words he was about to utter. "Very well," she croaked. "I will attend this Beres Caple if you wish it, only—only could we please return home first? I feel completely out of my depth and long for home. Is Beres Caple so very soon?"

"It is in two weeks' time," he admitted.

"So there is time for us to return home first?" she asked with a catch in her voice.

461

He opened his mouth, frowning, and Sabina tensed, expecting his refusal. It did not come, instead, he shucked his tunic over his head and emptied one of the jugs into the basin. "Very well." His reply was short and clipped but it completely took Sabina's breath away.

"We will?"

"If that is what you want."

Sabina sank down into a chair, the relief was so great. "Thank you," she said simply. "And this time you will tell me how I am supposed to deport myself at Beres Caple."

"That is easy," Jeffree interrupted her as he soaped his hands.

"It is?"

"You simply allow me to order you some new gowns," he said, scrubbing at the back of his neck. "Then keep your eyes on me and me alone."

Sabina considered. "That is all?" she asked. It could not possibly be that simple.

His gaze flickered as he appeared to consider. "When I lose, tell me my opponent is a filthy cheat, and when I win, smile and say it is inevitable. See, perfectly straightforward."

"What of the banquets and such?"

"What of them?"

"You must have noticed how stupid and awkward I am, Jeffree," she said frankly. "I sit there like a stone while the conversation flows about me."

"If you want to join the conversation you talk, if you don't, then simply eat your fill." He shrugged. "That is what I do. Besides, we could just dine in my pavilion. I do not care. In fact…" He considered her a moment in silence. "I should likely prefer it."

Sabina turned this over in her mind. "If I do not…exert myself," she said slowly. "If I do not make the smallest effort to—to shine, then how am I to retain your favor? Answer me that, Jeffree de Crecy."

He made a sound in the back of his throat. "Sabina…"

A knock at the door once more interrupted them.

"I am sorry to interrupt, Sir Jeffree," Wilton said apologetically, holding out a sealed letter. "The rider said this was urgent."

"Who sent it?"

"The seal is your uncle's, but the rider said the letter was from Sir Charles Ellis."

Sabina's heart plummeted as Jeffree nodded toward the table and bade Wilton to set it down there. She continued to gaze at the letter as though it were a coiled snake while Jeffree finished his ablutions. The door quietly closed behind Wilton as Sabina's mind raced.

What could an urgent note from Sir Charles betoken? Had he discovered her sister's bizarre revenge upon his son? Her heart was in her mouth by the time Jeffree had pulled on a clean tunic and broken the seal. She watched his eyebrows rise as he scanned the first few lines. Then his gaze flickered to her and then back to the letter.

Sabina felt frozen to her chair. "Is all well?" she heard herself ask with a croak.

He shrugged a shoulder. "Charles writes without his usual clarity. He must have dashed this off in a hurry." She nodded but could manage no response. His gaze dropped to the bottom

463

of the page. "Well, this corroborates our decision of mere moments ago. We will set out for Ganfordshire at first light." His expression was grim.

"Has his son been found?" she forced herself to ask.

"No, but Charles writes he has uncovered some type of plot or conspiracy against Leland," he answered with a frown. "He was clearly in a highly agitated spot when he wrote it, and he begs for my help in uncovering some villainy." He hesitated a moment and then offered her the letter.

"No, no." Sabina shook her head. "Sir Charles and I are not on such intimate terms that I should read it."

"Maybe not, but we are," Jeffree replied forthrightly. His words robbed her of all breath for an instant.

"It would not be right," Sabina insisted, clutching her hands together in her lap.

He frowned but set it down on the table. "Come and wash now; this second jug is for you."

When she removed her wimple and stood over the washbasin, he stood behind her and wrapped his arms about her shoulders. "Do not look so tense and pale," he murmured against the top of her head, gently squeezing her upper arms. "It little signifies if you find favor with the Queen or not."

Sabina nodded and leaned back against him for an instant. She wondered if she should mention that business with Sir Horace from the previous night, but Jeffree bore no visible scrapes or bruises from the incident that she could comment upon. "How is your side?" she asked instead.

"A little sore," he admitted, releasing her and leaving her to her wash, "but hardly worth the mentioning."

25

They were halfway down the staircase when Jeffree had a presentiment of disaster about the night ahead. He had half a mind to turn back, but as they were packed in on all sides by nobles jostling to get in line for entrance to the Great Hall, it would take more effort to turn about and leave now for the impetus of the crowd was moving forward.

He glanced at Sabina, but she seemed calm enough in the flood of courtiers, for tonight's feast was open to all, not just the competitors and their families. The King had spent lavishly, and minstrels wandered up and down the staircase strumming lutes and singing to keep everyone entertained as they waited for the large studded doors to open.

Jeffree was distracted momentarily as he looked about to see if that bastard Kentigern had turned up for this closing feast. As winner of the joust, by far the most popular event, he ought to be in attendance as a guest of honor. However, Kentigern was notoriously taciturn and frequently skipped such celebratory events. Jeffree had just come to the conclusion that he was not present when he became aware that Sabina was exchanging words with someone. He whipped about his head at once.

"Sir, as I say, if you could just remove your foot, for you have torn my hem," she was explaining when Jeffree reached over and shoved the oaf's shoulder hard enough to send him reeling into one of his friends.

He wheeled around at once, and Jeffree saw his eyes widen when he saw who it was addressed him. "Sir!" he bleated, and if Jeffree was not mistaken, he quickly changed his mind about what he had been about to say.

"She asked you to remove your foot, you mannerless churl!" Jeffree snarled. "Now apologize!"

The fellow's eyes darted to his companions, who were all agog, his color rising hectically. "As to that, sir, this area is reserved for courtiers, not their servants. You would have done well to tell this woman to use the other stair—" He got no further for Jeffree had a firm grip of his throat.

"You tell me you expect my wife to use the servants' stairs?" he asked in a low, menacing voice, squeezing hard enough to make the fool choke.

His eyes nearly popped out of his head. "Y-your wife, sir?"

"You are addressing Lady de Crecy," Jeffree growled. "Now apologize to her."

"My apologies, Lady de Crecy," he wheezed. Jeffree released him and he slammed into the bannister, clawing at his throat.

"Fie, sir!" one of his friends started before seeing the nasty gleam in Jeffree's eye. He gulped and lowered his gaze as Jeffree extended his arm to Sabina. She placed her hand on his sleeve and he felt his blood start to cool at once. It was strange but it put him in mind of how she rested her hand on his chest at night. Now he found himself lying awake, waiting for it and unable to sleep until she did so.

A sidelong glance assured him she was not disturbed by the encounter, though her color was rather high. In their immediate vicinity, they had created something of a buzz and he heard his name whispered along with "lately married" and several turned heads. By the time they had entered the hall, Jeffree thought himself to have simmered down enough to take his seat, though Sabina had to hold her skirts awkwardly to accommodate the ripped hem.

The first three courses were the usual rich, finicking dishes he so disliked, swimming in wine and sticky fruit glazes. Jeffree pushed his food about his plate and resigned himself to a dissatisfactory meal. By the sixth course, he realized that the attention they were garnering was not dying down. If anything, it was growing. Sabina, however, appeared to be weathering the storm of speculation well and making a good supper.

By the time the eighth and final course had been served, Jeffree was impatient to give his bow to the royal dais and retire for the night. "We've an early start on the morrow," he said, leaning in so Sabina could hear him, for it was rowdy company tonight and very loud. "What say you to returning to our rooms?"

"Right willingly," she replied at once, as though she had only been waiting for him to say the word. They both stood up from the bench, and Jeffree could feel all eyes at their banqueting table swivel toward them.

"You do not retire so soon, de Crecy?" one young knight called out. Jeffree did not know his name. He glanced at him tight-lipped but gave a nod.

"Oh, to be newlyweds," someone else tittered. Jeffree ignored this for 'twas plainly a woman's voice.

"Nay, do not leave yet!" boomed another knight de Crecy vaguely recognized. "For I have not yet had the chance to ask your lady wife how she enjoyed being made tourney queen!"

A frozen silence met these bold words for an instant as Jeffree slowly turned to see who had the temerity to utter such words in his presence, let alone his wife's. He was pleased to see that unlike the wretch on the stairs, this knave was of solid build, and he vaguely recognized him from the tournament circuit. As he walked toward him there was a strange buzzing in his ears.

467

"What is your name?" he asked almost softly, for he felt a strange sort of calm suddenly descend on him. It was only right that he should know the name of the man he was about to kill with his bare hands.

The other puffed out his chest. "Throckmorton is my name, Sir Alain Throck—" He did not get any further, for Jeffree had planted his fist in the other man's slablike face. Throckmorton, for all his solid build, went flying through the air and collided with the surface of the table behind them with a terrific crash, sending plates and goblets flying, landing unceremoniously in a dish of roasted swan.

There was the sound of several ladies screaming, but Jeffree barely heard them. None of them was Sabina, and in any case, his quarry was before him, flailing around, his face ruddy with anger and clearly up for a fight. Jeffree welcomed the fact and launched himself at him.

It took three fellow knights to wrench him off Throckmorton and a few more besides. Some of the royal guards had pulled their swords and were waving them about, though Jeffree heard one of Roland Vawdrey's cronies tell them irritably to put them away. "For gods' sake, no weapons have been drawn, save your own. Throckmorton was asking for a good hiding, in any case, the bloody fool."

"Make way! Make way for the King!" came the calls from behind the wall of spectators.

"Get out of my damned way!" came Wymer's belligerent voice. "Can hardly see what's afoot with everyone crowding in and obscuring my view!" As if by magic, the crowd parted and the King of all Karadok strode into proceedings.

"Ah, de Crecy," he said almost fondly, slapping him on the back. "This is not like you, de Crecy, not like you at all." He sounded so cheerful about the fact that one might have wondered if he much preferred this newer version. The King surveyed Sir Alain's stretched-out bulk with interest. "Out cold, is he?" He turned around to look at one of the royal guards who was still clutching a spear. "Do something useful, can't you, and throw some water in his face." The guard scurried off, and Wymer turned back to Jeffree. "He's split your lip," he commented. "Not a bad brawl from what I could see."

"Lucky blow." Jeffree scowled, touching his mouth.

"Maybe so, but he's a capable fellow, is Sir Alain," King Wymer mused.

"He's a bloody fool!" Jeffree snarled, earning a few gasps from the crowd.

"His blood is still up, Sire," said an apologetic voice, and Jeffree realized it was Sir Ned Bevan who seemed to have adopted the role of spokesman on his behalf. Jeffree glared at him, but Bevan did not seem remotely discomposed.

"Saw the whole thing did you, Bevan?"

"I did, Sire."

"Well, you might do me a good turn and come and give a first-hand account to the Queen. She is spitting mad that I've told her to stay put on the dais."

"Nothing could give me greater pleasure," Sir Ned assured him smoothly as Sir Alain gasped and sat up on receiving a bucket of water to the face.

The King turned back to Jeffree. "I'd take yourself off, if I were you," he said dryly. "The Queen will expect a heavy price to be paid for such rude interruption of her entertainments. I would

469

not want to be in your shoes when she thinks of one she deems fitting."

Jeffree shrugged. "Whatsoe'er the price, I shall pay it. Where is my wife?"

"Here!" called a small voice.

Jeffree turned his head and strode down the line of spectators until he spotted that godsawful wimple. Reaching into the crowd, he dragged her forward. She came quietly enough, and he towed her toward the big double doors with every eye in the place on them.

*

It seemed as if they had barely reached their rooms before a missive was delivered by two palace guards demanding fifty gold ducats in recompense for the damages and for bringing ill repute into the palace halls. There was also some ominous mention that Sir Jeffree must pay the Queen's forfeit at some future date, no longer than a twelvemonth. Jeffree scribbled a few words pledging himself to this course of action and returned it to them before shutting the door.

He and Sabina washed and undressed in complete silence, extinguished the candles, and climbed into bed. In the dark, Jeffree listened to her breathing and wondered belatedly if she might have been upset and hiding the fact. She did not like people staring at her after all. He pursed his lips, then winced from the painful split on the bottom lip. Throckmorton must have been wearing a signet ring, damn him.

"Well," Sabina's voice said out of the darkness, surprising him. "I think you have reignited the Queen's interest in me," she observed with a humorous inflection to her voice.

"What?"

"I will admit, though, it was not as much fun as I once thought it would be, seeing you beset on all sides," she said in an odd voice. "I don't know why. Maybe I just do not like seeing you at anyone's mercy."

"The only person who has me at their mercy is you." She fell silent at this. Was he being too blunt? He waited.

"What you said before, about retaining my favor," she said quietly.

"Yes?"

"You don't have to do anything out of the ordinary. I mean, you do not have to exert yourself. There is not the smallest need."

He pondered this. Was she saying he had her favor already? All this talk of favor and regard was not cutting it with him. He wanted the words they had both already said, admittedly on different occasions. Then again, she had made it plain it was actions rather than words she wanted. Mayhap starting fights was not exactly proof of his more tender feeling. He groaned slightly and rubbed his brow.

"Does your side pain you?" she asked sympathetically.

"No," he lied. It hurt like hell, but that was the least of his problems. He had no notion how to set about repairing relations with his wife.

"If you were not so sore…I could console you," she said quietly in the dark, and Jeffree caught his breath.

"I told you, it doesn't pain me," he said swiftly.

She gave a muffled laugh at that, and Jeffree felt a pang, for he did not think he had heard that sound in a while.

*

As though of one accord, they both turned inward to face the other in the shadowy bed. Sabina heard his breathing turn shallow and marveled that she had that effect on him. She shuffled in close and kissed his brow, then his cheek. "Is your lip still bleeding?" she murmured when his lips gently met hers.

"I don't know," he answered hoarsely. "Does it taste of blood?"

"A little, perhaps I should avoid your lips." He groaned as though her words displeased him. Sabina slipped her arms about his neck, and she felt his hands run down her braids, tugging them and pinning them to the small of her back. "Do you want me on top, Jeffree?" she whispered, voicing her suspicion after last time.

"Gods, yes," he murmured. "Like before. I want you to squeeze me with your thighs and direct me."

Sabina gave a startled laugh. "As though you were my horse, you mean?" she teased.

"Nay, not your horse, but your stallion," he corrected her.

"Why, Jeffree..." she started, but stopped when she heard his ragged breathing and felt a wave of heat wash over him. Was he embarrassed? It was almost endearing how awkward he was with words sometimes. Instead of teasing him, Sabina ran her hand down his stomach, reaching boldly between his legs to take him in hand. He was already very hard.

"Gods, Sabina!" She took her time cupping and stroking him until he was bucking into her hand. "I need—let me touch you too," he demanded harshly.

"I like your hands where they are," she admitted. "Though you could tug my braids a little tighter."

"Don't tempt me," he gritted out, and she felt him yank on her hair, making her gasp.

"It seems I like it though, just as you like me on top."

"I do," he admitted raggedly. "Please," he all but begged, "take me inside you, wife."

She clambered at once on top of him. She knew she was more than ready from his words alone, but she reached between her legs, in any case, to check she was slippery enough for him to fit, and his breathing hitched.

"Are you touching yourself?" he wheezed.

"Yes." He groaned and Sabina bit her lip. "Do you wish it was your fingers, Jeffree?" she whispered.

"*Yes*. No. I wish my lip wasn't busted open. I wish I could taste it. I wish…"

"What?" Sabina panted, wondering at his gasp.

"I wish you were sat astride my face," he admitted hoarsely.

Sabina's eyes widened at that image. "Jeffree!" she choked out.

He groaned, dragging on her braids and thrusting up. "I cannot wait any longer, do not ask me to."

Sabina made haste to maneuver herself above him. She had barely aligned their parts before he was gasping, "Now? Tell me."

"Yes," she sobbed as his hips surged forward, and he was there, thrusting into her core, where she ached for him. "Yes," she repeated as they jostled against one another, falling into a rhythm.

"Oh gods, don't stop. Don't stop," he chanted.

Sabina's eyes fluttered shut. "Yes, Jeffree," she encouraged him, pressing her thighs into his hips insistently as he had requested. "Harder." He grunted and complied. "Both," she panted. "Pull my hair too." There was the briefest pause, and then she felt his hands twist to pull on her braids, dragging her head back as he thrust up into her. Why did that feel so good? She sobbed and suddenly he had let her hair loose and was kneading her buttocks, rocking her against him, increasing the friction.

"Keep doing that," he uttered harshly.

Doing what? Sabina wondered, but speech was beyond her now, for pleasure had her in its grip. She moaned low and then, with an astonished gasp, shattered apart completely. When next she surfaced, she was blinking against Jeffree's heaving chest as he shouted his own release. His hands shifted over her back, pulling her tight against him.

"Your injuries," she murmured groggily, reminding him.

"Can't feel anything right now," he panted. "Except your sweet, tight cunny."

Her eyelids flickered, and if she had any breath in her body, Sabina realized she would probably be a little shocked at such forthright words.

When it could not be put off any longer, they disentangled, and Sabina dragged herself out of the bed to take a wash. She was wrung out. No sooner had she joined him back under the covers than she felt the bed shift and Jeffree moved, pressing his body against her back, his harsh breathing at her ear. "You please me," he muttered. "Your body, your words. I want to look at your face next time."

Sabina turned her head, even though she had no chance of making out his expression in the dark. "What?"

"Your face," he repeated tightly. "I want to gaze at it as I give you my seed. I want you to say my name when I'm deep inside you. I want—" His words broke off, and she felt his hot breath against her neck. "I want you to tell me—" The words were gravelly, hard to make out. "That I'm the best lover you ever had. Do you hear me, Sabina? The best and last you'll ever have."

His words robbed her of what little breath she had left. "Jeffree," she murmured.

"But I can wait," he added, dropping a kiss on her shoulder. "I will wait for you."

Her eyes drooped down and the next thing she knew it was morning.

26

The next morning, Sabina woke to an empty bed and realized Jeffree must have already set about their preparations to leave. Wilton brought her hot water and her freshly laundered brown dress. Someone at the palace laundry had taken the trouble to attach new cording at the wrists and hem to replace the old, frayed stuff. A very tidy job they had made of it too; she almost wished they had time for her red dress to be similarly repaired before their departure. Almost half the hem was hanging off thanks to that incident last night on the stairs.

It was far too early for Hugo to be up and about, so having packed her few things, Sabina broke her fast alone. She had just finished her last mouthful of toasted bread when she heard the door bang and Jeffree appeared in the doorway.

"Good morning," she greeted him and, to her annoyance, felt her color rise at the sight of him. Then she noticed his irate expression. "What has happened now?" she asked with dismay. "Not another fight, surely?"

He huffed and started pacing about the room. "Not a fight, no," he said tersely, "but I finally ran into that bastard Kentigern!"

Sabina pushed back her chair, unable to mask her expression of alarm. "What happened, Jeffree?" she asked with misgiving.

He ran a hand through his curling, fair locks. "I—I told him I would be revenged by giving his wife the crown at Beres Caple," he admitted with loathing.

"Oh. Is that all?" She was relieved. Heated words were not so bad.

He glared at her. "What do you mean, *is that all*?"

"Well, you see Hugo explained it to me."

"*Hugo?*"

"Cousin Hugo?" she ventured, seeing his furious expression.

He relaxed slightly. "What did he explain exactly?"

"Well, just that you knights are always doing peculiar things like that." She shrugged. "So I know now that I should not set any store by it."

Jeffree still looked annoyed, so she made haste to direct him to the place Wilton had put out for him and the large platter of roasted fish. For some reason, she had thought things might be different between them this morning.

Really, she chided herself. *Did you think this husband of yours was going to greet you with a kiss on waking? Start making you flowery speeches?* She smiled wryly to herself. Jeffree was just not made that way. Already she could see he was going to be in a foul temper all morning.

"What are you smiling about?" he asked grumpily.

"Why should I not smile?" she replied. "When sat opposite such a handsome husband." She had been aiming to tease him out of his mood, and Jeffree could not have looked more startled if she had started spouting poetry. His blond brows snapped together, and his cheeks turned rather pink.

Clearing his throat, he reached for the bread. "We leave in a half hour," he muttered. "The horses have been made ready."

"I am all packed," she told him brightly.

Soon they had left the capital far behind them. Despite the straight roads and blue skies, Jeffree seemed to be traveling under a thundercloud, Sabina reflected with a sigh. In truth, it ought to be her sat moping in her saddle. She still had the worst misgivings about what they were going to find on their return to Ganfordshire.

This plot that Sir Charles had written to Jeffree about, what could it be other than Isemay's bizarre revenge against his son and heir? Mayhap Sir Charles had been deliberately vague in the letter so as not to alert her that he knew. If Jeffree were to demand she prove her innocence, what could she say?

Guilt would likely show plainly in her countenance, and then all love would die in his bosom. *Love.* She pondered the word a moment. Did she believe that Jeffree truly loved her? She thought so, in his own peculiar, grudging manner. Would that fledgling love prove durable though, in the face of such a betrayal? She did not know.

She was uncomfortably aware that if *he* had acted thus over one of *her* family members, she would be very angry indeed. She *would* consider it a betrayal for someone to speak to your face of love whilst knowing some wrong was being done to your kin. Then again, an inner voice pointed out, Leland Ellis was not beloved of Jeffree. They had been raised together but were not close.

It did not matter, she argued back. They had practically been raised as brothers. Most brothers fought. It did not mean they would tolerate outsiders doing them wrong. She spent an uncomfortable day's reflection and was almost relieved when night fell, and they arrived at their first inn.

Despite being morose and taciturn at supper, in the privacy of their bedchamber he sought her out at once and she gladly gave him what he wanted.

"You are a disgusting, selfish, arrogant, pompous, loathsome toad." Sabina punctuated each failing with a kiss to his lips.

Jeffree lay still beneath her, his hand shifting over her lower back, accepting her accusations without question, receiving her kisses with every evidence of pleasure. By the end of her litany, he was no longer passive. The fact she drew her head back incited a growl of displeasure. He rolled her under him, pinning her hands beside her head.

"You're wrong, Sabina," he said huskily. "I am *your* disgusting, selfish, arrogant, pompous, loathsome toad."

She gave a breathless laugh. "You're ridiculous." And he captured her lips again, this time in a long, drugging kiss. When he drew back, she could see his eyes gleaming even in the dark.

"Say it right," he insisted, his hands roaming over her full bosom, stroking and lightly pinching her there. "Say it right and you can have my tongue."

"I can have your tongue whenever I want it," she pointed out, trying for his own arrogant tone.

"So bold," Jeffree replied with a groan. His head fell forward and nuzzled her neck. To Sabina's shock, his tone was almost approving. "Spoken like a true de Crecy," he whispered, kissing along her jaw. "Tell me then, wife. Tell me that you want it."

That was going a little far, too fast. *A true de Crecy?* She loathed the majority of the de Crecys, didn't she? She should remind him, but it was hard to muster her thoughts when her heart was beating so fast. Of course, in Jeffree's book, this was high praise indeed.

Her heart gave a lurch. *Was he trying to praise her?* "I want it," she blurted, startling herself. Jeffree gave a low hiss. Before she could lose her nerve, she grasped the hair at his nape and tugged on it. "It is mine. Give me my due."

479

He did not make her wait and applied his tongue both to her mouth and then between her legs with a lascivious thoroughness that had her squirming. Soon she was having to muffle her cries with her hand or the rest of the inn would know what they were about.

In the aftermath of their enthusiastic coupling, she had stroked his back and racked her brains for words of love to whisper into his ear. She realized she was almost as bad at this as he. Instead, she remembered his demands from the previous night and told him he *was* her best lover.

He had lifted his head at that. "Truly?" His gaze snared hers.

"Can you doubt it? You are very generous and giving in bed. I never realized…well, that relations could be like that…" Her words trailing off, she gave him a shy smile instead.

His eyes scanned her face, and whatever he had seen there must have reassured him, for he relaxed back against the pillow bearer. "Good," he murmured, tugging lightly at her braids. "Now go to sleep, we have an early start."

Before falling asleep, Sabina wondered with amusement why it was that she no longer minded so much about Jeffree's lack of polish. Even his awful, ungrateful manners did not really grate with her as they should these days. Why was that? she wondered. It was not that he had changed. Wherever he went, he left a group of disgruntled and offended people. Toward her, though, he could show consideration, though it was rarely accompanied by handsome words.

Perhaps, she pondered, it was down to her previous experience. Miles had been so charming to all and sundry, even taking in her parents with his easy ways, but under all that smooth charm, there had been no substance, for he had been a faithless snake.

With Jeffree, there was no pretense, but there were other things…like loyalty and passion.

At the inn the following morning he knelt down and applied a stiff brush to the dusty hem of her dress. Glancing up, she thought Osborn's eyes would pop out of his sockets he looked so shocked by this act of service. Jeffree straightened up and moved away before she could even thank him.

Her heart swelling, she realized there *was* a sort of charm to her husband after all.

27

The first day's journeying set the pattern for the rest of their four days on the road. Jeffree could not rouse himself from his sullens during the day, but it was quite a different matter when they reached the privacy of their inn chamber for the night.

On the second night, he did not even wait until after they had taken their supper. As soon as they were shown to their room, he shut the door and was all over her.

Sabina opened her mouth, but he knew just how to stop it, pushing her back against the door and crowding her against it. "Jeffree!" Her shocked gasp did not deter him one bit.

"Give me this," he said tersely as he lifted her against the door, pressing his hips into hers for comfort. "I need it."

Sabina's head tipped back, and she stared up at him. "Like this?" She faltered, looking scandalized. "But what if someone hears us?"

Jeffree huffed out an indignant breath. She really thought he would dishonor his own wife by fucking her against a wall like some trollop? Sadly, the mere thought of it made his cock throb so hard he could barely string two words together to deny such baseness.

Sabina licked her lips. "You—you will have to be quick," she cautioned him breathlessly. "And quiet."

Holy fuck, she would actually let him? He drew back his head to stare down at her. "Sabina," he groaned as he reached down to start bunching up her skirts. "Gods, wife…"

Before long, both of them were desperate and shaking. Jeffree covered her mouth with his to muffle her cries, or maybe it was his own he was seeking to quiet. All he knew was that when he finally stopped trembling and grunting and reached that blessed plane of sweetly spent, he still could not get enough of the press of her body or the cool, sweet taste of her mouth.

He did not ever want to leave the haven between her thighs and pressed deep when he should have pulled out. "Stay with me," he implored raggedly. What else was she supposed to do when she was still impaled on his cock, her back pinned to a heavy oak door?

Instead of calling out his nonsense, Sabina wrapped her legs tighter about his hips and slid her arms around his shoulders, petting him there, making small, soothing noises, and comforting him.

Muttering a prayer of thanks, Jeffree took her mouth again with thorough deliberation, rocking his hips and wringing the last from his softening cock. He was a little worried about his preoccupation with his own wife, but what could he do at this point? It seemed he was lost to all shame.

Later that night after they had eaten and washed and had another enthusiastic bout between the sheets, he did not even have to think about the words he needed to give her afterward. They tumbled out of his mouth. "I'm glad you seduced me, wife," he murmured. "And lured me to your bedchamber."

Sabina had made a choked noise in her throat. "What are you talking about?" she had asked in a muffled voice as he played with her braids and tucked her in close against his body.

"Enticing me to climb up to your window," he reminded her in a husky whisper.

She snorted. "*You* were the one allegedly spotted climbing my shrubbery," she reminded him.

"I could not stay away," he agreed.

The next morning, remembering his nonsensical words, he was embarrassed as hell and awkward at breakfast, scowling at Osborn and cursing a servant who spilled his ale. He had an uncomfortable notion Sabina knew exactly why he could not meet her gaze, though she let him off the hook and did not even allude to it once.

On the fourth and final night, Sabina had upbraided him again during their lovemaking and once again it had excited him beyond all reason. "You're such an arrogant swine," she had gritted out. "It's a good thing you're so pretty, or I would not suffer you in my bed!"

He had gasped at her words and thrust up his hips with a harsh groan. "*Sabina!*" Even thinking of it afterward made him shiver and burn for her. Why did he like it when she took him to task? He did not know; he only knew she was the one person he would tolerate it from.

After they had cleaned up, he had given in to temptation and dragged down the sheets and explored her lush body in the candlelight.

"What are you doing?" she asked with a yawn.

"Not cold, are you?" he asked with sudden concern.

She snorted. "On a warm night in July?"

He ran his hands over the globes of her arse and then shifted down the bed and kissed them both in turn.

"Jeffree!" Sabina's startled yelp made him frown. "What *are* you about?"

"Just thinking what a pity it would have been if the smooth perfection of your buttocks had been marred by a harlot's brand."

"I don't know about a pity," Sabina responded critically. "But it would have been a travesty of justice and hurt like hell!" He murmured his agreement as he ran his hands over them again. "And it's disgusting that you would have gotten away with it scot-free too!" she continued darkly. "While I was branded and paraded through the streets barefoot or stuck in a pillory! *Men* don't get branded for harlotry," she finished crossly.

"My crest might look well here," he mused, tracing his finger over her bottom.

"What?" Sabina turned about to squint at him suspiciously and he realized he had spoken the thought out loud. "You want to brand me like one of your cattle now?"

He grew a little red. "I don't own any cattle. I spoke without thinking."

"You—" Words seemed to fail her for once and she stared at him. "Sometimes you are so odd, Jeffree de Crecy."

He cleared his throat. "It was naught but an idle thought... I did not mean it. You know I would never let anyone burn your flesh."

She shook her head. "Maybe I should add this remark to the one about my ropelike hair?"

He cleared his throat with a frown and hurried to extinguish the candle. Thinking about it afterward, he realized that speaking *any* words while stupidly sated was likely a mistake. He could not count on himself not to talk like a lovesick fool.

485

28

They reached Morecotte by late next morning. Penny and Lancer both came running to welcome them home. Lancer's curly dogs bounded around their legs barking as Osborn led the horses into the stable.

"That Sir Charles Ellis has sent word over these last three days to check if you was back, Sir Jeffree," Sabina overheard Lancer report to her husband as Penny chirped away in her other ear.

Sabina felt sick dread once more rise up in her stomach as she followed Penny inside the house. During the journey, she had managed to mostly push it out of her thoughts but there could be no more burying her head in the sand. They were on the brink of disaster.

On the threshold she almost started, for she had forgotten all of the new furnishings that now filled the house. Sadly, in her current mood, she could take no pleasure in them.

"You look tired, milady. Let me heat you some water for washing off your travel dirt."

"Thank you, Penny, I would be most grateful." Sabina started up the stairs, before pausing on the third step. "I don't suppose my sister has sent me any word in my absence?"

Penny shook her head. "That she haven't, milady."

Sabina sighed and carried on up to wash and change. She had just finished putting on a clean dress when Jeffree came into the dressing room.

"Here you are," he said, looking her over. "I wondered where you had slipped off to."

Sabina noticed he had not changed and still wore his boots. "Are you off somewhere?" she asked with misgiving. Was the newfound accord between them to be shattered so soon?

He nodded. "I had better see what Charles has uncovered."

Sabina gulped. "So soon?"

His brows lifted. "You think I would be better employed elsewhere?"

"No, of course not," Sabina mumbled, casting down her comb and starting her first braid in a haphazard fashion. So rattled was she that the result fell far short of her usual standard. She had just fastened the loose braid and started on her second when she heard Jeffree's sharply indrawn breath.

"What are you doing?" he asked in an annoyed voice.

"What does it look like?"

"Extremely untidy!"

Sabina shrugged a shoulder. "No one will know as they won't see them under my headdress."

He practically vibrated with annoyance at her answer. "*I* will know!" he retorted tersely.

Again, Sabina shrugged, reaching for a ribbon to secure the end of her second braid. He strode across the room and practically snatched it from her hand.

"Give that to me!" He tutted. "Sit down on that trunk."

Sabina lowered herself onto the flat surface and sat watching his face as he picked up the comb and ran it through the length of her hair. He was fully absorbed in his task, his expression intent and curiously reverent as he dressed her hair, separating it into three equal strands and carefully weaving them together. With each pass, he adjusted the tension to keep it as he wanted it until he reached the very tips of her hair. Then he fastened the end and ran his thumb up and down the thick braid.

"That is something more like it," he said at last. "Now turn around so I can do the other side."

Obediently, Sabina turned about and faced the opposite direction while he repeated the process on the left side of her head. When he had finished, he stood there a moment, before reaching out to run his hand up and down the back of her head. Sabina closed her eyes at the slow caress. She would not cry.

She felt suddenly desperate that he should not see Sir Charles and let their tenuous happiness be destroyed. His hand slid about her jaw and tipped her chin up. He gazed down at her with such a strange expression in his blue eyes that Sabina caught her breath.

When he spoke, however, his tone was down to earth. "You will have to pin it about your ears yourself," he said gruffly. Sabina nodded and his thumb stroked absently across her jaw as he frowned down at her. "What is it?" he asked suddenly, making her draw in her breath.

She shook her head. "Nothing, I am just a little tired." She thought he would take his leave then, but he lingered in the doorway as she coiled and pinned the braids.

"Does that not hurt?"

"No."

"People say horses have no feelings in their mane and tail," he replied. "But that is not so. They feel well enough when someone pulls their hair about."

"Maybe some are just used to ill-treatment. When we were children, we had one old servant who used to comb our hair so roughly she would jerk our heads right back. Isemay used to wail."

"And what about you? What did you do?" he asked curiously.

Sabina paused in the act of draping her veil over her head. "What makes you think I did anything?"

"Just a suspicion. Tell me."

"Very well. I put a frog in her bed."

He smirked. "Of course you did."

Sabina's throat closed over. "No one hurts my sister when I am around," she said thickly, but Jeffree had already departed.

As soon as she heard the door slam, Sabina ran down to the stables and had Osborn saddle up Blitha.

"I only just took the saddle off her," he protested.

"I am not going far and I will return soon."

Osborn tutted but did as he was bid. "Tells me to unsaddle 'em, then they both goes tearing off again!" she heard him mutter under his breath. She supposed it made a sort of sense that Jeffree's servant should also have such a dreadful attitude. They would neither of them put up with the other if not so.

A quarter of an hour later she was slipping up the backstairs at Tipton Hall and knocking softly at her sister's bedchamber door. "Isemay?" she called softly, for she did not wish to go through the rigmarole of a visit with her parents just now. "Are you within?" She thought she heard movement, and after pausing to give her sister a few moments' grace, she pushed the door open and got the shock of her life.

There, lying in the middle of Isemay's bed and propped up on one elbow, was Leland Ellis.

*

"What are *you* doing here?" Sabina gasped, falling back against the door.

"It is not what it looks like," he warned, "whatever that may be." He still looked pale, but then perhaps he always had, with those coal-black curls and that tall, slender frame. He certainly did not look like he was on death's door anymore.

What in heaven was he doing in Isemay's bed? "Where is my sister?" she asked suspiciously, gazing about the room as though he might have stashed Isemay somewhere.

"Off mixing me another draught of foul medicine," he answered with a shudder. "A good thing her revenge did not include poisoning me, though at times," he added darkly, "I have wondered!"

Her revenge? Sabina stared at him. *So then he knew?*

Leland shot her a speculative look. "Close the door behind you unless you want Hildeth or the good Samuel to know everything." He leaned forward and poured himself a draught of whatever concoction Isemay was dosing him with, drank it down, and pulled a face. "You see, I accept my punishment. I take it you knew about Isemay finding me half-dead in the forest."

"Yes, but..." Sabina sucked in a shocked breath. "Is it possible," she began, her head reeling, "that your memory has been returned to you?"

Leland shrugged his shoulders. "I was really only confused for a couple of days," he admitted. "Bruised and battered. Hendry's thugs practically stove my skull in, gods rot them."

"Hendry?" Sabina covered her mouth with consternation.

"He that lieth with dogs…" Leland shrugged. "It was inevitable, I suppose. Do you know, an old hag told me only last month that I would get what was coming to me." He tilted his head and reflected on the matter a moment. "She cackled about it too, despite the fact I had tipped her quite handsomely."

"I think that is just stock in trade for wise women," Sabina answered without thinking. Leland laughed, then winced. "I think a couple of my ribs are broken," he admitted. "Do not tell Isemay."

"But why did Alfred Hendry's thugs attack you?" she asked as Leland cautiously rearranged his long, spare limbs, moving up the bed into a sitting position.

"I think it was a card debt," he answered. "Or simply because things did not turn out favorably that day at Ganford Chase, thanks to you. One or the other, take your pick."

Suddenly Sabina remembered the back bedroom at Morecotte had had a mattress on the floor and recent signs of an occupant when they had cleaned house. "You were staying at Morecotte!" she gasped. "After you left the duke's residence."

An expression of disgust passed over Leland's face. "For two nights only," he muttered. "What a filthy hole that was! That abandoned hovel your sister stashed me in was a distinct improvement."

"Excuse me!" Sabina objected. "Morecotte happens to be my rightful home. It is no longer filthy, and if it makes you feel any

491

better, Jeffree dealt very roughly with both of Hendry's henchmen and threw them into the water trough."

She tried not to dwell on the fact that Lancer must have been one of Leland's attackers. Penny had never said he was a good man precisely. "The best of a bad bunch" was how she had described him. Lancer had turned over a new leaf, Sabina told herself uneasily. Besides, Leland had more than deserved a good kicking after his dreadful behavior that day at Ganford Chase.

His eyes drifted shut as though moving around had given him a headache. "Did he really?" he murmured.

"Yes." Sabina nodded slowly. "And if you remained at Morecotte for two nights, then it must have only been a matter of mere hours after they assaulted you that we turned up there."

Leland's eyes sprung open at that. "To think I must have missed you by so short an amount of time. How funny." Sabina did not know about that; she eyed him curiously. "It is certainly strange how things turn out, to be sure," Leland mused.

"And yet, if I had not cheated Hendry at cards, then I daresay I should still have been there the next morning and then Jeffree would have thrown *me* in the water trough." He laughed softly. "More than likely it all turned out for the best."

"All turned out for the best?" Sabina echoed disbelievingly. "I think you are mad, Leland Ellis! Your father is beside himself, and as for my poor sister…" She trailed off distractedly. "The gods only know how this is going to turn out for her. How has she managed to keep you hidden here?"

"Hidden? My dear, I am here under official sanction, have you not heard?"

"What do you mean? My parents are aware you are here? I don't believe you!"

"Oh, but it is true. After all, we are man and wife now."

"Man and wife?" Sabina shrilled.

Leland winced. "My head, my dear Sabina, it is splitting."

"How can you and Isemay be…*man and wife*?" she asked with horror.

"Because your enterprising sister dragged me to a priest at Ganford Church and had her faithful Samuel act as witness," he explained. "It was all part of her revenge plan. Did she not tell you the second part of it?"

"No, she did not!" Sabina rasped hotly. "I never would have allowed such a thing to happen! How could Isemay have been so rash?" She sank into a chair with a moan. "This is dreadful. A *disaster*!" Leland's dark eyes dwelt on her with amusement. "Tell me," Sabina asked with sudden suspicion. "Had your wits returned to you when she carted you off to be wed?"

He gave her a crooked smile. "Of course, though it was true I scarcely recognized her at first. I had to wait for the swelling to go down around my eyes, and when it finally did, I took her for a peasant girl. She looked so different out of all her bridal finery, and we were in a tumbledown shack after all."

"And when you *did* recognize her?" Sabina prompted as he lapsed into silence.

"It sort of came on gradually, then all at once," he answered thoughtfully. "I was put on my guard then, of course," he admitted, "but so defenseless and weak, I was just grateful her vengeance did not include slipping a knife between my ribs as I lay incapacitated at her feet. I was feeling damnably sorry for

493

myself," he sighed. "At some point, I just wanted to roll over and die. But recognizing Isemay gave me the kick up the arse I needed. I started paying attention to something other than my own self-pity."

He smiled as though one recalling a fond memory. "She spoke sweet words, but the expression on her face when she thought I was not looking spoke of murderous intent." His smile broadened. "I realized she meant to be revenged on me and decided I did not want to die after all but to find out what she intended to do to me."

Sabina watched him speechlessly. "Am I to understand that you exchanged wedding vows quite willingly with my sister?"

"Oh yes. I knew what I was doing alright."

"Yet you have not told this to Isemay?" Sabina asked him, narrowing her eyes.

"Oh, certainly not. Why spoil her fun?"

Sabina stared at him long and hard. "You will tell her though, at some point?"

"It depends."

"On what, pray?"

Leland hesitated. "The usual things: expedience, convenience."

"You are so selfish!" Sabina burst out.

"But I am honest, you must give me that."

"You are not even remotely honest!"

He laughed again. "No, no, you must not say so."

"You lie, you cheat at cards…" Sabina started wrathfully, only to find the door bursting open.

"Sabina!" her sister reproached her. "Why are you flinging accusations at his poor head when you *know* how ill he has been?" Isemay hurried forward purposefully. "He is pale as milk from all your haranguing!"

"My love, I am quite well," Leland protested feebly, raising a hand to his brow and adopting a die-away air.

"You are horribly fatigued!" Isemay tutted, pressing him back onto his cushions with solicitous but heavy-handed care. Leland inhaled sharply though he voiced no complaint.

Sabina rose from her chair. "Isemay—" she started, but her sister rounded on her ferociously.

"He must be left in peace and absolute quiet for the next hour at least and then he can take his next dose."

Leland groaned faintly, and Sabina allowed herself to be bustled out of the room. It occurred to her that the cruelest course of action would be leaving Leland to Isemay's not-so-tender ministrations. Her sister was evidently trying her best, but gentle she was not.

"I will be back shortly," Isemay promised Leland before shutting the door firmly behind them and ushering her sister into the bedchamber next door.

"Married?" Sabina squawked as soon as they were alone together and the door closed. "Are you *mad*, sister? To such a man? To the man that wronged you so *grievously*?"

Isemay lifted a finger to her lips. "Quiet down, sister!" she hissed. "Do you want Mother to come running?"

Sabina glanced over her shoulder nervously. "Does Sir Charles yet know his son has been found alive and well?" she asked hoarsely.

Isemay shook her head. "No one knows outside our family, and Leland is not yet well. I am nursing him back to health, and he is growing touchingly reliant upon me."

"Oh, *Isemay*, what have you done?" Sabina demanded. "Tying yourself to this man for life!"

"I told you, I mean to take you for my role model now," her sister said, sticking her nose in the air.

"How on earth have I influenced you to compel Sir Leland into marriage?" Sabina squeaked.

"I mean to make his life a misery and make him pay for what he did."

Sabina stared at her. "That is not why I married Sir Jeffree!" she burst out.

Isemay looked momentarily disconcerted. "Is it not?"

"Of course not! I would *hardly* embark on such a reckless course of action! I only married Jeffree at his insistence. He demanded I take responsibility for his tarnished reputation!"

Isemay waved this aside. "Very well then, I took Jeffree for my role model," she said, sounding unconcerned.

"You took *Jeffree* for your role model?" Sabina repeated, quite thunderstruck.

"Yes, for I vowed that Leland would make reparation for those terrible accusations he made against me. I have thought it through, and the only way for my pride to be restored to me is for him to marry me himself and thereby show everyone that he

496

believed my conduct beyond reproach. That is how Jeffree restored his reputation, was it not, after you dragged it through the mud?"

Sabina slumped against the wall. "This is dreadful," she pronounced hollowly. "This is *all* quite dreadful. What is to become of us?"

Isemay looked around her. "Where is Jeffree anyway?" she asked, as though she had only just noticed the absence of her brother-in-law. "Did you come by yourself?"

"He has gone to Ganford Chase," Sabina said hollowly.

"Oh, what for?"

"To see his uncle and Sir Charles, I expect," Sabina replied, feeling nettled. "Sir Charles has been riding out hither and thither in search of his son. Apparently, he has been as far as Halfordshire in search of him."

Isemay did have the grace to look a little guilty at that. "I daresay the news will soon leak out that Leland lives still."

"Let us hope that Sir Charles does not swear vengeance on our poor blameless father's head!"

Isemay looked concerned for all of two heartbeats, then her expression relaxed. "He can hardly do that, not when his godson is wed to you. That would be very poor form, and I understand he is something of a stickler for convention."

Sabina pursed her lips. "And just how long do you suppose you can keep up this ruse, Isemay?"

"What ruse?" her sister huffed, blowing a lock of her dark hair out of her eyes. "There is no ruse. We are legally wedded and there is nothing anyone can do to prevent me taking charge of him!"

"What of Sir Charles?" Sabina asked, plunking her hands on her hips. "He will oppose this match to the utmost!"

"And what if he does?" Isemay answered with spirit. "Leland has reached his majority. He is over one and twenty."

"If his father were to cut Leland's allowance you would be left with nothing to exist on! You know how straitened our own father's circumstances are. Do you suppose he can support you both indefinitely?"

Isemay rolled her eyes. "Do you imagine I have not thought of that? Leland says he is to inherit some money from his maternal grandfather on his twenty-fifth birthday. We have only to eke out our existence here for a sixmonth before then."

Sabina absorbed this a moment in silence. "Well, that is something," she admitted grudgingly. She allowed her sister to lead her downstairs. "I must say his memory loss seems remarkably *patchy*."

"It is strange, is it not?" Isemay agreed absently. "He seems to recall practically everything apart from those fateful events at Ganford Chase and the days surrounding it."

"And the details of your own wooing apparently," Sabina pointed out.

"Oh yes, but there is not really anything for him to remember in that regard, is there?" Isemay said, scrunching up her face.

"Well, then, you do not think it is strange that he recalls some things and not others?" she asked pointedly, for she did not think it was right that Leland should string her sister along by pretending he was still her victim. "What will you do when he remembers all?"

"Maybe he never will," Isemay suggested hopefully.

Sabina came to an abrupt standstill. "Is that what you want?" she asked incredulously. "Would you not prefer open honesty between the two of you? Recollect, Isemay, his father was present that fateful day as were many others of his acquaintance. What if they were to remind him of the role he played in ruining your wedding day to Bethencourt?"

"I have already thought of that," Isemay assured her blithely. "I will simply tell him that he was madly in love with me by that point and did not want me to wed another."

Sabina opened her mouth to denounce this plan when it occurred to her that Leland Ellis would probably find this version of events highly entertaining. "What a tangled web," she said hollowly as Isemay tugged her down the last few steps of the staircase.

"Well, you need not lecture me, sister. Did not you and Jeffree play along with the wicked tales Alfred Hendry told of your midnight trysts?"

"That was quite different!" Sabina huffed. "By the way, what did you tell our parents when you turned up with him on their doorstep?"

"Why, that I saved his life and he fell madly in love with me, what else?"

By some miracle, Isemay managed to sneak Sabina down to the side entrance without them being discovered by their mother.

"Anyway, never mind about me," Isemay hissed, catching hold of Sabina's forearm before her sister could make good her escape. "Tell me quickly, how goes it with you, sister?"

"Oh, Isemay." Sabina sniffed dolefully. "I have likely damaged Jeffree's reputation beyond all repair." She gave a brief account of her less than salubrious court debut. Her sister was almost

499

awed that she had worn her awful brown dress in the royal palace.

"I don't know how you can have done such a thing," her sister admitted. "But as for ruining Jeffree's reputation, no, no, you have that all wrong. Folk round these parts used to think him horribly cold and stuck-up, whereas now…"

"What?" Sabina asked almost fearfully. "Now what are they saying about him?"

"Well, that he's married a local lass, so he cannot be all bad. Then, too, there is that business of his paying off the blacksmith's apprentice to marry that Selwyn girl and raise her child."

That pulled Sabina up short. "Pardon?" Her heart beat faster. "What did you say?"

"Oh, had he not told you about that? He gave them the money to set up their own forge anywhere outside of Ganfordshire. The whole village is talking of it." When Sabina could not find any words, Isemay continued breezily, "You are taking far too bleak a view of things, you know. It seems to me that Sir Jeffree is coming along nicely."

Sabina gaped at her. "What on earth—what are you talking about, Isemay?"

"So, his odiously superior manner slipped a few times, and he lost his temper at court. What of it?"

"Isemay!" Sabina drew herself up. "You do not seem to understand that Sir Jeffree is a knight of renown who has worked hard over the years to maintain his—"

"Stuffy reputation?" Isemay concluded.

"That remark is beneath you, sister."

"Pffft!" Isemay responded.

"Isemay!"

"Pshaw! I daresay he has seemed more human in the month since he has married you than in the thirty years preceding it."

"He is only twenty-eight!"

"Then he is not too old to make an exhibition of himself, is he now?" her sister responded serenely. "It is not like you to look on the bad side, and besides"—she shot Sabina a level look— "if you do not like people saying his wife looks like a dowd, then mayhap you should have some new dresses made up."

Sabina glared at her. "You are as bad as Mother!"

Isemay folded her arms. "Sometimes Mother is right."

As this was the one thing both knew was guaranteed to infuriate the other, there was a coolness to their leave-taking which was not altogether unsurprising.

Sabina felt shattered on the ride home, and when she led Blitha into the stables, she noticed Radax was not in his stall. She made her way back into the house with a heavy heart.

"Ah, there you are, milady," Penny hailed her. "I just set out some of my freshly baked cheese pies on the table for you and the master's supper."

"Thank you, Penny. I do not think—" Hearing horses' hooves, she broke off. "He is back!" she exclaimed with relief, for suddenly the only way forward seemed obvious to her. A full confession. It was the only way out of her current mess.

"I'll fetch the ale," Penny said, scurrying toward the buttery.

However, when the rider entered the house, they found it was not Jeffree at all, but one of the duke's servants delivering a missive to Sabina. She opened it at once.

Wife, she read.

Doubtless, you will think it a fool's errand, but I have been sent to Wynstay Marshes after some information Sir Charles received from a former servant of Alfred Hendry's. I will see you on the morrow. JDC

A former servant? Sabina read the words several times before lowering the letter. She tried to remember the other two attendants Alfred Hendry had that day. A toothless old villain of a man sprang to mind and another hulking brute in the same mold as Lancer. If they had been involved in Leland's beating, they would have known he was abandoned in Langley Woods. They must now simply be spinning a yarn to get money out of Sir Charles.

Sabina groaned. Wynstay Marshes was a good day's ride from here. Jeffree was being optimistic thinking he would be back tomorrow. If he was, it would be late tomorrow. If only he had come home first, she could have warned him it was a wild goose chase!

"Will I set up the bathtub for you tonight, milady?" Penny suggested, clearly trying to cheer her up.

"Thank you, Penny, that would be wonderful."

After her bath Sabina lay awake in Jeffree's large bed for a long time, worrying about her sister's rash marriage, Sir Charles Ellis's inevitable reaction to it, and what her husband would say when he learned all. When she finally drifted off to sleep, she could still feel the worry twisting at her gut.

The next morning she woke with the same sense of dread, even before she could bring the cause properly to mind. A letter arrived for her as she tried to force some bread down. She felt a lurch of fear, but when she turned it over she saw it was sealed with a large letter *V* for Vyse.

On opening it, Sabina found it was full of news from Crispin and Jasper, who had filled many pages about Feste's and Brisis's goings-on. Clearly, her brothers-in-law were as enamored of their hounds as ever. Crispin had even attempted a drawing of both dogs which showed some talent, for she could plainly tell which was which even though it was only drawn in black ink.

At the end, there was a neat paragraph added from the Lady Maud which was extremely civil for the reserved lady. Apparently, all of them were well and would expect news of how the newlyweds were settling into life together. Sabina thought she would wait for a few weeks before attempting to respond to that query. Perhaps she could get away with a drawing of Lancer's scruffy hounds?

A cough at the doorway had her looking up to find Osborn lurking there. "Oh, Osborn, I thought you must have gone to Wynstay Marshes with your master," she exclaimed, lowering her letter. She was not terribly surprised that he had made himself scarce the previous evening. In her opinion, Osborn always did the least work possible. Considering how difficult Jeffree could be, she thought his servant got away with rather a lot.

"No, milady." He coughed and took a few steps closer, lowering his voice. "Er, Sir Charles Ellis just called by."

"Sir Charles? But he knows Jeffree is not here," Sabina pointed out in startled tones.

"Exactly," Osborn said with a nod. "I told him you was *indisposed* but that you would let the master know Sir Charles wanted to see him as soon as he returned."

Sabina regarded him blankly. "You did?"

"Seemed to me Sir Charles was in something of a rare taking. Quite white about the mouth he was, and shaking with fury. Seemed to me," he repeated, rocking back on his heels, "that the master would not want you to be—er—*put out* by him when he was in such a temper."

Sabina was astonished. Osborn had made it quite plain that the change in Sir Jeffree's circumstances had hugely inconvenienced him personally, yet here he was making excuses for her and shielding her from Sir Charles's wrath. "Thank you, Osborn," she said faintly. Really, she could think of nothing else to say.

Osborn gave her a hard look and seemed to be weighing up his options. "Only I called in at The Blue Boar last night after Sir Jeffree left." His shifty eyes resolutely avoided hers, roaming instead all around the room. "There was—er—some talk of the houseguest staying up at Tipton Hall." His eyes met hers briefly, and Sabina's heart thudded. *Oh gods.* "Old Roper was there," he continued slowly, "as used to work here along with the Lancers."

"Old Roper?" Sabina heard herself repeat numbly. A wheel turned somewhere in her mind. "Wait, was he the toothless old man who—?"

504

"That were him. He's been hobbling up to The Chase the last few days pouring all manner of confidences in Sir Charles's ear."

"Was it Roper gave Sir Charles the tale about Wynstay Marshes?" she asked.

"Aye, that it were. He's an opportunistic old villain and no mistake. He were lurking last night in the tavern, and I have no doubt he went haring straight up to Ganford Chase with the tale as soon as it were done."

Sabina stared ahead of her blindly a moment as she took this new disaster in. "Thank you for telling me, Osborn," she uttered at last.

"I knows me duty," he said mildly. "Seems plain to me where it lies these days." He gave her a nod and left the room. Sabina blinked. Well, perhaps Osborn had recovered from his dislike of mistresses at last.

She remained where she was awhile, her heart thudding painfully in her chest. Clearly, the cat was out of the bag when it came to Leland Ellis's whereabouts. When Jeffree came home there would be hell to pay. Sabina rose unsteadily from the table, determined to keep herself busy this day until her husband's return.

29

It was not until late evening that Penny came flying up the stairs to tell her the master was back and asking for her. Sabina abandoned the inventory list she had been checking and rushed downstairs. Her heart gave a leap when she saw him in the Great Chamber. She hurried inside and made haste to close the door behind her, wasting no time to blurt out, "Isemay has done a terrible thing!"

Jeffree checked whatever words had been on his lips and eyed her warily a moment before scrubbing his hand down his face. He walked over to the small table and poured himself a drink. "Can we not reassure ourselves that all is well with one another before we start this discussion of your sister?" he asked, his tone surprisingly neutral.

"All is not well with me!" Sabina pointed out with alacrity. "That is what I am attempting to tell you."

"No, I mean—" He broke off. "Oh, very well, then." He flung himself down in a seat. "Tell me."

It was only at this point that Sabina noticed he looked bone-weary. Her conscience smote her at once. "What time did you set out this morning?" she asked with sudden concern.

When he did not answer, she knew immediately it must have been ridiculously early. "Oh, Jeffree, no wonder you are dog-tired!" She hurried to his side and dropped down to her knees to start pulling off his boots.

"Osborn can do that!" he said sharply. "You are not my servant."

"I know that," she answered patiently, "but doubtless Osborn is occupied stabling your horse." He did not argue with that, most likely because he could not. She tugged and pulled at his boots until she had removed them both. Then she fell back onto her haunches, gazing up at him. "Are you well?" she demanded without preamble.

A reluctant smile tugged at his lips. "I am," he replied. "Come up here." He patted the arm of his seat. Instead, Sabina promptly dropped into his lap. His arms closed about her at once. "Give me the greeting I want," he demanded with his customary arrogance.

Sabina rolled her eyes but leaned forward and kissed his cheek all the same. When he growled, she gave a huff of exasperated laughter before pressing her lips boldly to his. Jeffree's hand immediately closed about the nape of her neck, holding her where she was as he molded his lips to hers.

A banging on one of the doors made them both freeze and reluctantly part. "That is surely the outside door..." Sabina muttered distractedly, rising from the seat and batting away her husband's hands at her waist.

"Let one of the Lancers get it," he grumbled.

"I can hear Penny now," Sabina admitted, biting her lip. She could also hear another voice upraised in anger. *Oh gods.* It was Sir Charles.

The door flung open and Sir Charles Ellis stood there, pale and quivering with rage, an apologetic Penny hovering close by, wringing her hands.

"Right sorry I am, milady, but I could not—"

"Ah, you are home this time I find, madam, and your husband also," Sir Charles said, pushing rudely past the bewildered servant.

Sabina was spared from answering this as Jeffree had appeared suddenly beside her, looking reassuringly tall and solid despite his stockinged feet.

Sir Charles regarded her with hard, angry eyes. "I see you have not sent him forthwith to Ganford Chase as you promised!" he practically hissed.

Sabina had scarcely opened her mouth before Jeffree replied, "I am just this moment arrived and would not let my wife speak one word of news to me before now."

Sir Charles cast a quick glance over Jeffree's travel-worn clothes and, accepting this to be truth, clenched his mouth shut tight, giving a nod of his head.

"Now apologize," Jeffree said harshly.

"I fully intended—" Sabina began before he silenced her with a pointed look.

"Not you—him."

Sir Charles made a startled noise in his throat. When he saw Jeffree's expression, his own reformed into its habitual icy hauteur. "It was not my intention to cause offense," he rasped. "I trust you will allow that my current circumstances are enough to try the patience of any mere mortal."

"There have been developments, then?" Jeffree interrupted him, sending a quick keen glance between Sir Charles and Sabina.

Sabina felt her face grow very hot. She reached out a hand to pluck Jeffree's sleeve. "Could I—?"

"I must speak with you alone." Sir Charles's words cut across her own, preempting her. His breathing was ragged and the color in his hollowed cheeks, hectic. "There has been—such duplicity," he gasped. "Wicked treachery afoot—" He staggered and Jeffree was forced to grab a firm hold of him.

"Good gods, what ails you, Charles?" Jeffree demanded in bewilderment, half hauling his godfather further into the room.

To Sabina's eye, it almost looked like the older man had gone off in a faint. "I will fetch some brandy-wine," she called, running toward the pantry.

By the time she had fetched it, Sir Charles was slumped in a seat before the fire, half swooning with Jeffree loosening the clothing at his neck. His eyes met hers briefly above the older man's gray head. "He's gone off in a faint," he muttered. "Probably been pushing himself too hard. He's usually on some fast or other and rarely ever eats a square meal."

Sabina nodded, sloshed the brandy-wine into a goblet with hands that shook, and passed it to Jeffree. He hesitated a moment, and instead of administering it, he set it down on a small table. "Tell me quickly," he said.

She did not need to ask to what he was referring. "Isemay found Sir Leland in the forest two days after our wedding, insensible. He was badly beaten and she feared close to death. She managed to get him to a nearby abandoned cottage with the help of an old family servant who was sworn to secrecy. Between them, they nursed him there. His memory was gone and Isemay..." She hesitated, licking her suddenly dry lips, throwing a look of appeal at Jeffree.

"Formulated her plan to be revenged on him," Jeffree concluded grimly. Sabina nodded her head, avoiding his shrewd gaze. "What did she do?"

509

Sabina took a deep breath. "She convinced him they were sweethearts, who had been eloping when set upon by enemies," Sabina admitted wretchedly. "Then, once he was healed, they set out for Ganford Church and were wed there with Samuel, the servant, standing witness."

Jeffree's expression grew tight. "I see." He glanced down at his godfather, who was groaning and moving his head fretfully. "I hear Osborn in the passageway," he said, surprising Sabina with the sudden change of subject. "Fetch him. We'll get Sir Charles up to bed."

Grateful for the distraction after her confession, Sabina ran to summon Osborn and then watched helplessly as Sir Charles was carted up to bed by the two men. On impulse, she turned back to fetch the forgotten goblet of brandy-wine and a candlestick, carrying them slowly up the stairs held out in front of her.

Following their murmured voices, she gathered they had taken Sir Charles into the larger of the back bedrooms and stood outside the room awaiting them there. The old man would not appreciate her barging in on him being prepared for bed. Accordingly, she waited until Jeffree emerged. He started on seeing her in the shadowy passageway, but took the wine from her without a word, passing it back to Osborn, who was following in his wake.

"Give this to Sir Charles then fetch him some meat broth from the kitchen."

"I can fetch it," Sabina quickly offered, but Jeffree caught her elbow.

"No," he said, steering her along the passageway. "Osborn can do it."

He led her straight to their bedchamber and, to her surprise, took the candle from her, setting it down. "Let's go to bed," he said abruptly.

Sabina blinked and opened her mouth. "But should we not—"

"I don't want to talk about it. Let's leave it for now."

Seeing the tired look on his face, she relented at once. "Very well," she agreed. "Though you will need hot water for washing."

"Have Penny bring it."

Sabina hurried at once to the head of the stairs and called for the maidservant. When she returned, Jeffree was already undressing. When water was brought, he washed with his customary thoroughness, and no other words were spoken between them. Sabina did likewise and climbed into the bed, feeling a jittery mess.

When Jeffree joined her moments later, he drew her into his arms and let out a ragged breath. A moment later she felt his fingertips brush her eyelids. Was he checking if there were no tears? Then he steered her head to his shoulder and her hand to his chest as was his custom, and she listened to his breathing even out.

How could he fall asleep? she marveled. After hearing some of the goings-on? Why had he not demanded to know the level of her own complicity? All the harsh questions and accusations she had expected to fall from his lips had not even found utterance! She was dumbfounded. Was it simply that he did not have the energy for it at this hour?

By some miracle, she managed to fall into a light doze, comforted by his presence, and when she woke again, it was with a start. The room was now illuminated by candlelight and

Jeffree was propped up on one elbow regarding her. "I think you were more tired than I," he observed.

She cleared her throat. "I have not been sleeping well," she admitted. "What time is it?"

"Somewhere around midnight. Perhaps you should sleep some more."

Sabina shook her head. "I would much rather make a clean breast of it," she said, sitting up and hugging her knees.

His eyes flickered, but he did not move a muscle. "Were you in on it from the start?" he asked quietly.

"No!" she said quickly. "I swear to you, Jeffree, I knew *nothing* about it until I followed Isemay the day before we left for Caer-Lyoness. By that point, Leland was healing and on the road to recovery—"

He waved a hand and she lapsed into silence at once, waiting for him to indicate she could continue. "I believe you," he said, confounding her. "And even if I did not... She had every right to take her revenge. It is all Leland's fault we are in this position again."

Sabina's eyes widened. "It is?"

"Does this not remind you of last time?" he asked irritably. "My thinking you were complicit in some sort of plot, you forced to defend yourself."

Sabina swallowed. "You believed me last time too," she remembered.

"I'm weary of it," he admitted. "The mess is not of our making, and I do not want us getting dragged into things again."

512

"If we had not been dragged into it last time, then…we would ne'er have been wed," she pointed out painfully.

He was silent a moment. "I suppose that is true. That all seems a long time ago to me." Sabina did not point out that it had been little over a month and a half they had been married. Instead, she waited. "I also want to make a clean breast of things, wife," he said suddenly and reached out his hand to her. Sabina placed her own in it without hesitation.

"I wish I could go back to the time when I first met you," he started with a frown. "I can't tell you how much it bothers me that I do not remember the first time at the Bishop's Palace. I *should* remember it, and I am furious with myself that I do not. If I could go back and take my blinkers off, so that I was not blinded by my own consequence, then I would do so. There I said it!" He threw a challenging look her way, but when Sabina opened her mouth to make reply, he forestalled her.

"Nay, more than that. I *should* have been spotted climbing through your bedchamber window," he insisted. "If I had any damned sense, I would have pursued you from the first. I wish to gods you had spoken the truth and you *had* been my harlot that day!"

Sabina's jaw dropped. "Nay, Jeffree, that is too much—" she spluttered but got no further.

"Breaking that foolish vow of mine was the best thing that ever happened to me," he insisted before halting. His face flushed and he started again, correcting himself. "No, I should say, your claiming to be my lover was the best thing. I will never regret that you did so or forget it. That moment is burned in my brain, was from that very moment. I cannot tell you how often I think of it still. It is a treasured memory of mine."

Sabina was astonished. "I think perhaps you remember it slightly differently now," she quavered, thinking of his shocked expression at the time.

"If I could go back, I would proclaim it was so, and tell everyone that my intentions toward you were honorable."

Sabina coughed. "I am not sure they would believe you, after the salacious tale Hendry told."

Jeffree waved this aside. "I would explain you were being stubborn over a foolish vow you had made. Tell them I was having to break down your resolve."

Sabina stared at him in fascination before giving herself a little shake. "It scarcely matters now," she pointed out. "For that is all in the past."

"That is not so," he argued. "For I mean to set things fully to rights. At the next family gathering, I will set matters straight."

"What do you mean?"

"I will let them all know how prized you are by me. That they will show you due deference or feel my wrath."

"You will do no such thing!" Sabina started hotly, imagining a room full to the brim with haughty de Crecys. "I can imagine nothing worse than being made a spectacle for a second time in front of your family!"

"Very well, then, at the next royal tournament." Jeffree shrugged. "I will go down on one knee in front of the crowds and proclaim myself your knight to command and yours alone."

"Jeffree!" Sabina gasped. "If you do anything of the kind, I will never forgive you!"

514

"What? Why?" His brows drew down and his frown grew thunderous.

"Because," Sabina said hotly, crossing her arms, "I would not like seeing you humbled." She glanced away from his expression. "It is one thing for me to call you an arrogant toad, but I do not like anyone else to get the better of you. It would make me—" She did not get the chance to finish the statement for he had snatched her into his arms.

"The crowd would love to see me humbled by a woman," he said against her brow.

"I don't care what the crowd wants, and you will *never* be humbled at my hands!"

"I am humbled by my feelings for you every damned day," he growled. "I go hot and cold all over at the idea I might never have—" He choked on his words. "If you had not taken my fate into your hands."

"No, Jeffree," she said reassuringly and grabbed hold of his upper arms. "You deserve some credit there. I would never have insisted we wed. That was *all* your idea."

His shoulders relaxed. "That is true," he conceded, breathing out raggedly. "You would have left me in the lurch if you'd had half the chance."

"I did not know then what a good husband you would make," Sabina said, half defensively, half placatingly.

"Hmm," he rumbled, drawing her close against him. "Really? Even when I put you through things like that wretched business at Fulford?"

"You mean Meliora," she said dryly. "Your first love."

515

"She wasn't anything of the sort!" he said, twisting his head to glare at her. "She was naught but a—foolish boyhood fancy."

Sabina pictured Meliora's stern, autocratic face and had to suppress a gurgle of mirth. "I doubt anyone would ever describe her as that!" she gasped.

"Are you laughing at me?" he asked, his eyes narrowing. He slid an arm about her waist and drew her body closer to his. "You are my first and only love, as well you know."

She sobered instantly. "And you are mine too," she conceded softly, reaching up to stroke his hair from his brow.

He scowled. "I had better be."

"Of course you are. Miles was just…a horrible misstep." She glanced up at him to see how he took that.

He grunted, grabbing a feel of her arse to comfort himself. "Neither one of us chose wisely the first time," he admitted after a moment's squeezing.

"And neither of us chose at all the second," she pointed out, pulling a face.

"It was fate," he answered at once. "You were meant to be mine."

"Fate?"

"What else?" He slid his hands up to her waist. "It really does not bother you that I am not gracious?"

"Not now that I know what is in your heart," she said fondly, laying a hand on his cheek. "For once I told you that I wanted actions rather than words you have been very good at those, Jeffree."

He pulled back to regard her doubtfully. "I have?"

"Yes. Why did you not tell me what you had done for Delia Selwyn and her child?"

"Who?"

"The blacksmith's niece."

"Oh yes. I meant to tell you at some later point. I was not sure you would approve."

"Why would I not? It was very touching and considerate of you."

He shrugged a shoulder. "You might have thought me a little high-handed. I just wanted to make things comfortable for you. It did not seem right to me that—well, anyway. I made enquiry and it turned out that Selwyn girl and the blacksmith's apprentice were courting. They practically snatched my hand off at the offer of a fresh start."

"Yet you did not see fit to mention any of this to me?"

"Why should I? You wanted actions, not words, you said."

She bit her lip. "But, Jeffree, how am I supposed to know about your actions if you do not tell me of them?"

He shrugged again. "I supposed that eventually you would hear they had left the area and be glad of it."

Her heart swelled within her breast. "Jeffree…"

"You asked me before who my closest friend is," he said raspily. "It is a question I had never pondered before, for I never cultivated friends. My mother once said perhaps my wife would be my greatest confidante." Sabina stared at him. "It seems, in this respect, she was right."

517

Tears started in her eyes. "Jeffree…"

"I know it is not the same for you," he carried on calmly. "I do not expect you to give me back the same words. You have your sister and—"

"I dearly love Isemay," Sabina responded at once. "But recent events have shown me that we are *not* likeminded in the slightest! She is the most reckless person I know, indeed, some of her actions seem almost terrifyingly foolhardy to me!" Jeffree snorted and Sabina lifted her chin. "What?" she asked.

He shook his head. "Just remembering a rash claim made by a beautiful young widow that she had played the whore for me."

"That was entirely different!" Sabina insisted. "I did that to save Isemay, *not* initiate some crazed revenge plan!"

"Mmmm." He sounded skeptical.

"Beautiful?" She faltered, only just picking up on his description.

"Extremely beautiful." He lightly touched the mole above her top lip. "It took me a little while to notice, then once I had seen you without your wimple, your appeal grew apace, and now, I find you the most beautiful of all in my eyes."

He looked so sincere that it stole all the breath from her body. "Jeffree…"

"Though, if you ask me, you and your sister are a reckless pair and need to be kept a close eye on. It is fortunate you are both safely married so your parents can rest easy in their beds at night." Sabina gasped faintly at this description, but he ignored it. "Anyway"—he squeezed her hand—"return to what you were saying."

"What was I saying?"

"You were about to tell me who your closest friend is, now you have decided you and your sister are too alike for comfort."

Sabina made a noise of disagreement in her throat. "You are so provoking sometimes."

"An arrogant toad?" he suggested, quirking a brow at her.

"*My* arrogant toad," she corrected him.

"Tell me what I want to hear," he ordered.

"It is you who are my greatest friend," she admitted.

"That's good," he said gruffly.

"You are also my true love, Jeffree de Crecy," she added quietly. "True to me as no one has ever been before in my life."

Jeffree pulled her into his arms, tucking her head under his chin and holding her tightly. "You are mine as well and the best thing that ever happened to me, but…I am not good at showing it before others," he finished uneasily.

Sabina wriggled out from his tight embrace and tipped her head to one side. "I think other people *might* be able to tell," she admitted with a laugh in her voice. "You are not as subtle as you imagine. Even Osborn now seems resigned to my importance in your life."

"Osborn?" he scoffed.

"He spared me a rare scolding today from Sir Charles," she said and felt Jeffree tense. "For when he showed up here in a white-hot temper, Osborn gave my excuses and did not let him in."

Jeffree grunted. "Maybe I will increase the knave's wages after all."

Suddenly Sabina remembered Lady Maud's words. *Jeffree has turned out so very reserved and Leland so very wild.* "I do not know what is to become of Isemay and Leland," she said, shaking her head. "They both seem determined to be the ruination of each other." He made no comment, catching her braids and twirling them around his hand. "Leland has his memory back, but is pretending not to," she admitted. "It is like some sort of game to them both."

Jeffree grunted again. "It is not our affair. Let them entrap one another if that is what they are determined to do."

Sabina nodded slowly. "Jeffree," she said quietly. His hand stilled and he met her gaze. "I want you to know that breaking *my* vow was the best thing that ever happened to me too. When I swore I would never be wed again, I little knew you were waiting for me. If I *had* I would have demanded a new gown and ran up the drive to Ganford Chase that day instead of dragging my feet."

He smiled at that, and it quite transformed his face. Her heart squeezed in her chest. She had the strongest suspicion that she was the only person in the whole world who had seen such a smile from Jeffree de Crecy.

"You could not have run fast enough. At that point, I have been waiting for you for twenty-eight years," he murmured. "I just did not know it then."

Sabina slid her arms around his neck. "Sometimes your words are not so bad, Sir Jeffree. Mayhap you just need practice saying sweet things to me."

"Let's find out," he suggested, and together they sank back into the bed.

Epilogue

Three Months Later

Sabina was nervous. The tailor from Greater Ganford had finally delivered her new finery. He and his two assistants had carried armfuls of gowns and cloaks up her stairs along with undergarments of the finest quality. She had given very little instruction as to their making up, merely sending an assortment of sumptuous brocades and satins from Jeffree's own stores.

Isemay and her mother had added a list of things they thought essential for a grand lady. When Sabina had cast an eye over it, she had felt so daunted by the many things mentioned that she had quickly put it out of her mind, along with the number of Jeffree's coins that had had to accompany the order.

The only thing Sabina had put her foot down about was refusing to order any formal headdresses. She was done with anything structured, however much her mother recommended a steeple henin and her sister argued for one with double horns which were said to be the latest fashion.

Sabina had known exactly what she wanted and she did not care if it was fashionable or not. She wanted a netted gold caul to wear over her thickly coiled braids, so they could still be plainly seen on either side of her head. Then she wanted a simple white linen veil to wear on the back of her head, to denote her married status. Nothing more, nothing less.

Then she had tried to put it all out of her head for the tailor had wanted a ridiculous amount of time to fulfill the order. So long had he required that Sabina had been forced to attend her second tournament at Beres Caple still wearing her former

521

attire. How fervently then had she wished she had ordered new clothes as soon as she was married.

She had felt the insult to Jeffree's reputation most keenly, though he assured her it did not signify what anyone else thought. She had ordered the gowns already and he was satisfied with that. Still, Sabina had felt conspicuous and ill at ease among all the fine company. She knew only too well that people were still whispering about them and must think him a miser or a cruel husband.

When it came to the crunch, Jeffree had not been able to go through with his revenge over Lord Kentigern at Beres Caple. Despite preparing Sabina for the eventuality, at the last minute he found he could not ignore his own wife sat in the crowd politely clapping. His revenge had fallen by the wayside and he had awarded Sabina the tribute.

She had taken the flowered circle without a murmur and balanced it as best she could atop her bulky headdress. It had not sat right, but she kept a hand up to hold it in place, feeling her face turn very red as everyone turned to look at her and clap. She had not even known if she was supposed to nod or bow. She had attended only two tournaments and she had been crowned at both of them! Which was truly an odd boast she could make, now she came to think of it.

By the next tournament, Sabina vowed she would be dressed as grandly as the highest lady in the land. She knew that, in Jeffree's mind, she could not aim high enough in her aspirations. What a pity Isemay would not see the result for a couple of months, Sabina thought, for her sister had journeyed the previous week to her new home in Sutton St. Bolston, where Ellis Hall stood.

Sir Charles had initially been beside himself to find that not only his godson but also his heir had been snared by a designing Burrell female. It had taken weeks before Sir Charles had been well enough to leave the back bedchamber at Morecotte, for he had been very run-down and ill.

Over those ensuing weeks, Isemay had been a frequent visitor and won him over with her pretty ways and her love of music which was the one indulgence he allowed himself. He was also reconciled to Sabina, though she did not fool herself that they would ever be friends, at least they could be civil to one another.

His good friend the Duke of Bethencourt had also deigned to visit and could not praise Isemay highly enough, making it plain he thought the maiden, if anything, was far too good for the likes of wild Leland Ellis. The duke seemed to enjoy lamenting his own broken heart to anyone who would listen, and Sabina thought he was enjoying playing the disappointed lover to the hilt.

By the time Sir Charles was well enough to set forth for his home in Sutton St. Bolston, he had been accompanied by both his son and his new daughter-in-law. Everyone was relieved to see that, despite his healed body, Leland showed no sign of picking up his old crowd and seemed more than content in his new bride's company.

Sabina still did not know that she would trust her new brother-in-law as far as she could throw him, but after seeing the way his dark eyes softened when they rested on Isemay, she was forced to concede he did seem genuinely attached to her.

Isemay would approve of the new gowns, Sabina thought, and the tailor her sister had insisted she use had certainly deserved his reputation. Now the gowns had arrived, they simply took her breath away. His team had remained for over two hours checking the final fit of each garment and making minute adjustments so they draped exactly as they should on Sabina's form.

Each one she had thought was more lovely than the last. She stood now in the final dress. It was of the finest pale blue silk, closely fitted at her bodice and waist, then flaring out from her hips into voluminous skirts decorated sumptuously with gold embroidery.

"Should we not take the gown off you now, milady?" Penny enquired, looking the dress over uncertainly. "For surely its like is for parading about at court, not at home?"

Sabina shook her head. "You would think so, Penny, would you not? But you see, Sir Jeffree expects me to dress like this every day from now on." The two women exchanged doubtful glances. "Well, we shall see," Sabina concluded uneasily. "I will certainly need a few plainer gowns for days when I am just at home."

"And for in the winter, milady," Penny pointed out. "You would freeze to death in such thin stuff on a cold day in February."

Sabina nodded. It was naught but the truth, though Jeffree would likely expect her to order a bunch of heavier brocades lined with fur, knowing his tastes. Well, she would cross that bridge when she reached it. "We need to find chests deep enough to store these other gowns inside, Penny," she answered, pulling a face. "I will have to sacrifice some of my old ones. Do you think you could repurpose any of them for yourself?"

Penny's face brightened. "Right gladly, milady." Over the next hour, they threw open the trunks and made room for Sabina's new clothes, making a pile of her old ones to pass to Penny.

"This brown kirtle will likely need to be rehemmed," Sabina remarked, noticing the state of its skirts.

"'Tis of no matter, milady, for I'm a whole head shorter than you," Penny pointed out.

"That is true enough."

Penny was cheerful at the prospect of alterations and soon bore off her spoils looking well pleased, while Sabina sat on her bed and undid the parcel containing her new headwear. To her delight, the package contained not only two gauzy veils as white as snow but also two golden hairnets woven from the finest golden thread.

How delicate and pretty they were. On impulse, Sabina unpinned the starched linen wimple she habitually wore, casting it over a chair. Moving across to the looking glass at the end of the room, she immediately donned one of the gold net cauls about her head, so that it stretched over her coiled braids and then pinned the white veil to the back of her head.

Sabina turned her head this way and that to examine the effect. She looked nice, she thought with a nod, definitely more youthful. Isemay would certainly approve, though her shoulders and neck felt very bare after wearing a wimple for over two years.

Certainly, this way you could appreciate the flattering neckline of her new gown and Jeffree would be able to glimpse her braids through the gold netting, she thought. He should like that, considering his preoccupation with them. That was something which had not abated one whit in the past three months.

And that was not the only thing. She had realized that not only did Jeffree like her on top, but combative speech *inflamed* him. He liked to be heaped with insults as much as praise in the bedchamber, where they were starting to know each other's likes pretty well by now.

Jeffree was just as keen to learn what she liked, and he tended to take her at her word, so she now simply told him what she wanted without hesitation. It seemed he would deny her nothing and really, what was the point in playing coy when he needed instruction and she needed…well, *him.*

As for his next day embarrassment, she had also found a way around that. The best thing to do was to simply tackle him first thing before his defenses were up. That way she could get an *I love you* out of him before they had even left the bedchamber. He would gaze up at her as she straddled him, his blue eyes so adoring that Sabina sometimes had to look away.

When she did this, he would invariably reach up and turn her face back to his and when he tipped over, he would do so with a hoarse cry, his eyes very blue. By the time they went belowstairs he had an almost benign look on his handsome face and would sometimes even whistle a tune.

They had started out that morning the same way and Sabina thought of it now as she started down the stairs, a faint blush on her cheek. She had only reached the halfway point when she heard Jeffree's voice upraised and calling for her. "I'm here," she answered and paused as he strode into view.

His brow cleared when he caught sight of her, but whatever words he had been going to utter seemed frozen on his lips. He stopped stock-still, staring up at her before finding his voice.

526

"Come down here to me, wife," he said at last. "That I may take a better look at you."

Feeling strangely nervous, Sabina complied, halting on the bottom step so her eyes were almost level with his own. "What do you think?" she asked, turning slightly to the left then right so he could get the full effect.

"What do I think?" he repeated hoarsely. "I think that if you had worn *this* dress to the Bishop's Palace, then I would have begged for an introduction to you on my knees."

Sabina laughed. "You are too fulsome in your praise, sir." She dropped her voice and raised a hand to the swell of her bosom. "Indeed, you put a poor widow to the blush."

"You put *me* to the blush," he countered, "for I can see your glorious hair and you know full well it is a weakness of mine."

Sabina caught her breath and held his gaze. "But how should I know that, good sir, for this is our very first meeting, is it not?"

His gaze caught fire before he glanced exaggeratedly around. "But where is your aunt, for I understand she is your chaperone this eve? She is very remiss to leave such a beauty roaming these halls alone."

Lately, they had been indulging in a very silly game that involved rewriting their history together. It had meant that last time they had stayed at Tipton Hall, Jeffree had been forced to make a most uncomfortable climb up to her old window involving an aged apple tree and some ivy.

He had barely made it through the narrow frame in one piece, and Sabina had laughed so hard that her mother had rapped on their door demanding an explanation for all the commotion. It had been worth it though after Sabina had consoled him on his scratches and kissed them, every one.

Jeffree had been wonderful in the role, declaring he had been struck with love at first sight of her and promising to marry her the very next day if she "would only take pity on his most ardent love and devotion." Sabina had not resisted him for long, though she pointed out he was taking gross advantage of her naivety. "For what if someone saw you climbing through yonder window? My reputation will be in tatters."

"I care not," he had declared. "I will take full responsibility for ruining you, but I must have you now." Sabina had sighed and agreed only the flintiest heart would send him back out of such a tiny window.

Of course, the next day he had been very bashful, which for Jeffree meant going about being rather short with everyone and refusing to make eye contact while the tips of his ears glowed red. Still, it had been worth it, and remembering it now, she bit her lip. "Alas," she sighed. "My aunt has not ventured far and will likely return at any moment."

"Then let us not squander this opportunity, madam," he improvised, seizing her hand and raising it to his lips. "Let us fly now together and seek out paradise in each other's arms."

Sabina bit back her laugh and fluttered her lashes. "Nay, sir, I dare not, for I have heard tell of your fearsome reputation."

His brows snapped together. "My reputation?" her husband echoed, sounding more like his true self than the romantic version.

"Aye, for all of Ganfordshire knows of Jeffree de Crecy's hot, lusty nature," Sabina answered serenely.

Jeffree's face relaxed and he gave a short laugh. "Well, in that case…subterfuge is useless." He stooped suddenly and Sabina found herself slung over his shoulder as he mounted the stairs.

She gave a squeal of surprise. "Jeffree! What are you doing?"

"I am carrying you upstairs to the bishop's private chamber, where I shall ravish you within an inch of your life."

"Well! How shocking! You had certainly better marry me after this. That is all I can say!"

"Marry you?" Jeffree repeated thoughtfully. "Well, madam, let us see first how well you can please me. I should warn you, I am not easily impressed."

Sabina laughed. "Oh, you will marry me alright," she predicted. "You will be *begging* me to marry you before this night is over."

An Hour Later

They lay breathless in a heap in the middle of Jeffree's huge bed. Sabina ran her hands through his hair and bumped her cheek against his chest. "Well?" she prompted, lifting her head.

"I love you," Jeffree said calmly, if a little out of breath still. "Marry me."

Sabina gave a gurgle of laughter. "Oh, how the mighty are fallen," she sighed. "I will consider it."

He tightened his arms around her, squeezing her tight. "If you do not, then I will plague you with repeated avowals of love," he suggested lazily.

Sabina cocked an eye at him. Playful Jeffree still surprised her a little. She liked that no one else saw this side of him save herself. It was true, Osborn had walked in on Jeffree braiding her hair a couple of times, but her husband had been quite unabashed about that. Osborn had been more embarrassed than he. "Oh very well," she murmured. "I will marry you. Purely to save my family the embarrassment of a lovesick swain loitering about the place."

"My sweet Sabina," he whispered, pressing kisses up her shoulder toward her neck, "all that I own is yours."

Sabina tipped her head back. "Are we still play-acting? Only that last sentiment sounded rather like the real you."

He considered this. "This is me and that is me; they are all me."

"Hmmm." She regarded him doubtfully. "I don't know. I do not think the genuine Jeffree de Crecy would have ravished me in the Bishop of Ganford's bedchamber."

He snorted. "If I had known what was good for me, then I would have." A thoughtful look crept into his eye.

"What?" she asked curiously.

"I wanted to ravish you in that monastery that time," he admitted. "Or rather, I wanted you to ravish me."

Sabina gave a chuckle. "That was when you told me my hair would make a good rope," she reminded him fondly.

Jeffree looked faintly embarrassed. "So I did." His hand shifted up and down her back. "And you gave me my first kiss." He lowered his face and returned the compliment very tenderly.

"And you made out that you were not affected by it," Sabina reminded him as soon as he withdrew his lips. She placed her hand on his chest. "Even though I could tell how wildly your heart was beating."

He laughed. "Do not remind me." A puzzled look crossed his face. "I was such an idiot. Thank the gods you bore with me."

"You still pay me some odd compliments at times," she confessed, "but I do not really mind them."

"You don't?"

She shook her head. "Can I tell you a secret?"

"Of course. Anything."

"It is because I love you so."

He caught hold of her braids, dragging her face to his. "As I do you, wife."

Six Months Later

The Great Hall, the Winter Palace, Aphrany

Sabina had not anticipated the Queen's receiving chambers would be so busy, for all it was the beginning of the Solstice celebrations. She clung to Jeffree's arm and fingered the pearl and ruby necklace at her throat. How well it matched her new gown of red and gold brocade, she thought, catching sight of herself in a large, gilded mirror. She looked quite the fine lady these days, and she felt sorry that her mother and sister would not see her in her finery, for she was spending the Solstice at the palace with Jeffree's family this year.

She gazed about looking for the Vyses, who had said they would see them later in the day, but she could not see them anywhere. Jasper and Crispin were in high spirits, not so much for their court introduction, but because they would not be returning to Longacre afterward but traveling back to Ganfordshire to begin their squire's training in the new year.

Poor Hugo had been horrified to find two extra pallet beds shoved into his bedchamber and two smelly dogs, but he was far too much in awe of Lady Maud to object. It was quite a squeeze in the de Crecy chambers, but they were making do, as it was only for five days.

"What part of the celebration happens in here?" Sabina asked, looking around with interest, for she was finding the royal festivities to be a lot grander than the humbler customs back home. Suddenly, she realized the crowd was falling back around them, revealing a clear path to where Queen Armenal sat on her raised platform, resplendent in a burgundy gown and pearls.

"What—?" she murmured as Jeffree pulled away from her, deliberately putting space between them before turning gravely to face her. "Husband?" She could not quite keep the note of panic from her voice. "What are you—?"

"Ah, Sir Jeffree de Crecy and your good lady wife," the Queen's raised voice greeted them, cutting off Sabina's bewildered query. "But how wonderful it is to see you once again." Seeing Jeffree direct a bow toward the dais, Sabina dropped likewise into a deep curtsey to the Queen. "When last you were in our royal presence there was a little disturbance, no? Some unpleasantness in our hallowed halls, and Sir Jeffree, it was agreed that you owed me some recompense. Am I not right?"

Sabina felt a jolt of alarm for she had forgotten all about the forfeit Jeffree was supposed to pay for brawling in the royal banqueting hall.

Jeffree cleared his throat. "You are right, my Queen," he answered loudly. "I am prepared to make full reparation now before the witnesses here present."

The Queen nodded, looking pleased with his reply. "And how will you make this up to me, Sir Jeffree? I am all ears." Her eyes gleamed in anticipation.

Jeffree took a deep breath and Sabina felt her spine tingle in warning. What was he doing? Whatever it was, he looked for a moment a little…apprehensive? Certainly not like her proud husband. She glanced from him to the Queen and back again, trying not to show her perturbation.

"I will make you my defense and ask if the violence of my feeling was not justified," Jeffree replied, raising his voice to the rafters. Sabina blinked. What was happening right now? "I have been brought low by love for a fair, cruel maid who shows me no mercy."

Sabina's mouth dropped open as gasps rang out around the hall. "I dwell in darkest agony and torment, with no hope of my affection being returned. I have wronged her, but she revisits my wrongs back upon me one hundredfold and will give me no succor."

Suddenly, Jeffree turned to face her again and she met his gaze, her own full of blind panic. Was this some sort of Solstice mummery that she did not know the lines for? In front of her astonished eyes, Jeffree dropped to his knees like a supplicant before her.

She gaped at him. "Jeffree?" Gasps went up from the crowds around them, and the Queen clapped her hands together with glee.

"I am dying for love of you, Sabina de Crecy, and no one else can alleviate my suffering," he announced, and all around them, the buzz of conversation became so loud that Sabina's head reeled. The crowd pressed in around them, and the view of Queen Armenal was partly obscured.

Sabina could stand it no longer. She took three hurried steps forward and seized her husband's shoulder, shaking it. "Stop this, Jeffree! What are you doing?" she cried.

"I am making a spectacle of myself," he answered in his usual voice.

Just hearing his normal tones relieved her greatly. "But why?"

"Redressing the balance." He shrugged. "Everyone at court thinks I treated you with contempt for the first few weeks of our marriage. It is only right that they should learn the truth."

"The truth?" she squawked. "When have I ever spurned your love?"

"I want there to be no doubt, Sabina, of the regard I hold you in. That I adore you."

"Do n-not do this, Jeffree!" Sabina stammered. "Have you forgotten you said you would never prostrate yourself before a woman?"

"That was before I met you."

"Cease this now!" she said in desperation, her voice becoming shrill. All around them the once-hushed whispers were now deafening. "Simply *everyone* is looking at us!"

"I don't care," he said and lifted his arms to wrap them tightly about her waist, pressing his face to her bodice.

She couldn't even speak for a moment, just glanced about at the staring faces, her own growing hot and red. "Jeffree!" she whimpered in a strangled voice. "Have you forgotten where we are?"

Her words made no difference. She gazed across the murmuring chamber and threw an agonized glance in the Queen's direction. Queen Armenal was looking very agitated, standing up from her seat.

"I will listen to what Sir Jeffree is saying!" the Queen insisted imperiously. "I cannot hear through all these murmurings from you people!" she scolded her courtiers. "Silence, I say, or you shall all be ordered to leave! Now stand back, so I can see the de Crecys clearly!" There was an immediate sound of shushing through the hall and the press of people fell back once more. "Rise, Sir Jeffree!" the Queen commanded.

Sabina almost staggered when Jeffree released her and rose from his knees to stand beside her. His expression was grave, but he seemed calm enough.

"Sir Jeffree! Sir Jeffree, I say!" the Queen insisted. "I wish to know what it is you are saying to this wife of yours."

Sabina licked her lips. "Your Majesty," she started croakily, "he was merely—"

"I told her that I am dying for love of her," Jeffree announced so loudly he drowned her words out. Sabina gasped, her head whipping around to stare at him in disbelief. "I told her she is cruel," he continued steadily. "That she will not pity me. A drowning man that only she can save." Sabina's bosom heaved with indignation.

"I have treated her badly," he continued, glancing about the chamber. "You have all borne witness to that. To the kind of

535

husband I have made." He paused long enough for the crowd to murmur in cautious agreement. "I am jealous and unreasonable. I am demanding and quarrelsome. I am...unkind."

"Stop it!" Sabina burst out hotly. "This is not true!"

Jeffree swallowed again. "You see, Your Majesty? It matters not how I petition her. She will not soften her heart toward me, even though I offer her mine on a platter to do with it what she will."

"Jeffree...!" she protested weakly.

The Queen clapped her hands again, but this time it seemed with delight. "Yes, yes," she said gleefully. "Your proud heart, it has been conquered, Sir Jeffree?"

"It is no longer proud, Your Highness," he said in ringing tones. "It is only bleeding, pierced right to the core."

Queen Armenal gave a murmur of excitement. She was gesturing to a page who had pulled out a quill and parchment. Sabina had a horrible suspicion he was committing Jeffree's every word to paper. "Jeffree, for heaven's sakes," she spluttered.

"I am simply speaking the truth," he replied, just as loudly. "My heart beats for you alone and you will not accept my love."

So stunned was she by his words, that Sabina had not even noticed the Queen's approach until she was upon them.

"Lady de Crecy," Queen Armenal said sweepingly. "You must defer to me in this matter, for I have superior knowledge of the rules of courtship and of love and am likely the greatest authority in the land."

Sabina blinked at her. "Of course, Your Majesty," she murmured, dropping once again into a curtsey. "But there has been some misunderstanding—"

Armenal waved this aside. "Sir Jeffree has wronged you during the early days of your marriage," she said calmly. "He made you wear the rags. He disgraced you. He did not treat you with respect. You must make a list of the conditions you demand from him now. Make it clear to him what he must do in order to make you look upon him with favor. You may not be disposed kindly toward him, but he has made it clear he will go to the ends of the earth simply to earn a kind look from you."

Sabina shook her head, but the clamor about her was rising once more to a heavy swell. "There is really no need—" she tried to insist, but her voice was drowned in the noise of the crowd.

"Make your demands of me, wife!" Jeffree said in a voice that rang out. "I will deny you nothing."

Sabina gulped. "Really, I—"

"Jewels and furs are too dull and conventional for such a courtship as yours," Armenal ruminated, tapping her chin. An unholy gleam entered her eyes. "How would it be if you told Sir Jeffree to kiss your foot now in front of everyone?" Even as she suggested it, inspiration seemed to strike her anew. "Wait! I have an even better idea!" she crowed. "A spell in the stocks outside the palace! I am sure there would be plenty who would love to pelt the proud Sir Jeffree with the rotten vegetables!"

Someone in the crowd tittered, and soon this turned into delighted gales of laughter. Sabina felt herself turn hot with anger. "No!" she cried with a vehemence that struck everyone silent again. Her voice shook. "If anyone dared to do such a thing to my husband I would—I would—"

537

"Yes, what would you do?" the Queen asked, sounding most intrigued.

"I would make them extremely sorry they had even heard the name de Crecy!" Sabina concluded crossly.

The Queen nodded and turned back to Jeffree. "She is very fierce, this wife of yours," Armenal said thoughtfully. "I can see why it is you are suffering, now you have had the misfortune to incur her displeasure."

Sabina finally mustered the boldness to look at Jeffree again and found him gazing at her face with such admiration that it made her heart flutter. He looked as though every fiber of his being was focused on her, and he simply did not care what anyone else present thought about it.

"You don't want those things, Sabina?" he asked. "Maybe I deserve them."

"No, you don't, Jeffree," she said quickly. "I don't want that." She took a step toward him, placing her hand on his arm. "Please." She lowered her voice. "Enough. It was not your fault I wore my old gowns."

He shook his head. "I need to say these things," he told her calmly, then lifted his voice again. "To shout them from the rooftops if need be. From every town square. Jeffree de Crecy loves his wife to distraction. He begs for her forgiveness and strives only to be worthy of her."

"Did you get that last line?" the Queen asked her scribe. "It was rather a good one. But my favorite, it was the one about the town square." Her page nodded enthusiastically.

Sabina tugged on Jeffree's sleeve. "Please, husband." He shook his head. She could have screamed at this point. "Jeffree!" Sabina stamped her foot. "This is ridiculous and unwarranted!"

"Strike that last part," the Queen said, frowning critically. "It is hardly gracious."

Sabina strove for a more dignified tone. "Of course I forgive you, husband," she said calmly. "I accept your love and I return it. Why else would I put up with you? Are you satisfied?"

Jeffree swung her up into his arms. "I am," he said, turning to the Queen. "Is that sufficient, Your Majesty?"

Queen Armenal beamed and nodded with every sign of satisfaction. "Most satisfactory all round," she sighed. After a moment, realizing Jeffree had no intention of releasing his wife, she raised her hands and started politely clapping in a sign of royal approval.

The crowd followed suit, and Sabina gave up worrying and simply passed her arms about Jeffree's neck. This court was a ridiculous place, but she supposed at this rate they would certainly be getting their own dedicated panel in the Queen's tapestry. As for Jeffree, he was already striding toward the doorway.

"Well, I don't think the Queen thinks you're stuffy and reserved anymore," Sabina commented. "You put on *quite* the exhibition for everyone. At this rate, you will be known as the most chivalric, parfait knight in Karadok!"

"*That* was how I should have given you the tourney crown at Beres Caple," Jeffree responded, sounding smug.

"To think how you struggled even to kiss my cheek or think of a single word of praise in the early days of our marriage," she marveled. "Where are we going?" she asked as he started up the staircase.

"To our chambers. I want to try kneeling at your feet again. I think I liked it."

Sabina spluttered but, seeing the faint color rising to his cheeks, realized he was serious. "What about kissing my foot?" she suggested with a lift of her brows.

"Oh, I'll kiss anything you command," he promised. "In fact, I'm *dying* to."

Sabina sighed and rested her head against his shoulder. "You are certainly growing into that reputation I told you about," she told him.

"You mean my hot, lusty nature?" he asked after a moment's consideration.

Sabina laughed. "Indeed."

"Not until you," he said softly, echoing his words from a previous conversation. "I was never this way before you, Sabina."

She turned serious at once. "Because you love me," she said with a quiet conviction that made him smile.

"Because I love you," he agreed. "So much so, it seems I can even show it now in front of others." He cocked a speculative eye at her.

"What?" she asked with sudden misgiving.

He shook his head. "You had better prepare yourself for your next tourney crown, Lady de Crecy. From now on, all my wins will be for you, no one else."

And as it turned out, he spoke nothing but the truth.

THE END

If you want to read more about Karadok, then the next book in the series is Jane's story:

The Favourite

Alisander de Balon, fifth Viscount Bardulf, is a lot of things. Ambassador. Diplomat. Spy. He is also bored as hell at the Argent King's court. His only diversion these days is tormenting staid Jane Cecil, the Queen's favorite lady-in-waiting. Seeing her vexed amuses him more than any royal entertainment. Jane has finally found her place at court, and it is among the Queen's retinue. All she wants to do is faithfully serve Her Majesty, something she could do in peace if it was not for the Queen's countryman, Viscount Bardulf, who seems to delight in baiting her! Neither Bardulf nor Jane could have foreseen the sudden tragedy that leads to their hasty union, and certainly neither of them could have anticipated that they would fall so easily into different roles…that of husband and wife.

If you enjoyed this book, please consider leaving me a rating on Goodreads, Amazon, Bookbub or wherever else you leave your reviews. I would be very grateful.

You can find my website at: www.alicecoldbreath.com where you can sign up for my monthly newsletter and find out what I am up to.

Also, please do check out some of my other stories! Many thanks, Alice.

The Vawdrey Brothers Series:

Book 1: Her Baseborn Bridegroom

Book 2: His Forsaken Bride

Book 3: An Ill-Made Match

The Brides of Karadok Series:

Book 1: Wed By Proxy

Book 2: The Unlovely Bride

Book 3: The Consolation Prize

Book 4: Her Bridegroom, Bought and Paid For

Book 5: An Inconvenient Vow

Book 6: The Favourite

The Victorian Prizefighter Series:

Book 1: A Bride for the Prizefighter

Book 2: A Substitute Wife for the Prizefighter

Book 3: A Contracted Spouse for the Prizefighter